Praise for *Fall for*

"*Fall for Him* is the kind of rom-com that checks all of the boxes. Two characters with real, relatable issues? Check! So much tension and banter? Check! The perfect combination of laughs and spice? Double check! Andie Burke's sophomore novel is a true triumph, a book I haven't been able to stop thinking about. It's safe to say I fell for this book, and readers will too!"
—Falon Ballard, author of *Right on Cue*

"*Fall for Him* is enemies-to-lovers perfection all wrapped up with a beautiful forced-proximity bow. The chemistry between Dylan and Derek is sizzling and organic, and their love story will have you turning the page at lightning-fast speed. Andie's banter is god tier, her voice is a breath of fresh air, and I am a forever fan." —Lana Ferguson, *USA Today* bestselling author of *The Nanny*

"Even as Andie Burke competently tackles neurodivergent representation, complex pasts, and grief, this is a story about joy, queer family, and how the greatest love story ever told could be right next door. Spicy and sweet."
—Mae Marvel, author of
Everyone I Kissed Since You Got Famous

"*Fall for Him* is both a sexy romp and an exploration of self-love through complicated family dynamics, perfect for fans of HGTV and the shy nerd/confident cool guy dynamic of Levi and Nico from *Grey's Anatomy*."
—Rachel Runya Katz, author of *Thank You for Sharing*

"Romances don't come funnier or sweeter than *Fall for Him*. Burke writes with splendid candor and nuance, weaving a tale of forced proximity that will leave your heart bursting. Derek and Dylan may be a nightmare for the HOA in the story, but they are an absolute dream to read about!"
—Timothy Janovsky, author of *The (Fake) Dating Game*

Praise for *Fly with Me*

"A modern, tongue-in-cheek view . . . *Fly with Me* makes you laugh right before it makes you cry."   —*The New York Times*

"A one-way ticket to sapphic delight."   —*PopSugar*

"A soaring, swoony fake-dating tale."   —*Electric Literature*

"*Fly with Me* is a delightful tale full of beloved romance tropes. . . . Burke manages to center a nuanced look at grief while also maintaining the book's sexiness and humor."
—*Autostraddle*

"*Fly with Me* is a hug in book form. Opposites-attract goodness, top-tier banter, and delightful tenderness all combine to make Andie Burke's debut an instant favorite. I fell head over heels for Olive and Stella from the first page, and this hilarious yet beautiful story of love, grief, bravery, and acceptance was unrelentingly delightful. A celebration of queer love and joy from start to finish."   —Mazey Eddings, author of
A Brush with Love

"*Fly with Me* took me on a deeply emotional journey. This touching sapphic romance champions the healing power of found family, facing your fears with compassion and patience, and surrounding yourself with people who see and love you just as you are. Perfect for fans of Alison Cochrun and Abby Jimenez!"
—Chloe Liese, author of *Two
Wrongs Make a Right*

"Burke's writing is elegant and effortless and had me completely charmed from the first page. My cheeks hurt from smiling. *Fly with Me* balances the humor of a disaster sapphic fake-dating her hot pilot heroine with the heavy emotional weight of loving (and losing) family. Sprinkle in the perfect amount of tension and heat and Burke had me flying high."

—Ruby Barrett, author of *The Romance Recipe*

"A sizzling debut! In *Fly with Me,* Burke delivers a love story that is heartfelt, entertaining, and utterly romantic. I enjoyed every second of this wonderful read."

—Kate Bromley, author of *Ciao for Now* and *Talk Bookish to Me*

"An amazing sapphic romance . . . hard-hitting yet hopeful."

—*Culturess*

"Burke crafts a heartfelt, emotional novel about two women who must learn to trust themselves enough to fall in love. Recommend to fans of Helen Hoang and Abby Jimenez."

—*Library Journal*

"Burke skillfully balances sweetness and heat . . . readers will eagerly cheer on the charming central couple. Burke is a writer to watch."

—*Publishers Weekly*

"In this adorable yet heart-wrenching story of overcoming limiting beliefs, Burke weaves a classic romantic tale of fake dating while diving into the naked truth of trauma and mental illness."

—*Booklist*

"*Fly with Me* will undoubtedly make you believe in love! With its dazzling set of characters and opposites-attract romance, the story will take you to all kinds of highs that you won't ever want to get down."

—*Book Riot*

Also by Andie Burke

Fly with Me

Fall for Him

A Novel

Andie Burke

ST. MARTIN'S GRIFFIN
NEW YORK

First published in the United States by St. Martin's Griffin, an imprint of St. Martin's Publishing Group

FALL FOR HIM. Copyright © 2024 by Andie Burke. All rights reserved. Printed in the United States of America. For information, address St. Martin's Publishing Group, 120 Broadway, New York, NY 10271.

www.stmartins.com

Design by Meryl Sussman Levavi

The Library of Congress Cataloging-in-Publication Data is available upon request.

ISBN 978-1-250-88639-2 (trade paperback)
ISBN 978-1-250-88640-8 (ebook)

Our books may be purchased in bulk for promotional, educational, or business use. Please contact your local bookseller or the Macmillan Corporate and Premium Sales Department at 1-800-221-7945, extension 5442, or by email at MacmillanSpecialMarkets@macmillan.com.

First Edition: 2024

10 9 8 7 6 5 4 3 2 1

For the more than 18,000 health-care workers every year who experience workplace violence. To all of you who have gotten scratched, punched, or kicked during a shift only to shrug off your scars and file away your stories as just more wacky moments from the trenches.

Y'all are complete badasses.

But you deserve better.

Author's Note

I love that English uses the word *falling* to describe the initial rush of love, capturing the stomach-sinking danger of opening your heart over a chasm of *what if*. It feels like the greatest impossibility that anyone could love all those deep-inside, messy, jagged bits we try to hide from even ourselves. But after all, it's the impact with the ground that hurts, not the fall, so I guess that's why the best partners are the ones who cushion us as we . . . as we . . . yeah, sorry, the thread of that metaphor really collapsed there (pun intended). Anyway, this book opens with both a literal fall and an actual mess. When I wrote it, that's the way I felt. My wrecked brain was reeling from a health crisis, a relationship disaster, and a new ADHD diagnosis. Reflecting now, I see how grief impacted those days. Unresolved, complicated grief keeps its own timeline. And much like a home renovation project wherein hidden, expensive disasters are created when you try to fix the cosmetic parts only, sometimes you have to break things down entirely before anything gets repaired.

Pushing aside those two dreadfully tired metaphors, I'm writing this note because, along with what I hope are hilarious home-disaster hijinks, swoony sexy banter, and fun moments with a large goofy dog, Dylan and Derek face heavier stuff. There are discussions of losses of a parent and a friend, mental health battles, casual ableism/toxic teasing (confronted), the cost of being a grown-up parentified child, the effects of witnessing alcoholism, and untangling problematic family dynamics. There is also discussion of a health-care workplace violence incident.

Fall for Him, like my first book, *Fly with Me*, was written with the belief that life is messy. Even when life involves the joy of finding a happily ever after and a partner who loves those jagged pieces of ourselves, we don't get to be one thing at once. I wrote it at a time when I needed a reminder that people who feel like their bodies and minds and souls are being held together by caffeine and off-brand Scotch tape *deserve* to find and *can* find their **person**. Because when the ground beneath our feet is crumbling in every possible sense, sometimes we don't just need a safe place to land. We need a safe place to fall.

Chapter 1

The only warning had been a millisecond of ominous crunching before the kitchen floor collapsed beneath Dylan Gallagher's feet. He clawed against slippery linoleum, a muffled yelp erupting below.

"Shit. Shit. *Shit.*" There was nothing to grip. His legs bicycled in open air as he tried to keep his body in the flooded kitchen. Rushing water funneled around him, and another section crumbled. Dylan's climber instincts kicked in. He covered his head and bent his knees, bracing against the coming impact.

He landed in darkness with a painful, lung-rattling *thump*. Dazed and choking on dusty oxygen, he tested his arms and legs. Everything could move, thankfully. But everything hurt. Jesus Christ, everything *really* hurt. But it should hurt worse . . .

A softer than expected surface cushioned his spine. Something even softer was under his neck. Underneath the rubble it felt like a mattress? And a pillow?

Oh god. This meant . . .

Dylan had fallen through the apartment floor directly into Derek Chang's bed.

The realization sent him flailing toward a seated position until a slimy wet *something* dragged over his cheek.

"*Gah.*" He tried to scoot away, but his head slammed into the wall. A heavy weight pressed down on his chest, squelching his back into soaked fabric beneath him. He wiped drywall sludge from his face and blinked twice, vision still blurred from the eye-watering pain of his landing. A dog the size of a goddamn dire wolf was on top of him. *Not good.*

Another round of blinking cleared Dylan's vision enough for a quick scan of the room. It was dim, but not dim enough to prevent Dylan from seeing every exposed and rigid plane of his shocked neighbor's body. Dylan gave the animal a gentle nudge because the ribs beneath its giant paw were aching.

As the dog turned back to look at Derek, Derek seemed to unfreeze from his panic. He rushed to the hellhound that may have been assessing whether Dylan would make a tasty meal and lifted it off Dylan with almost preternatural strength. He set the dog in the slightly illuminated corner, away from the debris. "Oh my god. Are you okay, buddy?" Derek checked and rechecked the animal's limbs and joints, running his hands over the black-and-white fur while muttering. Dylan couldn't make out most of the words, but there was an unexpected catch in Derek's voice as he uttered each pained *"fuck."*

The creature itself appeared unconcerned with having just survived catastrophe. It sauntered away from Derek's evaluation and again approached the pile of rubble Dylan was still sprawled on top of.

"You're okay. Thank god." Again, Derek was speaking to the dog.

Water glistened over Derek. The leak must have happened first, waking Derek up and giving him enough time to get out of the way. *Shit.* Derek really was lucky he wasn't underneath when the ceiling collapsed. There wasn't any dust on his . . . *oh fuck* . . . Derek was only wearing tight black boxer briefs that showed . . . stuff. Stuff that Dylan, who had just fallen through a ceiling, should absolutely not be noticing. But nobody could completely ignore the outline of a dick when it was right in front of him, even if said dick also belonged to a complete dick. At least Dylan had fallen asleep in his jeans at his computer. He might not be wearing a shirt, but in the shadowy room, it wouldn't be noticeable that those jeans were suddenly tighter.

No, Dylan, remember this man is not for you.

Dylan had only been staying in the upstairs apartment for a few months, but the several mortifying run-ins he'd already had with Derek Chang had settled Dylan's opinion of him. And based on the parade of men who had been exiting Derek's apartment on a regular basis, even a version of Dylan not coated with demolished drywall muck was *not* Derek's type.

Whatever muscle responsible for cringing felt as sore and sprained as the rest of Dylan's body.

Running a hand over his slimy hair, Dylan forced his attention from the man in the corner and up to the gaping ceiling hole.

The lingering shock and exhaustion must have fried his brain because Dylan said the first (and absolutely most asinine) sentence he could have thought to say: "I think there's an 'It's Raining Men' joke in here somewhere."

The sound of dripping counted the silent beats passing between them.

A hoarse huff came out of Derek. Wait . . . was that . . . a *laugh*?

But with just *the best timing ever*, another small section of ceiling collapsed, sending yet *another* plume of dust into the space between the two men, prompting Derek to shield the dog with his broad torso.

The huff, or almost laugh, or whatever Dylan's overly optimistic brain had thought it was shifted to become a growl worthy of a morally gray hero in a fantasy novel. Derek straightened, and the small pillar of light from the hallway illuminated an infuriatingly attractive scowl so stormy Dylan was even more sure he'd imagined that initial laugh.

"Dad jokes? Really, dude?" Derek scratched behind his dog's floppy black ears. "He's traumatized now. Poor fella." Derek kneeled beside the beast, mumbling again in the tone an elderly auntie uses on a toddler before booping said toddler's button nose.

"*Traumatized*? His monster tail just whacked me in the face because he was wagging it." Dylan ducked away.

"He's *frail*." Derek slid his hand over the dog's spine. "Arthritis. And he's probably just happy he didn't get crushed to death."

"That Dalmatian crossed with a polar bear could probably withstand an entire iceberg."

Scathing. That was the word for the look Derek was giving Dylan.

"He's a *harlequin Great Dane American Bulldog mix*." Derek waited an inscrutable beat before frowning. "And he's old. And why the hell are we arguing about whether or not my poor, sleeping, elderly dog could have been hurt by half a ceiling and a whole-ass human man falling on top of him?" Derek's words were more bewildered than furious. "And the ceiling . . . *shit*." His hand kept petting the fur, but he was focused on the tableau of destruction. Every muscle in Derek's body tensed again.

Damn. How often did this guy go to the gym?

Dylan ignored the stinging, sharp pain that lightninged from his palm and pushed himself off the destroyed mattress. Between his hand and the dull agony around his ribs, he felt lucky to make it upright without actually crying, and he offered himself the manliest sort of mental self-congratulations on that feat. He could almost imagine his two oldest brothers in his ear yelling *Shake it off. Shake it off. Man up.* Like every time he'd gotten clobbered in peewee hockey by one of the eight-year-olds who looked like they took baby doses of HGH.

Dylan pointed above him. "*Wait*, I think I know why it . . ." Slippery warmth dripped from Dylan's wrist to his forearm. The slice across his palm was leaking much more than he expected—spots sparked in his vision. What he was saying? A rubber band tightened around his sternum. It was so hot all of a sudden.

Nope.

"I—I-I think . . ." His ears popped like he was too deep underwater. His body vanished beneath him.

Derek's low voice grumbled, *"Oh Jesus Christ."*

Then everything went black.

Chapter 2

Dylan's chest heaved. Strong arms were wrapped around his waist and shoulders. His cheek was pressed into the crook of a warm neck. A neck that smelled like sandalwood and something sweeter too. The niceness of that scent almost overpowered the damp, moldy smell that was everywhere else . . . Everywhere else . . .

Dylan's awareness jolted. The moldy smell was the destroyed drywall. The large hand braced against the bare skin of his lower back belonged to . . . Derek Chang.

Dylan froze.

Froze. Like his mouth couldn't make words and his legs locked up. *Yep*, contact with a hot man had actually provoked a fight, flight, or freeze response. *Fantastic.* As his mental operations revved to functioning speed, Dylan yanked himself away, almost tripping over the mammoth dog sniffing his bleeding hand.

Derek tossed a tissue box to . . . well, *at* Dylan. "Please don't bleed on him."

Dylan covered the cut with a handful of tissues. "I'm so sorry." He grimaced at the ceiling again. "Not for bleeding on him. I didn't. But for this. I'll fix it."

"What do you mean you'll *fix it*?" Derek rubbed his forehead. "It's completely wrecked." He sighed. "Is the rest of you hurt? Besides the hand?"

"Uh . . . I'm fine." Dylan suppressed another groan as he moved. "Fine-ish. Mostly fine. Fine enough. And the ceiling's really only wrecked in that one spot actually. Wow, that was unlucky." He tilted his head.

"I have to call my insurance. You need to call your uncle's in-surance." Derek rubbed his chin, smearing the dust that Dylan had evidently gotten all over him when he fainted—

Ugh, he'd actually fainted, hadn't he? He had never been great with blood. The dizzying ache in Dylan's head and ring-ing in his ears didn't help.

"I guess we need to call the HOA, maybe? Since it's between the units . . . wait, no . . . we can't. Shit." Derek's mouth tightened and his troubled gaze went to the dog.

Why would the dog be what he was . . . oh . . .

Dylan's brain was bad at a *lot* of things. Dates—both the kind on a calendar and the sort with men. Timing. Figuring out how to use an avocado before it went from rock hard to brown mush.

And given the most recent events, it was clear his brain sucked at remembering to shut off the faucet after filling his makeshift sous vide tank when a work call interrupted him. But . . . there were other things that Dylan's brain could intuit very quickly. Like certain body language cues and patterns. He also had a very good memory for certain types of information, and he'd spent an entire day going over his uncle's HOA rules about repairs and renovations and ended up hyperfixating and reading the HOA's entire document.

Some combination of the twist of Derek's mouth and that pointed, apprehensive glance at the bear-dog made Dylan under-stand.

"You aren't supposed to have that dog here. They have strict breed restrictions, don't they?" Dylan said, not quite realizing how that would sound given the current predicament. He'd been trying to state a fact, but Felicity had told him he wasn't always good at getting tone right. "I meant—"

If possible, Derek's body went more rigid. Every taut muscle on display now resembled chiseled granite. His demeanor that had been a mixture of frustration and concern shifted. Dylan had never seen a mother grizzly bear in the wild when he lived on the West Coast, but now he understood that experience. The dark, attractive eyes that had betrayed surprising, heartfelt concern about Dylan being injured now flashed. "Given that you just wrecked my bedroom and fell through my ceiling, I'm not sure you're the person who is *supposed* to be telling me what I should or should not have in my apartment. Speaking of things that shouldn't be here . . . if you're not seriously hurt, I would appreciate you getting the hell out of here and leaving us alone." Derek folded his arms over his chest and took a protective stance beside the dog. "He's just visiting."

Did he think Dylan wanted to kidnap a creature that probably weighed as much as an undersized manatee? Derek flipped on a lamp on the table next to him, and reached down—not far given the height of the behemoth beside him—to rest his hand on the animal's head. Like Derek was guarding him or something.

Dylan shrugged and refocused his attention on the ceiling, seeing a detail he hadn't before. He made to push his glasses up on his nose, but they weren't there. After cursing internally, he searched the rubble and found half of the frames. He set the intact lens over his right eye. "That shouldn't look like that."

"Okay, since two hours after going to bed a human crashed through my ceiling and almost killed me and my dog, I'm gonna have to just say *duh.*"

"No, I mean . . ." Dylan got up on the bed, regretting the decision immediately as something sharp bit into his foot. "I need a flashlight . . . or can I have your phone?"

"I'm not giving you my—"

"Just for a second."

"Fine." Derek lobbed the phone at him.

Dylan's non-bloody hand caught it and swiped on the flashlight function. It took him a second to juggle the glasses lens, the phone, and the bloody tissues, but he saw it. *"Shoot."*

"What's wrong?"

"It wasn't just—" Dylan sighed, relief mixing with dread. The flood probably hadn't helped . . . Who was he kidding, the kitchen flood was almost certainly the catalyst for the exact timing of the disaster, but the damage he was seeing in the weight-bearing beam wasn't from this flood. Nope. This was long-term rot, maybe from a small leak over time that ruined the subfloor. So it wasn't completely his fault. Not that those facts would matter if his family found out about this. His family *really* couldn't find out about causing the flood. "So . . . uh . . . Do you own this unit?" Dylan offered the phone back.

"Yeah." Derek's black eyebrows knit together. "Why?"

"I need a better look, but see there"—Dylan pointed to the rotted joist—"I think there's an underlying water problem and a resulting structural problem that's been here a while between the two units. I'm guessing it's a failed plumbing joint, but I need more light and a better angle." He scanned along the intact ceiling and wall and saw a very subtle amount of bubbling.

Derek's eyes darkened as he muttered an oath. The dog snuffled against Derek's leg and leaned on his strong thighs. The weight of that big head in a crisis seemed like it could be comforting, if you knew the animal wasn't going to eat you.

"You still flooded the kitchen, right? I've heard dripping all night. It made it impossible to go to sleep. Now this problem just appears? Seems a bit coincidental for it to make your screwup not what caused this mess." Derek winced like he didn't mean to imply Dylan was a liar. Or maybe he didn't mean the accusation to sound as harsh as it did.

It didn't make it better.

Dylan was used to screwing up. Here was just one more person who thought Dylan was an idiot. And possibly a liar.

"You're right that the water issue tonight didn't help, but that . . . that's been rotting for a long time." Dylan rubbed his temples, weighing the mental and actual cost of his uncle and family finding out that he absolutely had done something incredibly stupid here. "Look. My dad's a general contractor. I grew up working for him every single summer and after school. I've renovated an entire house that was in much worse shape than this. I know this shit." God, Dylan's head *hurt*. He rubbed at a spot in the center of his forehead.

Derek's eyes followed his movements with an air of admittedly justifiable skepticism.

"That floor was a ticking time bomb, and I'm guessing the plumbing problem is between the two apartments." Dylan squared his aching shoulders. "The intake for my uncle's apartment is on the other side and I've already had his plumbing checked . . . so I think it might be . . ."

"A problem with the plumbing for my unit?" Derek's shoulders slumped.

Dylan nodded.

His uncle couldn't handle this. This entire situation was supposed to take stress off his uncle. If they found out about the flood, the family would just assume the entire thing was a typical Dylan screwup. His uncle also didn't have a bunch of money for a deductible with the other bills piling up. He probably wouldn't let Dylan pay for it once he found out the extent of the problem. Especially given that the problem had been present for a while. That massive tail *thwacked* Dylan in the leg again, interrupting his thoughts. Derek's gaze was fixed on the bed. If the layouts of the two apartments were similar but reversed, this unit was likely also a one-bedroom unit, meaning he was probably wondering where the hell he was going to sleep tonight. Dylan couldn't blame him. His own brain felt as soggy as his jeans. Goose bumps prickled the back of his neck. Christ, he wished he was wearing a goddamn shirt.

If Derek didn't want people to know about the dog, and Dylan didn't want people to find out about the flood . . .

In that second, Dylan made up his mind to do something really, really stupid. "What if I had another idea?"

Chapter 3

"You're offering to pay for everything *and* do the labor yourself," Derek repeated while scratching behind Gus's ears.

"Yeah."

Derek was good in a crisis. He could calm a room of screaming people during a cardiac arrest at work. Just a few hours before Dylan Gallagher crashed through his ceiling, he'd calmed his panicked mother and a collection of her shrieking Bible study friends while at the same time convincing a humane wildlife relocation specialist to come remove a very hyperactive family of bats from his mother's attic after business hours. She forced Derek to go home before the wildlife expert even got there since he had to get up even earlier than usual for his shift tomorrow. He was in bed barely fifteen minutes when the persistent dripping began.

So no. Derek was not sleeping. And he was not calm. He was awake and being a dick to the guy who could have just broken his neck falling through a ceiling. *His* ceiling, yes. But still. He'd lost it on the guy. Maybe it was because his heart was still thumping from those seconds he thought Gus had been hurt and that was why he couldn't process what Gallagher was saying.

"So . . . ?" Gallagher shifted his weight.

"Why? What's in it for you?"

"Uh . . ." Gallagher's voice was still dazed. "It's complicated. I just want to."

If this had been the first time Derek had seen Gallagher be absentminded, he might have been more concerned that the shirtless, possibly concussed man in front of him wasn't making sense.

"Again, why?"

"A lot of reasons." Gallagher shrugged, wincing as he moved. Bruised ribs? "The plumbing work might be more complex, but I can call someone for that. I'll do the drywall repair and even repaint your bedroom. If we can keep the extent of the structural damage from my uncle."

"How do I know you actually know what you're doing?" While nothing about his interactions with Gallagher inspired faith in his competence, Derek also had a very specific and incredibly personal reason to think Dylan Gallagher was an inconsiderate, self-involved ass.

"Just let me show you my bedroom, and I think I can convince you." Gallagher's tone was serious and urgent. "I really think we can work something out here."

"Um." Derek scrunched his face. "Nah, dude. I think we might have gotten our signals crossed here."

Abject horror flashed across Dylan's face. "Um . . . Yeah, no. *Believe me.* That's . . . that is absolutely not what I meant." Gallagher's ears turned magenta after a dismissively snarky huff. "I meant because I've been *renovating* the apartment for my uncle. That room's done, so you can see the drywall and painting work. I've got before photos too. *Christ* . . ." He rubbed his hand over his bare shoulder.

Derek never would have guessed Gallagher would have that many tattoos hidden beneath his typical uniform of that faded gray hoodie and paint-stained jeans. The intricate fine lines and circles covering his lean-muscled upper back were especially surprising. "Guess I'll get to fix up the kitchen now . . . I'll just frame it like it's a surprise from the others. Floors were a wreck anyhow. No choice now . . ." Dylan's eyes went slightly unfocused.

Derek's body was on the verge of collapse, and now his bed was an unsalvageable mess at two A.M.

Dylan Gallagher seemed to have no idea that Derek knew *exactly* who he was from the second he moved in. Although given that Gallagher couldn't remember the trash pick-up days or to close his sunroof in the rain, he probably didn't bother remembering how he'd treated Jake Murphy several years ago. Jake Murphy, the older brother of Derek's best friend, Olive. Jake Murphy, who was once *almost* Derek's . . . something.

Just having Dylan Gallagher in the building tugged on a wound Derek thought had healed, and now the man literally crash-landed into Derek's life. Yet for some reason, the longer Gallagher was around wincing and bleeding, the more Derek's ER nurse instincts urged him to get the guy an ice pack or a Band-Aid. And Derek did not want to be nice to Dylan Gallagher.

"I have to get up for work in . . ." Derek looked at his phone and groaned. "Three hours. I'm going to go crash on my couch, so you—"

"How 'bout . . ." Dylan stepped forward, still clutching the broken half of his glasses in a way that made him look like Derek's sister Michelle's douchebag New York City friend who wore a monocle unironically. "You stay upstairs. I'll sleep on the couch. I can put something in the kitchen where the floor broke to keep the dog out. Then you can get some sleep in an actual bed while I clean this up."

If Satan himself had offered him a bed, Derek might have sold his soul right then. Still, the idea of sharing a space with Dylan Gallagher made him feel unsettled in a way that tightened every muscle in his body. His arms crossed in front of his chest and his jaw clicked. Gus rubbed his nose on Derek's leg, annoyed Derek had stopped petting him.

Gallagher exhaled. "Stop being a stubborn ass and just let me take care of this. If I muck it up, I'll call a professional."

"Oh, *I'm* the ass? You're just going to do some shoddy bad flip work and fix the cosmetic stuff while—"

"I *do not do* shitty flips." Gallagher glared.

That must have hit a nerve.

Gallagher's grip tightened on that one half of his glasses, sending another streak of blood down his arm.

Goddamn. How deep was that cut? Did he even notice the blood?

Shaking his head, Derek headed into the hallway.

"Where're you going?"

"Your hand's still bleeding because you keep forgetting to hold pressure on it, and I'd rather not have your genetic material all over my apartment if I kill you for waking me up and wrecking my bedroom. C'mere." Even though Derek's general desire to be liked did not apply to Gallagher, he still didn't want the dude to hemorrhage, or faint again, or whatever. If Gallagher was Derek's only hope in handling this, he couldn't let the guy get gangrene or tetanus. No matter what had happened between him and Jake.

"I'm fine."

Giving up diplomatic negotiations, Derek yanked Dylan by his un-bloody arm into the bathroom. A guy who fainted at the sight of blood probably wouldn't know how or bother to properly clean out a laceration.

Derek twisted the faucet. "Look away. Just hold it under there for a second."

As the water hit the cut, Gallagher's low hiss prickled against Derek's bare skin. "You work at a hospital, right? The scrubs. I mean, you wear scrubs sometimes. Not now obviously . . ." His gritted-teeth gaze drifted downward but then shot back up to Derek's face as if scandalized by the bare skin and underwear.

Derek grabbed gloves from the first aid kit under the sink. "ER nurse." He was too busy mentally figuring out why he had felt the need to pull Gallagher into a full-bodied embrace to catch him before for a longer response. From an ergonomic perspective, Derek *should* have just eased the man's deadweight ass to the ground, but when Gallagher had gone all pale and limp, some bizarre instinct made Derek catch him as if Gallagher were some swooning debutante on Olive's newest TV show obsession. After getting her own well-deserved happily ever after six months ago, Olive converted from cynic to hopeless romantic. This must be her fault.

"Sorry . . ." Gallagher wrinkled his nose as if straightening the glasses usually perched there. "I don't do good with blood. Never have."

Derek must have missed the *thanks for not letting me fall on my ass* part. *You're so welcome, jackass.* "Yeah. Noted."

"Do you have to be a dick about everything?"

Derek *was* being a dick, but even without the personal history shit, *it was two o'clock in the fucking morning and his ceiling had collapsed.*

Ignoring the question, Derek focused on gently cleaning the wound. He dried it with gauze but frowned as it reopened again.

"What?" Dylan asked in a tentative voice very different from the one he'd just used to call Derek a dick.

Derek tried to make his voice less assholey. "I'll bandage this for now, but you probably need to go get stitches."

"Can't we just pour peroxide on it or something?"

"No. Do *not* do that. Ever. It does more harm than good. It's clean now. But it's going to keep opening—"

"It'll be fine." Gallagher pursed his lips. "I've had worse."

"Yet he still faints." The sarcasm kept popping out without permission.

"Remember that whole asking you *not* to be a dick about it thing?"

"Remember that whole falling through my ceiling at two A.M. thing?"

"Are you going to let me fix your apartment or not?" The patterns of black ink streaking across Gallagher's chest and shoulders flexed.

Yanking his eyes back to where they were supposed to be, Derek taped the edge of gauze into place and then snapped his gloves into the trash. "You can try. I *am* going to take you up on the place to sleep though, because if Gus doesn't sleep on a bed, he's stiff the next day." At the sound of his name, Gus lumbered in and stared at Dylan.

"Whoa wait, I offered the bed to you, not a *dog*."

"This *dog* is the only reason I'm not calling your uncle right now about the flood. If you can actually fix this and somehow pay for it, then fine. I'll keep it quiet. If you mess it up, you're going to have to get a professional to fix it." Derek couldn't afford to pay the $2,500 insurance deductible right now anyway. If Gallagher was right and there was a bigger issue, insurance might refuse to pay.

"Fine. The dog can use the bed too. Whatever." He studied Gus, whose tongue had lolled out. "It doesn't . . . shit the bed or—"

"No. I don't sleep next to an animal who shits the bed." Derek rolled his eyes.

Gallagher lifted his hands defensively. "I mean, you said he's old. Just asking. I might have some of my niece's diapers around, but I'm not sure they'd fit him."

Two steps into the hallway, Gallagher stopped so abruptly Derek's bare chest smacked into his tattooed back and his crotch collided with Dylan's surprisingly firm ass. To stop himself from accidentally tackling the guy, Derek's hand reached around, a palm bracing against Gallagher's stomach while the other grabbed on to the wall.

Gallagher twisted away as if contact with Derek's skin was painful. "Christ, can you put some clothes on or something?"

"You're the one who . . . ah . . . okay. Sorry about that." Derek probably *could* have stopped the cocky smile from spreading on his face. But he didn't.

The look on Gallagher's face was the same one he got from men catching themselves checking out Derek's body in locker rooms when they thought he wasn't looking. Since his rather momentous ascent to the sunnier side of puberty, Derek had never been shy. Olive might call him a smug asshole for it, but Derek had spent years working on this body, and he could damn well enjoy it when his hard work was appreciated.

"Something about me making you uncomfortable, Gallagher? I was just trying not to knock you over."

"No, ughhh, I just . . . like . . . whatever. Ugh." Dylan dragged his hand through his hair, flicking drywall bits in every direction. "Right. So I just remembered . . . I keep my keys on a hook by the door, so I don't forget them. I don't have them. Think the chain's locked too."

Shit. Well, there went Derek's remaining time to sleep.

"Who has an extra key?"

Dylan frowned. His face looked younger without the glasses even though Derek knew he was also in his midthirties. "I think the woman living above my unit does, maybe? Uncle Sean said she has extra keys for most of the units because her sister—"

Derek shook his head. "We're *not* going to knock on Carol Taylor's door at two A.M."

"Why not?"

"Because she's probably sleeping in a coffin after drinking the blood of her enemies."

"Huh?"

"Anyone else?"

"My sister, but . . ." He shook his head. "She's got exams this week. I'm not waking her up."

"Well, then I guess Gus's sleeping on the couch. I'll be on the pillows. You can take the floor."

"Wait." This time when Dylan appraised Derek's body, it wasn't with heat—it was a cool calculation. "How tall are you exactly?"

Chapter 4

Dylan searched for a place to grip along the intact floor. It felt sturdy enough. The useless pieces of his glasses were in his pocket, so he couldn't be sure, but the damage to the joists appeared fairly isolated even from this angle. Someone had cut out the drywall and done a poor patch job on the pipe to hide the problem. Probably whoever sold Derek the apartment. *Damn.* Such a shitty thing to do to someone.

"Can you pull up already?" Derek's muffled voice was strained. "This has got to be the dumbest idea anyone's ever had."

"I know you don't know me very well"—Dylan grunted, stretching the extra inch he needed to reach the best grip point. The bruising probably covering his entire right side hurt enough that he barely noticed the pain in his hand anymore—"but you can be assured this doesn't even scratch the surface of bad ideas I've had in the past."

"That's not actually very comforting, Gallagher."

Dylan balanced his weight as he prepared to pull up. At least Derek had thrown on a sweatshirt, so Dylan's bare feet weren't slipping on the skin he'd been caught ogling minutes earlier.

That hot, arrogant ass had known exactly what Dylan had been thinking while looking at him in the bathroom. And *sure*, Dylan's mouth had gone bone-dry as Derek's ridiculously chiseled muscles had actually rippled in front of him. Anyone would be disconcerted by a fitness magazine–worthy V-cut staring at them while sitting pathetically crouched on a toilet lid so the V-cut owner could gently tend their wound. Those stupid muscles had been taunting him to the point that even now Dylan couldn't get "U Can't Touch This" out of his head, and it would probably echo there every single time he saw Derek from now on.

Christ, he hated MC Hammer.

Dylan anchored the back of a borrowed hammer into the linoleum. As he pulled himself up, he was newly grateful for every hour he spent at the climbing gym over the last few years.

Once up, he slid away as if spelunking across a slippery cave cliff to the structurally sound hallway. The runner rug wasn't even damp. The uneven hardwood had sent the flood directly into Derek's bedroom rather than flooding the rest of his uncle's apartment.

Great for Uncle Sean. Doubly shitty for Derek. *Woof.*

"I'll unlock the front door."

The only response from below was a vaguely affirmative growl.

Those growls were going to murder Dylan.

After pulling on a T-shirt, he estimated having ten minutes to make the bedroom less awful. Clothes were everywhere. Especially the clothes in that no-man's-land category of clean enough to potentially be re-worn, but too dirty to go back in the drawers. His uncle's bedroom furniture was exactly the kind that was incompatible with his brain. Antique dressers with deep drawers that swallowed his T-shirts like a black hole. It was nothing like his perfectly designed closet at his own house, but he shouldn't complain. Not with everything his uncle was dealing with.

Although this certainly would be easier if Dylan's actual house wasn't contractually unavailable. He could have immediately jumped in his car and let Derek and the dog have Uncle Sean's entire apartment to themselves.

The unexpected surge in professional work stress over the last few weeks meant Dylan had started to make big mistakes again. Like forgetting to take his meds, and thus forgetting to do all the things that had made his recent life so much better. Flooding the entire stupid kitchen was bigger than any mistake he'd made in years, and it was difficult not to fall back into the old patterns and intrusive thoughts from before he'd gotten all the diagnoses that changed his perspective.

Breaking something sometimes doesn't mean you're broken.

Dylan mentally repeated the phrase his sister had gotten from a therapist over and over as he stuffed things into the small closet. He'd redone the closet already, but it was filled with Uncle Sean's boxes. The old desk in the corner had already become a catchall drop area of doom. After five minutes of quasi-tidying, *every* other surface was covered in random tools, tile samples, diagrams, and receipts. But at least the floor was clear now. Dylan yanked off the sheets and then remembered he had no idea where the hell he'd put the extra ones he bought last week.

He walked through the apartment grabbing forgotten cups and mugs he never seemed to notice until someone was coming over. *"Shit."*

After a thorough excavation of another crap pile next to the repurposed hall closet, he found the Target bag with the new sheets. Hopefully Derek wasn't like Chase, Dylan's California ex-boyfriend/quasi-boss, and could tolerate box store thread counts. If he was used to sleeping next to a furry . . .

"*Shit*. The dog."

Dylan set up the baby gate they used for his nieces and nephews in the hallway and filled a bowl with water. Derek might legitimately murder him if something happened to his allegedly "visiting" massive were-dog.

Just as Dylan tossed the comforter back onto the bed, the front door opened. He ran into the living room and scanned it. Yeah, he'd missed a lot of messy shit.

While walking in, Derek, whose apartment had been perfectly neat and minimalist except for the bedroom Dylan had wrecked, eyed the mess with cool skepticism. If the guy hadn't been such a royal pain in the ass since he first met him, Dylan might apologize or explain the chaos. But Derek's jab about fainting still stung more than Dylan's hand wound.

Derek's athletic shirt was snug against his shoulders. He was wearing very thin heathered gray sweatpants. *Christ*, was Dylan sweating suddenly?

Derek cleared his throat. That conceited half smile was back. *Jesus Christ on a Popsicle stick.*

"I wasn't checking you out." Dylan's mouth snapped shut too late.

"Sure you weren't." An exhausted yawn made Derek's smugness vanish. He left his keys on the small bookshelf by the front door. "Bed?"

The dog, for what it was worth, whined almost apologetically at Derek's curtly demanding tone.

Good hellhound.

Dylan's sweeping gesture to the door was somehow a blend of crossing guard and concierge. "Your accommodations are right through there, sir."

WHY DID HE SAY THAT?

Dylan's furiously pumping blood seemed to scald his ears. He had been trying to make a joke about Derek's tone. Zero out of ten for execution.

"Sir," Derek repeated with a cocked-eyebrow nod that made Dylan wish the polar dog had just eaten him when he had the chance so he didn't have to live through this moment. "Kay."

Dylan glanced to the front door—half to make sure it was locked and half to give himself an excuse to look away from Derek's pitying derision. "It was just a jo—"

The bedroom door closed. Derek (and the polar dog) had disappeared behind it without sparing him another word.

Dylan sighed. "That's fair."

Realizing he was speaking to a door, Dylan decided he'd

been pathetic enough for one night and grabbed his laptop to make sure there were no more emergency emails from Chase about the project. There weren't. Small mercies were the best kind he could hope for right now. Chase was in Singapore and was the kind of Stanford business school tech bro who thought that whatever time zone *he* was in should determine the hours for every coding minion (Chase's term) reporting to him. Dylan was *not* one of the aforementioned coding minions, but his contract with Chase's company required responses when system errors occurred. Even if those system errors occurred in the middle of the night and the subsequent distraction caused a major household catastrophe.

He headed to the bathroom and braced himself on the sink for a couple of breaths before looking at his reflection. Sludge coated his hair. He definitely needed a haircut before seeing his mother again. Grime coated his chest. His back right ribs ached but weren't excruciating. He'd probably have some impressive bruises tomorrow. At least the bandages on his messed-up hand survived the climb.

He shuddered. As a kid, his brothers tried to cure his blood-related passing-out episodes by showing him every gruesome hockey injury they got. Clearly, it hadn't worked.

Dylan rinsed his unbandaged hand and pressed the cold, wet palm to his cheek.

He might never recover from the humiliation of waking up in the brawny arms of the man Dylan's sister Felicity called Hottie McDickhead. Well, it had started as Dr. McDreamy when they first saw him standing outside Uncle Sean's kitchen window in those light blue scrubs that showed the perfect amount of bicep. The jogger bottoms had made it obvious how rarely Derek skipped leg day. Like never. What exercises even gave a person an ass like that? It was like his butt muscles had muscles. Dylan had whispered the word *dibs* to Felicity, just as Derek turned around and looked up at the window. When his eyes locked on Dylan they *actually glittered* with cold, highly perplexing rage.

"*What'd you do to that guy, Dylan? Key his car?*" Felicity asked as Derek drove off.

"*No clue.*"

They hadn't even met before, and Derek glared at him like he thought Dylan tortured kittens or listened to Creed or something. He couldn't blame Derek for being an asshole tonight, though. Dylan *had* fallen through his ceiling.

Dylan groaned. "Of all people, I had to wreck the apartment of the grouchy local homosexual Adonis." Dylan pulled on his old and favorite Stanford hoodie from the back of the bathroom door.

At least he could make it up to Derek by tackling the worst of the mess now.

The longer water sat, the worse the damage could be.

Dylan could get a few hours of cleanup done and then sleep in the bed after Derek left for the hospital. Maybe this roommate situation could work for long enough so that his family wouldn't know about the flooded kitchen. He could almost hear his brothers' guffaws in his head.

He pocketed Derek's keys, grabbed some contractor-grade trash bags, popped in his earbuds, and headed downstairs.

✳✳✳

Dylan was closing his fifth sack of trash when a strong hand nudged his shoulder. Dylan whipped around and pulled out an earbud so he could hear what a very angry-looking Derek was saying.

"What are you doing?"

"Water damage gets worse, and I had a lot of caffeine and that accidental nap before the whole disaster happened so . . ." He shrugged.

Derek's eyes darted to the stacks of items next to the towels in the corner. "You went through . . ."

"Oh right." Dylan *had* been a little surprised at what he found under the bed. Honestly, he didn't really know people had DVDs anymore. He'd found several large decorative baskets containing a collection of TV shows and movies. And they were *alphabetized*. Like he was an actual serial killer.

"I—ugh. It's—" Derek's cheeks and neck went deeper into that not-unpleasant rose color.

"The water saturated the baskets, so I had to take everything out. I was surprised that there were three different collector's editions of *Burlesque* to choose from, but I'm not judging. I was always more of a Meg Ryan kinda guy . . . when I watched those kinds of movies . . . with my sisters, I mean."

"*Burlesque* is an underrated masterpiece," Derek said solemnly.

"Is it the one with the legwarmers and 'Maniac,' or the one with Jessie from *Saved by the Bell*?"

"Neither." Derek's flush was either fury or embarrassment, hard to tell. "Those are *Flashdance* and *Showgirls*."

Dylan shrugged. "Kay. If you say so."

With an outraged grunt that was far too adorable to be scary, Derek glared at him. "Now, why the hell did you decide to just start going through my shit without asking me?"

"You said I could." Dylan pointed toward the hallway. "Oh, and the bins with the books are completely fine because they had better lid situa—"

"Most of those are my best friend's." The words rushed out more quickly than necessary.

"Some had your name written in the front." Dylan bit his lower lip hard to stop himself from laughing at how flustered Derek was getting about the hundred dog-eared and broken-spined romances that were mixed in with a few classics, as well as a book called *The Joy of Gay Sex* . . . which seemed like it had some pretty good information. "The . . . uh . . ." Dylan gestured to the opaque fabric box that was, unfortunately, not water fast. "Um—toys, I decided to let you handle yourself. Water got in there, so it might just be a trash and replace situation."

"Goddamn it, Gallagher." Derek grabbed hold of Dylan. For a second, Dylan was *very* confused about what was happening and why Derek was looking like he wanted to tackle him to the ground between the box of ruined sex toys and the stack of rescued Nora Ephron movies . . . not that part of Dylan would have minded . . .

But Derek's fingers tightened and slid to his elbow.

"Ouch. I'm not judging you for the dildos, *Christ*, let me go."

"I'm *not* attacking you." Derek's other hand cradled his wrist. "You bled through your bandage."

"Aw shit. Again?" Dylan's shoulders lifted dismissively, but he didn't look at his hand. "It's fine. Doesn't hurt that bad."

"You need stitches." Derek's tender frown contrasted with his irritated tone.

"It'll be fine." Unless the hand was in imminent danger of falling off, he wouldn't be going to a hospital. Dylan hated doctors. "So . . . uh . . . where's the monster?"

"Asleep in his back-up dog bed." Derek's head twitched toward the living room. "My dog walker knows the deal with Carol, so he'll be around later today at the normal time."

"What exactly is the deal with Carol, and what do you mean the normal time?"

"Carol Taylor is the bane of my existence," Derek said with his face a complete deadpan.

"Is elaborating possible? Carol's the one who drives that pink Mary Kay Cadillac, right?"

"Carol Taylor, HOA tyrant, hates big dogs, and—um—she didn't like the previous owner of my unit. She *specifically* hates Gus because of a bad experience with a Great Dane. Not Gus, because Gus is a *gentleman* with better taste than to have his paws anywhere near a person who sells MLM products."

"Out of curiosity, why is an enormous but purportedly gentle-manly harlequin Great Dane Bulldog mix here at all?"

"Because he belonged to my best friend's brother who died seven months ago."

Well *shit*, now Dylan felt like an asshole. No wonder Derek was so protective.

"I'm really sorry about your loss." Dylan had never been good at this stuff. But his sister Felicity was in her psychiatric clinicals right now, and she had given him some tips at human-ing recently. "Do you . . . want to talk about it?"

Derek's head snapped up. "The fuck?" Derek eyed Dylan as if he thought Dylan was an alien. "No, I don't want to talk about it with you. I just want you to get out of my apartment."

"What about—"

"I get off work at seven thirty tonight. We can talk about the logistical details for fixing stuff then. Back to Carol. I have her schedule mapped out for my dog walker. In addition to being a complete autocratic wackadoo, she keeps to a strict routine. If she sees Gus around, the deal is to pretend that Olive is here visiting and will be back in an hour. There's no rule against short-term visits. She's knows some vague details about Olive's situation and has a soft spot—soft for Carol—for peripherally famous people."

"Peripherally famous? Olive is—"

"My best friend." Derek snapped his fingers. "Keep up, Gal-lagher."

"Best friend. Olive. Peripherally famous. Visiting. Gus. Got it."

"Do *not* go through my shit again." Derek pointed overhead. "Can you just please focus on the big hole in the ceiling? Is that possible?"

"Sure. *Great* idea." Dylan crossed his arms over his chest. He hadn't been stupid enough to expect effusive gratitude, but he *had* spent the last however many hours making sure that Derek's "shit" wasn't ruined. He rarely felt time pass while hyperfocused on a task with an audiobook in his ear, and so he was surprised at how many hours had flown by. Hyperfocus was how he had gotten most of the reno work on his uncle's apartment done already. It was why he could spend twelve hours straight coding and get a week's worth of work done. It was a perk of his brain. Felicity had told him it was important to recognize the perks.

But Derek certainly wasn't recognizing any perks of having Dylan around, and all Dylan was getting for those hours was being treated like the scum of the earth. Again. Dylan twitched his head toward a bag in the corner. "That's trash. The linens are in the dryer. I think they're salvageable. The comforter . . ." He pointed to another bag. "Is there. It seemed too big for your washer and dryer. I was going to take it to a laundromat."

Derek's expression softened. "So . . . it was just the stuff under the bed that was ruined?"

"The mattress is probably dead too."

"It sucked anyway. I'll get a new one." Mirroring Dylan's posture, Derek crossed his arms over his chest, but when Derek did this, it emphasized how broad he was. "Thanks. For cleaning up. I'm going to shower."

Dylan had never heard the word *thanks* said in a way that sounded more like *GTF away from me*.

"I'll . . . uh . . . just go upstairs then."

"Try not to wake Gus."

"Kay . . ."

"Oh, and thanks for putting the water out for him. He appreciated it."

That thanks *was* genuine.

As soon as Dylan arrived back at his apartment, exhaustion hit him with the weight of . . . well, a ceiling collapsing, probably.

After a quick cleanup trip to the bathroom, he toppled into bed.

The pillow smelled unfamiliar but not unpleasant. It brought him back to that moment when he'd regained consciousness, held tight to a quite bare, well-muscled chest. A chest that smelled just like his pillow.

Chapter 5

Derek's eighth cup of coffee was now lukewarm. He wasn't sure which would be worse—falling asleep and getting fired for it or shitting his scrub pants from guzzling tepid caffeine juice. Stomach ominously thundering, he sat at the charge nurse computer at the center of the nurses' station and scribbled down the names of the evening shift nurses. When he looked up, the two women listening to his story were gaping at him.

Olive's swivel chair creaked as she leaned an elbow on the desk next to his. "Are you talking about the guy who moved in above you a few months ago?" Her hair was bushier than usual, rebelling against her scrunchie-twisted bun.

"Yeah." He nudged her wild strands away from his writing space.

This was the first five minutes any of them had sat down in twelve trainwreck-shift hours.

"He's the one who looks like Clark Kent but *really* like if . . . ooh, if Jonathan Groff had a baby with Matt Bomer, and he became a slightly edgy librarian? That guy? Tattoos?"

"Oooh." Joni rolled her chair over from where she'd been finishing up orders at the provider workstation. "You had me at slightly edgy librarian." Derek's brain was made of overcooked oatmeal, so he couldn't interpret the wordless female glance she exchanged with Olive.

After Joni had moved to town last fall, she and Olive struck up an immediate friendship. If Olive liked someone, Derek almost always liked them too, and sure enough, now Joni generally came over to Olive's anytime they all hung out. It was good for Derek to have another single person on hand to balance out the love-drunk mushiness Olive and Stella displayed during their first months of official coupledom after their bizarre "fake dating" beginning.

Derek reflexively swigged his (now cold) coffee. His lower intestine barked louder than Gus ever had. "Uh—white dude, midthirties. Brown floppy hair. Glasses. Freckles. Yeah, I guess he has some tattoos now that you mention it." He shifted his weight and avoided eye contact.

Olive turned to Joni, mouth pushing into a knowing pout. "Derek thinks he's hot."

"I fucking do not."

"You fucking do too." Her sparkling eyes narrowed. "Possible emphasis on the *fucking*. I mean, hopefully. He's not exactly your usual type but that's not a bad thing. How many boring but smoking-hot generic jock dudes can there be on Tinder anyway?"

"Mean, Olive." He took a bite of the protein bar he'd forgotten about an hour ago. "And also, the limit does not exist."

"*Pathetic.* That Dylan guy though . . . I like him."

"Hmph."

Never mind about the always liking the people Olive liked thing.

She clasped her hands together like she was making mental plans for brunch dates involving stupid overpriced food and matching cashmere scarves or something else equally cliché. Her smile could make a cavity throb. "You know, I thought Stella was too good for me too."

"First of all, Dylan Gallagher is not 'too good' for me. Second of all, *no.*"

Joni's nod conveyed entertained agreement. Agreement with *Olive.*

Olive flushed with excitement.

If it hadn't been Olive's last shift before she left for her big trip, Derek would have called out of work for the first time in ten years. He even managed to get up early enough to pick up her cake from the bakery. Before the bakery, he'd had to walk Gus during the time Carol—aka HOA Karen or Parakeet Karen, depending on how Derek was feeling that day—went to water aerobics at the YMCA. He was too exhausted for this absurd interrogation. But he also couldn't tell Olive *that* or she would know he'd fibbed about getting permission for Gus to stay in his building.

This lie was only the third he'd ever told his best friend in their twenty-plus–year friendship, and compared to the first two, it was laughably small.

It was as if Olive's new relationship with her hot pilot girlfriend, Stella, had injected her with love radiation serum, and she was hoping its effects were contagious. Somewhat infuriating, but also . . . sweet? Really it was just so essentially Olive to want everyone in her life to be as happy as she was.

"So while Dylan fixes everything . . . it'll be Dylan living with you. Well, you living with Dylan. So . . . Dylan and Derek sharing that tiny apartment. Dylan . . . Derek . . . Derek . . . Dylan."

Derek glared. "*Don't* make the joke."

"But I want to make the joke," she whined.

"Do *not* make the joke."

Olive straightened. "I'm gonna make the joke."

He gently hammered his fist on the charge nurse desk. "Goddamn it, Olivia—"

"Not my name. And . . . *ahem*." She affected the voice of a smarmy stand-up comic, holding the end of her stethoscope like a microphone. "Sure seems like there's a lot of *D* in that apartment." Olive made a tiny drumming and cymbal crash motion.

Joni burst out laughing.

Derek covered his head with his hands and lowered his

forehead to the table. "I hate you. And him. I'm not going to sleep with him."

Dylan Gallagher was objectively good looking, but in that boy-next-door who's a regular in a *Dungeons & Dragons* gaming convention kind of way.

"Why do you *hate* him? Like, you've *always* seemed like you hated him, even when he just moved in. He seems pretty inoffensive. What did he do to you?"

Derek winced into the table where Olive couldn't see his face.

So . . .

Corollaries to the original lies count under the umbrella of *first* lies, thus Derek was not telling more lies when he answered. The truth would dampen Olive's glow. Any mention of her brother did.

Uh, so he went out with your brother once, and Jake was really into him but then the dude went off on him and made him feel like shit.

Nope. He would not be saying that. It was her last day here, and Derek loved seeing her carefree and happy.

"Well, for starters he walks around his apartment at weird hours, and oh yeah . . ." Derek's voice rose with indignation. "Can we get back to the fact that he fell into my bedroom?"

Joni offered a teasing smile. "I didn't realize it was your *bedroom* he fell into. Darn, I was going to say this was a rule thirty-four situation, but honestly, it's almost too easy."

Olive's mouth pouted upward in confusion. "What's rule thirty-four?"

Derek groaned. "It's a stupid internet saying that if something exists there's a porn of it."

"Out of curiosity, what were you both wearing when the fall occurred?" Joni said in the same sweet but clinical voice she used when asking octogenarians what creams they used for their hemorrhoids.

"Whose side are you on, Joni?" Derek asked.

Joni blinked her eyes looking like a mix of angel and Bambi.

"Oh my god." Olive smacked his shoulder. "What *were* you wearing?"

"I was wearing a man's sleeping attire, and he was wearing jeans."

"Is 'a man's sleeping attire' a euphemism for naked? Because then that really is the beginning of a porno." Olive's eyebrows almost reached her hairline.

"I had underwear on, you perverts." Derek rubbed that sore spot on his jaw that meant he had been grinding his teeth last night. He could not afford to break another molar. Although . . . Dylan's bed was surprisingly comfortable. Maybe he could get a mattress like it.

"And he was . . . just wearing jeans? No shirt . . ."

Derek really did avoid lying if he could help it, but his reluctance to answer was an answer in and of itself. For the next several minutes, Joni and Olive were laughing so hard he would probably have to put oxygen on them soon. Not that he would. They deserved what they got. Suffocate away.

"So is there only one bed in Dylan's apart—"

"Gah . . ." Derek waved his hand in a *can we concentrate on the important things* gesture. "That dude could have landed on Gus."

Olive's face sobered a little. "But he *didn't*. Gus is fine. Though, if it's a problem he's there with the repairs, I'm sure Stella's dad or my sister would—"

"Gus *is* fine. With me." Having Gus around reminded him of some of the happiest moments in his life. The evenings spent with Olive and Jake at Jake's house up North, having bonfires and cookouts and watching movies on his projector screen while newly adopted Gus gamboled along and snuggled with them under that big flannel blanket. He wished he had that blanket.

Joni grabbed some gauze from a packet beside her and wiped tears from her eyes. "Alright, now yes, back to the scenario at hand."

"It was not a scenario. It was just a scatterbrained neighbor flooding his kitchen and falling through a hole in the ceiling onto my bed."

"Oh my god. He landed on your *bed*? A half-naked man fell through the ceiling and landed on your bed while water deluged down all around you? Ahh . . ." Olive's eyes went wide. "Did you say hallelu—"

"No." He pointed at her mouth as if hexing her into silence. "If you were going to make the 'It's Raining Men' joke, Dylan already made it. It wasn't funny then, and it's certainly not now."

Undeterred, Olive snickered. "Sounds like a kindred spirit for me." She wrapped her arms around Derek's shoulders. "I was so worried about leaving you for a few months, but now I feel much better. If he cooks for you, you'll *have* to marry him."

"I would rather marry *literally* anyone." And by anyone, he meant no one. That was never going to be his future. Not with Jake gone. Olive squeezed his neck harder until Joni was paged overhead and a call bell rang. His two evil friends scurried off in opposite directions. He swirled the dregs of his coffee.

Olive smiled more now than she'd ever smiled since Jake's accident. She was still savagely sarcastic and cynical, but those cracks of deep unhappiness beneath the surface were gone. She deserved that. She deserved everything after what she'd gone through during Jake's coma. Olive deserved to be so stupid happy.

It made those two lies almost worth it.

If she ever found out about what had happened between Derek and Jake, she would *lose* it. Not just because she'd be pissed about the lying. She would hate that she wasn't there for Derek when his heart was broken too. She would be furious at herself for not seeing what was going on. He didn't want her to see him that way. It wasn't like there was ever a good time to drop it into conversation: *"Hey, so NBD, but I got drunk and slept with your brother, lied to you about it, and then we hooked up again two weeks before he went into an irreversible coma, and by the way I've been in love with him for twenty years."*

Hell to the no.

Lately, Olive had subtly (for Olive) hinted that Derek should consider deleting a few apps or thinking about dates serving purposes beyond basic needs. But Derek was fine with his personal life. Just because Olive had a happily ever after didn't mean that was possible for him. The small glimpses he'd gotten of happily ever after had wrecked him . . . twice.

Casual was his only option. It was the safe option.

Something about the way Dylan Gallagher had looked at Derek this morning had made Derek think that casual was not that guy's thing.

Derek's phone vibrated. He hoped it would be a text from his mom because, after a weirdly short The bats are gone. Everything's fine text from her this morning, she hadn't replied to any of Derek's other questions about how the rest of the night had gone. But the text was not from his mother. He scanned the screen and swore.

Parakeet Karen.

Chapter 6

CAROL

I noticed Mr. Gallagher's nephew going in and out of your unit several times carrying what looked like tools.

CAROL

Now, while the HOA cannot regulate how each individual owner chooses to do renovation work, it is strongly encouraged that you vet large-scale repair work with the board given the potential for complications that could potentially impact multiple owners, say with plumbing or electrical. If you choose not to do this and there is a problem, you face fines for that choice.

CAROL

You can also receive fines for noise complaints.

CAROL

I would appreciate the respect of your PROMPT response to my concerns, Mr. Chang.

Derek avoided quick replies when he was furious, so he slipped his phone in his pocket.

Ten minutes later, while grabbing crutches from the supply room, another barrage of messages came through. Still none of them from his mother.

CAROL
Also, I heard a very loud crash and what I believe was a howl from your apartment.

CAROL
While I understand that your female friend visits you sometimes and that this is not prohibited, her dog cannot be present in your apartment for a period longer than 24 hours straight per HOA bylaws.

CAROL
I did knock, and no one answered.

CAROL
Given that I am concerned about your friend who must be in the unit because why else would her dog be there.

"Jesus Christ." Derek growled as a flurry of text alerts interrupted his attempt to reply.

CAROL
I hope you understand that I have your friend's best interest at heart.

CAROL
After all, anything could be wrong.

CAROL
And there was no answer in the apartment.

Derek's thumbs tapped so hard against the screen he had to remind himself that shattered screens from rage-texting probably weren't covered under phone warranties.

He could easily imagine Carol Taylor beating on the door while wearing one of her electric purple Florida palm trees shirts paired with those clementine-colored stirrup leggings and Crocs—her chosen post–water aerobics uniform. Her brassy blond hair would be sprayed into that signature aggressive half bob while she sang the song of her people . . . i.e., nosy white lady complaints.

> CAROL
> This situation is why you gave me an emergency key. Wellness checks are permitted under certain circumstances based on section 10.7.1ab of the HOA handbook.

"Shit. No. No. No." Derek swiped across the screen. He closed his eyes and sighed. There was nothing else to do. He swiped to Gallagher's name. He'd only given her that key after she'd cornered him at an HOA meeting—the only one he'd ever attended—and told him a sob story about how the two apartments once flooded and the previous owner of Derek's unit had lost everything when they couldn't gain access to shut off the leaking pipe and that the water had nearly drowned one of her birds. That story seemed more ominous now.

> DEREK
> Need distraction. HOA Karen is trying to get into my apartment.

Three dots in Gallagher's message box appeared and then disappeared several times.

> DEREK
> I need you to keep her from finding out Gus is there.

DEREK
Gallagher! Can you fucking help me or not?

DYLAN
In a tight spot . . . literally. Got situation covered. And in the future can you possibly refrain from cursing at me when I'm trying to fucking help you? I'm hiding from a scary old blond lady who is brandishing what looks like a rolled-up copy of The National Review like a baseball bat.

DYLAN
I swear to Christ if I get beaten to death by fascist trash, I will haunt this building. And you.

Derek suppressed a chuckle. A fuzzy photo came through. Gallagher obviously had one of the newest iPhone models like Derek's younger sister had, because he was able to take a photo in near darkness. It was grainy, just like the ones Amy took of her sleeping kids. The photo showed a portion of a large black snout and a shoulder that must have been Dylan's. His T-shirt was covered in drool. Derek squinted at the photo. There was a box behind him labeled MICHELLE'S DANCE SHIT.

DEREK
Are you in the closet?

DYLAN
I swore I never would be again, yet here I am.

Derek chuckled in spite of himself.

DYLAN
Related topic. Are there canine dentists? I think
something died in your dog's mouth.

DEREK
Where's Karen?

DYLAN
From what I can hear, she's been snooping through
the kitchen. She opened your bedroom door, but then
I heard her in the main room, so I don't think she saw
the hole in the ceiling.

DEREK
Okay.

DYLAN
Of course. You're so welcome for this. Yes, I can
really feel the gratitude.

"Snarky ass—"

"Who's got a snarky ass?" Olive asked. "Aside from me."

"My neighbor."

"Dylan . . . ?" she said in a suggestive voice.

"Yeah, he's—" *Shit*, this is why lying sucked. It was never just one lie. A lie always turned into more lies. "He's doing some of the work fixing the hole, and he's hiding from my snooping neighbor who thinks we need to run all renovation work through the HOA."

"That was a surprisingly detailed response. Hmm . . ." Olive wrinkled her nose.

"Yeah." He kept his face neutral.

Derek had been the one to teach Olive back in middle school

that the first sign someone was lying was giving too many details while answering a question that should have been simple. He was off his game.

They left the supply room, and he handed off the crutches to the nurse who needed them. He sat back down in the nurses' station and set his phone on the desk where he could see the screen.

Olive dropped into the chair beside him, her lips pressed into a worried frown. "Just how bad is this apartment situation?"

"It'll be fine. Got the repairs handled. Well, Gallagher does. I guess."

"It's really shitty this is happening. The sublet just moved into my place or I'd say you should go stay there. You have a deductible with the insurance, right?" She stared at the staffing paper instead of meeting his eye. "I know after everything you did for Michelle things have been tight. Can I—"

"Gallagher says he's going to pay in and do labor. I'm good."

But at the mention of Michelle, a new worry tugged at him. He needed to get to the bottom of Dylan's financial situation. He might not like the guy, but he didn't want him to fall into the same debt hole Michelle had fallen into. Being hounded by collections assholes wasn't something he'd wish on anyone. Even a man who fell through his apartment ceiling at two A.M. While Derek didn't usually put any stock in his apartment complex's very active gossip mill, with what Jake said about his . . . encounter . . . with Dylan, he couldn't entirely discount the whispered rumors that Dylan Gallagher was some eccentric, deadbeat nephew mooching off his uncle after a vague career upheaval.

"You're *sure* you're good?" Olive asked.

"Yup." He forced a smile. "I'm good. It'll be good. Maybe all the work fixing it up will help the shithole sell eventually. So, are you all packed? Ready for tomorrow?"

"Mostly." The concern hadn't left Olive's face.

She hadn't ever *said* she didn't approve of what Derek had done for Michelle, but he knew. She probably wanted to remind him that his youngest sister was no longer the seven-year-old in a ballet leotard she'd been when their father died. He *knew* that.

But Derek also knew he needed to fix things if he could. He'd failed Michelle growing up. He couldn't be everything she needed after their dad was gone. How could anyone expect him to let a few bills ruin her life?

Olive tapped on his desk, interrupting his thoughts. "Can Stella and I come see Gus tonight?"

"You just want to scope out Gallagher."

She pressed an affectedly innocent hand to her chest. "I just want to see my dog. How *dare* you assume . . ." That melodramatic sigh was definitely overkill. "That I, your best friend, would have ulterior motives . . . like trying to check out your hot neighbor to be sure that said neighbor is worthy of your future hand in marriage. Outrageous accusation."

"I hate you."

"Noted. So—"

"I'll order pizza. Make Joni come too."

A buzz from the desk.

> DYLAN
>
> I think we got lucky because she's not wearing those turquoise glasses she normally wears. I can see her through the crack in the door.

> DYLAN
>
> Why the hell did you give this lady a key?

> DEREK
>
> She was crying about her birds.

DYLAN

Her birds? She has birds? Like she has birds in her
apartment? Living there? On purpose?

Derek smirked, imagining Dylan's face all furrowed like it had
been about Gus. He was afraid of birds too? Big dogs, sure. But
birds? *This* was what he was concerned about? Not the fact that
this busybody had just been snooping through Derek's apartment
like Derek had something to hide. Derek *having* something to
hide was neither here nor there. She was still an insufferable pest.

When he looked up, two faces stared back.

Joni pushed some of her red hair out of her face and exchanged *another* bemused, knowing look with Olive. These
women and their damned looks.

Olive's grin widened.

Joni shook her head. "Here we go again."

"You all have no idea what you're talking about."

DYLAN

The entire right side of my ass is asleep because
your polar bear is cutting off blood flow.

DEREK

Cutting off blood flow to your ass? You're still in the
closet?

DYLAN

Why the hell else would I be complaining about my
ass to you? Your dog just fell asleep on top of me. If
he starts snoring, the jig is up.

A weird sensation came over Derek when he considered
Dylan's ass and exactly how it had looked and felt in the soaking wet jeans last night.

Nope. That's a big dripping pile of N-O-P-E.

DEREK

Who says "the jig is up" anymore?

DYLAN

Can you focus on getting bird lady out of here rather than my choice of idioms please?

DYLAN

DO SOMETHING

Groaning, Derek swiped to Karen's—crap—to *Carol*'s number.

"Hello, Mr. Chang. I've been waiting for your call." Carol's voice was closer to her parrot's trilling squawk than should be possible. Was it like when people looked like their dogs?

"I've been working in the hospital."

"Now, everything looks okay in your unit—"

"You're in my unit?" Derek feigned shock. "I'm sorry, why are you in my home without an invitation?"

"If you read my texts, you'll know that I was concerned there was an emergency—"

"*Carol.*" Derek's current mental health nursing diagnosis could be termed an *acute lack of fucks*, so he didn't bother to be polite. "Your desperate need to be nosy is not a god-damn emergency. Get the hell out of my house before I call the cops."

"Well, I *never*—I was just . . ." She inhaled a flustered breath and then heaved a few affected sobs. "I had the *best of intentions*."

"I'll bet you did. I want to hear the door closing behind you."

"Fine." A door slammed.

"I'll be coming by your unit tonight to get my key back."

"I have that key for your safety. For the safety of the neigh-boring units. For my *birds*."

"Pretty sure I'll feel safer if you don't have it anymore. Your birds will survive."

"I'll be bringing up your rudeness at the next HOA meeting."

"Cool. Maybe I'll come and bring up the whole illegally entering my home thing."

The artificial waterworks seemed to stop. "Mr. Chang, if I catch that dog living with you, I'll have no choice but to have the board fine you the maximum amount. That sister of yours was always pushing the rules too."

Derek's teeth clenched. "Since you were just in my apartment and didn't see a dog, I think I'll be okay."

"There was food and a water bowl by the door."

"As you said, as long as he doesn't stay longer than twenty-four hours in my apartment, you can't fine me."

"If you're doing unlicensed or unpermitted renovations, I *will* find out."

Derek stiffened. He hadn't thought about permits. Honestly, all he'd thought about last night was getting back to sleep and getting away from Dylan Gallagher. The illegal breed fine was intentionally exorbitant. If Carol figured out a way to make his financial life more miserable, he wouldn't be able to pay his mortgage. He'd have to go to his mom. It would take her CPA brain about five seconds to figure out he was broke because he paid off Michelle's credit card bills without asking her permission.

God, his life was a mess.

Movement caught his attention. Olive stood at the other end of the hallway, reading something in his expression that had nothing to do with Dylan.

"Is everything okay?" Olive mouthed.

Nodding, he turned down the phone volume so Olive couldn't hear Carol's bleating about obscure ordinances and HOA bylaws.

Olive hadn't moved past that hypervigilant anxiety of always waiting for the next catastrophe. After her brother's accident and everything else that happened with Jake, he couldn't blame her.

He muted his side of the line. "It's just the usual bureaucratic bullshit from Carol." He channeled all of his remaining energy into a normal eye roll with an entertained grin that would be the typical response to Carol's antics.

Olive's worry lines relaxed into a smirk. "Ask Parakeet Karen where she got those yellow Croc heels. They're amazing." She stifled giggles.

Derek's spluttered response was the kind of laugh hiding something sadder. Olive could always make him laugh. He had been so focused on figuring out the logistics of keeping Gus, he hadn't processed the idea of her being gone for months.

Olive turned to answer a question from a passing radiology tech, thankfully distracting her from the phone call and the fact that the emotional impact of her leaving for a while was hitting him all at once.

He couldn't think about this now. Olive deserved to fly off into the sunset with her gorgeous girlfriend without worrying about anything, including Gus. How bad could things get in eight weeks? Gus had been Jake's dog, and Derek was the only person Olive truly trusted with him.

Derek was the one who could handle things. He could handle this.

Goddamn it.

"*Carol.*"

Carol paused her rant. The furious cheeping, squeaking, and clicking in the background meant Carol was surrounded by her Hitchcockian collection of feathered creatures.

"If I choose to do any work on my home, it's my business."

Carol ended the call with a disgruntled harumph.

DEREK
Coast should be clear.

DYLAN
Yeah. She's gone. My ass is grateful.

DEREK
Can you just stop updating me on the state of your ass?

DYLAN
k.

A smile Derek hadn't realized was on his face faltered at the response. Lowercase *K* with a period. Yikes. Had a small part of him been hoping for another snarky clapback? That was stupid and made no logical sense.

Both Gallagher's ass and his clapbacks should be nothing but an annoyance. All of Dylan Gallagher was an annoyance to Derek. Where had that smile even come from?

When he lifted his face from the screen, Olive's attention was back on him. Gray eyes doing a full-on X-ray of his brain. "Order enough pizza for five because if you don't invite Dylan down, I'm going to go upstairs and introduce myself on my own terms."

Derek growled.

God, he was going to miss her.

Chapter 7

Dylan hadn't been lying about his ass. His first attempt at standing ended in keeling over and banging his head on the closet door because his right leg was completely numb. The creature shook his head as if displeased his pillow moved.

How the hell did he end up in a cramped closet with a massive dog napping on top of him? Dylan was still groggy from having slept much longer than he meant to after Derek grumpily kicked him out of his apartment this morning. All of Dylan's phone alarms were useless given that he'd left his phone charging in Derek's apartment after the awkward exchange about the DVDs and books. Luckily, he had also forgotten to return Derek's key. With Derek's warnings about not touching his stuff without permission a persistent echo in Dylan's aching head, he went down to slip inside and grab the phone. But the dog sprawled in the entryway startled awake just as Dylan tried to step over him.

Avoiding accidentally stomping on tail or paw, Dylan crashed into the tower of trash bags while the dog yelped so loudly that anyone within a two-mile radius could have heard. After grabbing his phone, he heard Carol's clacking footsteps outside and the jangle of her own extensive set of keys. Dylan coaxed the dog inside the closet with peanut butter cookies from his pocket, and once the snack—the snack that was supposed to be Dylan's—was gone, the dog spent the first five minutes of hiding oozing foul mouth slime onto Dylan's shoulder until he was convinced that there were no more available snacks. Then, he nestled onto Dylan and went limply into doggie dreamland. All one hundred and thirty pounds rested on Dylan's right hip.

Thus the ass pain.

The blood flow returned like an attack of thumbtacks. He squinted at his phone, checking if there were any more messages from the *other* major pain in his ass.

The blurry words reminded him that ordering glasses needed to be priority one, since he couldn't drive without them. Knowing his brain, he stopped everything else and pulled up the webpage. Priority-one things had to be handled the moment he thought of them. With the thousand trips to the hardware store ahead of him, clear vision was essential.

The main issue outside of Dylan's scope of experience was the complex plumbing. He had found one source of a leak along the plumbing supplying Derek's unit. Derek's unit was technically a garden-style basement, which meant the water entered from the main supply between Uncle Sean's apartment and Derek's. As he suspected, a former owner had done a cosmetic repair to hide the problem. Since Derek had only lived there a couple of years, it must have been done by the person who had flipped the apartment at some point in the years before. Dylan's dad could rant for hours about amateur house flippers who prioritized cosmetics over workmanship. Which was why Derek's jab about flippers had hit a nerve.

"Band-Aid solutions lead to big-scale disasters." The unofficial Gallagher family business motto, and Dylan had enough experience to know exactly what he could and could not do himself at a professional level. Dylan shuddered to think what he could not see behind that far wall beneath the bubbling drywall. But if a *Gallagher* called an outside-the-family plumbing company there was at least an 80 percent chance of it getting back to his dad and brothers.

His phone was in his hand like he was supposed to be doing something . . .

He pushed a finger toward his face as a reflex and nearly poked himself in the eye.

Ack. Right. Glasses.

Priority one. He didn't look up from his phone until the rush order confirmation email notification came through.

Dylan had done so many things to help himself function, but after last night, his mind was loud again. He'd forgotten to take his ADHD meds at the right time, so now he had the choice between taking them and enduring a potentially sleepless night or not taking them at all and feeling like everything was chaos again. He'd spent thirty-two years with his mind roaring like a freight train. He'd managed to make it through, even excelling in certain areas. But the last few years since his diagnosis showed him how it felt to have his thoughts quiet . . . It was hard to go back. He was about to head upstairs when he saw the mess created by the door when he'd tripped over Gus. One of the trash bags must have ripped open.

He'd almost gotten everything cleaned up again when one of his many typical alarm reminders went off on his phone, signaling that it was his usual dinner time. This meant he'd spent over an hour down here after being held hostage in the closet.

A cold and damp thing nudged his hand. *"Gahhh . . ."* Gus's nose. As he wiped at the nose mark, a streak of blood along the bandage caught his eye. The cut had opened *again*. Trying to follow Derek's command that Dylan *"not bleed on any of his shit,"* Dylan went to the bathroom sink again. He swallowed once, trying to get rid of that imagined metallic taste in his mouth, and then splashed cold water on his face with his uninjured hand. When he was sure he wasn't going to throw up or faint again, he left the bathroom with Derek's small first aid kit.

Why was blood so hard for him?

Well, he knew why, but it still made him feel like a wimp.

Dylan was raised in an above-ground swimming pool's worth of toxic hetero masculinity. Self-disgust was baseline even without his squeamishness. His brothers tormented him when they came home with injuries, and Dad only halfheartedly discouraged it. *"Harmless teasing,"* Dad would say to Mom when she worried. Mom was a cafeteria lady, so she saw bullying on a regular basis.

Yeah. *Harmless.*

Ears ringing, Dylan grabbed a weird, cactus-flavored (*seriously?*) electrolyte drink from Derek's fridge and a bag of froufrou pea crackers from the cabinet along with the pack of bandages and walked into Derek's living room. He sat down on the carpet. The bruised areas on his ribs demanded a pound of ibuprofen, but the blood had to be handled first. He gulped the drink and crunched a few crackers, blinking away spots in his vision. When his head cleared, he risked looking at his hand. Sitting was better in case he got woozy again. The dog trotted over beside him and whined. Feeling the creature deserved a reward for being so well-behaved in the closet, Dylan tossed him a cracker. Pea was listed as an ingredient in the dog food in the pantry, so it couldn't be toxic.

As Dylan peeled the gauze off his hand, the door opened. Derek was flanked by two women. All three wore scrubs, and all three immediately honed in on the open wound.

Gus broke the tension by ferociously attacking the woman with the slightly fuzzy brownish-gold hair. Derek's best friend probably?

The red-haired woman took a step forward. She had a beautiful, ethereal face with Caribbean blue eyes that were fixed on Dylan's hand. She looked like an actress who would be cast as a forest nymph or an elf in a book adaptation.

When she opened her mouth, Dylan half expected Elvish to come out of it. "When exactly did this injury happen?" Although her question was clinical, her voice was gentle and soothing, which made Dylan feel even more like a dying Frodo when he first sees Arwen in the forest and the light goes all gauzy and white while he's gross, gagging, and being absorbed into the shadow realm.

Derek's eyes flashed as he towered over Dylan. "I thought I told you to go get stitches today." Not gentle or elf-like.

Before Dylan could give Derek the indignant retort he deserved, the red-haired woman crouched next to him. "He's right that this really should have been sutured." Her head tilted as she examined the hand. "It's probably going to scar . . . but I don't think there's any tendon injury."

"I *told* him—"

"He also needs a tetanus shot," called out the woman still being gently kiss-mauled.

Dylan closed his hand. "I . . . I can't drive without glasses." He couldn't hide the defensiveness in his tone. "It'll be fine."

"The hospital is literally a block and a half away," Derek said, his tone more of a grumble than a dig.

Ears burning hot, Dylan pushed his aching body up with his un-gashed hand and squared his shoulders to Derek. "Look, I've been a little busy and—"

"Okay." The red-haired woman patted Dylan's upper arm. "I think we got off on a bad foot—or a bad hand, as it were." The corner of her mouth quirked upward. "Health-care workers tend to jump on a crisis."

"It's just a cut."

She winced as if she were too polite to tell him he was being reckless. "In any case, I'm Joni. And that's Olive."

"Happy to meet you," Olive said with fur muffling her words.

"We just ordered pizza, and we'd . . . *all*"—Joni's head twitched at Derek—"we'd *all* love for you to join us. While we wait, do you mind if I look at your hand?" Her lips pursed for a second. "I also have a sneaking suspicion that you have a rib injury, too, from the way you're moving."

Joni's voice was coaxing but firm. Christ, how could anyone say no to her when she sounded so calm and reasonable? Derek stalked away and was pacing in the kitchen with an enigmatic mix of frustration and maybe . . . concern on his face?

Olive stood and brushed off her scrub pants. Her smile had an almost catlike wryness about it, but she genuinely seemed to want him to stay too.

All Dylan had wanted to do when he'd been stuck in that closet was to escape back upstairs and into the familiar silence, but now . . . it had been so long since he'd just had pizza with friends. Even if in this case they were someone else's friends.

So Dylan nodded.

In thirty minutes—or less—like the old commercials, a tall stack of Il Forno Pizzeria pizza boxes arrived, including a smaller box on top. Dylan's hand was freshly bandaged after swearing he would watch for signs of infection and dosed with medication by his rather overqualified care team. They'd all seemed relieved when he'd explained he'd gotten a Tdap booster before his brother's last kid was born. It was weird to have complete strangers fussing over an injury that any other Gallagher would have—once literally—poured a Guinness on and then kept going. But . . . it was almost nice.

Damn. Was he really that pathetically lonely?

Olive grabbed the small pizza box on top and placed it in the oven. "That one's gluten-free for my girlfriend. Her flight was delayed."

In unexpected social moments like these, Dylan had to remind himself how to human. He'd been sequestered in his uncle's apartment for months now.

"Where's she flying in from?"

"Fort Worth. She had a job interview out there." Olive's cheeks went pink with a kind of tender reverence. "She's a *pilot*."

"That's cool," Dylan said. "Wow. Does she—"

Derek bopped Olive on the nose with a breadstick. "Be careful about getting Olive on the topic of Stella. They're still in the honeymoon phase."

Honestly, it was only recently that hearing about successful relationships didn't make Dylan want to shrivel like a bunch of sour grapes. While his brothers were all getting married and having kids, he'd had a series of failed relationships when he lived on the West Coast, the last of which involved a colleague. But it wasn't until that one truly disastrous setup date here that he'd gotten mostly content with being single and embracing his hobbies instead. It no longer stung to hear about someone happily in love. Maybe everything he was doing for his mental health was helping him grow.

Olive grabbed the breadstick out of Derek's hand with her teeth, looking more like a lion than seemed possible. Although Derek's words had been snarky, his face was all reflected joy as his best friend tore into the breadstick carcass. He'd never imagined the guy who barked at him whenever he put out recycling on the wrong day or parked slightly crooked could make this face. His dark eyes glowed warmer with each of Olive's laughs.

Dylan's heart gave a perplexing, jealous hiccup.

Derek might love his best friend, but the guy was still a dickhead to him. At least most of the time. It shouldn't matter how good he made Dylan's pillow smell. Not that he was still thinking about that.

Dylan took a bite of pizza. "So Olive, Gus is staying here because you're traveling?"

"Yep." Olive rifled through the stacked boxes.

While Olive was distracted, Derek fixed Dylan with a pointed tense head shake and then made a motion that either meant *Cut it out* or *I'll kill you*. Either was possible.

"Uh ... where are you going?" Dylan said, trying to keep the conversation going while he worked out what Derek meant.

"Stella has a few interviews all up and down the East Coast. We're going to explore a lot of the cities we've never been before and then visit Maine and Canada for a few weeks. Gone about two months in total." She pulled out the last piece of veggie supreme. After a bite, she grinned at Derek. "I'm really lucky Derek's willing to keep Gus since the fella's not really up for big car trips anymore. Tough on his big doggy joints, according to the vet." Olive scratched behind the areas of gray peppering the dog's floppy ears. His tongue lolled out as he lifted his head to her from where he was sprawled over her feet. "Aren't you glad to be staying with Uncle Derek?"

Dylan nodded "Yeah, he's lucky to have Derek so attached to him, especially with Derek's neighbor—"

"Falling through the floor and almost landing on him." Derek handed Dylan his beer as if to say *Drink this and shut up.* "Yeah, oh, and that other neighbor is really up in arms about the *repair work.*"

Oh . . . So Olive had no idea that Gus wasn't technically allowed to stay here at all. Interesting. Another secret Derek Chang was keeping . . .

Dylan picked at his bottle label. If the dog was hers, it meant that its previous owner—the one who died—was *her* brother. This meant that Gus's former owner was probably pretty young. Far too young to have died so suddenly. *Shit.* Well, now Dylan felt even more like a jerk for almost spilling the beans about the HOA dog situation.

"What are you going to do if Parakeet Karen gets upset about the renovation work?" Olive picked mushrooms off her veggie pizza and plunked them onto Derek's plate.

Derek shrugged, eating Olive's mushrooms as if this was what they did every time they got pizza. "Invent some other plausible explanation for why Dylan is coming over at all hours of the day. Bandwidth thieving maybe?"

"I mean, you guys could pretend to be dating," Olive said with a suppressed smile.

"No. No. No." Derek's eyes did that angry glittering thing that both scared Dylan and made him feel a little . . . something else. This viscerally negative response only further delighted Olive. He waggled a finger at her. "Not in a million years. I mean it. Don't even say that out loud. Not even as a joke, Olivia."

She stood to face him, crossing her arms in mock defiance. "That's *not my name*."

"Olivia."

"Darryl."

"Olivia."

They locked into a fierce, silent glare battle.

Dylan leaned toward Joni. "Are they always like this?"

She grabbed another piece of pizza. "Yep. You kind of get used to it and then eventually find it endearing." She arched an eyebrow. "Most of the time."

Chapter 8

Joni and Stella each called out a last goodbye to Dylan as they left Derek and Olive standing alone in the shadows at the bottom of the stairs that led up to the sidewalk. Awkwardness knotted beneath Dylan's sternum as he looked away. Derek's forehead rested on his best friend's shoulder like he was breaking at the thought of her being far away for even a few months. It seemed like they had been through a lot together recently.

Dylan scanned the room to make sure he wouldn't forget anything here this time. Tonight had been fun, but what was he supposed to do now? He'd slept until late afternoon before coming down here to get trapped in a closet. They had one functional bedroom between the two apartments, and because of the text he'd just gotten, he needed to give Derek more bad news as soon as he came back inside.

The shuddering sound coming from the doorway might have been Olive crying.

If Dylan had picked up that giant ladder he'd wanted to borrow today from his brother, he could have escaped back up into his apartment through the still-gaping hole. Moving now would wake the dog hibernating on his right foot and probably ruin their moment. He kept his glances at the door as covert as possible. Derek's shoulder muscles beneath his T-shirt actually rippled as he tightened their hug.

Dylan tensed.

Any time he was around Derek Chang, Dylan was transported to his days as a preteen baby gay when his older brothers brought their hot varsity hockey teammates over during summer vacation. He had felt like his attraction was as obvious as if he had a blinking neon sign above his head spelling out *"I want to do butt stuff someday."*

Ever the self-preservationist, thirteen-year-old Dylan spent most of those hours hiding out on the family computer in the living room learning to code. This was unfortunately right next to a window looking out on the backyard where the hockey team's pickup football and conditioning work consisted of stripping off their shirts and engaging in a sweaty group exercise routine so overtly homoerotic all it needed was a few ancient Spartan uniforms to be a shot-for-shot recreation of the movie *300*.

And back then there had been the real terror of the ill-timed teenage erection. He could hide those more easily while sitting behind a computer desk. At least when he got older, he had some control over such things. Maybe he should be thankful for those hours trying to write programs. They had given him a successful career. Although, he had gotten inexplicably aroused by binary for a while during his first year of compu-sci classes.

Man, that Pavlov was a prick.

Derek mumbled something, and Olive mumbled something back. After one more short hug, he ruffled her bun. She kissed him once on the cheek and left. When Derek turned back to the room, his eyes were glassy.

Dylan snapped his head back down to focus on Gus. Dylan never wanted to be the type of person who had so much internalized toxic masculinity he felt weird around another dude crying, but yeah, this was awkward.

Mostly because he was still supposed to *hate* this guy. This guy who just spent twenty minutes saying goodbye to his best friend in this tragic, tender way and eating her mushrooms, and all of it made Dylan want to tuck the man into bed, brew him chamomile tea, and put on that strange dance movie he had three copies of.

This was probably worse than thinking about him in bed for other reasons.

Well, not worse.

Certainly different.

The fact remained that Derek had always been an asshole to him even before he crashed through his ceiling. He'd yelled at him for taking too long at the shared mailbox. He'd lost his shit once when Dylan was doing the initial work on Uncle Sean's apartment, and he was "making a racket" at nine A.M. How was Dylan supposed to know he worked nights sometimes and had been trying to sleep?

And then there was what happened during that unexpected downpour back in May.

Dylan had been working on Uncle Sean's bedroom for hours, so he'd had his earbuds in, the addictive audiobook making the time fall away as he finished the last sections of drywall repair. He'd only noticed the pounding from the front door because it vibrated the entire apartment.

Derek stood there.

Soaking wet. Looking like he's just gotten back from a run.

As that memory replayed in his mind, Dylan recalled how much he hated Derek's thin workout tank and mesh shorts that left little to the imagination. He'd hated that model-perfect, smug face that had several inches of height on Dylan.

Unfortunately, Dylan's own face had always been an open book. Derek hadn't missed any of Dylan's "hatred."

Could anyone blame a guy for looking?

Probably not, but the worst part was that during those delusional ten seconds of silence, Dylan had wondered (read: lost his mind) whether Derek could be coming up to ask him out or maybe even for other stuff . . . Yeah, it must have been Dylan's baseline sex starvation sending his thoughts straight to that bottle in his bedside drawer which lately had been only for *personal* use.

Derek had leaned suggestively on Dylan's door, letting water sluice down his corded biceps and forearms and *smiled*.

Derek's smile showed Derek knew *exactly* what Dylan had been thinking—just like he knew last night too—and he made Dylan feel even smaller.

That smile scoffed as if to say *"Dream on, loser"* very loudly.

"Gallagher, did you know your Jeep's sunroof's open, and it's raining on your laptop?" Derek had pointed to the parking lot. "A friend of mine noticed as he left earlier. Just texted me about it."

Obviously, Dylan didn't know. He was so annoyed at himself and how he had been caught gawking that he couldn't stop himself from muttering "A *friend*. Suuuure. Riiiight," under his breath.

"Yeah. *Friend*." Derek scowled.

Maybe it was because Dylan was frustrated (in every sense) and exhausted or maybe it was because Dylan's years-long relationship with Chase had also turned out to be exactly this kind of "friendship," and Dylan had just gotten the wrong idea somehow, but Dylan stared back at Derek and shrugged.

"*You* of all people have something to say about my behavior in my relationships?"

Huh?

While Dylan was in one of the longest sexual dry spells of his life, was this jerk seriously implying that Dylan *never* could have success in this area? Who just says something like that to a complete stranger?

Hiding actual hurt and trying to parse the full meaning of the insult, Dylan glared. "What? *Me of all people* because I'm nothing like the bonanza of blond, brainless, beefy, boring . . ."

Derek cocked an eyebrow.

"What?"

"Just waiting to see how long you can continue the insult alliteration." Derek's tone was infuriatingly unfazed.

"What the hell did I ever do to you? Just say 'Hey, Dylan, your sunroof's open' like a non-complete asshole would."

"Again . . . Not sure I'm going to take lessons from *you* on how *not* to be an asshole."

Dylan was too confused to come up with a biting response. "What's that supposed to mean?"

"Some people need to work on their memory, in more areas than one," Derek said in a low mutter as he walked away.

"Yeah, I'll work on that." Maybe Derek was referring to all the times he'd put out trash or recycling on the wrong day. Still, this guy barely knew him.

Baffled and furious, Dylan slammed the door behind him and ran down to grab the laptop. Unfortunately, he locked himself out of his uncle's apartment without his car keys or phone. After climbing in the Jeep via the aforementioned sunroof and moving the laptop, for the sake of his dignity, he'd walked three miles to Felicity's school in the rain to borrow her spare key, rather than give Derek the satisfaction of asking to borrow his phone.

All of this being why Dylan could *never* forget he *hated* Derek.

That hatred was for the best.

Hatred meant no temptation to investigate any other feelings or fantasies that had been triggered in the last twenty-four hours since seeing Derek in his underwear. *Again*, soaking wet. What was it with muscles and water that made Dylan want to lick up the column of that strong neck and—

Shit. *HATRED.*

Broken, water-damaged laptop. *Not* thinking about neck licking. Chest licking. Or . . . no goddamn licking.

He needed to leave this apartment ASAP. After quietly extricating his foot from under the dog's head, Dylan gathered his cleaning supplies.

The front door shut.

Don't look at Derek. Just don't look at him. "You should get your stuff and come upstairs because—"

"Why can't I sleep down here?"

"For one thing, your mattress is outside on the curb, and—"

"Crap."

"And ... umm ... so ... I ... while you were talking to Olive, I found out I have to turn off the water for the entire apartment. Plumber says shutting off that one part isn't enough." *Christ*, making eye contact seemed impossible, but not looking at Derek just made Dylan feel more awkward. "Sorry about that. And I have to show you something else."

Derek's jaw clenched.

Dylan led him to the spot between the kitchen and the bathroom. "Anyway, it looks like that person tried to do the repair themselves and then did a shoddy job of it. Over here too." Dylan showed Derek a place on the wall where the drywall seams were uneven and visible. He traced a finger across the white paint. "They did a patch job. I'm a little worried about what we're going to find behind this wall, to be honest. I've seen work like this before when people don't intend to live in a space. They just make it look pretty to sell. Bad repair techniques don't last. Most of the water damage ran down the couple of rotten beams, but I think a lot of it is behind this wall and into the foundation of the building."

"Shit. Shit. Shit." Derek directed the words at the wall. He touched the same spot Dylan had, sliding a finger over the unevenness, bubbling, and soft drywall.

Well, at least he wasn't cursing at Dylan this time.

"What am I going to do?" Any cockiness had vanished. He was any defeated homeowner contemplating how financially fucked he was.

The unfortunate answer in this case being super supremely fucking fucked.

"Did you do an inspection when you bought the place?" Dylan kept any judgment out of his tone.

Derek's knuckle kneaded the crease between his eyebrows. "My sister bought it. Bought it from a 'friend' who was flipping it. It's a long story. She . . . she couldn't pay the mortgage anymore three years ago, and otherwise the bank would have foreclosed."

"So you bought it as-is."

"Essentially."

"Well, damn." Dylan leaned on the wall but then stopped, remembering the legitimate concern that the walls weren't structurally sound. "Do you think your sister knew about the problem?"

"I don't think so. She was having a tough time. Had just had surgery. Thought it was move-in ready because of the fresh paint." Derek's sigh seemed ambivalent, but he didn't offer more details, and Dylan didn't want to pry. "So how much?" Derek's voice was raspy. "Don't sugarcoat it, Gallagher."

"I . . . I . . ."

"You said you grew up doing this stuff with your dad. How much?" Gus curled up on the floor next to the bedframe, and Derek's hand found his fur like the dog was a life raft. Some of the anxiety vibrating off him stilled. "How much? Please?" The last word was barely audible.

"I genuinely don't know. I'm still going to fix all the ceiling shit and the beams in the subfloor. That's my fault, and I admit it. I'm not sure what insurance would cover either way. The plumber will give us a fair estimate, and then we have to, you know, check if there's a mold situation." Dylan grimaced.

Derek's cheeks paled. "Mold."

"I don't know about numbers. I told you I'd cover the stuff that would be my uncle's responsibility as long as we don't involve him at all."

"You really think we can keep this a secret from him?"

"I'd really like to try." The back of Dylan's neck heated.

"Why?"

"Personal reasons." Dylan didn't really want to explain his uncle's situation with a stranger. Especially a stranger he didn't trust.

"You really want me to believe *you* can pay for all—" Derek gestured to the hole in outrage. "It's just . . . gah. Putting it on a credit card is not the same as paying for it, you know?" Derek's mouth shut. He swallowed twice, like he hadn't meant to say it. Or hadn't meant to say it like that?

But he did say it. Why would Dylan say he could pay for it if he couldn't? Damn, this guy really did think the worst of him. Did Derek think he was fleecing his uncle or that this was a scam?

What the actual hell?

"No shame in needing a place to crash or having debt and needing family to help you out. Doing reno work in exchange for a place to live makes sense as long as your uncle's not getting a raw deal." The tinge of reproach in Derek's voice would have been more than enough to make Dylan feel ashamed about needing a place to crash or having debt had that been the situation.

Wow.

No wonder Derek thought the idea of him getting laid was a joke.

Dylan could explain he was a software engineer—a successful one—and owned his own company and could get his week's work done in a few hyperfocused hours. He *could* explain that Uncle Sean needed to sell the apartment next year, but it was in terrible shape from years of neglect when the family didn't realize how bad things were getting. Dylan's brothers and sisters were all preoccupied with family, kids, work, or school, so *he* was the only one with the time to do this. The only one who didn't have anything else in his life besides a dopamine deficiency that seemed to be fed by home renovation work.

Honestly if this was what Derek believed about him, then to hell with this guy, with all the crap Derek put him through with the mean looks and snipes already since moving in. He'd give this condescending, douchey, muscly ball sack the bare minimum of explanation.

"No, I'm not freeloading. Yes, I can afford this." Dylan kept his tone almost robotic. "I'll fix the ceiling and the rotten joists and the stuff I *contributed* to breaking, and you can figure out the rest after talking to the plumber."

"You don't have to be a dick about it." Derek said, with a weird intentional callback to Dylan's words last night. Was he making a joke? "Look, I didn't mean—"

"Yeah, right. I'm the one being a dick here." Dylan sniffed. "Just grab your stuff and you can have the bedroom with Gus so his joints don't hurt until I finish with your ceiling or we can turn your water back on." The oversized dog was beginning to worm his way into Dylan's heart too.

Derek's eyebrows pulled together for a moment, but then he shrugged. "Fine."

"The ceiling has to stay open until the plumber fixes the underlying problem."

"*Fine.*"

"I'll text the plumber I have unless you've got a guy."

"Your guy is *fine.*"

Dylan crossed his arms over his chest. "Well, fine."

Derek stood up from the bedframe and mirrored Dylan's pathetic attempt at the over-the-chest-arm-crossing power move with his own version that was anything but pathetic due to his having pectoral muscles worthy of the Marvelverse. "*Fine.*"

Chapter 9

"You have to get up," said the voice of a man who would probably be dead soon if he didn't let Derek sleep longer.

Derek pulled the pillow over his head and smacked the hand trying to snatch it away.

"I know it's four thirty in the morning, but—"

"Four thirty? Go awaaaay."

"I was still up working when I saw the message. Plumber said this was the only time he could fit us in. He'll be here in twenty minutes."

Derek groaned. This wasn't that much earlier than he often woke up to go to the gym, but for whatever reason, Derek slept like a rock here. He couldn't remember the last time he had slept so deeply.

"Sorry. Can you repeat all that?" Derek logrolled himself into a seated position, and a shirt thwacked him in the face.

"Can you, like, not sleep mostly naked here?"

"Kay." Derek pulled the shirt over his head, hiding a smile. That hint of attraction was back on Dylan. Derek steeled his features to neutral before sliding his arms into the sleeves.

Dylan was wearing another of his collection of T-shirts covered in so many paint splatters and holes you couldn't make out the word across the chest. The arching black lines of a tattoo were visible just above the back collar. His hair fanned out on either side of his face beneath a backward Orioles cap. His bright-blue eyes were on display because he still wasn't wearing glasses.

"Sorry, dude. Didn't know my body would make you un-comfortable."

"It doesn't, and stop calling me *dude*." Dylan took off his cap and smoothed his hair back like it was bothering him before pulling it back on again. The hair looked exactly like it did be-fore. "I need caffeine." Gallagher hustled out.

Derek shook the sleep from his head and looked down. He'd kicked off the comforter at some point and his dick was evi-dently more awake than he was. Maybe *that* was what had Gal-lagher all flustered. It wasn't exactly a subtle presence. Derek hadn't considered that sleeping in his underwear would be weird. He'd just done what he always did. He wasn't *trying* to make the guy uncomfortable. Gallagher needed to communi-cate his needs better. Damn it.

And maybe not wear that hat ever again.

Seeing Dylan's hair fanning out under the cap made Derek want to touch it.

Yikes.

Must be early signs of Stockholm syndrome. Dylan's de-struction of his apartment forced him into captivity. Derek was a sad, lonely, heterosexual pirate seeing a manatee as a mer-maid.

That was what this—er—response was.

Once he was dressed, Derek felt better than he had in days. He hadn't had a single nightmare. Strange, but welcome. He'd might even feel up to hitting the gym. He'd missed several workouts, and that probably explained the pent-up energy he was feeling around Dylan.

He'd probably need to up his weight to manage the stress after the conversation with the plumber.

Mold.

The word struck fear in his heart.

When Derek emerged, Gallagher was sitting on the couch wearing noise-reducing headphones and furiously typing on his laptop. The hat was beside him, resting on the back of the couch with the Oriole side facing Derek. The hat stared, as if it knew the image of it on Dylan's head had turned Derek on in a completely inexplicable way.

"*Kinky,*" Olive would say if she were here.

Which she wasn't. Derek checked his watch. Olive should be getting in the car to go to the airport. Derek smothered the urge to smack the hat off the couch. If he did, they'd probably never find it again. Gallagher's uncle's apartment was a cluttered disaster. Not dirty except for the areas in the bathroom that were unfinished, but exactly the kind of chaos that drove Derek bananas. It was like the guy never actually moved in. Or maybe his uncle just never moved out, and maybe that was why he'd been indignant about Derek's freeloading assumption.

What was he *supposed* to assume? He saw the guy at all kinds of weird hours doing all kinds of weird things, but this was the first time he'd even seen him with a laptop that wasn't covered in rainwater. He must do *something* in between all the renovation work, but none of it added up.

Derek yawned. One of those enormous Olive-type yawns.

The yawn movement must have caught his eye, because Gallagher snapped his computer shut. Gus lifted his head and perched it on the back of the couch to look up at him. Next to the hat. After a second, he looked back at Gallagher as if to inform Derek, "*This lanky, mop-topped human is my new best friend.*"

"Traitor," Derck said in a low grumble.

Dylan pulled off the headphones. "What?"

"Nothing." Derek shrugged. "How'd you pull off getting a plumber here before five A.M.? Who is this guy? An ex?"

God, why did he say that?

"No. My uncle." Emotionless. Not cold exactly.

"I thought you didn't want Sean to find out."

"Different uncle."

"How many uncles do you have?"

"Irish Catholic family on both sides. I have a crap ton of uncles. If you really want me to blow your mind, ask me how many cousins I've got just in a twenty-mile radius." Still not a damn hint of a smile.

Derek couldn't imagine having that much family so close. The only two cousins he'd met on his dad's side lived in Taiwan. His mom's family wasn't nearby either. They lived in New Jersey near the Korean Presbyterian church Derek's great-grandfather had once been the pastor of. His mom always talked about never being able to get away with anything as a teenager because of the number of aunties nearby watching her every move. Guess that was what Dylan grew up with too.

"I thought you didn't want any of your family to know about the kitchen flood?"

"This uncle was the lesser of the several evils." Gallagher's lips pursed together as he squinted up at Derek. His shaggy curls covered the parts of his face usually obscured by thick black frames.

"When are you going to get glasses?"

"Ordered. Mind if I get a few hours of sleep in the bed when we're done with the plumber? I had to catch up on a few things overnight." Impassive.

"Look, I'm sorry I assumed that you—"

"Assume whatever you want. It really doesn't matter."

Derek hated to admit he loathed the shift in energy between them. That playful sarcasm that had been a bit like Olive's had blunted into a mechanical monotone. Derek did not like this at all.

Dylan stared expectantly. "So . . ."

"So?"

"Do you need the bed this morning?"

"Oh. Uh . . . No, I don't." Derek shook his head and bent to unpack the duffel of Gus's things. "Where'd—"

"The leash is by the door. I took him out overnight. Guess since I was up, he figured it was a good time for a walk." Gallagher pointed at the duffel. "If that's all just Gus's stuff, where's yours?"

Derek shifted the oversized bag to reveal a second, smaller one beneath. "Just this." His attempt at a chuckle might have sounded more like a grumble. "Not looking to move in with you, Gallagher."

"Kay." Gallagher gritted his teeth so hard Derek was almost sure the guy's jaw popped. "Yeah. The quicker we're done with this the better."

The silence was stiff enough you could hang wet jeans on it.

Derek's shrill alarm jolted both men out of their silent standoff. "Sorry. Parakeet Karen Schedule alarm."

"What is . . . you know what, never mind." Dylan grabbed his hat. "I'm going down to wait for my uncle. Can I use your keys?"

"Sure." Derek tossed Gallagher the keys with more force than he meant to use, but Dylan caught them easily. "Good catch, slugger."

Dylan's bemused expression was the same as the one he'd worn while analyzing rotten floor joists.

"Because the hat."

"Right," Dylan said as he opened the door and left.

And Derek was suddenly wishing that he had been crushed to death by the floor collapse, so he never had to experience uttering the words *good catch, slugger* at a man who clearly thought he was a vapid brainless meathead.

✳✳✳

Derek grabbed a respirator from the box at the door. He had to hand it to Gallagher. He could be tidy about some things. All of Derek's salvageable stuff was in neat stacks in the living room with labels. Everything had been easy to find last night, but he hadn't been in a mood to appreciate it. Something caught his eye. A broken picture frame with a Post-it on top.

> This was under the couch in the living room.
> It looked like it had been broken a while ago.
> All glass cleaned up.

The photo used to be one of Michelle's favorites. Her first recital where she was a flower in some ballet he didn't remember. Both of his sisters wore matching pink lacy costumes and held their arms above their heads. Amy's smile was wry in that almost-preteen way, but Michelle had taken dance seriously from her first class. Had she broken the frame and just left it there?

Probably . . .

Derek frowned.

Buying this apartment had been one bad decision in a series after Michelle's second failed knee surgery. It wasn't her fault the medical bills had piled up along with other less-essential credit card bills. That crack Derek had made about credit cards had really been about Michelle. He shouldn't have said it, especially since it seemed to have touched a nerve. But it was probably just his own guilty conscience not wanting anyone, even Gallagher, to go through what Michelle had just gone through after her own career crisis. But now, because of Derek's own asshole words from before, he didn't feel like he had any right to ask for specifics about Gallagher's situation. Anything he asked would probably just seem like more of the same unfair assumptions and accusations.

Hearing voices from in his bedroom, Derek placed the photo back on the pile and headed down the hallway. Gallagher stood next to a small, grizzled white man with thick glasses. He looked absolutely nothing like the prototypical American-TV version of a plumber. He looked like an accountant in a jump-suit.

"—is the problem." *Oh*, so when Dylan said Irish, he'd meant *actually recently from Ireland* Irish with a thick accent. "Hallo there. Are you the owner here?"

"That depends on how bad the diagnosis is." Derek's heart pumped faster.

"Well, son, it could be worse."

"That's a good start, but I'm sensing a *but* coming." Derek braced like he was watching a lingerie-clad blonde run into the Appalachian woods at three A.M. while knowing an axe murderer was on the loose. The jump-scare killing blow was coming. Everyone in the room knew it.

Dylan did the hair smoothing/hat thing again. Was he deliberately avoiding making eye contact with Derek? Was Derek being paranoid?

The small man climbed down the ladder and extended his hand. "Liam Byrne. Nice to meet you."

"Not Gallagher?"

"No, his mum's my baby sister. She's a Byrne." He laughed. "See." The man pointed to Gallagher's deep-blue eyes, sweeping the hair away. "The Byrne eyes."

Gallagher swatted his uncle's hand with a guarded smile.

Eyes twinkling at his nephew, Mr. Byrne tucked his pen in his clipboard before returning his focus to Derek. "We don't have all the details yet with the walls still up, but I can give you the important points."

Maybe the lilting accent would make the words, *You might as well just light your bank account on fire* less of a stab in the gut.

"I won't lie to you. It's going to be expensive. A lot of home-owner's policies have specific portions ruling out paying for slow damage building up over a long period of time. My best guess is that slow drip from several of the joints—shoddy work." The same word Dylan had used. Liam exchanged regretful, knowing looks with Gallagher.

"Fuck . . ." Derek flinched. "Sorry."

"I'm Catholic, but not a saint. You got a real motherfucking mess on your hands here, but it could be worse. For starters, seems like this here kid fell through the floor at the exact weakest spot when this joist gave out. Bad luck on one hand, but I reckon it's lucky he didn't break his neck, so we'll call it a win. This joist pulled away and crumbled into mulch. Bad sign."

Derek swallowed. He had been regretting not having coffee, but now he was regretting not having a whiskey before this conversation.

"There only seems to be one joist that's rotten. My nephew was right about that. I'm willing to give you a family discount on my diagnostic services today, because young Dilly can sweet-talk and I heard you bought the place to help your sister. But you'll still have to pay for labor and materials."

Derek nodded. He hadn't missed the way the nickname made Gallagher shrivel.

What followed was a long discussion of numbers and metals and timelines that left Derek's head spinning. Being an adult sucked.

After the small plumbing Irishman left, Derek rested his forehead on the wall. What he really wanted to do was punch the damn thing down, since it would be coming down anyway.

This apartment was less than eight hundred square feet. The amount of money he'd have to spend to fix it was dizzying. And that wasn't counting the mold abatement costs, which could be a few more thousand.

"Um . . . you okay?"

Derek hadn't even noticed Gallagher come back in the room. "No."

"I know it seems like a lot, but we'll get it done."

Something about that "we'll" gave Derek the energy to stand

straight again even if the pity in Dylan's expression made his stomach sink. "What's next?"

Gallagher's face shifted, mirroring the gloomy resignation that Derek imagined was on his own. "Now I have to call the three Icemen of the Apocalypse."

"Don't you mean Horsemen?"

"You'd think so, but that wasn't what they put on the T-shirts." A growl rumbled in Gallagher's chest as he pressed his phone to his ear.

Chapter 10

DEREK

If you can press snooze seven times, you could maybe consider changing your alarm time.

DYLAN

Your feedback is important to us. Please stay on the line and a customer service representative will be with you shortly. In the meantime, fuck off. Your dog woke me up at two thirty in the morning when he howled in his sleep.

DEREK

He has very vivid puppy dreams. And wow with the jokes today. Can't imagine a worse way to wake up, except maybe a ceiling collapsing on top of you.

Dylan peeked out the front window several times to give himself an excuse to not look at Derek. This was the first time they were intentionally standing in the same room for longer than ten minutes since the bad news–heavy conversation with Uncle Liam. Uncle Liam had asked Dylan to have an architect second cousin do a quick check on the structure to make sure everything was safe before any other work started. Waiting for that report meant that Derek and Dylan—and Gus—had spent the last two weeks living in under seven hundred fifty square feet.

The distinctive sound of three red Chevy trucks rumbled into the parking lot.

"So, like, the first rule of flood club is that you can't talk about flood club," Dylan said, fidgeting with his hair and risking a glance at Derek.

Derek blinked.

"Have you only seen movies that involve spunky female leads and romantic grand gestures?"

"I know what *Fight Club* is, dickhead, but I just don't know why you're quoting it. Also, did you borrow one of my DVDs?"

"Um. *No*." Dylan huffed as if the very idea was ludicrous and definitely not what he had turned on for background noise when his earbuds died last night while doing prep work downstairs. Christina Aguilera's performance was underrated, and the world didn't deserve Cher. Also, that Cam Gadget or Gidget or whatever dude was hot.

Despite not wanting to, Dylan called in the big guns for the brunt work, but his brothers could only all come on the weekends. Given that they were adding more joists based on the structural report, he was grateful they were coming, but still.

"I just meant, if you could *not* mention my part of the kitchen flood thing to my brothers, I'd be grateful."

"Okay." Derek looked out the window as Dylan's three brothers came up the steps.

And *there* it was. Every girl at Dylan's high school made that *same face* when they saw the giant hockey players. Dylan had played hockey too, but he'd been fast, not a big enforcer on the ice. Every Gallagher boy played hockey despite the fact that their father had clearly hoped for baseball players based on how he named his first three sons.

"*Those* guys are your *brothers*?" Derek whistled.

"Shocking, I know"

"No, there's definitely a resemblance, but huh."

Huh?

"Yep." Dylan adjusted his glasses—one of the three pairs he'd ordered so he would never have to be without them again. He braced for the usual comments.

Derek gave him a funny twitch of the eyes. "It's just—"

"Yeah, they're incredibly tall, and people think they're good looking. Brooks even played a season for the Capitals farm team before blowing out his knee. For the information I'm sure you're most curious about . . . they're straight, happily married, and yes, I'm very aware I'm the runt of the family."

"No, that wasn't—but actually—"

"As I said, I've heard it all before."

The apartment door flung open, and his three brothers yanked him into noogie-accompanied hugs.

Anderson grabbed the baseball cap from Dylan's head and tossed it to Brooks, trying and failing to entice Dylan into a game of keep-away. They could keep the damn hat. As Calvin, the brother with manners, shook Derek's hand, Dylan went back inside to look for his phone.

Dylan sucked at hiding his bad mood. With his brothers around, Derek would probably pick up on the fact that everyone in the family thought he was an absent-minded screwup. He'd never brought friends around his brothers because it was always the same. Derek might be practically a stranger, but he already had a portfolio's worth of evidence that Dylan was a screwup. And even before the ceiling collapse catastrophe, he inexplicably hated Dylan.

"You didn't tell us we'd be helping out Big J's buddy, Dilly." Brooks said, giving Derek a bear hug worthy of a long-lost family member.

Dylan froze. *What?*

Derek smiled, but his smile faltered after meeting Dylan's gaze.

"You guys all know each other?" Dylan managed to keep most of the trepidation out of his voice.

"*Big J*, Dilly," Brooks said.

"May he rest in peace." Anderson's normal irreverence shifted into genuine regret.

Calvin's voice was a little quieter. "Jake Murphy, Dyl. The goalie Brooks played with on the high school state's team. You know, the one *they* . . . with you . . ." His head twitched toward Brooks and Anderson with a little cough about as subtle as being mauled by a pack of hyenas. Dylan might have preferred the hyenas to revisiting the night he met Jake Murphy.

"Oh . . ." Of course he remembered Jake Murphy. What happened to him had been huge news after his accident. *Shit. Shit. Shit.* "Jake Murphy. Right."

No. No. No. This meant that Gus's owner and Olive's brother . . .

Oh god. A hallelujah chorus worth of obscenities scrolled through Dylan's brain as more pieces fell into place.

And Dylan was back remembering a night he never ever wanted to relive.

Three and a half years ago, he'd flown home from California for Christmas. Anderson and Brooks strong-armed Dylan into attending a "Team Christmas Happy Hour" and then *literally* pushed him at Jake Murphy, an admittedly incredibly tall, hot aerospace systems engineer, and left. The rest of the team seemed notably absent.

After a few minutes of the kind of small talk that never came easily to Dylan, he'd tried to escape the clumsily orchestrated, very obvious setup with a polite, "Really nice to meet you."

Jake flagged down the bartender in the way that only hot people seemed to know how to and paid for Dylan's drink before Dylan could even protest.

"Your brothers might be knuckleheads . . ." He gave Dylan's brothers who were obviously watching the interaction a small eyeroll before focusing all of his attention back on Dylan and lowering his voice. "But I'd love to buy you dinner." His mischievous movie-star grin was magnetic. He was the person that everyone in a room was always aware of. "I know a great place around the corner." Jake's strong hand on his shoulder and his easy confidence were impossible for Dylan's recently dumped self to resist.

The dinner had started out good, but the entrées hadn't yet arrived before Jake had finished his third Scotch in between fielding text messages he said were work related.

Dylan had grown up watching his uncles down booze like that—the kind of experienced, charismatic drinkers who knew how to minimize slurring. How to use charming smiles to hide exactly how hammered they were.

Dylan excused himself to the bathroom to give himself a few minutes to figure out how the hell to get out of this. He was walking back to the table and wasn't trying to look at Jake's phone screen, but a photo—a decidedly not-work-appropriate photo, unless he was in a *very* different industry—caught his eye. He couldn't see Jake's face to gauge his response, but nothing in his posture seemed surprised. The evening had turned out just like every date Dylan had gone on in Palo Alto with Chase, and the few men before Chase, and fewer men after Chase.

As Dylan stepped forward to stand next to the table, Jake slid the phone into his pocket. "I hope your boss has better boundaries than mine. It's almost Christmas, and I can't get the man off my back."

After a couple speechless seconds, Dylan found their server and paid the check, including the ridiculous bill on Jake's drinks. Jake followed him outside, smile wide, eyes more unfocused than ever. "So can I call us an Uber? Since you bought dinner, want to have dessert at my place?"

He could *not* be serious. All of Jake's handsome charm had vanished in Dylan's eyes. Now he could only debate both the ethics and physics of depositing a sloppy six-foot-five hockey player into an unfortunate Uber driver's car. Would Jake even be able to unlock his door? It was twenty-six degrees outside.

By the time Dylan figured out where Jake lived and had safely foisted the man onto a couch there, both Dylan's patience and the deep cleaning security deposit fee on his rental car were long gone.

"Sorry about tonight. Had a bit too much I guess. Bad day at work. Lost track of . . ." Jake glugged down some of the water Dylan had gotten for him. At least Jake no longer sounded in danger of needing an ambulance for alcohol poisoning. "When can I make it up to you? Or you could stay, and I could make it up to you now . . ."

"Are you fucking seriously coming on to me right now?"

Although not usually a yelling person, Dylan was very jet-lagged and very angry.

He lost it.

A lot of the things he said weren't just about Jake's behavior. They were also about Chase and the gay tech dating scene in general. And about people using alcohol as an excuse for crap behavior. About Dylan's uncles and the shit Dylan had watched them pull at family gatherings while drunk exactly like this.

Jake sat and took it all. No arguments. No excuses.

When Dylan opened the door, Jake spoke in a defeated voice. "I really am a piece of shit. Think I was waiting for rock bottom to try to get better."

"Maybe try to do better." Dylan's voice was hoarse from the yelling. "And stop *choosing* to be a piece of shit."

Once Dylan was back in his car, guilt hit. The guy clearly had an actual problem, and he felt like he'd kicked the guy while he was down.

When Dylan made it back to his parents' house, Anderson and Brooks were on the porch smoking special-occasion cigars.

Anderson grinned. "How'd it go? He's a great guy, right? You know I don't swing that way, but ya gotta admit the guy's like Ryan Reynolds–level hot. Right? Not that I'm into that, but I mean, everyone thinks Ryan Reynolds is a good-looking dude. Nothing gay about appreciating Ryan Reynolds, right?"

"Jake's the only gay dude we knew, but he's a stand-up bro, bro." Brooks nodded vigorously. "Ran into him at a Caps game last spring and been trying to get him to be our goalie ever since. He does a ton of charity work on the side too. Best friends with his sister. Your type of guy, Dilly."

After enduring several more *Jake Murphy's the best dude ever* stories, Dylan finally opened his mouth to speak.

But Anderson interrupted him, his voice weirdly serious. "Felicity said you were alone all the time when she visited. If she's worried about you, we're worried about you. She said you hadn't decided if you'd stay in California after quitting that job. Just wanted you to see you had options here. You had fun tonight, right?"

Their bizarre, genuine concern took away all the anger about what had happened during dinner. "Uh . . . sure. Don't think I'm his type, but he seems like a nice enough guy."

He never told them what happened.

Someone said Dylan's name, interrupting the cringe memory spiral he was on.

"I'm sorry, what?" Dylan blinked away the memories to find Derek standing in front of him.

Derek was smiling. Dylan hadn't seen Derek smile since Olive left, and Dylan's chest hitched.

There was such a contrast between Derek's smile and the memory of Jake's. Both men were categorically and objectively attractive. But beyond that, there was no comparison. Jake's had been all intentional charm and charisma; Derek's smile was *real*.

"I said . . . Anderson, Brooks, Calvin, and *Dylan*," Derek's attention shifted to look at the brother's each in turn. "So, your sisters' names are—"

"Emily and Felicity," Brooks said.

"Well, goddamn," Derek chuckled but stopped when he turned back to Dylan. "You okay?"

Anderson shook his head. "Don't worry about Dilly. He zones out sometimes. Always in his own head."

The anxiety over what Derek knew about the date occupied Dylan's thoughts as the five men carried loads of gear up to Uncle Sean's apartment.

While prepping the materials and area to replace the joists, Derek and the three oldest Gallaghers bantered about workouts and debated which of the local gyms was the best. Derek fit right in with the other three. He was like the long lost "D" brother. Yet for the first time, that didn't bother Dylan. Dylan liked that Derek fit right in. He didn't feel left out or excluded. Something about having Derek there made Dylan feel *less* awkward.

∗∗∗

Once the joists were in, Cal passed around Gatorade bottles his wife had sent over. They all stood in Derek's apartment looking at the damage that would need to be repaired.

Quiet panic filled Derek's eyes again. The same panic Dylan had seen when Uncle Liam was telling him the estimated cost. A strange impulse to wrap Derek up in his arms and tell him it would be okay came over Dylan. Maybe it was just because Derek stood much closer to Dylan than was necessary even given that all five men were crowded into Derek's small kitchen.

Dylan retreated to the far corner of the kitchen pretending to check he had all his tools in his toolbox.

"Well, here's hoping this is your rock bottom, dude," Cal said, tapping his plastic Gatorade bottle on Derek's as if it were a beer bottle.

Derek nodded and gulped down Gatorade.

Rock bottom. It triggered another flashback to the night with Jake.

That night hadn't just been *Jake's* rock bottom.

It had been an emotional turning point in Dylan's life. He'd decided after leaving Jake's house that he would not be someone's rock bottom. He needed to stop thinking about *himself* like he was something broken.

In a way, Jake *had* been the reason he'd moved back to Maryland. While still reeling from the failed date the next day and needing a break from his family's holiday chaos, Dylan had gone on a walk and fallen in love with an old stone house. A week later, Dylan was under contract and making arrangements for shipping his stuff back east.

He was still deep into renovations a year later when Jake texted him out of the blue. There had been a string of apologies and explanations about how he'd gotten his life together. Even a thank-you. Said he was sober for the first time since high school.

Dylan truthfully told him he wasn't interested in dating. Fixing up the old house had become his whole life, and it was coinciding with getting his ADHD diagnosis and new meds and a fresh perspective. Dylan was healing from a life spent feeling broken, and he knew Jake Murphy wasn't the right partner for that journey. Especially with all of Dylan's trust issues with intimacy. It wasn't worth the risk.

When he heard about Jake Murphy's accident, Dylan was genuinely shocked and sad. Now the embarrassment of the entire situation felt like a cinder block in his gut. Did Derek know details about the disastrous date? He couldn't imagine why Jake would tell *anyone* about what happened. Unless he'd lied about it?

"Waiting for a text from someone special?" Brooks nudged Derek in a brotherly way. "You've been checking your phone like that all day."

"Oh, uh—no. That wasn't . . . um . . ." Derek cleared his throat.

"Yeah, my mom had a family of bats in her attic so I was just checking in to make sure they didn't come back."

"What a good guy, amirite?" Anderson gave an encouraging twitch of the head at Dylan. "Checking on his mom."

"Yeah," Dylan said because there was nothing else he *could* say with the Three Icemen of the Apocalypse facing him down. But something in the way Derek answered made Dylan think of that moment when Jake put his phone away.

And it shouldn't matter anyway if Derek was fielding all the dick pics. Dylan needed to get everything fixed up between the two apartments so he could get back to his life and as far away as possible from Derek Chang. Dylan had been keeping strict boundaries the last few weeks, hoping he would get used to having Derek around and stop feeling intensely attracted to him. Unfortunately, the more he was around Derek, the clearer it was that Derek wasn't actually an asshole, despite how he first treated Dylan. Every second Dylan spent with him tempted him to make a very stupid decision that would probably end in the kind of heartbreak he'd successfully avoided for the last several years.

Brooks hooked an arm around Derek's neck. "Any chance you'd want to come to the annual Gallagher Grill-Out Summer Barbeque? It's in a few weeks, and we'd love to have you."

Dylan choked on his Gatorade.

Anderson patted him on the back. "You should definitely come, dude."

"Really?" There it was again. That perfect, unexpected smile on Derek's face threatening to make Dylan backslide in a way that would probably break him worse than the fall had. "Sure, when is it? I'll check my work schedule."

While Anderson, Brooks, and Cal talked over each other to give him the details, Dylan tried to ignore the tightening sensation in his chest.

This was not good.

With everything else going on Dylan hadn't had a chance to come up with a good excuse for missing it. If Derek was going, he'd have no choice but to go.

But maybe if Derek was there, his brothers would behave. Maybe this Grill-Out would be different.

Maybe.

Chapter 11

DYLAN

FYI—Wal-Mart has the deluxe extra-large giant shower caddies on sale today. I used to not understand how anyone could need a caddy that big. The more you know, I guess.

DEREK

Self-care is important. And snarky attitudes cause wrinkles.

DYLAN

Self-care requires three types of sunscreen? Our bathroom has more tiny bottles than the trash can next to Ozzy Osbourne's hotel minibar in 1973.

DEREK

So feisty with your super-current cultural references. On the topic of me being high maintenance, did you get a laundry detergent that you find *acceptable*?

DYLAN

Yours smells like chemicals. I can't sleep with that smell.

DEREK

It smells like "fresh rain mist."

DYLAN
The type of fresh rain mist that's made of acid and going to rot our bodies and erode cliffsides.

DEREK
Says the man who ate a leftover Taco Bell Crunchwrap for breakfast.

DYLAN
Any burrito can be a breakfast burrito if you believe hard enough.

"He has to be doing this on purpose," Derek muttered as he collected mugs and half-full glasses from literally every surface of the apartment. Did he just fill one then forget about it—he counted—sixteen times a day?

Over a month into this weird situation, and their time in the apartment rarely overlapped. Gallagher spent most hours in the kitchen demo-ing the rest of the floor or downstairs checking the progress of the mold abatement crew who had finally gotten started after several issues. He'd found a few other pipe problems in Derek's kitchen needing more repairs Derek would have to pay for and more time stuck up here.

As frustrated as Derek was, he had to admit he was impressed by how much Dylan knew. He could remember a ridiculous amount of information like product numbers of flooring or exact measurements without always needing to write things down immediately.

And yet sixteen water glasses in a little over thirty-six hours?

The front door opened. Dylan walked in wearing a respirator mask under his chin. His safety glasses were perched on his head, holding back a white-flecked birds' nest of hair. He started when he noticed Derek standing near the cabinets.

He grimaced at the dishes. "Shit, sorry. I was going to clean those up. My uncle called, so I just—"

"It's fine." Derek didn't care about the dishes. He cared whether Uncle Liam had been calling to deliver more bad news about the small money-eating hell pit beneath them. "What'd he say?"

"They said a few more days on the bedroom mold abatement. My uncle said the pipes in the bathroom are fixed, and he's going to send you an invoice. Two of the fixtures on the tub were not installed properly, so you're going to need to pick new ones."

Derek sighed.

"The drywall work's going to be pretty extensive. I have an order in from a supplier who can get some of the materials wholesale if you're good with not having a lot of choice? If you come down, I can show you what I mean."

"Alright." Derek petted Gus once and followed Gallagher downstairs.

Dylan gave Derek an overview of the work that had already happened and outlined the next steps. The living room area was crammed with stuff, but they had set up his bedframe there with an air mattress hoping that it would be possible for him to move back down sooner rather than later given that the crew had isolated the mold area. But since Gus was terrified of the air scrubbing machines, and Derek still didn't have functioning plumbing, moving back down seemed several weeks out. After Dylan finished his explanations, Derek grabbed a gallon bag of large breed dog food from the pantry. As they stepped up to the sidewalk in front of the building, Derek realized his blunder.

The telltale squeak of rubber Crocs against Carol Taylor's doormat made both men freeze. They wouldn't make it back down the stairs to his apartment without her seeing them. If they walked around the sidewalk toward the entrance to Gallagher's apartment, she'd see the bag of dog food.

Derek whirled around. "I'm sorry about this." He wrapped his arms around Dylan so that the bag of food was hidden between them. Dylan's back was pressed into the small brick wall beside the apartment building. Derek made sure his voice carried to Carol while he continued to "embrace" Gallagher, you know, in a friendly way. "Thank you so much for helping me—uh—"

"Unclog your toilet?" Dylan matched Derek's volume.

Carol's car door opened.

Derek made an *Are you kidding me* face at Dylan, who replied with a look that clearly stated, *If you're going to make me hug you to hide dog food, I'm going to make the world think your epic dumps broke your shitter.* Dylan followed that expression with a small challenging nod.

Derek kept his voice serious. "Yes. Thank you so much for that."

"My pleasure." Dylan's body shook with suppressed laughter. He spoke louder. "I'm always happy to snake a fella's drain if he needs it."

Derek clamped his lips shut.

Carol called out to them. "Mr. Chang, if you needed to borrow a plunger, you could've asked me for one." She wasn't more than five steps away from them, but Carol's typical voice volume was a shout. "Mine's pretty old, but with the right leverage it still works just fine."

Dylan lowered his voice to a whisper. "Hear that? Hers is old but it works just fine with leverage."

Derek locked eyes with Dylan. "Stop."

Dylan was a breath away from absolutely losing it.

"Mr. Chang, did you hear me? Mine's not quite as flexible as some of them they make these days, but it gets the job done."

Dylan's face could best be described as a kid on Christmas morning.

"I'm g-good. Th-thanks, Carol." Derek's attention narrowed in on Gallagher's face. If he looked anywhere else, his composure would crumble. He braced a hand on the bag of food pressed between them. He had planned on turning so that he could maneuver the food between his back and the wall, but something about watching Dylan Gallagher try not to laugh stopped him. His glasses had slid an inch down his nose.

"Olive was right about your eyes," Derek said before he realized that it was a weird thing to say.

Carol's car sped away from the curb, but neither man moved.

Gallagher's expression softened. "What about my eyes?"

A husky voice broke the silence. "Well . . . well . . . well. Been watching this from across the street waiting for Crocs lady to leave. She scares me."

Derek pulled away from Gallagher. "Oh hey. Um . . . so . . ."

"Hey there, both of you." Hudson shook Dylan's hand and winked at him. "Hudson Gregory." Hudson's blond curly hair was still shower damp and his light-green hospital surgical scrubs were as tight as usual. "I'd been kidding when I'd said we should invite your cute little neighbor down next time, but I'm definitely *down*. If you know what I mean?" Hudson's eyebrow made a suggestive motion astronauts on the Space Station could probably see and interpret.

"*What?*" Dylan gaped.

Mortified, Derek stepped away from Gallagher, hoping the ground would open and swallow him whole. The dog food slipped. Derek and Gallagher attempted to catch it at the same time, heads knocking painfully. Dylan grabbed the bag and held it to his chest like a shield. His blue eyes coolly assessed Hudson, taking in everything on display through the thin tightness of Hudson's scrub pants.

Hudson smiled genially. His slightly clueless niceness was grating in a way it never had been before. *Maybe* it was because Hudson had just casually implied that he and Derek had once discussed inviting Gallagher (a *complete goddamn* stranger to Hudson) into a threesome . . . but who could say?

Hudson smacked Derek playfully on the ass and then checked his watch. "Sorry I'm a little earlier than usual."

Dylan stood rigid, arms still locked around the dog food.

Hudson's movie-star smile turned confused as he did a similar up and down of Dylan. He pointed to Dylan's toolbelt, respirator, and safety glasses. "Is this a costume thing? You should've told me, Derek. I can do costumes. Derek knows. Don't you?"

Derek had shriveled into a husk of his former self.

"Uh . . . no . . . just, no." Dylan clutched the bag of dog food tighter. "I'm just helping Derek—uh—with some renovation work around the apartment . . ."

"Oh . . . that makes more sense then. Guess I got the wrong idea from the little sidewalk snuggle. No biggie." Hudson had never been afflicted by petty things like shame. He turned back to Derek. "I know we didn't make a definite plan for tonight, but you said you were off like usual, so I thought I'd stop by—"

"Right . . . okay." Gallagher pointed to the sidewalk that led to the door to his uncle's apartment. "I'll just take this to Gus."

"I'll be up in a—"

"No need to rush on my account." Gallagher shrugged and walked away.

Derek couldn't focus on anything else as Gallagher went around the corner.

"You okay, man?"

He'd forgotten Hudson was there for a second. "Oh . . . Hey, sorry. I'm actually having an apartment crisis right now. Everything's demolished. I'm actually staying with . . ."

Hudson smirked. "You know when you said 'not in a million years' would you want to have a hookup or a threesome with that guy, I don't think I *fully* understood what you meant. I thought you meant he *wasn't* your type, but . . ." A knowing nod. "I think I get it now. Good for you, dude."

"Huh?"

"Call me if you ever want to hang out again." He clapped a hand on Derek's shoulder. "Good luck, man. Dylan seems like a really nice guy."

"Sure, I—well, it's just that . . ."

"Don't worry." Hudson shook his head. "We've had fun. I've always known what this was. No hard feelings, bro." He checked his watch. He was probably on call later tonight. Derek's proximity to the hospital was part of what had made it easy to fall into the situationship with the surgeon in the first place. He'd completely forgotten Hudson was coming back into town this week. Hudson gave Derek's arm a final squeeze before reshouldering his gym bag and heading in the direction of the hospital. Instead of watching him go as Derek might usually have done, his attention returned to the spot where Gallagher had disappeared.

Derek's nights with men had established expectations. As a rule, Derek prided himself on his communication skills. He was always ready to spell out what he wanted. He was clear with what he was offering. Yes, Derek was a cocky bastard, but everyone left satisfied. *No one* got hurt. No one *ever* got hurt because it wasn't about deeper feelings.

A small voice that sounded like Olive's whispered in his brain—*DEREK never got hurt.*

Irritation brimmed at the edges of his consciousness. He just didn't really understand who he was irritated with.

His phone dinged.

> Mom
> Haha. No, the bats haven't taken me hostage. They're still gone. Just been busy with a few personal matters.

> Nothing to worry about. But do you remember where
> we put the information about the freezer?

He swiped across his phone. His mom answered before the first ring finished.

"What happened to the freezer?" He dragged a hand through his hair, unable to tear his eyes from that spot of sidewalk.

"It started leaking. It's fine, I just—"

"I can come over and take a look at it."

"No need. W—" She hesitated for a second. "It's all cleaned up. I just remember you reorganizing some of the files, and I couldn't remember where the appliance warranty paperwork ended up."

He frowned. "Shoot. It's in a couple different places because, I think, when we recarpeted your office we never moved some of those boxes back."

"I'll look around for it tomorrow. Nothing urgent."

"I'll be over in a few minutes. I have to work tomorrow, so it's better for me to come now if you need it soon. It's been forever since I've been over there."

"Oh . . . yes, that makes sense. Are you good with letting yourself in?"

"Of course. Did your Bible study get moved to Tuesdays again?"

"No . . ." Another weird hesitation. Why was she acting so cagey? "Just meeting a friend for dinner." She paused. "So . . . have you heard from your sister lately?"

He knew which sister she meant from the way she asked the question.

He felt for his car keys in his pocket. "She's not answering my texts. I know she was staying with some friends for a while last year after—"

"How *is* the apartment?" Her tone shifted from hesitant into that slight mix of disapproval and concern.

"I'm making some updates actually. Should be in great shape soon." No lies there, but also nothing to set off his mother's financial alarm bells.

"Glad to hear it." A muffled voice came through the line. "I have to get going for the reservation but thank you so much for offering to look for the paperwork." Her voice had brightened so much he almost dropped the phone.

"Anytime."

"Oh, I found an old envelope of your photos when I was looking through boxes. I'll leave them out on the counter."

Before Derek could say anything else, the call ended. He squeezed his keys in his fist until the edges imprinted into his palm. The call had been weird, right? There had been no other word for it. He tried to remember why he was staring so intently at the corner of the building before recollecting that he'd been about to follow Gallagher back up to his apartment and explain about the other weird conversation he'd just had.

He winced. Had Hudson been implying that Derek and Dylan were together?

Together together?

Shaking his head, he strode down toward where his car was parked.

Chapter 12

Not in a million years.

The words echoed through Dylan's brain.

Yikes.

He knew that he wasn't Derek's type, but he didn't need it thrown in his face. Hudson was practically a male model. His scrubs tested the limits of seam strength, particularly in and around the groin area. He'd waited until Dylan had left to make the comment but had one of those voices that seemed to carry. So Dylan heard it loud and clear. And fully understood the implication.

After the dog walker picked up Gus, the mess in Dylan's brain made it impossible to tackle the mess in the apartment. After feeding Gus his dinner, Dylan gave up and hopped in the shower. Why was it sometimes so easy to remember all the things that he needed to do while he was in the shower? He needed to wash out the glasses and mugs so that Derek would stop the passive-aggressive tidying. Dylan's mother always did the passive-aggressive tidying thing, and it drove him bananas. Dylan could get everything done if he managed to focus. He needed to run out for laundry detergent that didn't smell awful.

Not in a million years.

He wished he could stay in the hot shower for a million years so he wouldn't have to face Derek and pretend he hadn't found out Dr. Abercrombie & Fitch had discussed inviting Dylan down to join in whatever those two got up to and Derek had rejected the suggestion like it had been ridiculous.

A million years.

Dylan pressed a palm against the tile. He'd already decided that things with Derek were a no-go, so why did it sting? The rejection should have been no surprise. Because of the way Uncle Sean's kitchen window pointed, Dylan had a front-row seat to the type of men Derek had over. He and Felicity had even made something of a game about inventing backstories for the men emerging from the garden apartment door when they hung out there. Unsurprisingly, none of the well-muscled men looked like Dylan. Seriously, what in the *Grey's Anatomy* hot-people bullshit was going on at Derek's hospital?

He forced himself to give his body a final rinse and shook out his hair in an attempt to slough off that instinctive feeling of worthlessness. Awkward social interactions created small fractures in his mental armor. Every crack allowed old insecurities to slide right back into his brain.

Shit, his fingers had crinkled into raisin flesh.

He needed to get out. Dishes. Cleaning. Laundry. He said he'd take out the recycling too. Ugh. Dylan nearly slipped on the tile because he wasn't paying attention and knocked Derek's towel to the floor. He'd come back and grab it when he started laundry. He could put Derek's other things in too. He'd probably get to it before Derek got back from whatever he was doing...

With all the muscles between those two, they were probably into some kind of weird gay tantric-Sting-level shit. This wasn't an outcome he'd considered when he helped get Derek's bed set up in the living room.

Dylan shuddered and eased the bathroom door open enough to be sure he was still alone in the apartment. No sounds except for Gus's snoring. Dylan's ears strained, but he 100 percent wasn't trying to hear if there was noise coming from the apartment beneath him. He absolutely wasn't.

The mirror had completely un-fogged, which meant he'd been standing half-naked longer than intended. After a frown at his reflection, he slipped on his smudged glasses.

Olive was right about your eyes.

What the hell had *that* meant?

Muffled vibrating came from the couch cushions. His phone must have fallen out of his pocket. The text wall from Chase used more than the typical amount of profanity and exclamation points. Grumbling, Dylan adjusted the towel he was wearing and grabbed his laptop.

Chapter 13

DYLAN

Gus is whining. The dog walker took him out like usual and then I fed him, but he's still restless.

DEREK

Put on a movie for him.

DYLAN

You dog likes movies?

DEREK

Gus is a connoisseur of many forms of media. I brought one of his favorites up. Probably still in your uncle's DVD player.

Derek put the manila appliance information folder on the counter and grabbed the Kodak-yellow photo envelope sitting there. This must have been one of the last rounds of film he ever developed. As soon as he saw the photo on top, he froze.

Oh. *These* photos . . .

How far had his mom been digging in the boxes? He smiled at the photo on top—Olive and Derek flanking a barely teen-aged Michelle in front of gilded stage doors at a New York City theater. He'd forgotten his camera that weekend. They had bought a cheap disposable on the way to the city. Michelle wore a heavily sequined costume and cradled roses. That elite intensive was *supposed* to be a first step toward an impressive career. *God*, he missed those intense, confident grins Michelle had worn so often before her injury.

For the next month they broke out that camera during big moments. Apprehension knit in his gut as he flipped through photos shifting from cheesy NYC tourist shots to a townhome in Baltimore.

Derek fell in love with Jake when Derek was a skinny, pimply teenager, but he hadn't seen Jake for years while Jake went to grad school in Massachusetts or when Jake was working that first job. He was always traveling then. Jake only came back to the town house for short stretches. Derek suspected he'd gotten it so Olive wouldn't have to worry about rent while racking up nursing school student loans. He had told her he *needed* someone to keep an eye on it while he traveled. What a load of bullshit. He was always doing things like that for her.

Olive had a group of friends over that night. Derek saw Jake across the room, looking just as tall and devastatingly hot as he had when Derek had been a closeted, pining teenager. But when their eyes met, Jake threw Derek an unfamiliar and irresistibly charming smile. That wasn't the smile he'd *ever* used on the scrawny sixteen-year-old kid he taught to drive. But after a moment, Jake's expression lit with a sudden spark of almost-shocked recognition.

He downed half of whatever was in his tumbler glass. "Well, it's Derek Chang. As I live and breathe."

Derek managed a cool chuckle in response. "If it isn't Jake Murphy. Olive's absentee roommate-slash-landlord."

"Is that really all I am?" Jake's cocky smirk nearly stopped Derek's heart. Was this really happening?

"Yup." Pretending that this was *any* hot guy, Derek plucked the drink from Jake's hand. The straight gin burned his throat, but he suppressed his grimace, trying to look cool.

"Oh my god." Olive jumped on her brother's back. "Historic moment. It's been years since you guys saw each other. Derek said he didn't believe you still existed. And this is perfect. Look what I found today." She grabbed a disposable camera from the counter, and it took Derek a second to remember when it was from. "*Oooh.* Three photos left." She pushed Jake and Derek closer together and clicked the button before tossing the camera in the basket with her keys.

With an annoying burning behind his eyes, Derek slid the photos back into the sleeve.

He went upstairs. He'd grown up in this house, and one of the closets still held some of his old boxes. He didn't even know why he was looking for it or why he'd stuck the folded piece of lined yellow paper into the book he'd had with him that night. He never finished reading that book.

> Derek—
> Guess you were still on your walk when I woke up??
>   Look—didn't mean for last night to happen. But I don't regret it either. I'm not in a great mental place right now, but I want you to know that last night meant something. Well, guess I'm saying it meant something to me. But I also really meant it when I said I'm <u>not</u> a good enough guy for you. I wish I was. Maybe I will be someday? You're also Olive's best friend, so this is complicated no matter what, but really <crossed out scribbles> you deserve better than just some shitty-ass maybe/someday guy. Sorry I had to duck out without seeing you. Early flight. Call me if you need anything as always.
> —J

Derek slipped the worn yellow paper back between the book's pages.

That word *someday* had been Derek's excuse for years.

Someday Jake would be ready. The word *maybe* never seemed to register like it did right now.

When Jake moved to Frederick, the three of them grew closer than ever. A year and a half before Jake's accident he joined a local hockey league. Got sober. Adopted Gus. There was a little less work travel. It *seemed* like Jake was trying to put down roots.

Was Derek naïve for seeing it all as a sign that *someday* was coming?

Yet even then, apprehension was always mixed with hope. Loving Jake had become a default. It had come as easily as his love for Olive—though it *felt* very different. Or at least, he thought it was different.

Casual became his default setting for everything else. Sex was sex, and he could have good sex whenever he wanted it without jeopardizing what *might be*. That had been his mode with Hudson and every other guy Derek had spent time with. Then after Jake was gone . . .

Nothing seemed like it mattered.

He had Olive and Amy and Amy's kids, his mom, but . . . he didn't have Michelle anymore. He didn't have Jake anymore. He slipped his phone out of his pocket.

For a moment, he was struck by the strangest impulse.

He wanted to call *his dad* to ask him what he should do.

It had been years since Derek's subconscious had been this much of an asshole.

Fuck you, subconscious.

His thumb hovered over Olive's name before realizing he would need to explain a *lot* of other things to make any of his current feelings make sense.

Maybe all he needed was a friendly voice.

He dialed Amy. The sister who currently answered his calls.

A voice that wasn't his sister's answered. "Hi, Uncle Derek."

"Hey, buddy." He grinned at his oldest nephew's precocious and oddly world-weary voice. "Is your mom around?"

"Yeah, she's—"

Sounds of a tussle over the phone came with his sister's muffled voice. "Noah, they're going to send me to jail if you keep calling NASA and demanding—"

"It's me, Ames."

"Oh." She exhaled in warm relief. "Thank god."

"Why's your kid calling NASA?"

"He wants them to lower the age of their internship program." Her wry voice rose into a carrying reprimand. "He doesn't realize that getting put on the FBI watchlist at age seven will probably mean he's blacklisted."

Something unknotted in Derek's chest. She sounded just like his dad when she said stuff like that. It was the same way his dad used to complain about Derek's clothes or haircuts or music choices. Exasperation mixed with pride.

"Hey, have you heard from Mom or Michelle?" Amy said.

All the released tension balled up again. "I'm at Mom's now actually. She called me tonight asking about paperwork. And—um—no, I haven't heard from Michelle in about . . ." He put the phone on speaker and swiped to messages, scrolling through several screens of unanswered texts to find the last one from Michelle. "Six months." *God, had it really been that long?*

MICHELLE
I told you not to.

"Really?" Amy paused. "Yeah, I mean, you know Michelle. She gets wrapped up in something and forgets the world exists."

"She's wrapped up in something?"

"Just assuming." Amy cleared her throat, her tone shifted back into her normal dryness. "Mom, however, has been acting weird for weeks. Sneaky. *And* she took an unplanned vacation day last week, according to her assistant. First time in her entire career."

"Maybe something came up at church?"

"I don't think so. Something's off. I'll let you know what I find out."

"You say that like you're planning on hiring a private detective or something."

"Hmm."

"That was *not* a suggestion."

"You're no fun."

He restacked the boxes he'd moved out of the closet. "Have *you* heard from Michelle?"

"Oh, you know Michelle these days. She vanishes for a bit and then pops up with stories about following a rock band to Coachella or something. I'm sure she'll text you soon."

It wasn't until they got off the phone that Derek realized Amy hadn't actually answered his question. Sighing, he closed the messages app as if that would help him hide from the truth that all the women in his family were acting more bizarre than usual.

Derek *knew* Michelle would be angry he'd paid off the credit cards. He shouldn't have opened her mail in the first place, but those notices kept piling up. He'd just wanted to help. He couldn't fix her knee or her even more shattered heart, but he could give her a fresh start.

Instinctively, he went downstairs and began cleaning up his mother's kitchen. She must have been baking again. Now that *was* an odd sign. Maybe Amy was right.

The sink was full, which was also strange since it wasn't tax season, but he was glad he could do something with his hands. His family never used the dishwasher growing up, so he always did the dishes by hand. Dishes were oddly calming. A defined task with a simple, organized goal.

He needed to calm down before going back to the expensive

chaos of his living situation. And the chaos of Dylan. Maybe the dishes would also calm the chaos in his brain about that awkward conversation with Hudson. He just wished he didn't remember the exact expression on Dylan's face as he walked away.

Chapter 14

The front door swung open and Dylan blinked, tearing his eyes away from his laptop as panic surged. The apartment was pitch black except for the glow from the DVD menu for *10 Things I Hate About You*. Goose bumps covered him. Probably because he was still wearing nothing but a towel. He'd only moved long enough to put the movie on. Shockingly, it worked, and Gus chilled out enough for Dylan to get his work done. Dylan had been so focused on his work he hadn't felt time pass.

Something crashed to the ground in the entryway.

Dylan pushed the laptop on the coffee table and hopped up.

"Just move the toolbox out of the goddamn hallway," Derek said in a mutter.

Oh *no*.

The list of tasks Dylan was *supposed* to get done ticker-taped across his mind like those old inclement weather alerts framing prime-time TV shows.

"Shoot. I'm sorry. I got dis—"

"—tracted." Derek finished. "It's fine." He moved the toolbox to the side.

As some instinct made Dylan step forward, a yellow streetlight outside was just bright enough for Derek to see what Dylan was wearing, or actually, *not* wearing.

Derek gestured to his body with the hand that wasn't holding a laundry bag full of scrubs. "You give me shit about not sleeping in a shirt and you're just hanging out on the couch buckass naked watching a DVD menu."

"Towel," Dylan said feebly. It was *almost* a towel. All the full-sized ones were still dirty in the basket that Dylan still hadn't put in the washer.

"That's a literal washcloth, dude."

That *"dude"* was enough for him to remember what had set off this afternoon's bout of distraction. Anger boiled over, and he hadn't even realized he was angry. "Sorry, *bro*. Must be so awful to come home to this after your special time with your *friend—*"

"Special time with . . ." The lines of Derek's face knit into inscrutableness. "With Hudson?" Derek inhaled then exhaled once before speaking. "You're . . . jealous."

"Ha."

Great comeback, Dylan. Truly inspired.

Dylan snatched up the overfull laundry basket sitting at his feet and held it in front of the insufficient towel. "I don't give a crap that it seems like you've fucked every lacrosse player in a twenty-mile radius."

"This is about body count? Never thought you'd be the type of person to shame a guy for—"

"This is about you being an asshole when I make mistakes from the first time we even met." That *was* what it was about right? It was *not* jealousy. The anger was definitely not because he always ended up attracted to out-of-his-league men who would never want him *"in a million years."* He took a calming breath. "I'm sorry . . . I've just got a lot going on with the renovations and work—"

"It's fine." With a frustrated huff, Derek opened the door to the bathroom as if literally exiting their conversation. "Can you just *not* throw my towel on the floor? I get that you've got 'a lot going on' but is that too much to ask? I'm really not trying to be an asshole, but this is basic roommate one-oh-one."

"Shit. I'm really sorry. That was an accident. I really am being an asshole tonight." Dylan ran around the couch with the laundry basket, but he slipped on a stray sock.

He dropped the laundry basket and crashed into Derek, who tripped over the toolbox he had just moved.

Derek caught himself before his head hit the ground, but the only thing Dylan could grab was the lamp on the entry table—one of Uncle Sean's favorite antiques. He got both hands on the lamp to prevent it from shattering on the floor, but the cord caught on the bowl of spare keys and change.

Every naked inch of Dylan's body landed on top of Derek while a hailstorm of pennies pelted them both.

Derek's mouth had been set into a tight line, but then he laughed—actually laughed, scanning the jumbled mess of laundry they were basically swimming in.

"I swear I was just trying to get the towel to put it in the laundry basket, but I . . . shit, the laundry detergent."

Derek still didn't move except for a subtle twitch at the corner of his mouth. "Is the scent really that bad it bothers you right *now*?"

It took Dylan a second to understand what he was saying. "*No*, you smell great. Better than great." An understatement. Dylan would have let his head bow forward but it would have meant resting it on Derek's chest, although based on previous experience it was surprisingly comfortable for something that seemed chiseled from concrete. "No . . ."

Derek couldn't conceal his effort at holding back a smile. "Good to know."

"It's just I was supposed to go to the store, and I—"

"It's okay." Derek's throat bobbed. "Actually, I . . ."

A loud pounding sound came from the door.

Dylan scrambled off Derek, pushing the lamp back onto the side table as a carrying voice shrieked, "Mr. Gallagher? Mr. Gallagher? Are you okay?"

"Not again, Karen," Derek said in the tone people used when saying *Not today, Satan*.

Dylan slid into the door just as the door lock clicked open.

"*Shit.*" Dylan grabbed onto the rattling doorknob.

"Your door is stuck, Mr. Gallagher. Do I need to call the fire department?"

Derek threw the towel—okay, the *tea* towel—at Dylan's crotch.

Because Gus had no sense of self-preservation, he picked that moment to trot over. Derek caught his collar just in time.

"I heard a large crash down there and then shouting." More yanking at the door. "Are you injured? Is there an intruder?" Her tone shifted as if she believed Jack the Ripper lurked behind the door. "I'm on the phone to the 9–1–1 dispatch. I could have the police here in—"

With one hand keeping the undersized terry cloth in place, he let go of the doorknob without undoing the chain. "I'm fine, Carol," Dylan said. "Sorry for the loud noise. I just knocked something over . . . and I was yelling at the TV. Hockey game." He hoped his voice carried through her phone. "Please, tell dispatch I'm fine."

Carol looked him up and down through the slit in the door. "Are you sure?"

"Yes. I just got out of the shower."

"How were you watching hockey in the shower? And you're not wet." She said with another perusal of his body. "Just very cold, apparently."

Internally cursing, he hid his bottom half behind the door.

An urgent voice came through the speaker of Carol's phone. "Ma'am, did you say there was a man with a hickey in the shower?"

"*Hockey*, not hickey. He said he was watching hockey naked in the shower for some reason." Carol's voice echoed off the back alley behind the building. "I said *naked*. Damn bad service. I said he was naked and watching hockey, not naked with a hickey." She turned on the speakerphone as if the volume wasn't loud enough before.

At least its volume covered Derek's snort.

"Ma'am, can you please explain if you're experiencing an emergency?"

"Can you just tell the operator I'm fine?" Dylan sighed.

"He says he's fine." After a few more exchanges with dispatch, Carol ended the call. Her expression shifted from concern to suspicion. "Now Mr. Gallagher . . ." She kept her hand in Dylan's door so he couldn't shut it. She sniffed twice. Like a bloodhound. "I ignored all that equipment I saw you bringing in *and* the man setting up that ultra-highspeed internet connection."

Confusion outstripped his irritation. "What does the internet connection have to do with—?

"My sister told me all about those websites and how people make money with them. No judgment here. We all have to make ends meet these days. My sister might not understand that, but I do." She looked at him with pity. "But I need you to keep it down during quiet hours."

"You think I'm a—*oh-NO*, I'm not—"

"And since," her voice became low, almost conspiratorial. "And since I'm keeping your little secret, can I ask you a question?"

"A question?"

"Did you see any signs of a large dog while you were down helping Mr. Chang with his toilet earlier?"

An aggressive breeze made Dylan's nipples pucker painfully.

"A large dog? Not that I saw."

"But you'll tell me if you see it, won't you? It's really important we feel safe in our building after all."

"Sure." He yawned to disguise how bad he was at lying.

"Alright. Good night, Mr. Gallagher. You are quite handsome, aren't you." The knowing smile she gave Dylan caused the rest of him to shrivel as much as another certain part of him already had.

Derek tossed Dylan some clothes and collapsed into a chair

and covered his face with a pillow to muffle his laughter. "Not sure which is more surprising—that Carol Taylor thinks a fast internet connection means you're making amateur porn down here or that she's more okay with *that* than Gus living here. I mean, you? A cam boy? The way she said you were handsome. *Duuude*."

"Yeah, the idea of me being a porn star is *completely absurd*," Dylan said dryly. Dylan had been ready to laugh until the last bit. Derek was laughing a little too hard at the idea of him being an amateur porn star.

He could be a porn star if he wanted to.

It was just cold, damn it.

"C'mon, dude. Why aren't you laughing?" Derek's grin was infectious, but Dylan felt immune. "Sex work is nothing to be ashamed of. You should be flattered."

Dylan managed a few perfunctory chuckles before retreating to the bedroom. He'd never felt so glad to *not* be naked.

His mind was spiraling out of control. Everything was so loud. His meds wore off hours ago, and he kept forgetting the next step of what he should be doing. No wonder this was *hilarious* to Derek. He squeezed his eyes shut like he could hide from the memory of the overheard exchange with Hudson.

Derek knocked and called from the door. "I figured you'd forget to run out and get detergent. No big deal. You didn't respond when I texted to ask, so I just picked up some of that unscented organic kind you said you liked on the way back from my mom's."

Dylan should feel grateful, but the assumption that he wouldn't remember stung. It stung worse since Derek's assumption was correct.

When Dylan walked back into the kitchen, Derek was stacking all Dylan's abandoned mugs and glasses on the drying rack next to the sink. A thumping noise from the closet off the kitchen meant Derek had started the laundry. He could complete the necessary tasks like they were simple. Probably because for people with normal executive function, they *were* simple.

"You okay?" Derek slung a kitchen towel over his shoulder and crossed the bare subfloor to face Dylan. A charmingly crooked smile angled his face. "Joni's joke about you falling through the ceiling being the start of a porno seems even funnier now."

While Dylan's brain truly sucked at remembering to clean up dishes or buy laundry detergent, it was really good at figuring and creating new reasons to be anxious. Carol had offered to keep his nonexistent porn creation a secret in exchange for information about Gus.

What if . . .

What if *Derek* was just being nice and flirtatious right now to get him to keep Gus a secret? Or to get the repair done on the apartment? Dylan stiffened and leaned a half inch away. The part of his brain recalling that moment when Derek's body had pressed into his on the sidewalk to hide the bag of dog food wanted to match Derek's flirtatious tone. Normally he would have thought this entire situation was as hilarious as Derek found it. That same part of him had been low-key fantasizing ever since Derek mentioned Joni (of all people) making a joke that him falling through the ceiling sounded like the start of a porno. That part of him wanted to ask what Derek had meant by saying Olive was *"Right about his eyes."*

But this wouldn't be the first time Dylan had gotten the wrong idea. He could hyperfixate on a crush if he wasn't careful, and he was too attracted to Derek to think clearly. It was too easy to believe that Derek would never have even spoken to him if he hadn't literally crashed into his life. If Derek was flirting with him, it was probably because he needed him to keep up his end of their bargain.

"You're not actually a secret porn star, are you?" Derek tossed a dry dish towel at him.

Dylan caught it. "Not a chance." As he grabbed a mug to dry, the memory of Hudson's words clanged in his head, and so he said it. "Not in a million years."

Chapter 15

DEREK
Thank you for washing my scrubs! That new fabric softener is better on them too. I agree.

DYLAN
You're welcome.

Derek sighed. How did a simple period at the end of a text make a normal *you're welcome* text read like it actually said, *"You're welcome, asshole."*

After doing some stock room inventory at the very end of an uncharacteristically slow day, Derek lay down on a stretcher in the old, unused part of the unit. He needed a five-minute mental break. Not from work, although this was his sixth shift in a row. He needed to rake in every cent of overtime and shift differential bonuses to cover the most recent mold abatement invoice. The problem had been worse than expected, but if Derek could keep up this work schedule, he might be able to cover everything. The better-than-expected news about his financial situation didn't make up for the weird "emptiness" of his time in the apartment since the day Dylan definitely overhead the conversation with Hudson two weeks ago.

Derek still hadn't figured out how to apologize for it or if he should apologize, or if that would just make things worse. Dylan wasn't cold or angry. He was being nice and considerate—the bland niceness that was completely devoid of actual feeling. It was careful and boring and so different from the weirdly energizing quasi-hatred, quasi-something else from before. No repeat of accidentally naked-tackling Derek into piles of unwashed laundry.

Did Derek really miss that?

Yeah, he absolutely did.

Supposedly, the weather was amazing, but it wasn't like Derek could or wanted to take advantage of it. The nice weather did mean that they had discharged all but four of their patients. Which gave Derek just enough time to *over*think. Last night in that hollow polite voice, Dylan told him two more days of work, and then they could close up the hole between the two apartments.

He wasn't used to spending this much time in close quarters, but moving back downstairs made him feel strangely nervous. He'd always needed alone or semi-alone hours to recharge. But even though Dylan was quiet, he existed loudly. Or at least Derek *felt* his existence loudly. All reasons why Derek *should* be desperate to move back downstairs.

Needing a distraction, he shot off a few texts to his mom and sisters just to check in. His mom had said she didn't need him to come change her car's oil tomorrow like he always did. That was weird. If he wasn't completely swamped by work and the apartment disaster he'd probably be as nosy as Amy was being about it.

He closed his eyes. Why couldn't he just enjoy the silence? Like a tag on a new shirt, something itched at him.

Damn that Dylan Gallagher.

He'd gotten several texts from Dylan's older brothers about that family grill-out in a few weeks, but Dylan hadn't mentioned a word about it. That was weird too. Why was *everything* so weird? He had never known that the three hockey giants Jake played with were named Gallagher. *That* must have been how Jake met Dylan in the first place.

On the New Year's Eve before Jake's accident those three

Gallaghers and their wives had been at Jake's house for a few hours before they left to go to a family thing. Olive had already gotten pulled away due to some drama with her ex.

And this left Jake and Derek on the couch alone.

Derek had been a little drunk.

Jake had been sober for over a year at that point, but Derek didn't know it then. As the fire died, they commiserated about the sad state of the local online gay dating scene. To illustrate his point, Jake opened an app on his phone to scroll through the parade of douchebag dudes that he matched with until something on the screen made Jake freeze.

"Well *shit*." Jake slumped. "I guess there's my answer."

"Huh?" Derek looked over his shoulder.

"Nothing." He pulled the phone away.

"What?" Derek leaned closer. "One of those obviously catfishing stock photos? Show me. I live for that crap. Lemme see." Derek had (drunkenly) grabbed Jake's phone and scrolled through the profile of a *Dylan G.*

Jake shrugged off Derek's concern with a forced laugh. "Meh. Couldn't blame the guy for calling me a piece of shit and kicking me to the curb. Always been garbage at making it work with the good ones."

At this point in the evening, Derek's vision had blurred, but he'd blinked away the beer haze to look at the profile. Once then twice. Then one more time. "C'mon, this guy's a piece of shit. Not you."

"It's not a big deal. Just didn't expect him to come up on there." Jake tried to grab the phone back.

Derek shifted away and scrolled through Dylan G's profile enough to have the memory burned into him. Long enough to see all the times on the profile it mentioned *serious relationship* or *looking for long-term partner*, making Dylan G's goals very clear. "You're way out of his league. It just says he works in tech. Sounds made up. Like *The Bachelor* or on *House Hunters* when someone's a professional scrapbooker or some shit like that. He probably just owns a computer."

"I literally have no idea what you're talking about with *The Bachelor* or whatever the other show was."

"That's because Carrie Bradshaw was never on either show." In the rest of the profile photos, Dylan looked a few years younger, but Derek couldn't deny that the guy was . . . *something*. Still, if he had called Jake a piece of shit, the dude was dead to him.

Jake took his phone back. "I'm not sure your niche movie taste allows you to disrespect my addiction to HBO's finest prestige programming." After one last scan of the screen, he locked it.

Derek had never seen Jake be less than confident and self-assured about *anything* but especially about dating.

What the hell had *Dylan G* done to make Jake look like he'd been kicked in the nuts? Derek *had* seen a change in Jake over the year before that New Year's, but mostly Jake had seemed happier and healthier.

"Seriously, you okay, dude?" Derek asked. "You really liked this guy? Dylan G?"

"Nah. Of course not. Dylan G's just another asshole. Plenty more assholes in the sea." Mask of unconcern back in place, Jake had tossed the phone on the coffee table.

"Not sure that's the saying." Derek's laugh turned into a dorky hiccup.

Despite the gallon of alcohol his liver had to process that night, Derek chickened out from telling Jake how he felt. *Again.*

A little over eleven months later, Jake had his accident.

So when the actual Dylan G moved into the ground-floor apartment above him with the neighbors calling him the dead-beat nephew, Derek hated him on instinct. It still felt like Jake had *just* died. Derek couldn't fix him being dead. He couldn't even process it. But he *could* hate someone who hurt Jake.

The hospital room door squeaked open.

Derek opened his eyes long enough to see a flash of familiar ginger hair before he flopped back onto his stretcher. "Found me?"

The stretcher next to his squinched, and Joni's laughter filled the room. "I was hoping this was nap time. Group nap, kindergarten style."

"All discharged?"

"Yep." She nestled down, facing him. "No one in triage right now."

"Weird. It was so busy this morning."

"Do *not* say the Q word, Derek Chang."

"I've been an emergency nurse for ten years, Joni. You think I'm gonna say that word? No way." He rolled and leaned his head on his elbow.

Joni smirked. "I didn't mean to offend you."

"No offense taken. We should go get dinner this week. I need to get out of that apartment. We haven't since . . ."

"Since Olive left," Joni said quietly. "You still sleeping at Dylan's?"

"Yeah." Derek turned onto his back and faced the ceiling, letting more thoughts spill out of him because it had been so long since he'd spoken to Olive without needing to keep certain secrets. He needed to talk to someone. "I thought about going to my mom's for a few days, but she said the guest room's spoken for right now. I mean, that's not that weird. She's hosted women in crisis over the years, sometimes kids too, through a program at her church for the victims of domestic violence. But if it's that, why's she being weirdly cagey? My sister—the one who's still talking to me—also noticed and now's basically on the verge of hiding in my mom's shrubs with binoculars to figure out what's going on with her, and I don't want to get in the middle of that. My mom deserves her privacy if she wants it, you know? But I can admit it's weird. And *everything's* weird. And then there's Dylan . . ."

"That's a lot." Joni took a breath. "What's the trouble in roommate paradise?"

"Paradise?" Derek snorted. "Basically, having me there is hell for him. I think the guy *hates* me but is too nice to show it."

"I thought you hated *him*."

"I thought he . . ." Every time he remembered the hurt in Jake's eyes, he hated him. He had been so focused on listening to Jake being so entirely un-Jake-like that he hadn't really been *hearing* him.

He'd always seen Jake through his rose-colored crush goggles or through Olive's little sister perspective of thinking Jake hung the moon. He was a fantastic brother, but even Olive had made jokes about Jake's reckless behavior in other areas of life. Especially the dating and the drinking. Once, she'd even had to manage two boyfriends who had shown up at the town house on the same day when he was traveling.

Maybe Dylan hadn't been the one who was the asshole.

He covered his face as that sunk in, fitting into the version of Dylan he'd gotten to know.

Shit.

Obviously Dylan hadn't been the asshole in that situation.

It wasn't lovestruck regret in Jake's eyes. It was probably Derek's own jealousy that had made him interpret it that way. Nope . . . it had been guilt. When Olive was guilty, she had the exact same body language.

"Where'd you go?" Joni asked.

"I thought . . ." Derek rubbed his forehead. "I think . . . I'm pretty sure I was wrong about Dylan."

"What do you mean? Is he still fixing the stuff he said he'd fix?"

"Oh. No . . . not about that. And yeah. He's doing a lot. He's a machine."

"So . . . what were you wrong about?"

"It's complicated."

Joni played with the end of her stethoscope. "Maybe if I knew why you inexplicably hated him in the first place I'd understand?"

"It's really dumb."

"It's not dumb if it's something that's important to you, or something that impacted you."

Derek emptied his lungs completely before speaking again. "I think he dated Jake. And I think things ended badly."

"Whoa . . . *Olive's* Jake?" Joni sat up.

He nodded.

"Small world."

"I'd met his brothers a couple times before, but I never made the connection."

Joni studied his face. "I'm still confused."

Derek tried to explain. But because she didn't know Jake, she couldn't fully understand how bizarre it was to see Jake looking lost. Jake was the All-American superhero that someone would put on a magazine cover. Even more than that, Jake had been the one to teach Derek how to drive. Jake had been the *first* person he knew to come out to his family and basically dare the world to give him any shit for being gay. No one ever did. Jake always seemed to know what to do in every situation. While Olive babysat Derek's sisters, Jake had driven Derek and his mother all over town while they planned Derek's dad's funeral. Derek never asked him to do it. He just did.

"So, you thought Dylan might've hurt someone you loved . . . and because you, like Olive, are the most fiercely loyal person on the planet, you kinda decided to hate him for eternity without knowing the details?"

"Pretty much. It's just . . . Jake . . . he wasn't just Olive's brother, you know? Jake was . . ." Derek couldn't even pick the right word.

"Ah . . . okay. I think I'm understanding a little better now."
A different kind of pity infused Joni's voice.

"*Stop.*"

Small wrinkles creased Joni's forehead. She had one of those
faces. The kind that made deep dark secrets spill out because
anyone looking at her intuitively knew she wouldn't judge.

Very infuriating at the moment.

Her teal blue truth serum eyes bored into him, and something brittle inside his chest cracked.

She lay back down, giving him a needed break from the eye
contact. "How long were you in love with Jake?"

There it was.

"*Shit.*" Derek dug his elbows into his knees until they hurt.

"Did he feel the same way?" No judgment or pressure. He
also appreciated her calling him Jake instead of *Olive's brother.*

Derek sat on the edge of the stretcher and rested his head on
his knuckles. "Guess I'll never really know."

God, he sounded so bitter.

"I'm so sorry." She came to sit beside him.

"Me too."

"And Olive . . ."

"Doesn't know."

"But you tell each other everything."

He stood and paced. "Everything but this. Literally everything but this while Jake was alive, and then after he died . . .
fuck." He faced her with his hand out defensively. "She was having a really tough time. I couldn't fix it, so I needed to be strong
for her."

"I think you've filled that role a lot in your life . . ." Joni
frowned. "You didn't want her to feel like she needed to take
care of you while she was dealing with her own loss. So you
dealt with yours completely alone."

"Are you a witch?"

Joni grinned but tears gathered in the corners of her eyes.

"That's not the first time I've been asked, believe it or not. Probably partially because of the red-hair reputation for soul stealing."

Derek laughed in spite of everything else he was feeling.

"I understand why you didn't tell Olive, but I'm honored you're trusting me with this. Life is complicated. For the record, I think Olive would understand."

"Maybe."

DYLAN

FYI—I took Gus for a walk.

DEREK

Thanks! I should be back there soon. All patients discharged. Really appreciate it tho.

DYLAN

Derek scowled at that thumbs-up emoji and then dropped the phone onto the stretcher mattress like it had personally insulted him.

Joni's expression X-rayed him. "Everything else okay?"

"Just a completely normal text from Dylan I'm overthinking." Derek dug his fingertips into his upper legs. "I've been kind of a dick to Dylan since he moved in. And I'm pretty sure he didn't deserve that at all—except for the whole being partially responsible for destroying my apartment thing. But recently I've just been trying to be nice, and I don't know why I care about a stupid thumbs-up emoji anyway."

"You really lost me with the emoji."

"Okay, so this sounds like a silly thing to complain about, but lately he's been nice, but in the way people are nice to strangers, and before that, sometimes . . ."

He would *not* be telling Joni about the heat he sometimes saw in Dylan's eyes, and how a part of him had liked it. A big part of him.

Derek's hands balled together. "He's talking to me like a robot, but before, it was funny clapbacks and snarky jokes about my bathroom products." He'd made Derek laugh even when he was freaking out about the disaster.

"So I'll just leave the whole 'jokes about bathroom products' aside for the time being even though I'm curious . . . because, and I'm not sure exactly how to say this without just saying it, but did you *do* something specific to him since the night we were all over there? He wasn't treating you like that then. Olive and Stella were pretty sure he was into you, actually."

"I . . ." He couldn't tell her about the humiliating conversation with Hudson either. And the whole possibly accidentally implying no one would want to watch him do porn. And the assuming he was a deadbeat mooching nephew thing. Oh, and he might have accused him of lying about the water problem originating in Derek's plumbing . . . well, damn. "Thinking back . . . I might have been an ass at several specific points since then, yes."

"You could apologize?"

"I *could.*"

Joni grinned. Before she could reply, the door opened.

"There you are." Carolyn, a hospital social worker, popped her head into the room. "I just had a form for you, but I'll leave it on your desk. Boy, sure is *quiet* here today."

The word seemed to echo ominously after she left.

The forbidden Q word.

An urgent page overhead summoned Joni at the same time Derek's charge nurse phone rang.

Joni groaned in horror. "What. Did. She. Do?"

Chapter 16

When Derek climbed the stairs to Dylan's apartment, he had been at work three hours after his shift was supposed to end. His head was pounding, and he was still processing everything that happened since that conversation with Joni when they had *thought* the last part of their shift would be a breeze. Derek was used to the normal chaos of the ER, but the last few hours were less typical, though unfortunately not rare. There had been yelling, thousands of dollars' worth of equipment destroyed, and because Derek had pulled the tiny Environmental Services woman out of the way of the incident, the patient wielding the top of an IV pole like a club decided he *really* didn't like Derek's face.

Derek was trying to decide whether he'd have the energy to eat before collapsing onto the bed when a smell stopped him in his tracks. An amazing scent was coming from the open window of Dylan's apartment. If he didn't know that Olive was in Maine, he would have wondered if she was here cooking.

When Derek opened the door, Dylan launched up from the small table like a starter pistol had gone off. But without looking at Derek or saying anything, he flopped back down onto the couch and pulled his laptop over his legs and began hitting the keys harder than necessary. A section of his long hair in the back was stuck out at a weird angle as if he'd been absentmindedly twisting it like he did when he was anxious.

"What's wrong?" Derek asked.

"Nothing. Just needed to get back to work."

Derek scanned the room and found a plastic bag of meat sitting there. "So . . . should I put that in the fridge?"

"Not if you want to eat it warm."

"Eat it warm?"

"I was making food for myself earlier." Gallagher pointed behind him at what looked like a fish tank on the small kitchen table. "I buy the meat in bulk, and I just figured I could make some extra, but it can't stay in too *long* or the texture's weird." But . . . this wasn't the glacial Gallagher. This was the amusingly and genuinely irritated Gallagher from those first few days.

"So that bag of meat is for—"

"All you've been eating are those gross protein shakes and those weird Trader Joe's fancy snacks."

Again, he said this as if it explained why he'd kept a portion of the meat warm. This implied criticism was a bit ironic given Dylan's diet, but Derek would allow it if it meant steak.

"So you made me dinner?"

"I made *me* dinner and just pre-portioned some of the extra in a separate bag so it would stay warm. I put some of the mashed potatoes and mixed vegetables on a separate plate."

"You made me dinner and kept my portion of the meat warm? And there are plated sides?"

"If you don't want it, you can give it to Gus. He's been making sad eyes at me all night, but *someone* said he isn't allowed to have people food. Even Heath Ledger belting to a marching band didn't get him to chill out."

"His stomach is getting more sensitive, and I don't want him Dutch-ovening your bedroom." Derek's eyes flickered to the TV. Dylan had put the movie on again.

"Whatever. Just eat it if you want." Dylan pulled out his headphone case and began unzipping.

"You cook steak in a fish tank?"

"No." Dylan pulled the headphones on.

Well, just be like that then. He did a rude facial waggle that he knew Dylan wouldn't see given how intently he was staring at his computer.

DEREK
Why would someone cook in a tank of water?

OLIVE
Sous vide? Oooh super fancy. You've reached the "cooking for you" stage? I need to tell Stella.

DEREK
Nope. He's pretty adamant he made food for himself, and that he thinks I'm an asshole, but he's not an asshole so he left out a plate of leftovers.

OLIVE
Sounds like great foreplay.

DEREK
Gross.

OLIVE
Joni texted me about what happened today. It sucks this shit keeps happening. Makes me not want to come back to the ED TBH.

"Oh crap."
"What?" Dylan said pulling off one of the headphones.
"Nothing."
"Kay." Dylan restarted typing.

OLIVE
She thinks you could have a concussion.

DEREK
If I have a concussion, I won't be able to work. You
know they won't pay me for those days. I'll kiss my
differentials goodbye. I need the overtime.

OLIVE
I get it, but if you need help, can you just fucking ask?
I like your brain and don't want it to explode.

DEREK
You need to listen to your neuro lecture again if you think
a minor head injury is going to make my brain explode.

OLIVE
Just please text me if you start having weird symptoms so I can make Joni check on you.

DEREK
I do not need anyone fussing over me.

The three little dots appeared and disappeared. Olive was
probably trying to decide how much to yell at him.

OLIVE
I miss you.

Derek smiled sadly at the phone.

DEREK
Same. Tell Stella I say hi.

OLIVE
I will

DEREK
And I'm fine.

OLIVE
Okay. 😐

Sliding his phone into his pocket, Derek walked over to the end table. When Olive first cooked for Stella, she spent six hours ensuring everything was perfect. Given Dylan left a plastic bag of fish tank–meat cooking for an extra few hours and put scoops of two side dishes on a microwaveable plate, Derek didn't think the two situations were . . . wait. Why the hell should Derek even be thinking . . . Olive was *Inception*ing him. This was *not* foreplay. This was just steak, potatoes, and vegetables. Nothing was sexy about cauliflower.

Dylan and Derek were just reluctant roommates who crashed into each other's lives and barely spoke. No wonder Dylan didn't give a shit about him. Why should he?

As if Dylan had followed the train of Derek's thoughts, he sprang up from the couch and tried to pace in an area much too narrow for pacing. "I know we're not friends, and we aren't really even roommates except right now." Dylan growled at the window. "But I thought you'd be home like two hours and forty minutes ago, and I just think you could at least have texted to tell me you were going to be late."

"I'm sorry I didn't text."

"I know I don't have a right to ask—oh, wait, what did you say?" Dylan stopped moving and blinked at the blank wall.

"I said I'm sorry I didn't text. I didn't know if you'd still be—"

"Oh my god." Dylan bounded across the room. "What the fuck happened to you?" He stood in front of Derek with his hands held tightly to his sides, horrorstruck at Derek's face.

Oh, right . . .

Derek's right eye probably looked worse now than it had the last time he'd seen it in the ER bathroom mirror. He'd had to change into his extra clothes, which probably meant Dylan could see all the angry scratches on his neck too. He was usually quicker at getting out of the way, but that first blow had caught him off guard.

"Did you get mugged?"

"*No.*" Derek touched his eye reflexively. "It's fine."

"You look like you lost a fight with something with fists and claws."

Derek glared, puffing out his chest. "Why would you assume I lost?"

Dylan rolled his eyes. "Certainly not because you lack machismo."

Hey!"

"Christ, Derek, what happened?" Dylan's hand lifted to the eye. He traced a gentle finger along the area below the swelling. It should be weird. Right?

Derek shrugged. "A patient went berserk. It happens."

"What do you mean *it happens*?" Dylan was practically shaking. Such a contrast from the weeks of flat composure. "You were *assaulted*. Are you pressing charges?

At that, Derek barked a laugh. "We've all been assaulted."

"All of who—"

"Olive nearly got a chunk of her hair torn out one day. I think Joni got kicked just last week. And that's nothing compared to what we've seen happen to other staff members."

Dylan shifted forward, lifting his chin. All his attention remained locked on Derek as he pushed his glasses back up his nose to get a better look at the injury. Why did a small something in Derek's chest go soft and fuzzy? He'd seen Dylan irritated and detached, but he had never seen his freckles turn pink with anger. "That . . . This . . . this is not okay."

"Not a felony to assault a nurse."

"That's complete bullshit. Are you staying home tomorrow? This looks serious."

"My CT scan was *fine*, and I need the cash right now. Not really in a can-afford-to-call-out financial situation."

"You got *a CT scan*? That means they thought it was serious. What the actual fuck?" Despite his voice rising, Dylan didn't back away. Indignation seemed to freeze him to the spot. A spot so close to Derek's body that Dylan's arm kept grazing the drawstring of Derek's pants with every gesticulation.

"The scan was just a precaution in case something's wrong. CYA for the hospital." It wasn't the first time he'd gotten hurt on the job. Wouldn't be the last.

"CYA for the *hospital*? You should be getting—I don't know, like, hazard pay for this. That patient can't come back there, right? Like, they were arrested?"

Derek couldn't help it. He was laughing again. It was wild how little people knew about working in an emergency department.

"This isn't funny, Derek." Dylan grabbed his shoulders. "You're hurt. Can I get you ice? Frozen peas? A raw steak like in a cartoon? I think I have a little left uncooked in the fridge. This entire thing is ridiculous, and—"

"Dylan." Before he knew why, he was grinning. "I'm okay. *Really*. Stop freaking out." His chin dipped lower.

Derek had never called him Dylan before. It had always been *Gallagher* or *him* or *that asshole*, mostly. Only a couple inches of space separated them, and both seemed to realize their closeness at the same moment.

Dylan's tongue dragged over his lips as if indignation made his mouth go dry. Derek followed the movement with his eyes. Dylan's hand lifted toward Derek's face again, and Derek leaned a fraction closer.

"How bad does it hurt?" Although he'd just been yelling, his voice lowered into tenderness.

"It's fine. I iced it there. Barely even sore."

Dylan's fingertip traced the edge of the bruising again. The whisper of pressure from his touch sent a current of lightning down Derek's spine. His eyes closed. Something deep inside Derek's chest felt softer, but a different part of Derek was rock hard, and there was no hiding it in scrubs.

Derek opened his eyes and, shit . . . Dylan's eyes were so damn blue and so damn earnest. He reached up and pulled the thick frames off his face. The right corner of Dylan's mouth tugged upward into a crooked smile. That smile did things to Derek. Things he'd rather not admit.

"What did you mean about my eyes?" Dylan's voice caught on the last word.

"What? When?"

"You said Olive was right about my eyes . . ."

"Oh . . ." The room surged ten degrees warmer that it had been. "That you have really blue eyes."

The swath of freckles across his cheeks seemed darker. "Oh . . ."

Derek grasped the bottom of Dylan's T-shirt, his fingertips grazing the skin beneath. "If I do something stupid, can I blame the fact that I might have a concussion?"

Dylan ran a hand through his shaggy brown hair, head bowing as if hit with a sudden shyness.

Derek touched Dylan's chin, tilting his face toward him. "Tell me to stop, Dylan."

"*No.*" Dylan's mouth crushed over his. His soft, ready lips moved in a perfect rhythm against Derek's. Derek's hand combed through Dylan's hair as he matched him kiss for kiss. It was like they were competing for who could get more, sharing panted breaths whenever they parted.

And Derek wanted more, more, more.

Dylan kissed along his jawline and down his neck. His hands explored the muscles of Derek's arms and chest and then settled on the knotted drawstring of his scrub pants.

Derek twisted his fingertips through the tangles of Dylan's hair.

"I really need a haircut." Dylan's wry eyes flicked up to Derek's hand before he restarted nipping down Derek's neck.

"I like your—" His sentence was lost to an irrepressible moan as Dylan's tongue flicked over his collarbone with a teasing graze of teeth behind it. "Shit, Dylan. *Shit.*"

What exactly could that mouth do on other parts of Derek's body?

They crashed together once more. A thrill went through Derek as Dylan's own arousal pushed and pulsed against Derek's. Dylan was wearing tantalizingly thin gray sweatpants.

He needed those goddamn pants off.

Derek craned his neck to find Dylan's mouth once more. His hands slid under Dylan's shirt to explore his surprisingly muscled back before sliding down Dylan's spine. "If you want to stop, say the word."

Dylan pressed himself into Derek. The pressure was almost painful against Derek's cock. "I'll tell you to stop if I want you to." The sharp heat of Dylan's tone sliced through Derek. It almost sounded like . . . dominance.

Dylan paused as if the tone had surprised him too.

But after reading what could only be desperation on Derek's face, Dylan pressed his lips against Derek's again. His tongue pushed into his mouth, sweeping against Derek's, eliciting more fevered noises.

Derek cupped Dylan's ass forcefully, spreading and lifting him slightly.

"*More.*" Every throaty, guttural response out of Dylan felt like a trophy.

How much more? Derek wanted more of *everything*. More

tongue. More skin. More teeth. Derek dropped to his knees. He wanted to know what other sounds he could coax from the man in his arms.

A clicking sound from the front door broke them apart. A key turned in the lock.

Derek fled to the shadowy space just inside the bedroom doorway. The bounce and squeak of old springs from the living room meant Dylan must have hopped onto the couch.

The door swung open.

An unfamiliar female voice broke the silence. "Dylan Gallagher, I'm going to kill you."

Chapter 17

Dylan's dick was very, *very* angry about being hidden under a laptop.

His sister Felicity, thankfully, appeared entirely oblivious to Dylan's predicament since she was juggling a boxed air mattress and a sleeping bag along with her backpack. She answered the question he hadn't had a chance to ask. "Mom and I had a thing, so I needed to come here to stay for a few days. Sorry it's so late."

"How does that relate to wanting to kill me?"

"Oh yeah, that. You—" She picked up a pillow from the ground and tossed it at his head. "You asked the assholes to help with the beams, but you didn't call *me*? I had to hear about all this going on from *Brooks and Anderson*?"

"Felicity . . ."

She scooted an accent chair out of the way to make room on the floor. "I'm in school. Yeah, yeah. Yeah, but—"

"You were in the middle of a summer term you described as both overwhelming and soul-sucking, then you were on a trip to Kansas, so—"

"That doesn't mean I wouldn't help my favorite brother with a disaster. And where's the McDickhead? I thought he was staying with you?"

"I think I'm McDickhead." Derek emerged from the bedroom. Somewhat to Dylan's chagrin, he had changed out of his scrubs, but he was just as sexy in fitted black jeans.

"*Shit.*" Felicity cringed. "I mean, obviously *shit* about the you overhearing me call you that, but the reflexive '*shit*' was about what the actual fuck happened to your eye? Messing up your face is a goddamn tragedy." Felicity clamped a hand over her mouth.

"Uh, thanks?" Cracking up, Derek held out a hand to her. "Honestly, the McDickhead thing is fair. But otherwise, Derek's fine. You must be the F Gallagher."

"*Felicity* Gallagher." She dipped in an un-Felicity-like elegant curtsy and then pointed to the bruised eye. "What's the other guy look like?"

"It was a patient," Dylan said before Derek could answer. It was ludicrous patients could be violent and the staff couldn't do anything. The slightly overprotective brotherly side of him wanted to demand Felicity quit her nursing program immediately if there was any chance this could happen to her.

Infuriatingly, Felicity's response showed no hint of shock. "One of my classmates got pushed into a wall on one of her rotations. Shook her up real good."

"*What?*" Dylan said.

Derek gestured that she should sit down. "This one time, a patient's parent pulled an eight-inch knife on me because he was vomiting and I couldn't get him out of his dirty clothes quick enough."

"A knife?" Dylan said, incredulous.

The other two ignored his outraged spluttering.

Felicity sat in the chair she'd pushed aside to make room for her mattress. "When I was a tech in the nursing home one patient always threw her soiled briefs at us." She pretended to wind up like a baseball pitcher. "Surprisingly good arm. Luckily, I've got a smaller-than-average strike zone. And before you ask, like everybody does, I'm five feet, well, actually four eleven and a half, but I generally round up. And before you say the next thing that most people ask, yes, my older brothers did steal all the height genes before I came along."

It seemed like Derek could barely speak through his laughter at her mini-monologue. "I wasn't going to ask how tall you were. I was going to ask who won the nursing home battle of the briefs."

Her face crinkled up with disgust. "The old lady definitely won." She shuddered. "I think I took four showers that night."

Dylan vacillated back and forth between the other two passing stories between them like some trauma tennis match. "Why in the hell would anyone do this job? The money can't be worth it."

"It's not," they said at the same time.

Derek winked at Felicity with a steeling half smile. "It can be fun sometimes. And challenging. And *never* boring. We see the best and worst of people's lives."

"For me . . . " Felicity's head tilted back and forth. "I don't know. Seemed better than being a business major, which was what my second degree was in. Shocking that the English literature didn't pan out with career options."

Derek jumped over the back of the couch to sit beside Dylan, bumping knees and hips. "Not to change the subject, but out of curiosity, why did you say you wanted to kill your brother?"

"Oh right. Sorry about that." Felicity pulled off her favorite University of Kansas sweatshirt and tossed it at Dylan, revealing the new touch-up work she'd gotten done on the botanical tattoo sleeves snaking along each of her arms. Felicity's tattoos were more daring and vivid than any of Dylan's. "My mom and I—" but Felicity's explanation ended with an incomprehensible shriek that sounded a bit like *"ohmygodhesamazingcanihave himineedtopethimnow."*

Sensing the attention, Gus trotted right into Felicity's waiting arms. After ear scratches, he flipped over onto his back into that absurd, open-mouth, tongue-out, dead bug position that demanded belly rubs. *Christ*, Dylan loved that animal despite the hint of dog musk all over his bed. So far he had slept amazingly anytime he curled up with Gus to get a few hours of sleep while Derek was at work. The mattress also smelled like Derek. And Derek smelled like Derek. Derek, who was sitting so close to him right now.

He tried to focus on the conversation and not on his mental postmortem of those heated moments. *Don't be weird. Don't be weird. Don't be weird.*

God, he was going to be weird, wasn't he?

"Mind answering my question about fratricide before I let *another* Gallagher steal my dog's love and affection?"

Felicity chuckled. "Because of my brother's internalized misogyny."

"*Hey.*" The unfairness of that accusation refocused Dylan's attention into the moment. "Is it internalized misogyny or that I didn't want my sister sacrificing any of her study time?"

Derek waved a confused hand. "What are you talking about?"

"Dy-lan," she enunciated his name with the same inflection his mother used whenever he was in trouble, "only called our brothers to help with the joists when I'm just as knowledgeable even if I don't match their brute strength."

"Hey—"

"You worked with your dad too?"

Felicity beamed. "Yeah. I was barely out of diapers when they took this photo of me pulling on my dad's toolbelt. I was a big oops, so my parents thought they were all done dealing with babies by the time I exploded on the scene."

Dylan cringed. "I really wish you'd stop giving me those visuals."

"Your mom let you just go to work sites?" Derek asked.

"I was"—her green eyes flashed as she made air quotes with her fingers—"supposedly not a natural fit for typical childcare."

Dylan arched an eyebrow "When they tried to send you to preschool you pushed the other four-year-olds and threatened to feast on their flesh if they stole your teddy bear again."

"I was a four-year-old with a fourteen-year-old brother"—she twitched her head at Dylan—"who watched the *Lord of the Rings* movies—extended cut, obvi—basically every day of the summer. Like I was going to let that daycare bully Chad Saglio take Mr. Wiggles for a third time."

"See what I have to deal with?" Dylan shook his head.

Felicity's face went smug. "I screamed 'I am no man' and then 'I will kill you if you touch him.' It was a very dramatic moment. My earliest memory."

"You're such a liar. You just know you said that because it's on the official report they sent home when they kicked you out." Dylan shook his head. "You really did go through a major Eowyn phase, didn't you?"

"God, I hope you have that report framed somewhere." Derek laughed.

"My mom put it in my baby book. Sixth kid, so I actually think that's the *only* thing in there. But yes. It's emblematic." She affected a wistful posture. "Alas, my severe horse allergies kept me from becoming an actual Rider of Rohan."

"Allergies, i.e., you're afraid of horses."

"Am not."

"Are too."

Derek elbowed him in the ribs. "So . . . with the contractor work . . ."

"Oh yes." She grinned. "My dad built me this portable play space, but as soon as I could hold tools, I was learning. My carpentry skills are almost as good as Dylan's."

"Her tile work's better. She's more patient than I am with the boring stuff."

"If the nurse thing doesn't work out, you both should pitch a reality show for HGTV. Brother-sister nerdy reno team. You could build hobbit houses or something." Derek's eyes twinkled with his broad smile.

Dylan's heart galloped as if actual Rohan horse hooves were *clip-clopping* against his ribs.

Derek's attention flitted between them, his smile going even wider.

"What?" Dylan said.

"It's . . ." Derek shrugged. "It's just nice." He looked at Felicity. "You remind me of my best friend when she talks like that. That's all." He nodded once. "I think you'll do alright as a nurse. Won't take shit from anyone. You got a good sister, Gallagher."

Woof. Dylan was back to being called Gallagher, then?

Dylan hid disappointment by focusing on his sister. "Thanks. I sure do."

"You're probably lucky enough *not* to have sisters who show up at your doorstep whenever they fight with your mom." Felicity nuzzled Gus's head.

Dylan didn't miss Derek's small flinch. "My youngest sister Michelle more does the 'I'm going to make impulsive apartment purchases I can't afford' thing. Amy, my other sister, is literally the most cynical but also the most brilliant and functional human on the planet—she's a tax accountant like my mom. So, no. If anything, I'd have to crash on Amy's floor and risk waking up to an attack by my four nephews." He held up his phone, showing Felicity the wallpaper photo.

"They are so adorable. Although, Christ, her house must be loud." Felicity shook her head.

Derek swiped like he was going to find another photo, but he frowned as if disappointed by what he found on the screen.

Felicity snuggled closer to Gus. "Oh . . . so *Michelle's* the one who bought the place downstairs."

Derek's eyebrows scrunched together. "Yeah."

"Well, from what Dylan has told me, you were pretty nice buying this money pit from her, so I'll excuse the fact you treated my brother like a pariah when he first moved here. For what it's worth, Dylan is the most functional human *I* know. He makes better money than any of us as some kind of specialized programmer computer engineer for hire. Owns his own business. Seriously, it's borderline offensive how much money he makes given how many hours he has to work. You know he's fixing up this apartment for our uncle because my other brothers all have big families and my dad's busy with the business, right?"

"*Lissy.*"

Derek's mouth fell open.

Dylan couldn't decide if he was more outraged or embarrassed. "Lissy, you really need to learn to shut up sometimes."

"Oh Dylan, you shut up, or I'll feast on your flesh too."

Dylan threw back the pillow that she'd thrown at him. "Mr. Wiggles is toast next time I come to the house."

She clutched it to her chest and glared. "You lay a hand on that bear's fur—"

"You're just doing this for free?" Derek stiffened beside him. "All that work in the bathroom. The bedroom."

"*Dude*, get this, he's even paying Uncle Sean *rent*, and he leased his—"

"Felicity, cut it out. I didn't tell him, and it was reasonable for Derek to assume there was a different situation." Dylan stood and went over to the sous vide tank because he needed something to do.

Derek stared at Dylan. "I shouldn't have assum—"

"Forget it."

"Have you showed him photos of your—"

"Eat this, Derek." Dylan set a plate in front of Derek. "And I'll warm something up for the Rider of Rohan."

Eyes lighting at the plate of steak, Derek dug in.

Luckily, Felicity seemed to have gotten the message that Dylan didn't want to go into all that.

She gave Dylan an oddly understanding look when she took a plate from him. "So, Derek, how'd you like meeting the Three—"

"Icemen of the Apocalypse?" Derek finished between bites.

"Actually, I didn't realize I had already met them years ago. My friend played goalie on their team. Small world, right?" Derek speared a piece of steak with his fork and held it up to admire it. "This is amazing, Gallagher."

"Oh . . . thanks . . ." Dylan mussed his too-long hair absently.

"The goalie on their—oh . . ." Felicity's attention snapped to Dylan.

Dylan shook his head.

While Dylan assembled a plate for Felicity, Derek explained about meeting the three older Gallaghers at a New Year's Eve party.

Felicity blinked at Dylan as if to say *He doesn't know?* Felicity was the only other person who knew most of the story about Jake because she'd been with him when Jake called to ask him out again.

Dylan shrugged and sat back down next to Derek.

As Felicity bent to scratch behind Gus's ears, Derek winked at him, giving his thigh a small squeeze before picking up his fork again. As if nothing passed between them, Derek continued the story, describing an epic push-up battle between Jake and the older Gallaghers that Derek had ended up winning at the party.

Dylan couldn't focus on the story. His entire body was buzzing. Those wild seconds of *almost* were flooding through him, but the mention of Jake Murphy reminded Dylan of all the reasons this was a bad idea.

If Dylan wasn't careful, this entire thing would blow up in his face.

Chapter 18

An urgent text from Chase had Dylan buried in emails on his laptop. Felicity was snoring from the air mattress nearby.

Footsteps shuffled from the hallway bedroom, and a callused hand stroked down Dylan's neck. "Hey." Derek's freshly showered scent threatened to overpower Dylan's self-control.

"You're working?"

Dylan nodded.

Derek's thumbs rubbed a few knots from his tense shoulders. Every muscle had been locked up for hours. That kiss had been scrolling through his brain so much that he could barely concentrate on his work scrolling on the screen.

"Everything okay? Want to share the bed tonight? It's late."

"Ack. I'm sorry. Everything's totally fine. One sec." Chase's message was a notification that Dylan had made an inconsequential but not unnoticed error on a deliverable. Despite all the therapy, mistakes derailed his mood. He typed out a couple more words to close out the email and then sent the fixed file. On the subject of mistakes . . .

Felicity's appearance had given Dylan just long enough to overthink about what had almost happened between the two men. And how it might be the mistake that ruined all his progress with his mental health and his acceptance of his ADHD. But the potential mistake's hands were doing things to his neck muscles that felt like wizardry.

He closed his laptop and turned to face Derek. "My sister's staying here . . . so I just don't feel like it's a good idea to, uh, you know?" His attempt at funny and casual sounded more like frustrated and constipated. The back of his neck boiled beneath Derek's touch.

Derek wore that ribbed blue tank top and a pair of those fitted jogger sweats he'd been wearing to sleep. The clothes showed off his shoulders and ass in a way that made it hard for Dylan to avoid looking at all.

Self-control.

Derek's hands slid away. "I really was just talking about *sleeping*. Next to me, yes. Gus will be there too. Just for the record, I *always* meant sleep in the literal sense, not the euphemism sense. That's why I said, 'it's late,' but I guess that could've been clearer. I have to get up early to work again. *And* I wouldn't proposition you three feet away from your sleeping sister. Flirt, yes; proposition, never."

Felicity snored loudly and then rolled over.

Derek lowered his voice and spoke directly into Dylan's ear. "I feel like you're upset about something?"

"I'm *not* upset. Can we please talk about this tomorrow? I'm just really tired. Work stress."

He was also confused and sexually frustrated to the point of spontaneous combustion, but saying that out loud probably wouldn't be a good idea. His hyperfixation brain had launched him into a hyperloop round trip between arousal and anxiety. Jesus, he was a mess. *This* was why Dylan had avoided relationships since Chase. His mind seemed to crave the pain, like the masochistic suck of air over a cavity.

"Okay." Derek's hand rested an inch from Dylan's shoulder. "I know I was a dick to you for a while, but . . . if you need to talk about something, even work stuff . . . uh . . . just let me know. But just come to bed with me if you want to. If you're that tired it'd probably be better for you to be in an actual bed . . ."

Dylan's stomach needed to cool it with the damn butterflies. Hearing Derek say *"Come to bed with me"* was too much for him.

"Dylan?"

It was only the second time Derek had said his first name. The butterflies were swarming now. "Um—kay."

Derek's eyebrows furrowed. "Um . . . Kay?"

"Kay. As in *kay*, that sounds good. Bed. Good. Sure. Just have a little more work to do."

Derek opened his mouth to say something else, but then closed it again and walked away. "Good night, Gallagher."

"Night."

The door closed behind him, which left Dylan alone to analyze all the ways he could've handled that better.

Chapter 19

DYLAN
When you said you liked my mattress, I set a price
alert. they're on sale with expedited shipping.

DEREK
Thx.

DYLAN
Also, Felicity wanted me to ask you if Gus needs
doggie CPAP.

DEREK
Ha.

"You're not getting out of this." Felicity helped Dylan lift the
next sheet of subfloor into place.

"Huh?"

Felicity and Dylan had spent the last week and a half getting
the kitchen ready for the new floor. They'd picked up boxes of
leftover tile from their dad's storage unit yesterday, a gorgeous
luxury vinyl some rich person had changed their mind about
at the last moment, not caring that they'd be charged twice for
materials. Once the rest of the subfloor was down, they could
start the underlayment. He could have the tile done by the
weekend with Felicity around.

"You're absolutely not getting out of it."

Dylan pressed the screw gun into place and pulled the trigger. "I'm not getting out of *what*?"

"The Gallagher Grill-Out, obviously."

"Who said I *wanted* to get out of it?"

"*You* did. Every single year. This is your third summer being back here. And every single year you have an excuse. You said when I graduated and came back from Kansas, you'd come back. Lies. Two years ago, you had that 'bad cold' . . . in the summer. Last year there was an 'emergency' with the house." She gave him a skeptical frown. "I just don't think you can beg off again without Mom finding you and dragging you there. You come to Christmas. Why's this so different? Is it because—"

"I *do* come to Christmas, so I don't know why missing this is a big deal." Dylan reloaded the screw gun with a new cartridge. "I've heard from Derek that there are several intense summer stomach bugs floating around. They could hit at any time."

"My point is that since you're not getting out of it this time, you should just tell the others not to—"

"I *plan* on going. End of story." He didn't want to relive that part of his past. Felicity was too young to remember most off the worst of it anyway. "Can we talk about something else please?"

"Absolutely. Let's discuss your smoking-hot roommate. Guess he's not actually an asshole at all."

"He's still an asshole." His conscience made him add, "Well, not lately, I guess."

"Does he still have all those ab muscles like that day I saw him running? I feel like one would be willing to put up with a lot to get into the asshole's—well—asshole."

"Gross. Stop talking about assholes."

"You're the one who called him an asshole first."

"Stop talking about *literal* assholes. Metaphorical ones are fine."

"You're such a weirdo." She slid back to give Dylan room

to do another section of flooring screws. "Derek's been super nice. He makes me coffee every morning while you're passed out on the couch, cuddled up with your laptop like in those pictures Mom has of you with your Barney."

"You morning people are like magical, mysterious unicorns." He'd *thought* Derek wasn't a morning person, but he'd been very wrong. Even on the days he wasn't working, he was up before dawn and at the gym. "And why wouldn't he be nice to you? You're the coolest."

"Stop making me blush." She brushed a section of wild ginger wavy frizz away from her face. "Thanks again for letting me crash here even though it's close quarters." She crossed to the next section of floor to apply the adhesive.

"Are you ever going to tell me what Mom said?"

"It's embarrassing."

"Because I don't know what it's like to be embarrassed by family."

"Touché." Felicity adjusted the straps of her overalls. "*Fine.* She asked if I wanted her to pay for a few months of Weight Watchers as a birthday present slash nursing school graduation present."

"Woof." They picked up the next section and then fitted it in. "You know that you're—"

"Perfect the way I am?" Felicity's navy blue eyes sparkled. "I do actually. Honestly, I have mostly come to terms with my body, and I have fully embraced the intuitive eating life. I mean, I'm in great shape and work out three times a week. Should being a size fourteen mean I can't like my body? Unfortunately, from Mom's perspective, the answer is yes. But I think every Irish Catholic family needs a curvy, tatted-up, bisexual ginger with ADHD to call everyone else on their bullshit. Even the Gallaghers."

"Mom's mom shamed her for her weight all the time. Grandpa did too."

"Dad told me. You know, when I told her I started Vyvanse, she said she could never take amphetamines because she hated the diet pill kind her mom gave her back in high school. But she hoped that the weight loss side effects would 'help' me."

"No . . ."

"Yeah . . . I was like, *Mom*, my ADHD meds are not the same as the literal meth your mom gave you in high school to keep you a size two."

"What'd she say to that?"

"Oh, I didn't *actually* say that. It was one of those mental hypothetical arguments after the fact."

"Why didn't you just say it then?"

"It's Mom." She shrugged. "I just said weight loss wasn't my goal right now, and I didn't want her to comment on my weight anymore whether it was going up or down."

"Good for you."

"Meh, boundaries are really only about what *you* do. I can't change her. But what I could do is have an extended slumber party with my favorite older brother."

"Don't let Anderson, Brooks, or Cal hear you call me that." He handed her the screw gun. "I still wish I could talk to Mom about the—"

"Oh, our brothers totally know you're my favorite." She worked down the line. "We should probably keep moving so the adhesive doesn't dry."

Since Dylan knew that *she* knew that *he* knew how to put in a floor, he figured this meant she was done talking about this. Christ, he loved his sister. He was pissed at his mom, but Lissy could fight her own battles.

Once the subfloor was in, a very sweaty Dylan and Felicity sat next to Gus's enormous doggie bed. Gus had fled the screw gun noise to cower in the bedroom. He seemed so alarmed that Felicity found a YouTube channel designed for dogs and turned her laptop volume all the way up. Who knew there was

such a thing? This led Dylan down a mental rabbit hole of researching life solutions for big, elderly, monster dogs with delicate paws that hated hot sidewalks.

He realized he'd lost his mind when he started pricing out
dog treadmills.

Seriously, what had this animal done to him?

Felicity clicked her metal water bottle against his. "To luxury vinyl, and the rich people who change their minds." She
wiped her mouth on her sleeve. "So, did something happen
between you and Derek? Please note how I'm not asking about
assholes."

Dylan choked on a swallow of water. "Wh-why do you ask?"

"Just the way he looks at you sometimes when you're asleep
and half drooling on the couch cushions."

"How does he look at me?"

"Kind of like how I look at the garden at the parents' house
when the calla lilies start blooming."

"That's oddly specific."

"Speaking of which, I need to go back tomorrow because
Mom's probably getting everything ready for the barbeque and
needs stuff harvested. But this is neither here nor there. So . . .
Derek. There's a vibe. A sex vibe."

"You get a sex vibe when you look at calla lilies?"

"It's like you've never heard of Georgia O'Keefe." She nudged
him. "Can you just be honest?"

"I am not going to deny that the guy is . . ."

"Super hot. Like *celebrity swimsuit edition of a magazine*
hot."

"Right."

"Then why haven't you gone for it?"

Dylan shrugged. "You should've seen him with our brothers.
It was like they were going to kick me out of the family and ini-
tiate him, but that was actually weirdly nice in a way. But . . . he
was really close with Jake Murphy. Family-friend close."

"I still can't believe what happened to him. Brooks and Anderson were a mess about it for months, according to Mom. So sad . . . even though he was such a jerk to you. *God*, I still can't believe he treated you like that." She sighed. "Did you ever end up seeing him again after he called you to apologize?"

"No. I told him I wasn't dating. I'm still not dating. *Despite* what everyone in the family thinks, I don't need a boyfriend."

"Hmm. All right. Let's review." She ticked points off on her fingers. "You spent two years obsessively renovating a house you bought on a whim and then got bored when it was done and rented it out so you could come and *obsessively* renovate our uncle's apartment all while you amassed a bunch of hobbies but made zero local friends." She held up a hand to shut him up. "Yeah, yeah, we're all grateful you're doing this, but we're also all worried about you."

"I'm fine." He scrunched his face. "Doing this for Uncle Sean isn't a big deal."

Felicity took a long breath before speaking. "It *is* a big deal. So . . . back to what I was saying . . . now you have another project to drown yourself in, only this time there's a complication that won't allow you to avoid human contact. A complication who looks damn good in light-blue scrub pants."

Dylan didn't answer.

"Do you think *maybe* you've just gotten out of the habit of liking someone and *maybe* liking someone as hot as Derek scares you because of douchebag West Coast *Chad* and how he treated you?"

"Chase." He rested his head on the wall behind him. "Yeah, I'm especially not looking for that kind of guy again."

"And Derek seems like that kind of guy? The dude who bought a money pit for his sister—"

"I thought he did . . . at first. But you're right. I don't know. I just think after Chase and even that stupid night with Jake

Murphy, I think it made me realize how much I need to be with someone I completely trust not to lie to me."

"That's fair."

"And I guess there's a small part of me worried Derek's just acting nice or pity-flirting because he needs my help." He hadn't meant to voice this fear, but Felicity had that effect on him.

"That's the dumbest thing I've ever heard."

He chuckled. "Uh—thanks?"

"Just because Chad—"

"Chase."

"Don't care. You can't let a couple bad dudes ruin your willingness to trust anyone."

"The biggest *complication* right now is that we're literally living in seven hundred and forty-eight square feet. Shouldn't I wait to make any moves until it all going totally wrong doesn't mean I have to see his toothbrush every time I'm—I don't know, taking a shit?"

"You should really keep toothbrushes in a cabinet. Flushing causes—"

"Lissy, focus."

She gulped more water. "I think you feel like shit about yourself like eighty-five percent of the time, and you never acknowledge you're the best-looking Gallagher brother, and any dude would be lucky to have you."

"Okay, so—"

"While I can't deny your reno skills are good enough and a hot man might use his penis wiles to get your help, that's *not* what's happening here."

"I got stuck on *penis wiles.*"

"Don't we all," she said dreamily.

"Ew, please stop." He picked at a worn sticker on the side of his water bottle. "But also, thanks."

She grinned. "Let's go pick up the stuff we need for the underlayment, okay? I need to swing by to grab a preorder at Curious

Iguana, so we should do Café Nola for lunch first." She swiped at her phone. "Oh. Does Uncle Sean still have a key?"

"Why?"

"Dad says he's going to come by with him at some point this afternoon."

"*Shoot.*"

"I know you didn't want Uncle Sean to come back until the kitchen stuff was done, but I think Dad convinced him you had no choice about the floor. He still doesn't know the details about how bad it was structurally." She shrugged and then smiled. "But . . . we might not be back yet. Especially if we get lunch at Café Nola . . ."

"Uncle Sean still has his key, so they can let themselves in." Dylan ruffled her bun. "You just want Café Nola so you can ogle that tattooed server lady."

"You get to ogle your roommate. Don't judge my ogle-choices." She tapped on her phone a few times and then stuck the Specials Menu under his nose. "They have an avocado waffle thing this week ooonly."

"Consider your ogle choices un-judged. They have outside seating, so if the Parakeet Karen calendar says it's okay, we should just bring Gus along."

"I'm sorry, the *what*?"

∗∗∗

Dylan's mom brought his phone outside. "This was buzzing, luv."

Gus wasn't allowed in the house because of Mom's allergies, but the doggo had investigated the property, sniffing and peeing everywhere and appearing to be delighted to be off leash with wide open space. Dylan threw the tennis ball again, and Gus padded after it. He didn't actually fetch, but he did run over to the ball and nudge it with his nose until Dylan ran over and picked it up and chucked it again. Maybe Gus was the one making Dylan fetch . . .

"A haircut before Saturday, right?" His mother pulled off his Orioles cap and untangled a few knots before he could get away. His mom had left Ireland at age six, but he still heard a bit of Derry on certain words. "Your aunt Edna's gonna give me hell if my boys look like hooligans."

"Aunt Edna's a crotchety old bat, and if she comments on Felicity's tattoos again, I'm going to personally escort her off the property."

"Not sure your sister needs your protection."

"I know she doesn't. From anyone." He gave his mother a pointed look.

A shadow of guilt hooded her eyes as she watched Felicity take off her work gloves and haul another refuse bucket to the compost pile. She patted the phone in his palm. "Check your messages, Dilly. I'm going to look in on Sean."

Dylan's eyes widened at the screen.

DEREK

Where are you? Do you have Gus? The door to the unit was open when I got here. I'm freaking out.

DEREK

Seriously, where are you? Going outside to look.

DEREK

I can't find you or Gus. I'm going to start calling shelters to see if anyone picked him up.

DEREK

None of the shelters that were still open have him. Please, call me if he's with you.

"Oh shit." The message he'd typed for Derek about taking Gus on a field trip was unsent in the message field.

DYLAN

I'm so sorry. I texted you, but I forgot to send it. We brought Gus out to play on my parents' property.

DEREK

Gus needs his medicines and dinner.

DYLAN

I brought his food and his meds with us. He's already had everything. I really am so sorry.

DEREK

Why was the apartment door open?

"What's wrong?" Felicity picked up Gus's ball and threw it once.

"I hope you know a good lawyer because we might be arrested for dognapping."

"*What?*"

"Derek told me I could take Gus on walks and short car rides during the day, but I *might* not have sent the text message about taking him out here today."

"Ugh, double shit." Felicity didn't bother pretending she wasn't reading the rest of the messages over his shoulder. "Do you think Uncle Sean left it open?"

"Probably. No wonder Derek's freaked out. God, it's a good thing Gus *wasn't* there." He typed out an explanation about what probably happened with Uncle Sean.

"I'd be freaking out too."

"Christ, why didn't Dad check the door?"

"Uncle Sean's been getting more sensitive to that fact that *something's* going on with his brain. It's caused a few blowups."

"Derek's probably so pissed." He patted his leg. "Come on, big guy, I need to take you home."

Felicity shouldered her garden tool bucket. "Good luck."

"You aren't coming back to the apartment tonight?"

"Nah, I have more work to do here."

"Cowardice doesn't become you."

"Tell McDickhead I'm sorry too. And give him my number if you aren't going to make a move because I have a few gay friends who might be interested in that *asshole*, both metaphorically and definitely literally, if he's into that kind of thing."

Dylan whirled to face his sister.

Felicity's smirk was as loud as if she'd also shouted *"gotcha"* at the territorial protectiveness she must have seen on his face. "God, I was only joking. *Chill.* But hurry and get the dog back so you guys can kiss and make up."

"Shut up."

"Love you."

"Ditto." He loaded Gus into the back seat of his Jeep onto the astonishingly expensive car seat sling thing they'd found this afternoon at a boutique pet store. "Still coming over to help me install Derek's drywall tomorrow?"

"Sure. Dad'll give me a ride."

Before pulling away, Dylan shot off a final text.

> DYLAN
> I'm on my way. Be there in thirty. He ate dinner. Had water too.

> DEREK
> K. Can you bring him to my apartment?

That wasn't a good sign.

Chapter 20

Thirty-three minutes after Dylan's last message, Derek was pacing the front room that was packed with most of the furniture he owned.

The initial terror had calmed, so why was his heart still pounding?

It wasn't Dylan's fault his uncle left the apartment door open, and it was for the best Gus hadn't been there at the time. If he'd noticed the food and meds were gone, he would've figured it out.

Gus was fine.

Everything was fine.

Derek steadied his breaths against a mounting pressure on his chest.

Was *this* what a panic attack felt like? He'd never had one before.

But even before he couldn't find Gus tonight, he'd been stressed. The *all done* voicemail from the mold guy came right at the end of his shift. He'd rushed home to hand the man in hazmat gear a bank account–decimating check in exchange for having destroyed half his drywall. Since the okay to move in just meant *your apartment's not actively poisoning you and the machines that terrify your dog are gone*, the water would still be off for the plumbers. Plumbers who would be needing *more* checks. Derek's new mattress had been delivered yesterday. He *could* sleep here and shower at the gym. Maybe that would be better, especially because things with Dylan . . .

He braced against the wall, leaning his forehead on the cool back of his hand.

The familiar rumble of Dylan's Jeep jolted Derek out of his thoughts. He'd almost fallen asleep standing up. He blinked away the exhaustion and rushed to the door.

Gus's tail wags seemed happily tuckered out from his Gallagher-siblings adventure. After giving Derek a lick of greeting, he climbed directly into the newly set up bed and was snoring in seconds.

Worry etched Dylan's face. "I'm really sorry. It's totally my fault. I can call back any of the shelters you called to let them know what hap—"

"It's fine. Just text next time, okay?"

"Oh. Okay. Yes. Of course." His voice was relieved as he scratched the back of his head with the hand that wasn't clutching a gray canvas bag. "Thanks for being cool about it."

"I'm a cool guy sometimes," Derek said, attempting a casual drawl to hide any residual shakiness from his past panic. He scanned the doorway as Dylan shut the door behind him. "So is Felicity . . ."

"Staying at my parents."

"Ahh. Okay. So . . ."

"So . . . ?"

So, they were alone. Actually alone.

The memory of the last time they were alone hung in the air between them.

Dylan shifted his weight as he opened his mouth.

But Derek needed to say something first. "So . . . we haven't really had a chance to talk since . . . and for the record, if you didn't want to . . . like, I get it. I didn't mean to make things weird when I asked you to come sleep in the bed too. If I did and that's why you've been avoiding me, I'm really sorry."

There. He said it.

Dylan could take the apology or leave it.

Dylan looked at his shoes, scuffing one along the floor. "I got spooked and I don't know . . . I was worried you were only flirting with me because of needing my help. It—uh—wouldn't be the first time. A guy at my old company strung me along like that."

Derek was genuinely so shocked he couldn't think how to respond. Half of him was offended, but the other half was pissed that *anyone* would treat Dylan like this. *What the hell?*

Dylan scanned the apartment hallway, looking anywhere except at Derek. "And with the way you acted when I first moved upstairs, I thought . . ."

"*Dylan.*"

"I guess I just thought you never thought I was near your standards for a partner—"

"Dylan, no . . ."

"*Then* I overheard what Hudson said, so I've just been confused as to why you'd even be interested in—uh—sharing a bed with me in a million years. In any sense."

"The way I acted when you moved in . . ." Derek rubbed his temple. "It was shitty. It wasn't about you, not really, it was . . . I was just pissed at you for something I'm pretty sure was a misunderstanding. Look, I don't know what happened between you and Jake, but I don't believe for a second you would've *actually* called him a piece of shit." Derek flinched. Why did he say that out loud? *Crap.*

Dylan paled. "Jake told you about that?"

"Wait . . . *did* you call him a piece of shit?" Derek froze.

"Well, technically, I guess, yeah, but . . . ugh—it's a long story and I can explain—"

"What the *hell*, Dylan? You really got in his head." Derek glared. "God, I can't believe I was assuming that it all must've been a misunderstanding."

Confused hurt filled Dylan's eyes. "It's not what you think. I didn't want to tell you what happened for a lot of reasons, but—"

"Yeah. I can see why." The words spat out of Derek. That

fiercely protective loyalty Derek had always felt with Jake and Olive surged. He couldn't stop himself from getting angrier. He was too damn tired and too damn angry about everything right now. He knew he was lashing out, but Dylan was in front of him and there was so much Derek kept locked inside because he was the one who was supposed to be able to handle everything. He wasn't handling this conversation well. But he couldn't stop himself. "And just so you know, if you ever want to pull the *I'm not dating* card with a guy you called a piece of shit, maybe delete '*looking for a serious, longtime partner*' on your dating app profile first."

"My *what*?" Dylan shook his head. "I wasn't on apps when I told Jake . . . *Jesus Christ*, how is any of that your business anyway?"

"Because you apparently told my friend he was a piece of shit and then flagrantly lied to him and hurt him? How could you treat him like that? I know Jake wasn't perfect, but he was a great person. He didn't deserve—"

"Jake Murphy's a great person all right. Oh, I know." Dylan's scoff fell into a frown. He ran a finger over a spot of peeling paint on the wall like he was checking for something Derek didn't understand. "I'm genuinely sorry for what happened to him, but . . . he wasn't . . ." His teeth clenched. "Ugh. It was a long time ago, but I'm *not* a liar. I wasn't dating. And *Christ*, I wasn't on *any* apps when Jake called. I barely left my house back then. I have no idea why Jake would say—"

"Okay. Bullshit." Derek's body went rigid. "I *saw* your profile. C'mon, dude. Why are you doubling down on this?"

"Doubling down?" After a long exhale, Dylan glared. "Just believe whatever you want. I was trying to explain what actually hap—you know what, I'm done. It's *fine*."

Derek's hands curled into fists at his side. Yes, this entire conversation had gotten derailed, but all of his frustration boiled up at that "*it's fine*." Frustration about this stupid apartment.

Frustration about his sister. Frustration about all the years he spent putting Jake on a pedestal. Sure, there was obviously more to the story. And Derek was probably being super unfair. But Olive was gone. His mom wasn't returning his calls. And he just wished he could ask his dad what to do about everything, but he couldn't. And he couldn't stop himself from getting angrier.

Dylan paused at the front door with his hand on the doorknob. "I'm going upstairs. If you ever feel like giving me the benefit of the doubt about anything or maybe just not accusing me of being a liar for no reason like you already have several times before at this point, let me know."

"I *saw* the dating app profile myself. It's how I knew who you were when we met."

Dylan directed a dismissive nod at the door as he opened it. "Kay."

"Goddamn it, Dylan, if you ever say *kay* again like that, I'm going to . . ."

"What?" Dylan turned, eyebrows raised. "You're going to *what*?"

"I—I—" Derek rubbed his chin. That adorable quirk of Dylan's face punctured his pressurized anger. All of it was softly deflating. "I don't know. Like freeze your underwear or something."

Wryness blunted Dylan's scowl. "We're back to summer camp levels of maturity here?"

"Guess we are. You just shut down on me like a pouting teenager after kissing me. And now you're saying you weren't on an app that I saw you on with my own eyes."

"You think *I'm* the one who's immature?"

Derek gestured to the space between them. "You're the one who seems completely incapable of just telling me how you feel about anything like a grown-ass man."

"Because every time I want to, you make it clear that you

don't trust me or act like I'm a . . ." Dylan's free hand tangled in his wild hair, and he clutched the bag under his other arm tighter. "*God*, I thought my trust issues were bad . . . *fuck*. I just needed time to figure out if what happened was a mistake."

"Whether *kissing* me was a mistake?" Derek's stomach dropped.

"Kissing might not be a big deal thing for *you*, but for me—"

"Oh, so now you're acting like I'm some unfeeling asshole because I have an active sex life?"

"No, of *course* not."

"You say I won't give you the chance to explain? You never gave *me* the chance to explain how I felt about kissing you. And just because *I'm* not embarrassed about using apps for a little physical companionship doesn't mean what happened between us *didn't* mean something to me."

"That was a lot of negatives. What are you even saying?"

Was wanting to strangle someone and being desperate to kiss them again at the same time some new kink Derek's brain had concocted to torture him?

One of Gus's normal grunting snuffles interrupted the moment.

The endearing flash of concern in Dylan's face over something as stupid as Gus's old-man-dog sleep apnea was more than Derek could handle right now.

"You should go." Derek twitched his head at the door. "And also, maybe try not to accidentally steal my dog in the future."

Dylan stepped a foot outside the door. "Kay."

"And maybe look into whether some sucker stole your pictures to catfish people as Dylan G if you're sticking with that story."

"I'll add all that to my to-do list immediately. Right after I fix your busted walls tomorrow. And here." Everything about Dylan blazed.

A rush of desire and hope churned deep inside Derek's gut.

But Dylan didn't cross the room and take Derek into his arms for the angry make-out session Derek hated himself for wanting.

He tossed the gray canvas bag he'd been holding near Gus's bowls. "I bought this at the pet store today to make Gus more comfortable in my car. It should fit yours too, but you should be careful because the strap is tricky and there's a warning label." There was an absurd hilarity in hearing Dylan angry-bark safety disclaimers about a gift like some kind of robot crossing guard. Like even at his most furious, he couldn't repress helpful instincts.

Not that Derek was in the mood to laugh. "Cool."

Dylan tossed a spare key on the bed. "I got this made for you for upstairs. Bring me your keys at some point tonight if you want me to be able to get into your apartment tomorrow for that first drywall stuff."

"'Kay."

After several more excruciating seconds, the door closed behind Dylan.

He'd closed the door gently so he wouldn't wake Gus.

What a jerk.

Derek's phone buzzed, and he looked down. "Aw, shit."

Chapter 21

JONI
You still coming to pick me up?

DEREK
I'm so sorry.

He typed out an explanation of everything that had happened this evening along with a few more profuse apologies.

JONI
No worries at all. You've got so much going on. If you send me the name of that new place your mom just found I can pick up takeout instead, if that sounds ok?

DEREK
You sure you're good with staying in?

JONI
I'm tired too but not on tomorrow, so I'd love some chill hang-out time tonight. AND I've been really craving Korean food since we were talking about it today!

DEREK
That actually sounds perfect. My mom said it's the first time bibimbap in a restaurant came close to what her halmeoni used to make, so I've been hoping to try it. Can I text you my order and then Venmo for mine?

JONI

My treat. Call it a "condolences on your home catastrophe" gift.

DEREK

Well, I'd argue, but . . .

JONI

Good. See you in a bit. ☺

Gus lifted his head and peered back and forth around the apartment and then stared straight at Derek. Derek would like to say there was no way the look was an accusation, but Gus's face was very expressive.

"He's upstairs, doggo."

Gus stared.

"You probably think I should apologize, right?"

Shockingly, Gus did not understand anything other than the word "doggo," which made him wag his tail a couple times. After a huffed breath, Gus stretched.

"Well, he needs to apologize too."

After several more crackling stretches, Gus flopped back on Derek's nicest pillow.

He'd just changed the pillowcase too.

But Derek hated himself too much to remind Gus about the pillow rules.

Forty-five minutes later, Joni arrived on his doorstep holding a bag of food.

As the food smell roused Gus into bounding over to the door, a pair of citron leggings appeared at the top of the stairs.

"Just got done with the HOA meeting, not sure if you remembered but there was one tonight, and we were discussing your situation. I was just coming down to do a check on the mold abatement process, but—" Carol paused her fussy monologue and glowered at Gus.

"The mold inspection was done today."

"Mr. Chang, what's that dog doing here?"

Joni cut over Carol's accusation with her usual disarming smile. "Derek was watching him while I picked up our food." Somewhat impressively, nothing about that was technically a lie. "You must be Ms. Taylor. Derek told me how much you do around the building."

Carol eyed Joni with an apprehension like she was concerned that Joni might turn into a rattlesnake. Or maybe she was still worried Gus would break away from Derek's hold.

"I'm Joni, one of the doctors Derek works with."

"Oh a doctor? That's wonderful. I'm a local skin care entrepreneur." She gestured to her light pink shirt with *Boss Babe Goals* written in lurid cursive. "I'd *love* to talk to you about opportunities for a lucrative side hustle. These days everyone needs one, you know. Even doctors."

"I think I'm okay." Joni subtly handed off the food bag to Derek, which served the added purpose of getting Gus out of Carol's immediate eye line.

"Well, if you change your mind, let me know and I can talk to you about the entry-level sales kit, but in the meantime, any chance you could look at this mole I have on my shoulder? My sister pointed it out, but between you and me, I just think she's jealous I inherited our mother's skin, and she's stuck with our father's. All those hours in a tanning bed add up, you know."

"It must be nice to have your sister close by."

"Hardly."

"Oh . . . Um, okay." Joni's expression never lost the measured calm she used at work. "Actually, because of liability, I can't look at your mole, but I do have the name of a wonderful dermatologist nearby."

"Well, I'm *very* picky about health care providers. I've had to write so many Yelp reviews . . ."

"It's a good thing our community has so many for you to choose from." Joni pursed her lips. "Well, we're going to eat. I'll have Derek forward you that number." She closed the door behind her without another look back. She followed Derek into the kitchen where he was handing over her bowl. "Derek Chang, if you ever give that scary MLM lady my phone number so she can harass me about joining her cosmetic pyramid scheme, I'll kill you."

Derek offered her a look of exaggerated outrage. "I would never. And *Jesus.* You gingers and the death threats."

"You have another ginger threatening your life?"

"Dylan's sister. You'd like her." He still needed to get that stupid key back from Carol, but for now, at least she left without barging in to inspect the renovation process. They had done absolutely everything to the letter of the HOA's rules. If Carol tried to fine him, she wouldn't have a legitimate reason.

Unless she found out Gus was living here.

Joni settled down at the kitchen table and ate a few mouthfuls before speaking again. "Gosh, your eye *still* looks a little awful in this light."

"Always so flattering. Is that patient still there? I didn't have a chance to check the other board today."

Joni nodded. "I still wish you would have let me report this for concuss—"

"I need the money, Joni. If I'm concussed, I'm out for weeks. No differentials. No overtime. Being on disability would cut my take-home pay in half."

Her mouth pressed into a line. "I get it. I just hate it."

"Health care in America?"

"Yeah, that too." She sighed and scanned the room. "So . . . what's Dylan up to tonight?" She spun the lazy Susan in the center of his table around to find the salt. Dylan had left all of Derek's things perfectly labeled, so it was easy to find the essentials.

Derek snapped the disposable chopsticks with more vigor than necessary. "I think I blew that all up again too."

After nodding, Joni left the space for him to say more if he wanted to.

The entire weight of everything crashed into Derek as he stirred his food. He *had* made a lot of assumptions about Dylan. But tonight, he'd tried to fix things and talk it out, yet somehow that still ended in a fight because as soon as Jake got brought up, Derek flew off the handle. Maybe Derek was as much of a disaster as his apartment.

He had been bottling everything up inside him for months . . . maybe years. Had he ever actually even cried about Jake?

Thinking he had lost Gus tonight cracked an emotional levee he didn't remember installing. Then he'd screwed it all up with Dylan again, and for whatever reason *that* piece of it kept getting rehashed by his mind over and over again.

Joni rested a hand over his.

"I'm a disaster. This is disaster. All of it's such a goddamn disaster."

Joni nodded.

Everything deluged out in the form of a long, rambling monologue. He told her everything. All of it. Everything he'd left out before about Jake and Hudson. How when Gus was gone, he'd had what might have been an actual panic attack because Gus was all he had left of Jake. He told Joni what happened with Dylan before Felicity showed up. Even his worries about wanting to protect Olive spilled out. When he started to talk about Michelle and what was happening with her, his voice broke.

Old words in his father's voice echoed in his head. Derek *needed* to be the one to help her. He needed to help Mom. He'd helped Amy and her family as much as he could, but she barely needed him these days. He'd always known he failed his family in so many ways as a teenager. Derek was in his thirties. Wasn't he supposed to know how to help the people he loved by now?

Joni patted his shoulder.

Maybe if Derek could cry about this, he could fix it.

He'd rarely even talked to Olive about losing his dad since the year after it happened. It was too much. His father had died so long ago. Shouldn't Derek be past it? This was no one's responsibility except his own.

He breathed slowly, and Joni increased the pressure on his shoulders. When she released him, he felt lighter. Maybe this was all he needed.

No . . .

There was something else he needed to fix.

Chapter 22

Dylan was distracting himself from the monotony of laying flooring with another of Felicity's favorite audiobooks. The cuts and double-checking spacing became monotonous without the smutty fantasy males growling and chuckling darkly in his ear. Unfortunately, this reminded him too much of Derek and the fight.

After leaving Derek's apartment, Dylan called Cal. He admitted that yes, a couple years ago their two oldest brothers had asked their only gay friend (again, Jake Murphy) to tell them "which gay sex dating site was the most awesome" and then secretly made a profile for Dylan. All three brothers were sick of Dylan "acting like he was married to an old pile of bricks in the middle of nowhere" because, apparently, they "all thought you needed a reminder that refurbished stained glass can't love you back, Dilly, no matter how hard you rub it."

He'd hung up on him at that point.

Those dicks. Strangely well-intentioned, but Dylan still wanted to kick Brooks and Anderson in the balls. Maybe starting the barbeque with a well-timed nard-kick would set the right tone for the event.

First thing tomorrow, Dylan would apologize to Derek. He'd been oversensitive. After what happened to Jake, *of course* Derek put the guy on a pedestal. He and Olive had been friends since they were kids, so he'd probably looked up to Jake.

Tonight, Dylan had been the McDickhead.

Realizing he'd stopped paying attention to his audiobook, he paused to sip his drink and skipped back a chapter. At first,

Dylan thought the weird tapping noise meant his earbuds were crapping out. But the knocking was coming from inside his apartment, as in, directly behind him.

He spun around on his kneepads.

Derek stood in the kitchen doorway. Dylan wouldn't have thought it possible, but Derek looked like absolute shit. His shiny black hair stood up at weird angles, like he had tossed and turned instead of sleeping. The shiner around Derek's eye had faded to a sickly green and neon yellow, but now both eyes were bloodshot.

"Are you okay?" Dylan clutched his energy drink tighter.

"Those things are bad for you."

"I'll add it to the list."

"What list?"

"The list of reasons why my insides feel so screwed up right now. I think there's a lot of them." Dylan set the can down. He started to apologize, but it wasn't what came out. "I had one single date with Jake, and—look, what happened to him with that accident was awful, and I'm genuinely sorry for it. But did you ever consider that maybe there's a good reason I'm not telling you what happened? But whatever Jake told you, I didn't lie to him, and I hate how easy it is for you to assume the worst of me."

"I know it seems that way. But I don't think you're a liar. I think there's a lot of stuff I never processed, not that that's an excuse. I'm sorry."

"My jackass brothers were the ones who made that profile that I guess you saw. I had no idea it existed until tonight." Dylan's voice didn't sound bitter so much as resigned.

Derek sat cross-legged, just across the threshold into the living room. "Can I help with the floor?"

"Would you mind sorting those pieces into the two piles? We ended up with boxes that have a couple different patterns." Derek shuffled through the pieces of vinyl tile.

They worked in silence for twenty minutes before either spoke again.

"Kissing you wasn't a mistake, Derek. I was just stressed and scared. *I'm* sorry for shutting down."

"You don't have to be sorry about not being sure. You've been under a lot of stress." Derek's shoulders slumped. "Is the stuff about that asshole that used you at your old company why it's been all hot and cold with you?"

"Partly?" Dylan crossed his legs beneath him and took a deep breath. "Truth is . . . I promised myself a long time ago that I'd stop dating guys who were just looking for no strings. When I date people like that, I always end up feeling like a broken mess. I don't want to feel like that again. Also I'm living above you, and so . . ." He frowned. "I've seen the kind of guys you . . . spend time with. I'm not judging. I'm just saying . . . me and them. There's a stark contrast."

"What?"

"Seriously, does Shonda Rhimes run the HR department at your hospital? You expect me to think I can compete with sandy-haired surgical superheroes in skintight scrubs?"

Derek chuckled. "Always at the alliteration."

Dylan laughed in spite of himself. "Felicity told me I was being stupid."

"Good for her."

"She never misses an opportunity." Dylan twisted his hands together. "So after we kissed, I was annoyed at myself and feeling insecure. We haven't talked about this yet, but I have pretty debilitating ADHD. Diagnosed recently. Before that I had a bunch of other diagnoses, but none of the treatments worked. It messed with my head and led to some major insecurities . . . Finally getting on the right meds has helped, but I'm still trying to retrain my brain after years of bad coping mechanisms."

"I'm sorry you had to go through all that. I don't know what that must have been like, but I do get the insecurity part."

"Bullshit. Derek, you're the most secure person I've ever met."

"Sure, now I'm not a late-blooming emo kid covered with acne, but I guess something about you rejecting cuddle time an hour after—"

"Cuddle time?"

"Yes, cuddle time." Derek continued defiantly. "And then saying it might have all been a mistake. I felt like a rejected teenager again. I'm man enough to admit it when I want to be the little spoon, Gallagher."

Dylan winced at the use of his last name and sighed. "I'm sorry about doing that. *My* insecurity isn't an excuse for shitty behavior."

"I'm sorry too. I should've let you explain." A corner of Derek's mouth pulled upward. "So you *really* hate it when I call you Gallagher, don't you? I might be some himbo gym rat, but I notice shit."

"First of all, I'm pretty sure you listen to NPR while you lift weights since I heard Kai Ryssdal's voice when you connected your phone to that portable speaker last night and you carry your gym clothes in a *Public Radio Forever* tote bag. *And* you keep both *The Economist* and *Men's Health* magazines in your bathroom and have a million books in bins under your bed. There's no pretending you're a meathead. Not buying it." Dylan scooted himself closer to Derek. Just six inches and a brass threshold separated their knees. "Calling me Gallagher . . . just reminds me of all the times my hockey coaches said I need to act more like a real Gallagher. As in the other Gallaghers."

"Ouch."

"Just stupid childhood shit. It's why I prefer rock climbing to team sports. For what it's worth, I don't think less of you for working out a lot."

"The rock climbing explains the back muscles."

Dylan's gaze snapped to Derek.

That adorable eyebrow scrunch pulled at Derek's forehead. "I told you I notice things. And I noticed I really liked touching you."

"Touching me anywhere *specifically*?" Dylan took off his Orioles cap. He rested his elbows on his knees and leaned forward, letting his stupid too-long hair fall in front of his right eye. He was covered in dust and chalk.

"There's no chance Felicity's coming back tonight?" The edge in Derek's voice threatened Dylan's sanity.

"Nah." Dylan quirked a wry smile. "She was scared of facing you since she thought you'd be pissed at us for accidentally kidnapping your dog. She'll be back in the morning."

"Scared of *me*?" Derek pressed a hand to his chest. "But I'm a marshmallow."

"I don't even believe you eat marshmallows." Dylan pointed to Derek's abs.

Derek grabbed Dylan's hand. Their arms bridged the gap between them. At least, until Derek yanked and pulled Dylan on top of him. It was impossible to ignore the physical evidence of how much Derek seemed to want him.

"You could've dislocated my shoulder." Dylan rested his elbows on either side of Derek's head.

"Good thing I know a local emergency room doc." Derek's expression brimmed with addictive, cocky surety. *Christ.*

"The kneepads are an interesting look."

"They have their uses." Dylan knees hit the dusty hall floor on either side of Derek's powerful thighs. Derek grabbed him in a kiss.

Dylan pushed up the bottom of Derek's T-shirt. "Please tell me you're flexing."

"Maybe just a little."

Dylan touched Derek's zipper. "Is this . . . okay . . ." His finger strokes mapped the bulge beneath it. Derek's eyes shuttered as he nodded. Dylan flicked open the button and unzipped.

He slid the boxer briefs down just enough to let Derek's dick spring free.

"My hands are pretty dirty, but I think I have another idea." Dylan was close enough Derek could probably feel his heavy breaths against that very sensitive part of him. "I feel like I should be honest and say it's been kind of a while since I've done this."

"If you don't put my cock in your mouth in the next five seconds, I'm gonna . . . I'm gonna . . ."

Dylan slid his tongue over the slit, loving the way the touch muddled Derek's speech.

"I'm going to put your cock in my mouth when I fucking want to." Dylan hadn't missed how much Derek had liked that little bit of dominance before. Derek's brows furrowed like the pleasure withheld caused the best kind of pain.

Dylan pulled Derek's pants off, trailing pressured kisses and sucks along his thighs. He pushed up his shirt and eased it over Derek's head. Derek's groan thrummed against Dylan's mouth as he licked his way down from Derek's navel.

When he had put on his kneepads to work on the floor earlier, he hadn't thought about this alternative-use case.

Derek rose up on his elbows. As he opened his eyes, the heat behind them begged for more. Derek's teeth sank into his lower lip as Dylan positioned himself above Derek's dripping cock.

"Dylan . . . please . . ."

"I think I'll give you what you want. If you ask really nicely."

"Let me fuck your mouth, Dylan. Please . . ." The S of "please" sliced through the silence.

Dylan's tongue teased Derek's tip, relishing the taste of what was to come. "I could come just from doing this, you know? From licking you."

"Don't. Let me . . . I want to—"

The words ended in a moan as Dylan took as much of Derek in his mouth as he could. He sucked and then retreated to lap the dripping spot.

The hand twisting into Dylan's hair seemed unsure, but Dylan craved the roughness and pushed into the grip, wanting Derek fingers scraping against his scalp.

Derek thrust into him in an uncareful, seemingly involuntary arch.

Yes. Yes. *Yes.*

Dylan's entire reality was shrinking to the study of Derek's reactions. He learned which strokes made Derek seize up and shudder. He wanted the perfect body beneath him to lose control because of Dylan's mouth. Dylan's tongue. Dylan's splayed fingers wandering and digging into Derek's taut ass, coaxing him into a relentless rhythm.

"Dylan." Derek's exhales became guttural. Cursing, he snaked his fingers into Dylan's hair again, holding it tighter. "I'm going to . . ."

Dylan pushed their pace into a final fury, never pulling away. Derek's hand slid beneath the neckline of Dylan's shirt, holding on as his body jolted, giving Dylan everything he wanted.

Dylan's face lifted to enjoy the smooth satisfaction on the face of the man beneath him.

"Come here." Derek pulled Dylan up into a kiss.

Could Derek taste himself on Dylan's tongue? Dylan's core pulsed with the idea as his kneepads scraped the hardwood.

Derek wrapped spent, clumsy arms around Dylan's shoulders. *"Fuck."*

Dylan grinned against Derek's chest.

He was almost asleep when Derek spoke again.

"Want to go to bed?"

"Definitely."

"Definitely, huh?" Derek's grip slid beneath the back of Dylan's pants.

"Oh . . ." Dylan's body tensed, unexpectedly nervous again. "I think . . . Just sleeping though tonight . . . okay, babe? We're both tired."

That seemed to rouse Derek from his blow job–addled stupor. His eyebrows scrunched together again. This expression was quickly becoming Dylan's favorite. It was so earnest and trusting. Derek was all dusty from Dylan's work clothes but he didn't seem to mind.

"I'm not too tired to . . ." Derek palmed Dylan's fly.

"You're *so* tired that you're half asleep. I'm two-thirds asleep. *Mr. Manly-enough-to-ask-to-be-the-little-spoon*, I just want to spoon the hell out of *you* after I shower and get my work clothes off."

"*Kay.*" Derek grinned.

"Smartass."

"Oh, just wait. You are not ready for this ass, Dylan."

Dylan brushed a kiss across Derek's forehead. "Honestly, I'm not yet. Slow, okay? To be clear, I do like that . . . *all* of that. If it's something you like too. But it's been a while . . . and I realize I just sucked your dick off, so that might undercut my point . . . Although, it's nice to know that's like riding a bike."

Derek chuckled in response.

"You're okay with slow?"

"Of course." Derek's eyebrows wrinkled back to that utterly addictive inquisitive expression. "And . . . hey, I want to make this very clear . . . I'm up for whatever you're into here. And thus . . ." His mouth hovered half an inch from Dylan's lips. "I am ready . . . and willing . . . to endure as many perfect blow jobs as you need . . ."

The slight awkwardness of the moment broken, Dylan twisted away playfully. "*Endure*? You little shit."

Derek caught him in another soft kiss. "I think we've established that no part of me is little. And I also said *perfect*." Derek's gorgeous eyes went serious again. Those damned eyebrows would be the end of Dylan. Every tiny nuance of that movement made something flutter within Dylan. "Your pace is fine."

He smiled with an edge of that infuriating cockiness returning. "As long as spooning is acceptable."

"Yeah." Dylan smiled and inhaled as his head rested on the angle of Derek's neck again. They should get up. They both needed to get cleaned off and go to bed, but this man was so warm and solid.

"If there's anything you want to tell me, you can. Just so you know," Derek whispered.

"I do know."

"Good . . ." As if Derek could feel the anxiety humming through Dylan's head like morse code. "I'm up for anything. Not judging or thinking anything beyond that when you're ready for it, I'm gonna make you feel so damn good." Derek's fingertips traced up Dylan's spine and combed through his hair. "Just want you to keep that in mind. Kay?"

"*Kay.*" Dylan tightened his hold on Derek's body. "That reminds me, I need to go get my hair cut before Saturday. Saying it out loud so I remember."

"I like your hair." As if to demonstrate the point, he ran his fingers through Dylan's sweat-damp hair and then dragged them behind his ear and down Dylan's neck again. *Shit*, that felt good. "Why do you need to cut it?"

"Because my mom's going to yell at me if I show up to the Grill-Out '*lookin' like a fecking eejit.*' The Derry mainly comes out when she's yelling at her kids."

Derek shook with a drowsy laugh.

Dylan had thought the smell of Derek on his pillow was erotic but it was nothing compared to his actual body. The slight musk of sex and sweat mixing with whatever aphrodisiac concoction the guy used on his skin and hair. He'd never complain about all the bottles again.

"I'll cut it for you."

"Fuck off."

"I cut hair for years. Learned in high school. Always did Olive's hair and my sister's hair for dances and shit." Derek's eyes were barely visible with the subtle glow of streetlights from the window.

"No way."

"It's a long story. But right now . . ." Like a ridiculous core strength god, Derek sat up, cupping Dylan's jaw in his hands. He kissed him as if every inch of Dylan's mouth were precious to him. Christ, Dylan had *never* felt like this with a partner. When they pulled apart, Derek yawned. "Sorry . . ."

Shaking off the absurd apology, Dylan pulled Derek up. If they stayed there any longer, they actually would fall asleep. When they made it to the bedroom, Gus was on the bed. Derek must have brought him upstairs with him. The dog lifted his head and sniffed once, stretched, and then walked right out of the room without giving either man another glance. Dylan had never seen that dog move from the bed overnight. *Weird.*

"No fucking way," Derek said.

"Huh?"

"Olive thinks Gus can smell sex." He rubbed his eyes.

"You're shitting me."

"Nope. Gus started sleeping on Olive's couch when she and Stella started *dating.*" His voice put air quotes around the last word. "Olive was like," Derek imitated his best friend's slightly raspy voice, "'the poor dude had his balls removed, no wonder he can't handle all these bedroom pheromones'."

"Olive's a weirdo."

"Hey, he just left the bed while we came in smelling like blow job. Scientific confirmation for her hypothesis." Another yawn. And then several more.

"I feel like now I'm a little concerned about the number of science courses that nurses have to take. But I think we should stop talking because you're a zombie at this point." Dylan laughed and patted Derek's cheek.

When Dylan came back after showering, Derek's eyes were shut, yet he was somehow still smiling. Dylan slipped under the blanket behind Derek.

Derek shifted backward, pressing his back into Dylan's chest. Dylan's face leaned between Derek's shoulder blades.

"Little spoon?" Dylan said, the words barely audible so that if Derek were sleeping, he wouldn't wake him.

After the loudest yawn yet, Derek pulled Dylan's arms around him. "Goddamn right."

Dylan's grin spread so wide his cheeks cramped up before he fell asleep.

Chapter 23

The strangest part about the next morning was that nothing about it was strange. As usual, Derek woke just before dawn, but unlike the other times he'd woken in this apartment, there was no moment of confusion. Derek knew where he was. He knew who was lying beside him.

Derek rolled into the crook of Dylan's arm. Dylan's rhythmic exhales whispered against his neck as the violet light grew rosy.

A little while later, full-strength summer sunshine flooded the room. The air-conditioning had kicked on, making the sheer curtains sway. Derek must have fallen back into a much deeper sleep than he meant to. Dylan was stretched out, definitely taking up more than his share of the bed. And that shameless bed hog had stolen the comforter and tucked most of it uselessly beneath him.

Derek suppressed a snicker. Dylan's hair was wilder than ever. He had one fist tucked under his chin.

Waiting to touch him just made Derek want it more. Want *him* more.

As the room brightened, Derek could make out the logo on Dylan's worn green T-shirt. It had the name of a local climbing gym. Dylan had a little scar notched into the outside edge of his right eyebrow. Where had he gotten that? From climbing? Nah. If Derek had to guess, it was probably a childhood gift from a brother. All Derek's friends with older brothers sported a few scars from getting pummeled at some point during childhood. Did the other three always rag on him like they had the day they came over? Derek couldn't imagine ragging on a sibling. But of course, in his case, he was a lot older than his sisters.

He brushed a swath of Dylan's hair away from his sleeping eyes. His hair was a mix of dark brown and a subtle bronze color more prominent in sunlight. The color was nothing like his sister Felicity's bright red, but they shared the same texture. Partially—and slightly selfishly—Derek wanted to cut it to make sure some random barber didn't cut it too short. The memory of fisting Dylan's hair while he came apart inside Dylan's mouth was enough to make him need to adjust his boxer-briefs against an aggressive morning erection.

Dylan sighed in his sleep.

Despite the impulses of a particular part of Derek's body, he wanted to let Dylan sleep. The guy had to be zonked with all the work he and his sister had done on the floor this week.

When his full bladder and caffeine addiction became impossible to ignore, Derek eased himself out of bed. When his feet found the floor, reality dosed Derek with an unwanted and disturbing realization. He just spent nearly half an hour watching someone sleep.

What the actual fuck?

He'd never done this with anyone. It wasn't that he *never* spent the night with a partner after a hookup, but it was safe to say it had never felt like this. Morning had always been an ending. It had never felt like the *beginning* of something.

Feeling a chill he blamed on the air vent, Derek rubbed his bare arms. A few minutes ago, he hadn't been scared at all. A few minutes ago, Derek hadn't ever wanted to leave that bed.

He needed to think. Well, what he *really* needed was to take a piss. Derek eased open the door. Dylan's breathing stayed steady as Derek shut it behind him.

Later, as Derek drank his coffee surrounded by the chaos of tools, furniture, and the general mayhem of renovations, he realized why the morning felt so different. He hadn't checked his phone. He hadn't worried about Michelle. Or Olive. Or anything.

He'd been completely in the moment. Peaceful.

Gus stirred and stretched like a cat in the morning sunlight, the jingle of his collar making a small ache tug in Derek's gut. A roiling unease he associated with guilt . . . and something else.

Jake.

The tug turned into a yank. He hated himself for thinking about Jake when Dylan was so close. Gus lumbered over to sniff Derek's hand and beg for neck scratches. He adjusted Gus's collar to straighten his two tags. Behind the tag listing Olive's and Derek's names and numbers, there was the oversized, bone-shaped piece of blue metal she'd left there. IF FOUND, CALL JAKE MURPHY BECAUSE HE'S PROBABLY FREAKING OUT THAT HIS BEST FRIEND IS MISSING. On the other side it said IF ANYONE ASKS, THAT SQUIRREL HAD IT COMING above the phone number.

Derek sat on the floor. Gus laid his head in his lap.

Jake was gone.

A spot between Derek's eyes ached just like it had with Joni last night. As if the tears were stuck there. Telling her everything had taken away some fraction of the sting.

The AC rumbled on, and Gus shook out his head in confusion, jangling the collar and whipping his big floppy ears around. It might have been that sound or the prickling shiver from the overchilled air on bare skin, but the triggered memory's impact nearly knocked Derek over.

That Halloween was *frigid*. The old furnace at Jake's house couldn't keep up. The flow of trick-or-treaters had slowed, but Derek and Jake still wore the silly Power Ranger costumes Olive had picked out for all of them before she got the flu and couldn't come.

Derek touched Jake's shoulder. "Don't take that off yet. We

need to get a photo for Olive or she won't believe we actually wore them."

Jake got closer and smiled at Derek's phone. "Oh. That reminds me. Found something today Olive said is yours." He dug through a kitchen drawer and pulled out the old disposable camera. "Not sure it still works, but you could probably try to get it developed anyway."

"Two shots left." Derek held out the disposable like he had held up the phone. "I guess no time like the present. Smile."

Just before the shutter clicked, Jake leaned close, his voice low. "Do you want to stay?"

Unlike now when Derek sat in a room filled with morning sunshine, that old farmhouse was pitch black when Derek slipped out of Jake's bed. He'd realized he was caught when he heard Gus's jingling collar and that same ear-flapping sound. Gus leaned on Jake on the landing.

"History is repeating itself." Jake sat on the step, Gus resting a head on one of his knees.

"I just needed to go for a walk"

"At three A.M. when it's thirty-eight degrees?"

"Crisp fall air." Derek forced a casual smile as his fingers slipped on his first attempt at tying his shoelace.

"Last time was the same, Derek." Jake frowned. "Have you ever considered that you like the idea of me and us more than what it would really be like?"

"You have to know I've always lo—"

"*Don't* say . . . I'm not sure this is—"

"Jake." Derek stood, focused on the distance between himself and the door. "Please . . . let's just go on a date? It doesn't have to be a big deal. When you get back from your trip. If you want to."

"It's not a matter of me not wanting to. I just don't know if I'm—"

"You're what I've wanted forever. It's just new, and I've never been the stick-around-and-cuddle guy." Derek gripped the railing at the bottom of the stairs, feet glued to the floor as he looked up at Jake. "But I really want to go on the date we talked about last night."

"You're sure?" Jake glanced from Derek's coat to the door.

"Maybe I just want to be wooed?"

Despite Derek's attempt to be flirtatious falling flat, Jake smiled. "When I get back, I'm going to take you out on the best date ever."

Derek's stomach should have been full of that fluttering happy sensation he used to have every time he saw Jake, but instead it felt queasy. And he couldn't blame it on a hangover. This time they'd both been sober.

The farther Derek walked that day over fields of frost-covered grass, the more loudly his mind screamed for a redo. Part of him wanted to take it all back.

At the time, he thought it was a reflexive fear of relationships.

Cold feet. Both the literal and figurative kind on that blustery morning. When his feet went numb, he started back. Derek fell asleep on the couch, and when he woke up, Jake had left.

Jake was still on that last business trip when an envelope of photos arrived. The note explained he couldn't help getting them developed. Derek flipped through, oddly relieved that the *last* photo, not the Power Ranger one . . . the other one . . . must not have turned out.

The next time Derek saw Jake was at the Baltimore trauma center after Olive got the call.

He'd loved Jake for so long, but he couldn't wait to leave afterward both times. After a night sleeping beside Dylan, he'd *never* wanted to leave.

Derek dug his fingers into that damned tight spot above his

eyes. Was this another post-concussive thing? A sinus thing? He grabbed a tissue box from the side table and blew his nose.

When Jake was around, no one compared. After Jake's accident, Derek needed easy release and fun. If he actually stopped numbing and felt all his feelings, he might crumble.

Dylan had assumed Derek wasn't looking for anything real, and the more he considered this, he couldn't blame him for the assumption. Derek had hated feeling Dylan go hot and cold on him, but hadn't Derek also held back to hide his own growing feelings? Maybe part of him reflexively pushed Dylan away because the attraction felt so vital, so easy, that it became unwelcome proof things would never have worked with Jake.

And acknowledging that *should* have felt like betrayal.

But it didn't.

How had the memory of that that dark, bleary walk gotten lost in the hazy devastation after the accident? He'd known Jake wasn't right for him. Not in the way Derek had fantasized him being.

During his life, Derek had had three people he could absolutely depend on during the worst moments. His dad, Olive, and Jake.

If he had a therapist, they might ask if the fact that two of them were now dead made him feel . . . abandoned, maybe?

And *shiiiiiiiit.*

He had dumped so much on Joni during that conversation, which felt like days ago—not hours.

Derek blinked, eyes still dry.

It wasn't like Derek *never* cried. He was a man secure enough in his masculinity to be comfortable crying when the situation was appropriate. A well-timed Julia Roberts speech next to a priceless Chagall painting? He cried. That moment in *13 Going on 30* when Jennifer Garner is certain Mark Ruffalo is going to marry that awful weather lady and move to Chicago?

Eyes leaking like a damned faucet. The entire dead wife plot in *Sleepless in Seattle*? Sobbing mess. But even with every heartbreak gut punch, you knew what was coming at the end of a romantic comedy. You were guaranteed two people who were happy together despite everything. It was fucking beautiful.

Such a cliché to ask, but why couldn't life be that simple?

More specifically, why did *death* keep screwing him over?

An insistent whine came from the front door. Derek needed to get out before Carol left for her weekly Mary Kay minion breakfast. Derek grabbed shorts and a T-shirt from his duffel bag. He snuck back into the room to grab his sunglasses, lingering a few extra seconds to watch Dylan sleep.

Chapter 24

"*EW EW EW EW.*" Felicity's high-pitched shrieks from the hallway outside echoed off the walls of the bedroom. "Oh my god, Dylan, no . . . my eyes. My eyes."

Dylan leaped out of bed, grabbing his work jeans and almost knocking himself out trying to put on both legs at once. He stumbled into the living room to find Felicity in a state of nearly dissociative distress.

"What's wrong with your *eyes*?" He searched her for an injury.

She pointed toward the kitchen. "Derek's clothes are all right outside the kitchen and there are actual scuff marks from your kneepads on the ground from—and—" She gagged. "I'm your sister. Can you just keep your business less graphically obvious? I've been downstairs measuring for the drywall all morning while you slept like a rock. Sounds like Derek's in the shower, so I'm leaving."

"Lissy, I—"

She snapped at him, actually snapped with her accusatory fingers pinched an inch from his nose. "Lock it down while I'm around, Dylan. I've listened to a shit ton of true crime podcasts, so I can spot a crime scene when I see one."

He snorted. "Are you implying that two men engaging in consensual sexual activities is a *crime*? Because that sounds like homophobia." His terror from hearing her cries had turned into pure amusement.

Felicity's storm-gray eyes narrowed. "You fucking know what I mean. I don't want to come in and see a floor dust outline showing me exactly what goddamn position you prefer.

Boundaries." With a disgruntled yawp, she stalked out of the room and slammed the door.

He walked to the small stretch of hallway between the kitchen and the living room and exploded into laughter. Not only had the kneepads left rubber scuffing, but there were lines of actual chalk dust handprints right next to all of Derek's abandoned clothes. Derek's naked body had left a barely visible outline like a pornographic sawdust snow angel.

"Was that Felicity?" Derek leaned out from the bathroom. "What was—?"

"She'll survive. Went downstairs. Don't think she'll be back anytime soon."

"God, she scared the shit out of me." Derek cleared his throat. "Um . . . are you having some kind of respiratory distress episode I should worry about?"

"No." Hysterical tears blurred Dylan's vision. He shook so hard from laughter he could barely form words. "I think we broke her."

"How?"

"By leaving graphic evidence of our lewd acts."

"Um . . . *what?*" A white towel was tastefully draped around Derek's waist as he stepped into the hall.

Dylan gestured to the floor.

"Oh my *god."* Derek braced a hand on Dylan as he lost it for several minutes the same way Dylan had until he managed to hiccup out a few words. "Poor, innocent Felicity."

Dylan leaned his head on his hand. "You know, somewhere in here there's a joke about—"

"Uh-uh." Derek gave him a little shove. "New rule. You do not get partial credit for jokes. You make the joke or don't."

"Yeah?"

"Yep. None of this shopping it and feeling it out. That's weak shit. You gotta go for it." Derek smirked. "Like this . . . you know why you shouldn't have gay men working on expensive flooring?"

"Why?"

"Because no homosexual man can be trusted around that amount of high-quality hardwood."

"That was awful. I'm embarrassed for you." Dylan's forced grimace couldn't hide his laughter, so he caught the twisted front of the towel and drew Derek's hips toward him.

"Hey . . ." The soft way Derek's eyebrows pulled together drove Dylan wild.

"Caught you." Mischief edged Dylan's voice.

"You better let go."

"Technically, that's *my* towel."

"But it's *my* hardwood behind it." Derek's arms-crossed stance emphasized the cut of his pecs in a way that was, frankly, unfair.

"I think I proved last night that I know what I'm doing with all of the most important tools. A veritable genius in fact."

"Might need another demonstration of your skills to be sure your initial result wasn't a fluke." His expression was completely deadpan. "After all, there are a lot of techniques and variables that cannot be judged on a single task."

"Are you saying you need a few more demonstrations of my expertise to be assured of my overall level of tool mastery?"

"I certainly wouldn't say no to a new project with expanding scope." Derek traced Dylan's jaw with his thumb while his eyes laughed. "That's as far as I can go with the construction metaphors though. I don't think I've ever done any work with two-by-fours. Saws scare the shit out of me. But I can go to town on sex puns about drills or screws."

"Really?"

"I had a few catastrophes trying to learn shit off YouTube before I gave up. Never learned that stuff." Derek shrugged.

"My dad died when I was sixteen. He was sick for a while before that, so it wasn't like we were framing up walls on the weekends."

"I'm so sorry . . ." Dylan released the towel back to Derek, wishing he'd known this before. "That . . . god, that just sucks."

"Yeah." With a shrug, Derek shifted back into the playful tone. "I'm a whiz with that tiny hexagon thing though."

"An Allen wrench?" Dylan smiled.

"Yep. Expert-level Ikea furniture builder."

"Impressive." Dylan gave him a soft closed-mouth peck, hopefully balancing the playfulness Derek wanted with some tenderness. "I'm really sorry about your dad though."

"It was a long time ago." Derek looked down and adjusted his towel. "Did you see the text from your uncle?"

Derek didn't seem inclined to say anything else about his dad, so Dylan let it go.

"No, pretty much was a corpse until my sister's screams re-animated me."

Derek chuckled and mussed his hair. "Well, the water's back on in the bathroom downstairs, Frankenstein. Got the major pipes fixed this morning. Kitchen's plumbing still's a mess though."

"Oh . . . interesting."

"Interesting?

"Can't help but notice you could've easily gone downstairs to shower." He touched Derek's hair still shiny with water.

"Meh, I had to stick around to make sure you weren't dead. You didn't budge when I tried to wake you up after Gus's walk." He checked his watch.

"What time is it?"

"It's ten thirty."

"Shit, really? I meant to wake up . . ." Dylan rubbed his eyes. "I'm a heavy sleeper when I'm zonked. My brothers are loud, and we all shared a room until Anderson moved out."

"Four boys in one room?"

"Two bunk beds. It was loud. And so many sticky socks."

Derek wrinkled his nose. "Your mom must be a saint."

"Not with the way she yelled at us to '*Stop bloody wanking, or I'll be throwing every fecking sock in the house in the bin*'."

"Can't wait to meet her."

Dylan's gut tightened. *Right.* "You're still coming to the Grill-Out?"

"Planning on it. If you're still okay with me coming, that is?"

"I am. My family's just a lot is all." Dylan tugged at his collar. "It's just—"

The front door creaked open an inch. "I'm not coming in until I'm assured that all parties have their respective dicks put away." Felicity's tone threatened violent death.

"One sec, Felicity." Derek leaned close to Dylan's ear. "Can't let her see the bare hardwood."

Dylan groaned. "Go put some goddamned clothes on."

"You've been saying that since day one." Derek winked. "I still don't believe it's what you really want."

Felicity banged on the door again. "Can I come in yet? Uncle Liam's people accidentally locked me out of the apartment, and this nutty old lady in a flamingo shirt just called the cops on me, so I feel like that's more important than your gross sexy talk."

As if on cue, sirens blared outside.

"Shit," Derek and Dylan said at the exact same moment.

Chapter 25

Dylan's eye-rolling muscles were practically cramping from overuse. They'd been standing on the sidewalk outside Derek's apartment in the sweltering heat for an hour with the cops and Carol Taylor. It hadn't helped that Derek's apartment *did* look ransacked, so initially the officers had been skeptical of Felicity's story. The confusion was compounded by Carol's continued insistence that "any woman willing to mark up her body like that probably was into all sorts of substances—you know," meaning that Felicity's intricate tattoo sleeves, visible since she'd tied the top part of her jumpsuit at her waist, were somehow symptomatic of a drug problem.

Reluctantly, Dylan tuned back in to the conversation.

". . . fishy going on in the apartment. Mr. Chang is gay so why would he have some strange woman here dressed like a workman but with the body of a 1950s pinup girl?"

"Aw. Thanks so much." Only Dylan's younger sister could dramatically preen and bow while being insulted by a woman who looked like the physical embodiment of the state of Florida.

God, if only they could find a convenient sinkhole.

"You think this girl is doing actual construction work in that bright-red bra?" said Carol with a scoff.

"It's a *crop top* underneath my jumpsuit." She gestured to the sleeves tied around her waist. "It's ninety degrees outside, and I was unloading the drywall—"

"Do I look like an idiot?" Carol glared.

No one seemed to want to touch *that* question with a ten-foot stick.

"You're all sneaking around because you're running some sort of sex and drugs ring. I hear that man leaving his house at all hours." She gave Derek a sweep of stink eye. "I'm going to be living in a crack den soon, and you have to do something. Check behind that new so-called drywall. You'll see. I refuse to believe that this four-foot tall, busty, carrottop bimbo is here to—"

"*Five* feet tall. Ish." Felicity scowled. "You know carrottop is literally offensive to people with red hair, right? And crack den is pretty gross just generally."

"Jesus fucking Christ." Dylan immediately regretted vocalizing his bewildered exhale since it drew the unwanted attention of Carol. Dylan had, up until that point of the conversation, been leaning against a lamppost, minding his own business.

"And you, Mr. Gallagher—" She pointed at him. "I know you lied to me before about the dog because I saw that very animal in your vehicle last night. I've been watching out my window the last twenty-four hours. All of your going back and forth between apartments. You won't get away with this." Carol took this opportunity to point a neon-orange acrylic nail between Felicity and Dylan. "This one's probably raking in millions in dirty pornography money with that unnecessary, hyperfast internet connection. I heard *all sorts* of pornographic noises coming from his apartment last night. I can go into more detail when I file a criminal report."

Felicity's face screwed up. "*Please* do not go into more detail."

"Those matching tattoos could possibly be some sort of gang symbol." She gestured between Dylan's forearm and Felicity's wrist.

Felicity seethed. "It's the outline of Ireland."

"Didn't the Irish criminals in that movie with what's-his-name and that other one that showed his whosiewhatsit in that other film have matching tattoos?"

Derek, the two cops, and Dylan all stared blankly.

Felicity was quickest on the draw, pretending to hit an

imaginary game show buzzer first. "Who are Leonardo DiCaprio and Mark Wahlberg in *The Departed* for five hundred, Alex. Side note, y'all, I think a lot of Scorsese's overrated." She shrugged as casually as if they didn't have two cops trying to figure out if one or all of them should be arrested for breaking into an apartment that had never been broken into or for being in an illicit amateur porn ring that didn't exist.

"She sure seems to know a lot about that film, doesn't she?" Carol said with a sneer.

"Caught me there. Super suspicious to know about a movie that won a boatload of Oscars. Officers, just cuff me now." She held out her wrists.

Dylan kneaded his temples. "Felicity, can you please just shut up?" Couldn't he go back to bantering about blow jobs and making lumber euphemisms with Derek? He liked that part of the day.

"Sorry." Felicity directed the apology at Dylan. "He's my *brother*. And I can't *believe* I have to say these words out loud, but he's definitely not an internet porn star."

It took another twenty-seven minutes for the officers to accept that *yes*, Felicity was indeed there to help with drywall work. And also *yes*, the dust in her hair was, in fact, from working with said drywall and not from any kind of "coke-fueled hooker ring" or any other sort of "depraved shenanigans."

As the officers finally started to leave, Felicity posited—loudly—that the Depraved Shenanigans would make a great name for an Irish punk band.

While Dylan's sister's chosen anxiety response had always been explosive verbal diarrhea, he found it more annoying than usual today. "*Felicity*, for the love of god—"

"C'mon Dylan, can't you imagine someone being like 'Yeah, I'm going to see the Depraved Shenanigans tonight at the Vic. Sounds so killer."

Breaking away from her rant at the cops, Carol shrieked, "I

think she just said 'Let's *kill her*.' I'm not going to be safe at night in my own bed. Don't you see why I was suspicious?"

"*Lissy!*"

"Ms. Gallagher, you need to take this a little more seriously," one of the cops said before exchanging a look with his partner that said *nothing* happening was serious beyond their wasted time.

"I—I—" Felicity exhaled. "I was doing pro bono drywalling work for my brother's cash-strapped neighbor—"

"*Hey!*" Derek said.

Felicity gesticulated at Carol like a crossing guard hired to host a game show. "And now some random lady wants me arrested for having arm tattoos and breasts. I'm really doing the best I can here."

Carol actually stamped her foot. "Not for the tattoos and the breasts. For the drugs."

"For the last time, Carol, there are no drugs in or associated with my home." Derek braced a hand on top of his head as if worried it might explode. "Either of our homes for that matter."

Frustration must have outpaced Derek's amusement watching Carol being grilled by the police. Outwardly, he'd stayed the calmest until now.

"Go ahead and ask that one about his eye." Carol gestured to Derek's still healing shiner. "If that doesn't say violence, I don't know what does. Were you lying about snaking his toilet drain the other day? Is this some *Fifty Shades of Grey*–type debauchery?"

"How'd we get to S&M sex dungeon?" Felicity muttered.

"*Felicity.*" Dylan palmed his head.

"Not that it's any of your business, Kare—Carol, but I was assaulted by a patient while working in the Memorial Hospital ED."

The officers gave him a sympathetic frown.

"Can we go inside *please*?" Dylan asked.

"You know *both* those two are gay, right? Pretty coincidental."

Carol cut in with another aggressive round of acrylic talon pointing. It was as if she were selecting Keyser Söze in a perp lineup. "Living right on top of one another. Keeping each other's dog secrets. Maybe other secrets too."

The shorter cop doing most of the speaking pointed to his partner, the gruff cowboy-ish man built like one of Dylan's brothers. "What do you think about that coincidence, Officer Creager?"

"It reminds me that my anniversary's coming up next week. Thanks, Mitchell." Officer Creager spoke with a strong Maryland panhandle accent. "Ma'am, should I tell my gay husband that our gay meeting at a non-gay bar makes us suspicious? Are multiple gay men existing in the world in close proximity really something you're worried about right now? Right now, at this here second?"

Carol fumed.

"Have a good rest of your day, sirs and ma'am." He intentionally directed that singular "ma'am" at Felicity, not Carol.

Carol paced on the sidewalk, gesticulating so wildly that Dylan would not have been surprised if she took flight. "They say if you see something, *say something*. That's how community works. At least it did back in my day." Her outraged hand pressed on her chest, directly over the T-shirt flamingo's face, shielding its eyes from the scandal before her.

Officer Creager lowered his sunglasses. "Well, Ms. Taylor, if we find out you're *saying* something about *seeing* things you *aren't* even seeing again, we'll be *seeing* you right to the station and charging you for making a false statement to law enforcement."

The spackled-on, multilevel-marketed makeup couldn't hide how the blood drained from her face.

Meanwhile, Derek's lit up like . . . well, like someone giving up concealing well-earned schadenfreude. Dylan didn't blame him. Derek should schadenfreude that shit up.

Carol bleated her case until the officers' car door shut. As if telepathically connected, all three others bolted down the stairs and into Derek's apartment before the unfriendly pastel neighborhood despot could say anything else.

After collapsing onto the couch, Felicity opened her mouth again, but Derek pointed at her. "I do *not* want to hear the words 'depraved shenanigans' again for at least twenty-four hours. Too soon, F Gallagher. Too soon."

Felicity weighed this, tilting her head back and forth before nodding. "Fair."

Dylan collapsed onto Derek's queen-sized bed that was still set up in the living room. "Can I go back to bed and start over? *Shit,* I forgot to take my medication, so Carol's cop-calling saga took all my processing capacity for the day."

Felicity patted his shoulder. "Don't worry. Derek and I won't let Tropical Karen Barbie getcha."

"Wonderful." Dylan buried his head in Derek's pillow. Even though freshly washed, it smelled like Derek.

Felicity sank down onto the edge of the bed while Derek went into his kitchen. A few minutes later he came back with three souvenir Baltimore shot glasses and a bottle. He poured a small amount of one of Dylan's energy drinks.

Dylan sat up again, yawning. "I thought you said those toxic drinks rot my insides?"

"All the normal caffeine and alcohol are upstairs." Derek handed him a shot. "This is for medicinal purposes. I'm a nurse, and Ginger over there is almost one. Also, let me know if 'ginger' is offensive? And how old are you again? Is this much caffeine okay for someone whose prefrontal cortex is still developing?"

"Twenty-six. Just short, asshole." Felicity accepted her own nonalcoholic, medicinal, possibly toxic caffeine shot. "*Ginger* is fine. *Carrottop* and like that whole 'red-headed stepchild' expression are the two I loathe." She held up her glass. "A toast, since we're celebrating avoiding getting thrown in the slammer."

"Agreed," Derek said.

They clinked glasses.

"To Karen getting her fluorescent ass handed to her." Derek tipped his shot into his mouth.

"To gay cops and their upcoming equally gay anniversaries," Dylan said before sucking his down.

Felicity swirled her portion of neon liquid and raised it higher. "And to the Depraved Shenanigans."

Chapter 26

Derek was *stoned*. Not college-student-frat-party-bong-level stoned, but thirties happy-buzzed after a safe portion of a (mostly) legally and ethically obtained edible. After Derek complained that he was amped up from the caffeine shot, Felicity produced the small tin of the THC gummies she used for anxiety. Somewhat ironic, given how adamant they'd all been about there being no drugs in here. A few minutes later, she grabbed the TV remote and flipped it on.

Derek didn't remember the last time he had watched *Burlesque*, so Dylan must have put it on while he was doing work in the apartment. After the credits, Felicity queued up another movie without asking for input. She had such a strong sense of herself and what she wanted all the time. Despite their differences, the siblings shared a certain whimsy Derek found strangely addictive.

"I can't believe you have all these . . ." Felicity flipped through the DVD bin. "Good selection but not a lot of range. The BBC period dramas are excellent choices though. Why only a couple seasons of *Downton*? You have all of *Gilmore Girls* and *Friends*. And something called *Moonlighting*? Is that the with the guy from *Die Hard*?"

"Killing off Matthew Crawley and Sybil in the same episode was a crime against humanity. I like what I like." Derek grinned.

They were treating the bed like an extension of the couch behind it. Felicity tossed every disaster-survivor throw pillow and blanket onto it as well. At some point, pizza had gotten ordered. Derek was about to get himself a drink when Dylan brought him one of his favorite sparkling waters. The gesture tugged at him. Dylan could have easily asked him if he wanted water. Derek would have said he was fine. He never wanted anyone else to help him, even with such a small thing. But Dylan hadn't asked. He'd thought that Derek might need water and just got it for him.

Weirder still was the way Dylan had ended up with his head partially on Derek's lap. His eyes were closed, but every now and then he made a well-timed quip. Derek dragged his fingers through Dylan's hair absently as Meg Ryan pretended to orgasm over her sandwich.

"I just didn't know anyone had bins and bins of DVDs anymore. And *yes*." Felicity snatched one from the pile. "Oooh, I found the movies that aren't rom-coms. This is more like it. Jackpot."

"Those are my best friend's."

"She's got good taste." Felicity nodded approvingly.

Dylan chuckled. "I think if Felicity and Olive meet it might disrupt the space-time continuum."

"The world would never be the same, for sure." Derek smoothed Dylan's hair behind his ear.

Dylan shivered but kept his focus on the screen.

"Don't knock DVDs, Ginger Spice. I didn't want to be subject to the whims of the streaming gods for my entertainment. Just got rid of my VHS collection a few years ago."

"Geriatric Millennials." Felicity shook her head.

Dylan nudged his sister gently with his bare foot. "Be nice."

"So why rom-coms?" Felicity grabbed herself a slice of cold pizza.

Dylan's eyes popped open. It seemed like he wondered too, but unlike his sister, he rarely asked probing questions. The only time they talked about it, Derek deflected.

"Long answer or short answer?"

"I think it's safe to say I'm not getting any more work done today." Felicity fidgeted with her phone. "By the way, I texted Dad and told him to come Sunday instead."

"Good." Dylan shifted so he could better see Derek and interlaced his fingers with Derek's. "Long version?"

"Long, but pause for a second, I need another drink. I love these daytime adult slumber party vibes. Truth or dare for lazy old people, which just means *truth*." Felicity stood. "The small dose of THC helps. Let me know when either of you gentlemen feel like really getting this party started and I'll grab you a second seltzer water."

"She's telling both of us we're old and busted, ba—Derek."

With a curious mouth quirk, Felicity headed into the kitchen.

Dylan had almost called him "babe" in front of his *sister*. They couldn't be at the casual pet name usage stage . . . right? But why didn't Derek feel glad Dylan caught himself?

A slight pink colored Dylan's cheeks, but his ears made the embarrassment obvious. Fire engine red. No wonder Dylan liked his hair long. Which reminded him . . .

"Don't let me forget to go to my mom's house tomorrow for my shears."

Dylan blinked. "You're really serious about cutting my hair?"

"Yep."

"Okay, back." She set two cans down on the box acting as a side table, carbonation fizzing as she opened her own. "Story time."

"Context first. Sweet summer child, do you know what a Blockbuster is?" Derek knew this audience would appreciate the reference.

Felicity clicked her tongue. "I've watched historical documentaries where the archeologists referenced an ancient practice of venturing to a blue-and-yellow store to obtain—"

"The shade this one throws." Derek frowned scornfully.

"I'm well aware." Dylan grabbed his seltzer water.

"Longest story in the world." She gave him a hurry up

motion. "Can we move on from the context and the melodramatic pausing? Please? *I'll* be as old as Dylan by the time you finish."

"Alright, smartass." He tugged Felicity's bun. "The short answer is Blockbuster and bees."

Her nose crinkled. "Was this like a *The Swarm* situation? Or a Winnie the Pooh and honey situation?"

"It was an Anna Chlumsky situation."

"The pregnant woman in that Anna Delvey series?" Felicity said. "*Veep*?"

Derek's hand went to heart as if shot by an arrow. "Oh honey. In *our* day, she was one of the biggest child stars. Olive convinced me it was a tragedy that I hadn't seen *My Girl*."

"A nineties classic." Dylan nodded. "Not sure I ever saw it though."

"Derek, you're officially the *worst* storyteller when you're high. Accelerate."

"You good with spoilers?" Derek asked.

"For a movie that came out a million years ago? *Yes*."

There were only a couple things Derek had extremely strong opinions about—how to put the toilet paper roll back, socialized medicine, squirrels, capitalism in general, . . . okay, maybe there were more than a couple. But at the center of his mess of extreme opinions was the movie *My Girl*.

He stood and paced the only empty square feet of floor space. "So—*spoiler*—at the end Macaulay Culkin is literally murdered by bees. And we see his nine- or ten-year-old lifeless corpse in a goddamn coffin. Anna Chlumsky crashes his funeral and sobs that he needs his glasses because apparently her undertaker dad didn't give that dead, pale white kid his glasses. But she keeps crying that *he can't see without his glasses* and that he *needed* them."

Felicity grimaced. "I'm sorry, you're sure it's a kid's movie? Sounds really dark."

Derek gestured to Felicity in a vindicated, open-palmed sweep. "*EXACTLY. Thank you.* Seriously."

Felicity squinted at her phone. "Rated PG? What the hell, 1991 MPAA? What the hell?"

"The early nineties were dark, Lissy. Bees murdering a child? Not as scary as a Cold War during a Bush presidency."

"It should've been rated NC-17 for the minimum of seventeen years of therapy I needed after watching that bullshit."

Felicity threw her phone down onto the mattress. "So can you finish explaining how watching a Kevin McCallister snuff film led to the rom-com obsession?"

"I was inconsolable . . . for an hour." Derek grabbed his sparkling water and downed it like it was whiskey, but the excess carbonation caused a coughing fit.

"Aw . . ." Dylan grabbed his hand and rubbed his back with the other.

When the throat spasm stopped, he choked a laugh. "Olive's parents aren't the adults you'd want managing an intense adolescent emotional breakdown, so Olive called my dad. I cried for two more hours at home."

Felicity clasped her hands like a therapist facilitating an intervention. "How old were you exactly when this event occurred?"

"Uh—like twelve?" Derek thumped his chest with his fist. "I *feel* things. That okay with you, Dr. Marcia Fieldstone?"

"Dude, I *love* the feeling vibes." To emphasize, Felicity booped him on the nose before sliding off the bed to cuddle with a groaning Gus, who seemed annoyed that the volume of Derek's opinion had interrupted his nap. "So rom-coms . . . ?"

"I like happily ever afters. I want Heath Ledger—RIP—wearing a tight gray Henley waiting at my cool vintage Dodge Dart with a fancy Fender guitar while Letters to Cleo plays on my school's inexplicably dangerous-looking roof stage. I want *those exact vibes* in an ending." As Derek relaxed, he found himself nestled between Dylan's bent knees with his back against Dylan's chest. "And absolutely no goddamn bees."

"Amen." Dylan swept the smallest of kisses along Derek's neck, but then Dylan went rigid. He craned his neck as if verifying Felicity's attention was still fixed on Gus, and his hand slid away from Derek.

Derek tried not to react, staring at the TV without registering anything happening on the screen.

"Are you still afraid of bees?" Felicity said.

"No . . . I'm not."

"How'd you get over it? I need something to fix my fear of snakes."

"I guess I just stopped at some point." Derek slid off the bed to throw his empty can into recycling.

Meg Ryan sang off-key into a karaoke machine on the TV while Derek leaned on the kitchen doorway. His fear of bees had been debilitating for months, but until this second, he didn't realize he could pinpoint the exact moment he stopped being afraid of them.

Derek's thirteen-year-old self had been sorting his music into the new CD binder Olive had gotten him for his birthday when his dad knocked on his door. Derek had expected the usual joking complaints about the "whiny" music playing too loudly on his stereo or maybe mild parental harassment about a recent disappointing math grade.

But on this night, his dad sank down on the floor beside Derek's desk. "I never wanted to be this kind of dad."

Confused and already a little scared, Derek dropped the CD binder and sat on the floor facing his dad.

"I wanted you to be a normal kid in all the ways I didn't get to be." His dad scanned Derek's walls lined with the cut-out band posters that sometimes came in Olive's magazines. "My parents put so much pressure on me. I wanted you to be a kid. But now . . . I understand why my parents did what they did.

Their expectations made me stronger. They knew when they left Taiwan and came to this country that family is the most important thing, and no other help is guaranteed. But for you . . . that wasn't the kind of parents your mom and I wanted to be." He fell silent.

"Dad, what's going on?"

His dad's face seemed etched with more wrinkles than usual. "I'm sick, son."

Sick?

As if the word *sick* tied Derek's vision to a freight train zooming into endless tunnel, the bedroom around him faded.

"We hoped we could keep this from you a little longer. Michelle and Amy are too young to understand, so a lot's going to fall on you." He leaned forward, a hand on each of Derek's scrawny shoulders as if he needed Derek to understand exactly how heavy this would be. "Your mom's not doing well. Keeping this from you is making it worse for her."

Derek's head bowed over white-knuckled fists.

"Do you understand what I'm asking?"

At some point, Derek had started crying, so his mouth felt too full of salt and bile to answer. Derek's dad took off his thick-framed glasses and held them in his lap. He pulled Derek's forehead to his and let Derek cry as much as he needed to. Derek had no idea how long they sat that way.

Hearing Derek's mom call from downstairs, his dad got up to leave.

Derek stood and grabbed his dad's arm. "Are you going to die?" Only a stupid, punk thirteen-year-old would ask the question like that. Like it was happening to Derek and not actually happening to his dad.

But when his dad looked down at him, a little bit of his normal self had returned. "I'd say my odds are about fifty-fifty. You know . . ." He dragged his knuckles softly across Derek's face in a joking motion that he had used so many times before. "In

206 * Andie Burke

a casino, that kind of luck is unheard of." He thumbed Derek's nose. "Your mom doesn't approve of gambling, so don't tell her. But yes, Buddy, I'd bet on me."

Dramatic music swelled.

Derek blinked. At some point, Derek must have returned to the bed in his living room. Dylan leaned on him with his Ireland-tattooed arm resting across Derek's thigh. He could feel that arm's warmth through the fabric separating them.

On the screen, Billy Crystal ran through the streets on New Year's Eve. The movie was almost over.

He grabbed his phone and swiped to his text chain with his mom. She had been going through old albums recently and sent him a bunch of low-quality pictures of old photos. He scrolled up to a particular one. His dad, in his early twenties, smiling behind a tiny Derek holding up a red envelope on Lunar New Year. Preschool Derek was cheesing like the cash inside was a check from Ed McMahon.

His dad was ten years younger in that photo than Derek was now.

Dylan did a double take at Derek. *"You okay?"* He had mouthed the words so as not to disturb Felicity, who had apparently fallen asleep next to Gus. He kissed him once.

"Yeah." Derek shifted his body closer, smiling and letting their fingers tangle together. "I'm okay."

Chapter 27

When Derek woke up, he reached instinctually toward the other half of the bed.

Empty.

Derek was still in his clothes. The shorts and T-shirt were tangled and slightly sweaty from being slept in. He vaguely remembered falling asleep against Dylan's chest while Tom Hanks spelled F-O-X, and Dylan saying he should go take a "nap" in the actual bedroom. He must have made it upstairs.

He pried one eye open to check his phone.

DYLAN
You passed out at 5:30. I took Gus for his walk and gave him his meds and food.

DYLAN
The paint is wet in the bedroom downstairs.

Another set of messages came in this morning about an hour ago.

DYLAN
I got pulled onto a job late last night. Your dog found this confusing and seemed to think I needed more exercise. Took him for his walk, so if you see this when you wake up, you can just go back to sleep. Seems like you really need it.

DYLAN
Don't worry about Gus, he fell asleep after watching
Heath Ledger serenade Julia Stiles (3rd time tonight).

With a glowing sensation beneath his sternum, Derek rolled over and was unconscious in seconds.

The next time he opened his eyes, sunlight burned them. His hand bumped into his phone on the bed as he tried to move.

He'd slept close to fifteen hours total.

Had he *ever* done that before? The combination of helping Dylan with the repairs and working at the hospital, and the possibly lingering effects from that head injury, had taken a toll. At least after today, he had two more full days off before his next run of six shifts in a row.

He rolled over and clutched the comforter.

He loved Dylan's bed. It wasn't just the mattress. They had spent yesterday afternoon watching movies on the new one Derek had bought for his old, sagging queen bedframe, and it was fine, but it still didn't feel like this. He probably shouldn't have splurged on that higher-end mattress, but that cost was a drop in the bucket compared to the rest of everything. Technically, he couldn't afford *anything* right now with half his home bare studs and rubble.

Come to think of it, Bare Studs and Rubble sounded like the name of a postindustrial gay strip club. He'd have to save that one for Felicity.

These goddamn Gallaghers were rubbing off on him.

Quite literally in Dylan's case.

While Derek had always been ideologically against begging for anything in the bedroom, he was becoming increasingly obsessed with the idea of touching Dylan.

Going slow had given Derek plenty of time to imagine all the different scenarios he wanted. At least he'd gotten to spend half of yesterday snuggled up with him. It had been jarring how natural it had felt even with his sister there. That half of a gummy probably was part of it. He'd have to find out where Felicity got them.

Low sounds of Dylan talking on a phone call while typing furiously carried through the door.

God, he was *still* working?

Dylan needed sleep too.

Or maybe Derek could just help the guy relax . . . But slow. Derek could go slow.

He texted back and forth with Olive about what had happened with Felicity and Carol. Olive demanded to meet Felicity, and Derek promised that she would. He'd nearly dozed off again when his phone buzzed.

> JONI
> Want to jog in the park?

> DEREK
> You hate jogging.

> JONI
> So do you.

> DEREK
> You make a good point.

> JONI
> Meet you at your place in ten minutes?

> DEREK
> I'm upstairs actually.

> JONI
> Ah. Ok. Interesting.

∗∗∗

When Derek came down the hall toward the front door in his running clothes, he stopped so suddenly he nearly tripped. "Holy shit . . ." he said, taking in the scene.

He'd only ever seen Dylan work hunched over his laptop on the couch. But now, he sat at a fancy up-and-down desk inside what Derek had always thought was just a locked storage closet. It was the kind of thing advertised in *Sky Mall* or some shit. Four large monitors. He also had a laptop and a tablet. Every now and then he would stop to scribble something into the open spiral notebook in front of him. He adjusted his large headphones and gnawed on his bottom lip, making the lip look slightly bee stung in the screen light.

Dylan stretched his neck to either side with a small groan. His hair stuck out at all angles. There were three Diet Mountain Dew cans next to that cardiologist nightmare of an energy drink they'd all taken "shots" of yesterday. The drinks surrounded an apparently untouched bowl of apple slices spread with peanut butter.

At least the man had thought about consuming something with nutrients.

An alarm dinged on Dylan's phone. He silenced it and spun around in the chair. Seeing Derek evidently startled him, because he almost fell off the chair as he tried to pull off his headphones.

"Steady there." Derek grabbed hold of the chair before it toppled.

"Thanks." Dylan smiled sheepishly and then yawned. "Morning."

"This is some secret identity–level technology. A mini-Bat Cave." Derek scanned the equipment. "Why didn't I know this was here?"

Dylan laughed. "Definitely not as fancy as all that. I guess you've usually been at work when I've had to run meetings. If it's just emails the laptop's fine, but for this kind of crisis I need a real system. You sleep okay?"

"Like a rock. You've been at this all night?"

"Except for walking Gus and replaying his chosen entertainment."

"Thanks for handling stuff so I could sleep."

"No prob." He scratched at his hair. "Heading out?"

"Meeting Joni for a run." Derek paused. "Can I . . . can I grab you anything while I'm out? Anything to eat, I mean."

"Nah, I'll be fine. Stopped for a snack a couple hours ago after . . ." Dylan checked his watch again and then gave the untouched bowl of cut fruit a confused look. "I guess I never ate it after taking Gus out. Huh." The preciousness in his baffled and bloodshot eyes gave Derek a very confusing impulse to feed the poor man himself. By hand. Like he was a sad, homesick puppy.

Well, that was some weird, kinky shit.

"I could bring you back coffee? Also, do you even drink coffee?" Derek eyed the soda cans.

"Sometimes. I've got a good espresso machine at my house. The drip one here's shit but Uncle Sean won't get rid of it. I don't know how you and Felicity drink that sludge. I'm picky about coffee."

"Probably because you've never had to survive on hospital break room—wait, can we get back to the fact you have a house? You have an actual house somewhere?"

"Oh right. Guess we haven't talked about that either." Dylan took off his glasses, squinted, and then put them back on. "It's rented out right now, which is why it wasn't an option for me to stay there after the disaster."

"You're an onion, Dylan Gallagher."

The buzzing sound made Dylan's eyes shift to his phone. He silenced a call. "Before I forget, I got pulled into this thing with a new client. They want me on-site in Palo Alto for the next round of demos, and I'm not sure I'll be able to get out of it."

"Oh. Uh—how long will you be gone?"

"A week or so? It's not settled yet. It just means I probably won't be able to get the last stretch of work done on the apartment as quickly as I'd hoped." Derek's first thought hadn't been about the apartment work at all. He'd just been sad at the idea of Dylan leaving when they'd just gotten started with . . . whatever this was.

"No big deal on the timeline." Derek scanned Dylan's face. "Will you be able to take a break soon?"

"Should be. I hope you have a good run . . ." Dylan's eyes drifted back to his workspace as he yawned again. He seemed to get tunnel vision in task mode.

"I'll see you later."

"Oh." Dylan touched his back. "Real quick, still want to cut my hair later, or should I try to find a barber shop? I'm sure somewhere could fit me in."

"I'm definitely going to cut it. Just make sure to evict whatever squirrel's living in it now when you shower."

Dylan gave him a mock glare. "So mean."

"Sorry." Derek ruffled the hair as if actually trying to dislodge a small furry mammal.

Dylan caught his hand, and as Derek yanked it back, Dylan followed the inertia. Derek pressed his hand to Dylan's waist to steady him. As Dylan's chin lifted, their teasing movements stilled. Derek's thumb brushed over the sandpaper stubble on Dylan's cheeks, as his fingers held the angle of his jaw.

"I looked for you when I woke up." Derek couldn't believe he said this aloud.

Happy surprise lit Dylan's features. "Really?"

Nodding, Derek pulled him into a hug.

Another work call came in on the monitor behind them.

"You need to get that?"

"I'll call him back in a second. Snack first." Dylan leaned his full weight into the hug, pressing one hand into Derek's lower back and reaching the other up to cradle his neck.

Derek pulled back enough so he could see the shade of purple beneath Dylan's eyes. "Seriously, you going to get some sleep soon?"

"The update has to go out to California as soon as possible. The team needs to have the fixes to test everything before it goes to their jackass boss the next morning in Singapore."

"This is making my brain hurt."

Dylan squeezed Derek tighter. "Can we do the haircut around five? I can take a long nap and then shower, so I can human again."

"I like this plan."

Gus hustled over and whined at the door, which meant Joni was probably here, but with Dylan's body pressed against his, Derek was regretting make the running plan. Especially since mesh shorts were as unforgiving as scrubs. "That's probably Joni."

"Should we start taking bets?" Dylan said with a smirk.

"On what?"

"On how many times a redhead will interrupt us when you have a—"

"You're a dick, Dylan Gallagher."

Dylan's smug eyes flickered downward as he patted Derek once on the ass. "Enjoy your run, babe. Think about baseball."

Baseball only made Derek remember how adorable Dylan looked in that Orioles cap. "You're the actual worst."

"You really think so?"

"Be right there, Joni." Derek called to the door. Giving the too-tempting man a kiss, Derek shoved his hand into his pocket along with his keys and phone, hoping that would disguise the incriminating bulge. "Unfortunately, not at all."

Chapter 28

"I'm going to puke." Derek leaned on a bench near the rippling stripe of Carroll Creek.

"Deep breaths," Joni said, but then she gagged too. She flopped down on the grass as she tried to suck down the last drops from her water bottle.

"You said we were going to go slow."

Through her own huffs and puffs, Joni lifted an accusatory finger. "I *was* going to go slow, but you kept speeding up."

"No, *you* kept speeding up."

"Did not. Remember when you said *'I'm going to beat you to that bridge'*?"

"I was *joking*." The horizontal nature of the soft grass was too tempting to resist. He found a cool patch a few feet away from Joni. It was way too humid today.

"I didn't want to slow you down. Seemed like you were processing something. I was trying to be supportive. Goddamn it." Joni grabbed her stomach. "If I vomit and pass out, you're fucking carrying me back to my aunt's house. Why are there so many goddamn hills in this stupid state?"

"Can I remind you that you used to live in *Denver*?" He managed to lift his head to look at her. "I don't think I've ever heard you curse before." The harsh profanity jarred coming out in her ethereal, velvety voice.

"That's a story time." She wheezed a laugh. "In med school, I accidently said a particular word that begins with *C* and rhymes with 'bunt' and was overheard by a very verbally precocious three-year-old who had escaped from his mother during a vaccination clinic."

"Oh no."

"He ran down the hall singing the word over and over again to the tune of 'Old McDonald.'"

"Oh *no*. So . . . here's a bunt, there's a bunt—"

"Everywhere a bunt, bunt." Joni covered her flushed face. "I thought I was going to get kicked out of school. In my defense, I'd just had a run-in with an obstetric rotation attending . . . and my goodness, that guy was a real—"

"Bunt?"

"Exactly."

"So, no more swearing? Cold-bunting-turkey?"

Joni shrugged. "After that incident was never traced back to me, I thought karma was on my side." She looked in her water bottle again, as if to verify that it was still empty. "Are you going to tell me what you're working off? How are things with Dylan? Did you go up and talk to him after I left the other night?"

"Dylan's great, actually. Well, mostly. He's . . . never what I expect. Usually in this hilarious and completely disarming way."

"I'm sensing a 'bunt.'"

Derek huffed a laugh. "No bunts." After a few minutes of labored breathing, Derek rolled onto his side. "Can I ask you a completely hypothetical question that if you ever talk about it with anyone else, I will personally go to your med school and find that attending and reveal your secret?"

"Wow. You just immediately turned my deep, dark secret around on me to use as leverage. Bold." Exhaustion muted her feigned outrage. "You just said a lot of words, and I think most of my blood is pooled in my legs, but yeah, I'm not going to tell anyone."

Derek stood and extended his hand. "We need to walk, or we'll cramp."

"But ground is soft and wonderful, and legs are sad." She ran her hand over the grass with her bottom lip pouted.

"Up." He yanked her from the ground.

"Bossy." Once upright, her face went as serious as a flushed and sweaty face could be. "You can talk to me, Derek. I know it's been hard to have Olive traveling while your life has been in literal, actual shambles."

"*Hypothetically*, can you think of a reason why someone would be nervous about having sex, or mainly just like someone seeing them orgasm or whatever?" He rushed out the last part. "If this is TMI, I'm sorry."

"Not TMI." Joni was quiet, considering. She tightened her ponytail as they hobbled a few more steps. "I think there are a lot of reasons. Nervousness or discomfort with one's sexuality, former trauma or previous unhealthy sexual relationships. I mean, clinically speaking, there are medications or conditions that make it difficult to climax. Lots of reasons, most of which don't actually have anything to do with one's current sexual partner or overall interest in sex. This might be more particularly anxiety-provoking in men, given the way we treat male sexuality as a matter of course."

Derek nodded. "Makes sense. What do you mean by discomfort with one's sexuality?"

"Like . . . hmm . . . So, not to get all deep when I'm literally feeling drunk from how dead I am, but I'm het but aspec. So, in my case, I have to have a pretty strong personal connection with someone before sexual attraction grows. My sister calls this *demisexual*, but honestly, I just thought I was a little different. I didn't know this was a thing other people experienced until recently. My last boyfriend was pretty . . . confused. At first."

Derek scanned Joni, who was twisting her hands together. In his personal experience, every time he invited someone into knowing about his sexual identity, it felt like a small test with big stakes. It was like whispering *Are you going to be comfortable with my existence?* into a void and just hoping what came out didn't attack you.

He squeezed her shoulder. "Thanks for telling me and trusting me."

She mirrored his smile. "I'm comfortable with who I am, but it's easy to feel like your brain's broken when everyone else around you just seems to be sexing up everything that moves at the slightest impulse."

"Hmm . . ."

"Anything about that seem familiar?"

"It actually reminds me of when he was telling me about his ADHD. It was a major brainfuck before he was diagnosed."

"Could be related for sure. *Oh.*" Joni pointed to a small convenience store at the corner. "Let's stop there and buy more water before we get heatstroke. It would be humiliating to get carted into our own ER."

After guzzling about a liter of water each, Joni held the cold extra bottle to her sweaty forehead. "I just read something—oh whatever, my sister sent me a TikTok about something . . ."

He chuckled.

"People with ADHD have pretty high rates of sexual dysfunction and anxiety. It's reasonable it could be connected."

"He takes Adderall for the ADHD. Guess he used to be on other meds too."

Joni shrugged. "It could be a combination of things." She led him over to a bench and slumped down on it. "If you're asking all these questions . . . seems like you really like him. Hasn't been something I've seen you do over the last year. Not that I'm judging."

"After that night when I drama-vomited into all that delicious Korean food, it . . . it was like I needed that. I needed to tell someone everything. So . . . thanks. For being there."

"You needed to do a little honest processing." She scrutinized him. "Much healthier than holding it all in."

"I still miss Jake, but I'm recognizing that I built the relationship up so much in my head I didn't give anyone else a chance."

Her mouth quirked to the side. "And you're giving Dylan a chance?"

"Maybe just hoping he'll give me a chance . . ." Hopefully his post-run sweat hid whatever embarrassing blush was burning his cheeks. Now he just needed to get Dylan to be comfortable enough with him. He was okay with how things were, but he wanted to make sure Dylan trusted him. How did you even go about doing that?

"Olive's going to lose it when she sees this."

"Sees what?"

"That she was absolutely right about Dylan."

"Fuck off."

"When does she get back? Still pushed out to after Labor Day?"

"That's the current plan." He spread his elbows out, cradling his head in his hands. When he turned back Joni's smile had become enigmatic. "What?"

"It's just nice watching two people like you and Olive . . . find your . . . people. It's just nice to know that anyone can still have this. That this is possible."

Derek tilted his head. "Have what?"

"This lovesick-with-unquenchable-sudden-joy thing you're radiating right now." She made a small spiraling motion at his face.

"I'm not radiating shit."

"*Sure.*" She started down the path toward her aunt's house.

"What happened with the boyfriend that was weird?"

She shrugged. "I moved in with him. We were together for ten years."

"Were?"

"I came here. He wants me to move back though . . ." Her tone was so flat compared to the usual Joni. "We'll see."

"Hey, Joni. You know you deserve this too, right?" He gestured to himself in a similar swirly way that she had a few minutes earlier.

"An objectively attractive and muscular male body that probably should add in a bit more cardio to his fitness routine if he wants to force his friends into grueling runs in mid-July heat?"

"I take it back. You don't deserve this at all." He went serious again. "You know what I meant, dummy. You deserve stupid, lovesick, radiant joy. If you want it, I mean."

Her mouth brimmed into a tight smile. "So, what you're saying is that you admit to having stupid, lovesick, radiant joy?"

"Fucking hell." Derek turned back toward the sidewalk, leaving her on her aunt's porch steps. "Alright, you win that round. There might be a little stupid radiant joying going on, but lovesick? Hell to the goddamn never. I'm going home. Can't handle these ludicrous accusations." He waved to her over his shoulder.

"Derek?" She jogged toward him, her auburn ponytail swaying. "Thanks for saying that. About me deserving it too." She winced. "I'd hug you, but you need a shower, because joy isn't the only thing you're radiating right now."

"Rude, Dr. Sutton. Just so damn rude." With a smirk, he headed down the path leading to his street.

He was a couple blocks away from home when his weekly alarm went off on his phone. He felt bad he had to set an alarm for this, but he didn't want to forget. He swiped to Michelle's contact. Predictably, the call rang three and a half times and then went to voicemail.

"Hey, Michelle. Just, you know, my weekly voicemail. I love you, and I miss you. Call me or come by if you're ever back in town. If a call's too much, I'd be cool with an email. A text. Morse code. Whatever. I . . . I might have a new guy in my life soon. You'd like him, I think. He's funny. And a complete dork. Just . . . just let me know how you're doing some time, okay? Bye." Derek slid the phone into his pocket.

Chapter 29

Dylan swiveled back and forth in the chair, still groggy from his daytime five-hour nap, while Derek assembled his hair-cutting stuff. After he sent the file to Chase, he'd crashed. He had slept longer than intended, which was becoming a theme lately, but that probably meant he'd needed it.

It was the type of work he loved. A concrete task with clear benchmarks for success. It wasn't like those few years when he'd been in charge of a team. Management had been a unique kind of hell. He'd been pulled in too many directions, especially with budgets. There was also the administrative HR stuff, the people stuff, and then the development work. It never ended, but nights like last night were perfect. His parents thought he was irresponsible and reckless to give up his last job with its upward trajectory and big perks. But this wasn't a demotion or a step back. This was making a choice for what worked best for his brain. Just himself and his dev work and problem-solving.

When he woke up this afternoon, a note on his pillow said Derek would be ready to cut his hair whenever, but that Dylan should sleep as long as he wanted. At some point they needed to be on the same sleep/waking schedule more consistently.

He'd grinned like a fool when he saw the small heart next to Derek's name at the bottom. Derek Chang was a *heart-next-to-his-name* guy?

Dylan needed to *chiiiiiiiiill*.

Now he was seated in a chair in Derek's kitchen with a large mirror set up in front of it. The plumbers had gone home for the day, so they were alone in the apartment. Derek's hands combed through Dylan's shower-wet hair, and it was clear from the syncopated pitter-patter response of Dylan's heart he didn't have a single ounce of chill. He'd almost ripped the guy's running clothes off earlier and sucked him off again while Derek's friend was right outside waiting and probably wondering what TF was happening.

That was the kind of chill Dylan had right now.

No chill at all.

"Do you care what I do to you?" Derek made eye contact via the mirror.

Well, honestly, I'd prefer you ripped my clothes off.

"Uh . . . not too short I guess?"

Derek smiled. "How about I keep the sides short here and the back?" His hand dragged up the back of Dylan's neck, sending a thrill straight to his core. "Use the clippers?"

His head lolled down as Derek rubbed the base of Dylan's skull. *Holy shit.* His voice was punch-drunk when he found it again. "Sounds good."

Derek kneaded firm circles down an area of tension on either side of Dylan's spine. "You need an acupuncturist or chiropractor after nights like last night."

"It was worse before I got that desk. The up and down helps a lot. I use a wobble board sometimes too."

"Does that stuff help with the ADHD too? Like with fidgeting?"

Dylan tensed. "Uh . . . with me, if I'm super focused on a task, I don't fidget. I've got to be reminded to move, pee, and—"

"Eat."

"Exactly. It's why I set alarms to take breaks. I've got a whole system now."

"Smart."

"I do fidget and can't sit still if I'm bored. Meetings. Death-by-PowerPoint-type deals. Sales calls, really anything having to do with money. School in general. Super hard. That's what all the notes home from teachers said." He affected a tone of fussy displeasure. "Dylan may be exceptionally bright, but he can't sit still and is often rude to the teachers and his peers. His study skills are nonexistent."

"Can't imagine you being rude."

Dylan studied Derek in the mirror. "I didn't mean to be. I just didn't always notice things. My parents always thought I was scatterbrained and that my issues were disciplinary. But you can't spank the ADHD out of my brain." Dylan wrinkled his nose to pull his glasses back up where they were supposed to be. "That came out wrong. My parents weren't mean or abusive or anything. Well, I think spanking *is* abusive, but they didn't do it very often with me . . . They were just out of their depth, so they did the same stuff they were raised with. My mom's parents suuucked. My situation was fine comparatively . . ."

"So . . ."

Dylan really didn't like the mix of pity and curiosity on Derek's face. "You said you'd tell me how you learned to cut hair," Dylan said, tamping down on his discomfort with talking about what it was like to grow up with his family.

"Aha. I guess I should give you my credentials, shouldn't I?" Derek slid Dylan's glasses off his face and put them on the counter.

"Only if you want to. Honestly, given that you've massaged my neck in a way that is basically hypnotic, I'd probably let you do whatever the hell you want." Whatever was being sprayed onto Dylan's hair smelled amazing.

"Excellent." Derek started at the back. "I'm going to do a small fade here."

"Hypnotized, remember."

"Fair enough." The clippers buzzed. Derek's eyebrows pulled together in that irresistible scrunch as he worked. "After my dad died, my mom went back to work full time. She'd been working part time as a CPA for most of my childhood, doing the books for local businesses, that kind of thing, but then she joined a bigger firm to get better benefits."

"That must've been hard."

"It was a transition. My sister Amy was nine at the time and Michelle was six. They were both these two little angels. My mom would drop them at school, and then I'd pick them up and walk them home every day. Somewhere along the way, they got it in their heads they wanted to be ballerinas."

"Reasonable."

"I found a local studio—well, Olive helped because her sister took ballet classes. Olive and I were pretty much inseparable then. Emo high school misfits and all the clichés that go with that. Chuck Taylors. Dyed side parts. The works."

"Still don't buy you as a misfit."

"This area was different back then. I was gay. Also, I was the most middling student imaginable. And I was also about five feet two and ninety pounds until sixteen."

"Wow, you must've shot up fast after that. I was a late bloomer too, but no one did shit to me because they knew my brothers would kick their asses." Dylan laughed.

"So, the girls needed to have these hair buns for their classes and recitals, and their hair kept falling out." A small frown worried Derek's mouth as he changed the setting on the clippers. "When my dad got sick, he told me that sometimes I needed to take initiative because a lot was going to fall on my shoulders."

"That's a ton of pressure for a sixteen-year-old."

"Ha, I was *thirteen* at the time. But kind of like what you said about your parents . . . looking back, my dad was obviously terrified and barely holding it together. He loved my mom and sisters more than anything." Derek swiveled the desk chair back and forth to examine the evenness of the sections he had done so far. "I think he knew it'd get bad. Just don't think he knew it would get bad that fast."

"Shit . . ."

"It was absolute shit." Derek grabbed a pair of shiny silver shears out of a leather case. "One day, Michelle came out of class crying. Amy always let the bad stuff roll off her, so I could never get anything out of her, but Michelle was always a heart-on-her-sleeve kid. Even then."

"What happened?"

"A kid in her class kept singing some truly offensive rhyme and making fun of both of them."

"How badly did you want to beat up that kid?"

"Given that the culprit was an eight-year-old girl, I took a different route. I waited until the classes were done that day. Then I, an undersized emo boy in ripped skinny jeans and a thrifted concert T-shirt, marched into the studio to confront the teacher. Shockingly, the teacher profusely apologized and said the little girl wouldn't be welcome in classes again."

"Good."

"Wasn't expecting that. Usually, in my experience with teachers and stuff, white people tend to just brush off racism as 'harmless' when it comes from kids."

"That's bullshit."

"Yup." Derek pulled up sections of Dylan's hair and trimmed the ends. "The studio owner wanted to talk about Michelle. She thought that Michelle could be a rare talent. Said she had perfect turn out, amazing feet. An innate understanding of how to move her body."

"Wow."

"I had no idea what it meant at the time. But she also asked if my mom could start doing their hair before class because it kept coming down from their buns and getting in their way." Derek pulled a wet comb up through another section of Dylan's hair. "Unfortunately, this was March when this all happened."

"Oh . . . Tax season."

"Sure was. I couldn't bug her with my sisters' hair. My dad told me to figure it out on my own. I tried. Olive tried too.

Olive's hair was totally different, and really, Olive is still hopeless at her own hair. So, again, I marched into another place. In this case it was the salon three doors down from the ballet studio, and I begged someone there to show me how to do my sisters' hair. This was before YouTube tutorials. I didn't have a lot of options."

Dylan was surprised to feel tears prick at the corners of his eyes. "You're a good brother."

Derek ignored the compliment. "I hung out there while the girls took classes. Shari, a Korean woman who worked there, showed me how to work with different textures and ways to make it stay put and what products worked best. Stuff that wouldn't damage it. She taught me how to braid. I didn't even know what a bobby pin was. All that shit." Derek swiveled the chair the other way, facing Dylan away from the mirror. "To make the rest of a long story short, I started working at the salon. Shampooing, then apprenticeship. I went to school, got licensed. I worked four years full time as a hair stylist so I could stay close by while my sisters were young."

"When did you do nursing?"

Derek rubbed some other thick product onto his hand that smelled like lilacs and then pulled his fingertips through Dylan's hair. "When Olive started looking into nursing after undergrad, it made me think back to what classes I'd actually liked in high school. The girls were doing great, and my mom's job was less demanding at that point. I started thinking about whether I wanted to keep working at the salon or just do something different."

"Long time to be doing something you fell into."

"Exactly." Derek crouched slightly, so he was at eye level with Dylan in the office chair. He stretched out a couple of sections of wet strands. When their gazes met, this sweet twinkle came into Derek's eyes and one half of his mouth perked up. Appearing satisfied with the cut, Derek stood and pushed the hair back, twisting and spiraling his fingers to shape curls. "I always knew I liked using my hands. Science and anatomy interested me. I was really into The Discovery Channel's *Medical Mysteries* shows. I narrowed it down to physical therapy and nursing. I took classes at night, then I got into nursing school at the same place as Olive for the BSN program while she did the master's program. PT school would've taken a lot longer. Made the decision easy. I cut hair to make money all through school so my mom wouldn't worry about me. She could save for Amy's college and all of Michelle's dance classes . . ." Derek spun the chair around. "What do you think?"

Dylan's mouth fell open. It was just as Derek had described. He left the top almost as long as it had been, but whatever magic potion he'd used had tamed it. Instead of wild and frizzy, it was controlled and tailored. Honestly, Dylan thought his hair looked pretty damn hot. He stood to get a closer look in the mirror. "Shit, you're really good at this."

Derek unsnapped the cape around his neck with a nimble flick of fingers. "Yep, I am." He put a crooked section of hair back in place. His fingers lingered around Dylan's ears, his hip pushing up against Dylan's from behind. "I bet it's the best haircut you've ever had."

"Cocky asshole." Dylan grabbed his glasses from where Derek had put them on the counter.

"That too."

"I hadn't even thought about it, but it's probably good I won't show up to that meeting in California looking sloppy."

"Did the timing get worked out yet?"

Dylan frowned. "A week from Thursday. Just got the email before I came down."

Derek grabbed a broom and swept up the hair into a dustpan.

"Hey, I can do that." Dylan put his hand over Derek's to try to take the broom.

Derek shrugged. "It takes a second. You and your sister are literally replacing the drywall in my bedroom for the cost of materials. Just let me do this. Kay?"

"Kay." Dylan grinned.

Derek brushed hair off his shoulder. "You should change your shirt. That drape's old and some hair got through it in the back." He found Dylan a T-shirt from his clean laundry hamper. Derek must have washed some of Dylan's clothes with his own earlier.

Suppressing another of what Dylan was sure would be an extremely dopey grin, Dylan pulled off his shirt.

"What's that?" Derek said with genuine surprise.

Confused, Dylan looked down.

Derek snorted and he walked right over and touched the straight barbell at Dylan's nipple. "How did I not notice this?"

A small shiver went through Dylan as goose bumps rose all over his freckled skin.

"It was dark both times you've seen me shirtless, and it's pretty small."

"You really are like an onion."

"That's a good thing?" Dylan's eyes closed. Derek's fingertip was barely grazing the skin of his chest.

"Definitely a good thing. This piercing's hot as fuck."

Derek's hand trailed down the soft skin of Dylan's stomach. Normally, Dylan would have felt some insecurity with this kind of thing, but he was surprised to find his body leaning toward the touch instead of flexing away from it.

Smiling, Derek hooked two fingers through Dylan's belt loops, pulling him closer. "Tell me what you want. Even if it's just kissing. Whatever." There was no pressure there . . . but there was heat. Nothing about Derek's behavior over the past weeks had been what Dylan expected. And for the first time in possibly ever, Dylan wasn't nervous or panicked about the possibility of what could happen between them. Moments like this usually sent his brain into a boiling eddy of worst-case scenarios, but instead his mind simply simmered.

Dylan *trusted* him.

The silence held. Derek seemed to be giving Dylan the time he needed to sort out what he wanted.

What *did* he want?

Chapter 30

Dylan slid his hand around the base of Derek's neck and pulled Derek's mouth to his.

And like the previous time, every taste was better than the last and every graze of Derek's lips over his made him want more . . . more . . . more. He abandoned his glasses on the counter and pulled Derek down the hallway to the living room. He didn't let Derek get more than an inch away as he did. Everything sharpened with the firmness of his decision.

He wanted this.

Derek's fingertips dug into the muscles of Dylan's lower back. That solid pressure grounded Dylan. Made him feel more certain that everything about this moment was right. That *everything* about this man was safe.

They fell in a heap onto the bed. The sheets were fresh.

Of course they were.

Everything was perfect. The warm weight of Derek's body on top of his. The slide of Derek's hands over his shoulders as Dylan pulled Derek's shirt off.

Derek's cock was an enticing pressure on Dylan's thigh, and Dylan's own erection strained against his pants, practically begging to be let free. "What do *you* want, Derek?"

"I want to make you feel good. Just tell me what to do."

"Your hand . . . hand would be good on my dick. Maybe with you behind me." He undid the button of his pants with trembling fingers.

Derek pulled Dylan's jeans off with steady hands. His rather wicked smile relaxed any lingering tension in Dylan's chest.

"Do you have—"

"Yes." Derek kicked off his pants and opened a drawer on the nightstand, which, like most of his furniture, was crammed into that front room.

Christ. Dylan swallowed.

Derek opened the bottle and warmed some of the clear slippery liquid on his hand. "Tell me what I can do."

Dylan turned on his side, and Derek lay down behind him, molding their bodies together so that Derek's own solid arousal pressed against Dylan's ass. A low rumble in Dylan's throat. Derek slipped his thumbs beneath the elastic of Dylan's boxers and pushed them down. Derek's right leg lifted over Dylan's, tightening their bodies together. As Dylan ground his ass into Derek, he felt a satisfying shudder from the man behind him.

Dylan's tip was dripping so much precum, Derek really didn't even need the lube. He gripped the length and gave it a gentle, almost tender, squeeze.

As his body jolted and he moaned, Dylan felt Derek's smile against the bunching muscles of his back.

"Smug," Dylan muttered.

"How'd you know?" Derek's teeth grazed over Dylan's back.

"I . . . I . . . *fuck.*" Dylan moved his hips again, looking for every bit of slick friction. "You can . . . you could bite me if you want?"

Not needing to hear that invitation twice, Derek bit down on Dylan's shoulder, just hard enough to cause a tiny edge of pain as his hand sped up.

Dylan's entire body gave an involuntary thrust. "Jesus Christ."

"If you keep rubbing your ass over my cock like that, I'm going to jizz in my shorts like a horny, dry-humping teenager." Derek spoke through clenched teeth.

With a smug smile of his own, Dylan continued exactly what he had been doing.

Derek kissed up the angle of Dylan's neck and licked his earlobe.

Despite Derek's warning, Dylan pushed his ass greedily against Derek, the firm contact following the rhythm of his hand.

"Oh—" Derek's hand matched Dylan's urgency, but Dylan didn't want it to end.

Derek's mouth was on Dylan's shoulder again. He bit down a little harder than last time.

"*Fuck*. Don't stop . . ."

"I'm so close too, just keep it going with that perfect ass." Derek licked over the small indentations his teeth had left in Dylan's skin.

Without warning, Derek's other hand slid underneath Dylan, changing the angle of his body so he could touch that barbell. Derek fondled that pierced nipple between his thumb and forefinger, pinching it.

"*Christ!*" Dylan nearly roared it this time.

His body shook. He let sensation take over, every part of him erupting and unleashing and feeling that perfect moment of release.

When he opened his eyes, Derek's gaze met his. There was no smugness. Just a sweet, almost reverent smile.

Dylan rolled. A new need surged through him. A confidence he rarely felt in the bedroom bloomed within him, making him so hungry for more. Making him want to do and say things he'd never felt comfortable doing or saying with anyone else. He wanted the words that had only echoed in his fantasies.

Dylan didn't bother with the lube. Derek's cock was as wet with precum as Dylan's had been. He took the length in his hand. "This okay?"

"Y-yeah."

Dylan leaned his mouth to Derek's ear without letting his hand's rhythm falter. He tugged the sensitive lobe with his teeth and then spoke into Derek's ear. "I can't wait to feel that perfect cock fuck me against my bedframe."

Derek groaned.

"I want you to ride me so hard I'm going to feel you for a week."

Derek wrapped an arm around Dylan and pulled him close, leaving only enough space between them to allow for Dylan to keep that unfaltering pace.

"Dylan . . . oh, *god*."

Every movement of Derek's body begged him not to stop. Dylan's voice was still hoarse from his own climax. "I want you to bite me while you do it. I want you to leave marks next time." Every filthy word pushed Derek closer to the brink.

Giving in, Derek gasped. He came against the friction of Dylan's unmerciful hand and spilled himself on Dylan's chest. His body vibrated through those final guided shockwaves.

Dylan whispered increasingly depraved things into Derek's ear until Derek's body was absolutely still.

Derek's voice was a wrecked rasp when he spoke. "You know . . . I thought you were a good boy."

And again, that person that Dylan never thought he could be with anyone spoke again. "Oh babe . . ." He pressed a kiss to Derek's slack mouth. "That totally depends on your definition of good."

Chapter 31

Watching Dylan come was . . . *god*, the man was beautiful with his cheeks flushed and lips parted. He thought watching that mouth on his cock had been the hottest thing ever, but watching Dylan come . . . Holy shit. It was better than any porn Derek had ever seen.

The light from the door set all of the ink on Dylan's body in accentuated contrast.

"I want to know what the tattoos all mean."

Dylan laughed and stroked the back of Derek's arm. "They're all pretty nerdy."

"I had no doubt. If I was scared off by your dorkiness, I wouldn't have let you suck me off that first time."

Dylan snorted. "Hey, cool guy. Tell me again about your verbal dissertation about Christina Aguilera's character arc in *Burlesque* and how you feel like it's a modern retelling of the hero's journey—"

"I was half-drunk, and Olive baited me into it that night."

"Olive's a good egg."

"This one." Derek touched a tattoo near Dylan's shoulder.

"It's 'Gallagher' in old Irish in some fancy script my sister picked with the number six. All six of us got it on vacation the year Felicity turned eighteen."

"This one." Derek's hand dragged over Dylan's chest.

Dylan grinned. "Elvish. 'Not all who wander are lost.' Somewhat cliché, but I was in college."

Derek's fingers paused to play with the metallic ball. "Does it hurt if I do this?"

"Nope . . . had that since college too. Weird phase."

"This one looks familiar." Derek traced the symbol on Dylan's lower left ribs. "Oh, and what's the jagged line on your forearm?"

"That's the *Star Wars* rebel symbol. Also, a cliché, but oh well. I like it. On my forearm, it's the crack in Amy Pond's wall. An incredibly niche *Doctor Who* thing. Niche even in geekdom."

"Even niche for a dork? Impressive." Derek touched along the elastic of Dylan's tight gray boxer briefs, letting his fingers tease a few millimeters beneath the seam. Dylan's breathing hitched. "This?"

"Oh . . ." Dylan pulled the elastic down low, so the entire tattoo was visible. "Bridge Four symbol. Stormlight Archive. One of my favorite series of all time, actually."

"The big one on your back? All those lines and circles?"

"Ah . . . That one is probably the dorkiest. It's a line art rendering of a schematic of an Alan Turing design." He turned on his side, giving Derek a better look at the delicate ink streaking across it and over the lean muscles. Dylan's stomach growled.

"Have you eaten anything yet?"

"Uh . . ."

Derek pushed him over to the edge of the bed. "Go get your shit. We're going to get dinner."

Dylan just grinned at him.

"Go." Derek pointed to the door. "You're driving because my car's being weird."

"Kay."

Derek's face spread wide on reflex. "Kay."

⁕⁕⁕

Derek handed his menu to the server. Dylan hadn't even looked before ordering. "You've been to Sumittra a lot before?"

"Yeah, love Thai food." Dylan leaned forward with his elbows on the table. "And feminist prose . . . and angry-girl music of the indie rock—"

"How many times have you watched that movie?" Derek chuckled.

"It chills Gus out when the noise from downstairs makes him anxious. And Heath Ledger is a snack . . ."

"Agreed." Derek grinned. "I was asking because you didn't actually read the menu."

Dylan's ears went pink, and he rubbed his hand over the now shorter areas of his hair, pausing for a second as if he didn't immediately remember why there was less hair. "I'm the sort of person who orders the same thing over and over. Decisions are stressful for me." He coughed. "It's—uh—not that I don't try new things, I just find something I love and then . . . it's weird, I know it's weird. It's why I like watching movies over and over again when I fixate on one, come to think about it."

"Dylan, I wasn't saying it in a gotcha way, I was just asking. Not weird. It's fine." Normally, Derek might have been tempted to tease him a little, but he was learning Dylan's cues. Seeing when his discomfort seemed to be motivated by embarrassment—not even embarrassment, something sadder . . . like shame.

Dylan exhaled. "Okay, cool."

"Out of curiosity, was this a thing with an ex or something?"

Dylan fiddled with the corner of his napkin, flicking his thumb over it again and again while he spoke. "In the Bay area, a lot of people are big foodies because there are great restaurants and everything. It's actually how I got into the 'fish tank' cooking." Dylan's smirk sent a floaty feeling into Derek's stomach. "This guy just kept harping on it at every business dinner. How my taste is like a kid's. Guess it made me self-conscious. Still working through a lot of that stuff with my therapist. You know. We all have shit."

"I know I have shit." Derek leaned forward.

"I think everyone in the building after you drink too much coffee knows you have shit."

"So salty today with your new haircut."

Dylan wrinkled his face. "I'm always salty." He lowered his hand so that it was palm up in the middle of the table.

"I like it." Derek's hand pushed forward, leaving a sliver of space between their fingertips.

"I can tell." Dylan slid his fingers beneath Derek's.

Derek traced the lines of Dylan's palm, enjoying the way the man's eyes softened behind the thick lenses of his glasses. Every time Derek stopped tracing, Dylan's hand gave a tiny shake as if to encourage him to keep going. It was like when he was petting Gus, and that thought made Derek grin.

"What?"

"Nothing."

"Tell me."

"No."

"Well then tell me something else."

Derek squeezed Dylan's hand in his. "It's been a really long time since I've done this. Really, I'm not sure I've ever done *this*." He twitched his head indicating the space between them.

"Eat delicious Gaeng Daeng after cutting a hot computer nerd's hair?"

"Now who's a cocky asshole?"

"Still you." Dylan let the longer hair on top fall diagonally across his forehead. "And same. I had a few relationships in college, but it was more experimentation. Figuring things out."

"And recently?"

"I had one long-term partner in California, but things weren't great. I still work with his company. Chase—he's the manager of the main team I still work with a lot. And that's part of the reason I decided to start my own company. My anxiety and intrusive thoughts were out of control. A psychiatrist started me on some new meds, and Chase, that ex, took my mental health symptoms very personally. And the med side effects were . . . sometimes hard to manage."

Maybe Joni really was a witch.

Dylan sipped his water. "That's why trust is a big deal to me." His voice was confident and clear, almost rehearsed. As if he had mentally scripted this hypothetical conversation. "I have trouble trusting myself, so it's really important for me to trust a partner even with the little stuff. I . . . I need to feel safe. If I don't feel safe, I end up feeling broken."

"I get that."

"What about you?"

"Not a relationship guy before, but now . . . I don't know." Derek was not ashamed to say that he was utilizing all his various physical powers to smolder the shit out of the man in front of him. That unsubtle smolder broke the tension of the moment because Dylan seemed to be suppressing a laugh. "Also, I'm trying not to be a jealous jerk and ask whether this douchebag Chase will be at your meeting."

"He'll be there, but trust me, nothing to worry about." A flush spread over Dylan's freckled cheeks. "That *is* why I wanted to mention it before I went, though. Just since there's some history there you should probably know about it, especially since we still work together . . . but *jealous*, huh? Now are you saying . . ."

"Don't know exactly what I'm saying." Feeling more uncertain, not about Dylan, but about himself and what he had to offer someone, Derek stroked the pulse point of Dylan's wrist to remind himself that the person in front of him was real and things had been so . . . *nice* since they stopped hating each other. "Are you good with doing this?" Derek couldn't believe the words that were coming out of his mouth.

Was this really a *DTR* moment? There had always been something about Dylan. His disarming smile. The way they could banter but not feel unbalanced. He made that insecure, dad-less, emo teenager inside Derek feel safe. Just as much as the muscled-up cocky asshole side of himself was safe. It was like both halves of who he was and who he'd been could be real. Dylan was this anxious, overly self-conscious nerd half the time, but then he was also this brilliant and sharp-witted guy who could talk shit and take it too. Derek . . . liked them both.

Before Dylan could answer, a server brought them their appetizer and Dylan's tea.

Dylan poured tea into the mug. "I'm still kind of a mess. I'm figuring stuff out, but since we're on the subject of the past." His spoon scraped against porcelain. "I do also think I should say . . . I . . . uh . . . the thing with your friend. Jake Murphy. If you *want* to know what happened . . ."

Derek stiffened. "I shouldn't have made assumptions about it, and it's really not any of my business."

"I don't want you thinking the worst about me."

"I don't. *Really.*"

Over the last few weeks, Derek had thought about Jake a lot. Not just about the version Derek idealized, but about all of him. He didn't need to know the details to trust the man in front of him.

Derek cleared his throat. "I *do* want to know the story about your mysterious house. You still haven't told me what the deal is with that."

"Right. The house." Dylan's face brightened. "I was visiting home at Christmas and was on one of my 'prescribed mental health wellness walks,' and I found this gorgeous fixer-upper near my parents' house for sale, and I just bought it. Interest rates were low, and it had everything I wanted."

"Impulsive."

"Something I've always struggled with. With all the toxic stress of working in Silicon Valley, I barely had a personal life in California after breaking up with Chase and starting my company. It's why my brothers initially tried to set me up when I came back for Christmas. They were trying to give me a reason to come back for good. Actually, I found my house on that same trip back. But when I buried myself in the renovation, I barely felt the days turn into months until two years went by. Time just passed. My family noticed I *still* didn't have a life and that's why the app profile thing happe—*ugh*. I'm sorry to bring that up again."

"You don't have to apologize. Jake and the dating app thing . . . it was all a long time ago." Talking about Jake had gotten easier. But that added a new layer to his loss. A prick of guilt digging in deeper with each happy moment spent forgetting what he'd lost. Derek looked down, finding his hand in his lap, not remembering when he'd stopped holding Dylan's hand. When his eyes returned to the man across the table, Dylan eyed him with a new curiosity.

"What?" Derek tilted his head.

Dylan cleared his throat. "This might be a really weird question, but did you and Jake date? Or . . . anything?"

Derek's hand curled into a fist around his napkin. The server appeared to deliver their entrées, and Derek sent a prayer of thanks to the kitchen gods that their timing gave him another few extra moments to figure out what the hell to say.

"Jake is . . . was . . . you know, he was Olive's brother. Uh . . . we were *all* really close. She would've had a conniption if I . . . if we had started dating." He pushed a large bite of noodles in his mouth even though he was less hungry than he had been five minutes ago. Chewing gave his mouth something to do that didn't make him feel guilty. *Because you're lying by omission, jackass.* "Don't get me wrong, he was a great friend to me." He dropped his chopsticks on the side of the bowl and grabbed his water. No matter how much water Derek drank, he still had a weird burning feeling in his chest that wasn't from his dish's spice level. How could he even explain about Jake *now*? He didn't even know how he was feeling about it or what anything between them had meant.

"Oh okay, I thought . . . I don't know. Never mind. I don't always read nonverbal cues right . . . probably should mention that."

Derek's stomach roiled, and he wet his dry lips. He should walk his implication back because he *did* trust Dylan. Come to think of it, during that shockingly intimate haircut, he had just talked about his dad and his dad's death more than he had in *years*. More than he had even with Olive. He certainly never talked about Dad ever with his mom or sisters because it was too hard for them.

"How's your mom doing? I feel like you haven't been over there as much lately as you said you usually are. Did you see her today?"

"*No*, she wasn't there when I went by for my stylist kit. Normally, I come over around this time every month to help with yard work, but she said it was already done." Derek's face lifted, relieved by the subject change. But the reminder stirred a sense of unease. How long had it been since he'd heard from his mom? "I was supposed to go over tomorrow too, but I still haven't heard back. My sister Amy's trying to figure it out. I'm trying to not get in the middle of it for once."

"Probably wise if your sisters and mom are anything like mine. Is the sister you bought the apartment from still close by?"

Derek twisted his chopsticks in his food. "I don't know where she is right now."

Dylan's quiet nod left space for Derek to say more. But instead, Derek told Dylan a few of the best stories of his sisters growing up.

When they were almost done eating, his phone buzzed in his pocket, startling him so much that he banged his knee into the table. Three missed texts in the last four minutes, but he hadn't even noticed the other ones.

Amy

HELP. Babysitter puking her brains out. SJ and I are still in DC. Mom STILL not answering her phone dependably.

"Oh crap . . ."

"Everything okay?"

Derek's thumbs tapped on the screen. "So, how do you feel about kids?"

"To be honest, I feel like it's a little bit soon to have that particular conversation," Dylan said dryly as he sipped his tea.

Derek's open-mouthed horrified response only made Dylan chuckle.

Chapter 32

Dylan pushed his hands in his pockets as they approached the door of a Craftsman-style new-build house. It was about twenty minutes south of Frederick in one of those highly planned-out quasi-urban/suburban communities.

A minivan pulled up to the driveway, and the front screen door swung open, nearly knocking Derek over. A college-aged kid with a ghostly green hue to her skin ran out, gagging and heaving into a trash can. She hopped in the front seat of the van between retches.

"Bye, Joanna." Derek waved at her. A parental figure in the driver's seat waved back before pulling away. "Amy said they should all be in bed, so this isn't going to be anything except—" A pillow hit Derek in the mouth just before four boys, all wearing Spiderman pajamas, ambushed him, each grabbing a limb until he toppled onto the floor.

The resulting cacophony recalled that iconic Jon Snow moment in the "Battle of the Bastards" episode of *Game of Thrones*. Dylan leaned on the doorframe, leaving the other man to his fate. "I'm sorry, I thought we were babysitting children, not all of the superheroes from the Spidey verse?"

"Help, please?"

"Nah. I think you got it covered." Dylan smirked while eight undersized hands savagely tickled Derek.

"Your mom said you guys were asleep." Derek wrestled one of the wriggling bodies off his back.

The tallest of the four piped up. "We were pretending because Joanna was *really* sick."

"Throw-up is gross," the second smallest one said, sticking out his tongue for emphasis.

One of the middle-sized kids jumped back from the fray and leveled assessing eyes at Dylan. *This* kid looked uncannily like a young version of Derek. "Who's this asshole?"

Derek smacked him on the head. "If your mom hears you using that language, she's going to—"

"Blame *you* since you're the one who said it in front of me the first time." He feigned an expression of cherubic purity. "I'm just an innocent child."

Dylan rubbed his chin and appraised the boy. He got the sense he was the oldest even though he was not the tallest. "Are we living in this one's villain origin story or . . ."

"Very possible," Derek detached the smallest kid, who was closer in age to a toddler, from his neck and set him on the couch. "Line up, you four."

The four boys filed into a line, and like Dylan expected, the one who might turn out to be an evil genius stood in front with a defiant stare. "Is he your boooooooyfriend, Uncle Derek?" He used the same voice kids use when they overhear another kid getting called to the principal's office. "Mom said you didn't have a boyfriend. Dad says you never have boyfriends because you're on your phone too much, but he won't explain what that means."

Dylan pressed his lips together, choking down his laugh.

"Shut up, little man."

Derek tapped each Spiderman on the head. "Lucas, age seven." He tapped his head. "Noah, six; George, four; Sammy, two."

"*Christ.*" Dylan shook his head.

"That asshole said a bad word," the tall six-year-old said. Noah? Dylan would not be remembering these names. Well, except for Lucas's. He should probably remember the name of a kid who seemed destined for a future career in world domination.

"What's the asshole's name?" the second smallest looked at Derek.

"The asshole's name is Dylan," Dylan answered before thinking better of it and wondering if this was going to be his nickname in Derek's family. *Great.*

"*Mr.* Dylan," Derek said. "Or Mr. Gallagher."

"Are you Superman, Mr. Dylan?" said the four-year old, sidling up to Dylan and grabbing his arm, swinging it roughly. "You look like Superman when he's in disguise."

Dylan crouched down. "Sure. Want me to make you fly?"

"*Yes!*" shrieked the tiny voice.

Dylan launched him into the air and zoomed him around while the kid made all of the zoom-appropriate sound effects.

When he set the kid down, Derek was shaking his head. "You have no idea the mistake you've made."

Howls of "*Me next!*" erupted from the boys.

Chapter 33

Derek sank onto the couch next to a whimpering Dylan. His sister and her husband had just gotten home. Amy had ordered them to wait while the two young parents kissed their insomniac spawn good night.

"I'm never going to be able to lift anything again." He frowned at his arms. "They're done."

"On the bright side, think of all the money you saved by not needing to go to the climbing gym this week."

Dylan grimaced. "I don't think I'll ever be able to climb again. Agony."

"Quit whining." Derek put his thumb and forefinger around Dylan's bicep. "Come lift with me. I'll fix your spaghetti problem."

"Too mean," Dylan said through laughter. Dylan was actually really good with teasing unless that teasing made his brain, more specifically his ADHD or anxiety, the butt of the joke. "Even the littlest monster probably weighed, what—thirty pounds? I'm supposed to help with the barbeque setup tomorrow. Can you write me a nurse's note to get out of it? Just put that I was forced to zoom compact superheroes for two hours, so I have an urgent medical need to stay home, watch TV, and eat medicinal ice cream. If I can even hold an ice cream spoon ever again. Please?"

"Not a chance."

"I could pretend that my trip to California got moved up."

"I'm dragging you to that party tomorrow, Dylan Gallagher."

"So cruel."

Derek leaned his head on Dylan's shoulder. "I told you to tell the kids you needed a break. The 'just one more time' thing is a complete lie."

"They are relentless and cute. Well, Lucas is not exactly cute so much as—"

"Precocious."

"Sure."

"He's funny. He was a really intense baby too."

Dylan leaned on his shoulder. "Did you babysit a lot?"

"Yeah. My sister had him in college, so my mom and I helped out so she could finish her degree. She and Seo-Joon got married in their freshman year. Fell madly in love like my parents did. Didn't want to wait."

"That's sweet." Dylan linked his hand with Derek's. "So . . . your sister's really religious, right?" Dylan said, scanning the room, seeing a few pieces of mass-produced décor featuring that mix of words he associated with Bible verses.

"She goes to church. Thus why Lucas's mouth is a pretty big problem."

"She's always been cool with *you*? Like, should I leave?"

Derek shrugged. "She knew you were going to be here. Thanks again for coming. New people are always a hit with the boys in a crisis."

"All right. Just wanted to make sure."

They sat in silence for a while, Dylan groaning whenever he moved his arms.

Derek listened up the stairs, hearing that his sister and her husband were still in the rooms with the kids. "It *is* a little weird with Amy and Mom."

"Oh?"

"Like they go to a church that wouldn't be cool with me being in it. They say they don't agree with everything the church says . . . but I've always thought it's weird. Michelle agreed with me."

"I would think it was weird if I were you too." Fidgeting

more than usual, Dylan stood. He crossed the room and looked closer at a photo on the gas fireplace hearth. "Your family?"

"A million years ago." Derek joined Dylan.

"Amy's a carbon copy of your mom in this photo. Uncanny." Dylan studied the picture of Derek hamming it up with the cheesy smile that annoyed his mom and made his dad laugh. "The bow tie and suspenders are pretty cute. I think *you* look just like your dad."

He *did* look like him in that photo. The idea hadn't occurred to him, and his mom had never pointed it out. Too many of his most acute memories of his dad were from when he was sick. "I guess I do. Michelle looks like Dad too. Though obviously in this photo she's a baby, so she just looks like a baby. But when you meet . . ." Derek's mouth closed.

Dylan's voice was cautious when he spoke again. "Things with Michelle really aren't good?"

"It's all my fault. I was just trying to help her. Give her a fresh start. But I don't even know where she is. I messed things up."

"I get that." Dylan's hand pressed on his lower back. "You like being able to fix things. And you're good at it."

Derek shifted his weight, resting a slumped shoulder against Dylan's chest. "I guess I just always tried to take care of her. All of them." His focus narrowed onto his dad's face in the photo.

As footsteps sounded on the staircase, they pulled apart. Had Derek pulled away first? Amy had changed out of her fancy dress and let her hair down into a glossy black curtain to her shoulders. Seo-Joon was a tall presence behind her.

"Who wants a glass of champagne? I'll be drinking one to celebrate a successful kid-free evening." When Amy was irritated, she kept her voice deliberately flat in an almost Aubrey Plaza–like tone.

Dylan looked like a student facing a pop quiz at the mention of alcohol.

Derek grinned. "I think he thought people who have Bible verses on their walls don't drink."

Amy rolled her eyes. "My first night out since a human creature was cut out of my actual body—"

"Gross, Amy."

"—and it was cut short because the nineteen-year-old future Rhodes scholar I trust with the lives of my four genetic crotch goblins somehow missed the essential life lesson about parasites and gas station sushi." She rubbed at her temple. "I think that warrants a glass of something hopefully *actually* French since I'm a snob, midshelf because I'm economical, and very dry because obviously. Some Protestants take the story of Jesus turning water into a wine as a theological imperative." She held up her water bottle to her husband as if asking him to role-play Jesus in this scenario.

Seo-Joon smiled and left the room.

When Derek was halfway through his glass Amy leaned forward, giving his progress on the drink a cool evaluation. She turned to Seo-Joon. He nodded at her.

What the hell?

"The reason why our mother wasn't answering her phone tonight was because she was on an airplane. I finally got ahold of her while we were driving home." She swallowed the rest of her glass with a gulp more suitable for Natty Light.

"She's going out of town?" Derek asked.

Seo-Joon winced. "Just tell him, Ames."

Dylan downed his champagne as if even he could tell he would need it.

"Our mother is flying home tonight after staying at an Airbnb in Florida that the listing describes as 'a place to make your magical fantasies come true—a sensual romantic paradise just steps away from the sparkle of Disney World.' And yes, she sent me the listing . . . in case I needed a recommendation. I think hot tubs in bedrooms are a little gauche, but to each their own."

Derek spluttered into his glass, inhaling dry, midshelf French carbonation into his windpipe.

Dylan patted him on the back.

Amy looked like a cat about to present a human with a dead mouse with the manner of handing out a Nobel Prize. "So . . . she was staying at this sensual romantic paradise—"

"Please—" Derek's jaw twitched. "Stop saying sensual romantic parad—"

"With the bat man."

As Amy's revelation hit him, Derek inhaled a gulp of champagne that hardened to concrete in his trachea. He tried to stop the coughing fit that followed by downing the rest of his drink, but the carbonation made it feel like there were Pop Rocks up his nose.

"Your mom went to Disney World with Batman?" Dylan's hand stopped moving on Derek's back.

Derek pushed the glass back onto the table. *Mom went on vacation with some random man?* To a sensual romantic paradise with a bedroom hot tub—*Jesus fucking Christ,* he needed to burn those words out of his brain.

Before Derek recovered enough to speak, Seo-Joon smiled and spoke directly into his flute. "Not Batman, *the bat man.*" He separated out each word. "The one Derek called to help her get the bats out of her attic a while ago." After taking a second sip, he exchanged his mostly full glass for the empty one in his wife's hand.

"Oh . . ." Dylan's eyebrows rose. "Wait, so do you mean—"

"Because in this family we *love* surprises. Cheers." After another swig, Amy held up Seo-Joon's glass. "They eloped." And all the suppressed hysterics burst out of her.

Chapter 34

It was still dark out when Derek woke the following morning. His body was wrapped around Dylan's bare torso. Dylan had already been asleep when Derek had come into the bedroom. The workout zooming Derek's nephews combined with his sleepless night before made him zonk out. Derek had spent an hour on the phone with his mom trying to convince her that he was completely happy for her and none of this was weird.

Of course it was weird.

How could it be anything but weird? Would it have been less weird if he'd known she was dating? How would he have reacted then? Was she worried about how he would have reacted, and that's why she didn't tell him?

With the AC blasting, it was almost chilly after Derek had been hot half the night, but he didn't have the energy to reach and move the sheet over them. Instead he pulled Dylan closer.

The second time Derek woke, sunlight streamed in through a gap in Dylan's translucent curtains. His thoughts went right back to where they had been before.

His mom had eloped. Actually *eloped.*

"What are you thinking about?" Dylan words were drowsy, eyes still closed.

"How did you know I was awake and thinking?" Derek lifted his face from Dylan's chest.

"I feel you doing that adorable eyebrow thing."

"I don't do an adorable eyebrow thing. *Stop.*" His head settled back on Dylan's sternum.

Dylan smoothed the area between Derek's eyebrows. "Must've imagined it all the times."

Dylan had to have spent a fair amount of time in the climbing gym. He wasn't bulky, but everything was lean. He was the kind of man who was probably a lot stronger than he looked. Probably why he could spend an hour tossing around Derek's nephews.

Dylan's heartbeat thumped slowly, and his breaths evened out, like he'd fallen back asleep. Derek's thoughts returned to his mom. He was thirty-five years old. His dad had been gone for nearly two decades, and yet it had never occurred to him for a second that she would get remarried. *And* he'd been the unwitting matchmaker. Well, him and a family of *Eptesicus fuscus* brown bats.

His mom had always had lots of people around. Her Bible study. Her running club. Amy. Her grandsons. Before the apartment catastrophe, Derek was over there several times a week on a consistent schedule, usually to fix things and take care of all the basic maintenance tasks around the aging house.

Was he still supposed to do that now? Would her husband change the smoke alarm batteries and fix the pilot light? His mom was quite capable of doing all those things herself, but she still called him to do it anyway ... He had never really asked himself why before.

What were the rules now? He'd always just stopped by whenever. Was he going to go over to her house next time and see some other dude's clothes hanging where his dad's suits had been? Or would they move to another house?

"What time is it?" Dylan asked in a sleep-addled voice, stirring beneath Derek. "My mom wants me over there by ten to help set up."

Derek grabbed his phone from the table beside him. "It's seven thirty." Dylan's mouth pressed into a line. "Hmm . . ."

MOM
Can you come by this morning? We should talk.

DEREK
Will your husband be there?

MOM
No, he's got to stop in at the office.

DEREK
Okay.

✳✳✳

Derek sat at the counter clutching a mug of scalding tea and trying to nibble the corner of a cookie that appeared to be home (over)baked. His mom had always baked when she was happy, so this was a good sign even if the childish part of his brain felt conflicted.

When his mom came back downstairs, she held a box of files. "I was decluttering the office and found these—"

"Mom, I could've carried those."

"I am perfectly capable of carrying a box myself." Her skeptical expression shut him up in that way that only his mother could.

"*Oh.*" The files held everything having to do with the apartment. He meant to bring it to the apartment, but that place had never felt enough like home for him to want to spend time moving more shit into it. "Thanks for finding this."

"Looking to get rid of some of the clutter, but I didn't want to shred anything you needed. You're still fixing it up to sell?" She leveled him with an appraising stare.

"Hopefully."

She took a sip from a Disney mug—one he hadn't ever seen before. "Amy said Dylan seems very nice."

Derek burned his tongue on the tea. "He is. He's—uh—helping me with the renovations to the apartment."

She nodded. "Amy says you're just friends?"

"I . . ." He wasn't expecting this question from her. Amy, sure. But his mom didn't usually ask much about his relationships. Not that there had been any actual ones for her to ask about. "It's been kind of a shi—crummy few years, Mom. A lot's happened, and I don't know if it's too soon . . . I don't know . . ."

His mother let her teabag drip onto a saucer. "After your father passed, being a widow became my entire identity. I wanted to forget that another side of me had existed and could still exist in the future."

Derek swirled his tea.

"Years went by, and it wasn't just about grief. Being alone became a habit because I was afraid to try again. I was afraid to open that door because . . . what if there was *nothing* behind it?"

"And behind it was a humane animal relocation specialist?"

"Behind it was fun. Behind it was adventure. Behind it was *love*. Different, but just as real."

A strange burning seared his eyes.

His mother stared at the counter. "I guess sometimes habits—even if they don't feel good or even if they make you lonely—can get comfortable. At least they can *seem* more comfortable than trying."

"You were lonely all these years?"

"Mostly, I was too busy being a single mother trying to pay the mortgage to be lonely. I had the girls. And I had you here. I had you a lot longer than I had any right to have you." Her head bowed forward as she stirred her mug into an eddy. "I relied on you too much. I should've been encouraging you to do more or try things, but I didn't. I couldn't bring myself to push you farther away from the nest."

"I wanted to be here. I wanted to see my sisters grow up and help out. It made me happy."

She tapped her spoon three times on the rim. "Still, I know it wasn't fair to you. And I know it wasn't fair for you to find out about Ken the way you did. Although honestly, I'm not sure I've ever heard Amy as gleeful as when she got the 'Mom eloped' gossip before you."

Derek laughed in spite of himself. "I can see that."

"I just didn't know how to tell you. Since Olive's brother's accident you've been trying so hard to not let anyone know how much you're hurting. I know part of that was because of what Olive was going through, but I'd hoped you'd confide in me . . ." She twisted her hands. "You never did. I guess I should confess sometimes I would tell you things were broken at the house just because I wanted you to come over, so I could make sure you were still okay."

"God, Mom, I'm sor—"

"Why are you apologizing to me?" She gave him a half-serious, half-severe look. "I'm the one who married the bat man without telling her son."

"I think Dylan's going to be calling him Bruce Wayne until the end of time." He laughed, a real laugh this time. Dylan could always shake him out of a bad mood.

"I've been rethinking a lot of things lately. Ken's been helping me see the ways I was stuck in prejudice even when I thought I was just wanting the best for you. I really am sorry. And I think that's why I never told you . . ." Her gaze was a mixture of regret and appraising.

"Never told me what?" Derek tilted his head. "About getting married? It's really fine—"

"Not that." After another X-raying look, she paced back and

forth next to the island. "Jake Murphy came by here a few days before his accident."

"What?" He set down his mug, feeling oddly shaky to hear his mom say Jake's name. Jake had come by their house a couple days before his accident? He didn't know how to feel about that, except that he was surprised it didn't sting more.

"You were staying here before closing on Michelle's apartment."

He rubbed his chin. "Honestly, those weeks are kind of a blur."

"You never left Olive's side."

He nodded.

"I think you'd gotten called into work. You were working a lot of overtime back then too . . ." She flipped through the box of files. "I'd just found out what was actually happening with Michelle's apartment and everything you'd done to try to clean up that mess. So, the question just slipped out."

"Wait, what question?"

"I asked him if he was finally here to ask you out on a date."

"*Mom.* You *didn't.*"

She winced. "He seemed so startled by it that he said yes. Dropped his bag actually. His things went everywhere. He said he'd just gotten off a plane and wanted to surprise you and take you to get a late dinner. I told him he'd strung you along for too long since moving back to the area, and that if he was going to date you, he needed to show that he recognized how special you were and make up his darn mind."

"*Mom. God.*" Was it possible to die of delayed mortification over something that had happened years before?

"You know what he said?"

"What?"

"He said watching you with your sisters was what taught him how to be a better brother to Olive and his other sister. You know, I don't get the sense that those Murphy parents were ever very nurturing . . ." She paused to blink a few times and then continued. "Jake said he'd traveled all over the world and met all kinds of people, but you were the best man he'd ever known. The kindest best friend his sister could ever hope for. And right before he let, he turned back. He said that lately, the question wasn't whether or not *he* had real feelings for *you*. I get the sense that he saw what I saw even before Jake's accident."

"What'd you see?" Derek stared at a blank kitchen wall, his breath catching. "Why are you telling me this now?"

"Because after meeting Ken, I realized that for years I was using your dad as an excuse. Devotion seemed like a good reason to avoid even thinking about finding someone else. I think you've spent a lot of your life worried about losing people. You hold that door closed so tightly because it feels like you're protecting what you have . . ."

"Mom . . ."

"And I don't think that's just about Jake Murphy. I see it in everything you do for me and your sisters and Olive too. But really, it's about your father."

"I *promised* Dad—"

"It wasn't fair for him to ask that of you. You were a child. Might be hard for you to understand, but when he got sick, your dad was younger than you are now."

Derek's hands balled together.

His mom patted his fists once. "And maybe you need to start investing more in your own life."

"Now you're giving me accounting advice?" The question hadn't sounded as wry as he hoped.

"Giving you the advice I wish someone had given me." She took another long sip of tea. "Are you sure you can't stay for lunch? Ken should be back—"

"I have a thing with Dylan's family today or I would, I swear. I'm not avoiding meeting him."

Somehow his mother could sip tea skeptically. Her cup was empty when she set it down.

"I'm not *intentionally* avoiding meeting him."

"Fair enough."

A sound came from upstairs.

Derek looked up at the ceiling.

His mom set her tea down. "That woman in need I mentioned before is still staying here. Wait here a second."

"Okay?" He washed their mugs, a pang going through him when he read that underneath the painted image of the Cinderella castle on hers there was a personalization that read AN-GELA AND KEN . . . HAPPILY EVER AFTER.

His heart squeezed. He was happy for her. He really was.

But the loss of his dad felt more present than before. His mom could at some point get to meet Dylan, but his dad never would. His dad, who would have loved Dylan's sense of humor.

He dried the mug and set it on the drying rack. When he turned around, he was struck by the odd image of Jake standing in this same kitchen, having that conversation with his mom.

Jake was right.

He'd loved Jake, but it hadn't been what he thought it was. And Jake had sensed that from that first night they spent together.

He had never once thought about bringing Jake here as his boyfriend. Partially this was because they all already knew Jake as Olive's brother, but it was more than that.

He rubbed at a spot in the center of his chest as he remembered what he said at dinner last night with Dylan. More precisely, what he didn't say. Not telling Dylan about Jake had been nearly a reflex. But it wasn't fair. Dylan deserved that, especially have he had been so open about seeing his ex and everything about his anxiety and ADHD.

"I have trouble trusting myself, so it's really important for me to trust a partner even with the little stuff."

He needed to tell him. Something like the tiniest dose of panic surged through him as a reel played in his head of the future moments Derek could lose out on if he didn't earn Dylan's trust.

Aw crap, he'd given Olive so much shit about her fantasizing about Derek's future coupledom bliss. And Derek had been imagining seeing Dylan's house for the first time. He was wanting Dylan to meet his mom, and Derek couldn't wait to see what the deal was with this big Gallagher family party.

Derek sat at the counter and swiveled the stool, thinking about the lives they'd lived in this 1970s split-level through the framed photos, the books, the sparse knickknacks accumulated from family vacations that were sometimes fun and sometimes a disaster but always memorable. The throw blankets on that old basement sofa they'd used during movie nights or wrapped up in when home sick from school.

He'd never once imagined a *life* with Jake.

Had the pang over his mother's mug not been about Ken, but because he, for the first time in his life, wanted his own happily ever after? And maybe . . . he'd started imagining what that could look like without even knowing it.

After leaving his mom's house, he went straight to his apartment.

He dug in the closet Dylan had hidden inside with Gus and pulled out an old metal lockbox, thankful everything in there had been spared from the water disaster. Derek didn't keep many sentimental things, but this lockbox had been his father's. On top was a gold double photo frame holding his dad's two favorite wedding photos of Derek's mom—one in each of the dresses she wore. His parents' wedding had blended his dad's culture from Taiwan and his mom's Korean heritage. It was hard to imagine his mom's second wedding being a spontaneous elopement at Disney World of all places.

Derek rifled through the trinkets and found what he was looking for—a leather-bound graph paper notebook full of sketches. His dad had been planning on building a house for their family. He'd drawn out plans so many different times, because his imagination couldn't help but muse on giving his family the life he dreamed of for Derek's mom and his sisters. He was halfway through the notebook when his phone buzzed.

> **DYLAN**
> If I accidentally maim myself while throwing myself down the stairs to get out of this, will you drive me to Joni?

Derek grinned and placed the book back inside the box. They'd need to get to the Gallaghers' soon. He could tell Dylan about Jake after the party.

> **DEREK**
> No maiming. Needing stitches might ruin your haircut.

> **DYLAN**
> At least you have your priorities straight on the subject of me maiming myself. Cool.

> **DEREK**
> Glad you agree. Be up in five.

Chapter 35

Dylan led Derek up the long, winding driveway to his parents' house. Derek wore a subtly pink floral, short-sleeve button-up that was just tight enough to show off his pecs and biceps. For all the shit Dylan gave Derek about being cocky about his muscles, they were a constant distraction today. Dylan's own arms were still so sore he could barely lift them. Dylan's shirt was similar to Derek's, though it fit very differently. Derek had gone through all of Dylan's clothes in his uncle's closet and decided it was the only acceptable option. It was light gray with a subtle patten of Doctor Who Daleks you could only make out if you were up close. A gift from Felicity, of course. Dylan didn't know if he had ever done the *getting dressed with a partner* thing, but the experience gave him a peculiar thrill.

Derek eyed the line of fifty or so of every type of vehicle imaginable, including multiple vans bearing a variety of logos for every type of home renovation or repair. "I thought you said we were coming early to set up?"

"A weird thing about these parties is that everyone's family, so they all end up coming early to help set up for the party. Inevitably the party starts six hours early."

Derek laughed. "Well, lead on, then, since I guess we're already late."

The small brick rambler house was packed, so Dylan bypassed the front door and went around back, scanning the assembled Byrnes and Gallaghers for red hair. For all the stereotypes about the Irish, there were only a few gingers in his family. His mother, Felicity, and a couple of his nieces. The fenced-off pool sparkled in the morning sunshine and was full of a gaggle of Gallagher kids under the careful eyes of their parents. Felicity had instituted a new set of pool safety rules and etiquette since starting nursing school. Dylan waved to some cousins and Brooks and Anderson, who were tossing their kids around while splashing in the water.

"Why didn't you tell me to bring my bathing suit?"

"Because with the number of kids going in that pool today, it's gonna be more urine than chlorine by three P.M."

"Gross, Dylan."

"It's a fact." Dylan smiled. "I'll bring you back on another day if you want. Oh, also, if you go inside that fence, carry stuff in your pockets at your own risk. My brothers have a reputation for the well-coordinated ambush pool toss, but the rule is that it's only permissible if you're within the fence."

"How'd that rule start?"

"Felicity threatened to beat Brooks with a bat the last time he tossed her in the water and busted her phone."

"I think Felicity wakes up each day and chooses violence."

"You're not wrong."

"Meh . . ." Derek squinted at the two large hockey players carousing in the pool, dad bods on unabashed display in the lurid speedos they donned each year for this occasion. "I can take them."

Leaning closer, Dylan pretended to assess Derek's body. "While your physique is objectively impressive—"

"Aw shucks, hon."

"Combined, those dudes have a hundred and fifty pounds and three inches on you. Just like Gloria Estefan says, the physics is gonna get you."

Derek tried not to laugh but failed. "Why was that even funny?"

"Because you're biased in favor of my biting wit."

Derek's mouth grazed Dylan's ear. "Definitely think we've established I'm good with biting."

Dylan shoved Derek away. "My mother is here somewhere. Shush." He hadn't been sure what to expect today since Derek hadn't touched Dylan at all in front of his sister. But Dylan hadn't expected Derek to press a casual peck on his lips without any concern about who was watching.

When he pulled back, Derek winced. "Sorry, was that okay? I should have asked."

"Super okay." Dylan slipped his hand into Derek's. "It's all good."

"Okay, then. Cool." Derek exhaled like *he* was the nervous one or something.

An insect must have flown into Dylan's mouth without him noticing, because his stomach was doing a very disconcerting flittering like there were dragonfly wings inside while he tried to keep his mind on finding his immediate family and not on anything having to do with kissing or biting.

The pair walked to the large external garage workshop that was actually double the size of the tiny house. All of the adult Gallaghers contributed money for this event. In recent years the kid entertainment had expanded to include an enormous bounce house next to the garage. A few kids were in the bounce house while others climbed on the old playset that Dylan's father had built thirty years earlier. The elder of the Gallagher girls was probably inside cooking since she was a crunchy vegan and normally brought a selection of her own food for herself and her kids, but he didn't see Felicity anywhere.

"I didn't realize this was *an event*. Like an *event* event."

"Oh, it's an event for sure." A blur of orange hair in the distance cut behind the tent.

Inside, his mom was taking inventory of her Costco packs of paper plates and cutlery, pointing out things to his dad, who appeared to be taking a mental list of her instructions. She flipped through an old spiral notebook and checked items off with one of the colorful gel pens sticking out of her fluffy auburn bun, beaming like a kid at Christmas. She sent her husband off in search of something missing.

"Mom." After hugging her, Dylan put two hands on her shoulders to direct her attention. "This is Derek."

"Heard my son kidnapped your dog. Will you be pressing charges?" His mother leveled a hard glance at Derek.

"Oh, uh—no. Of course no—"

She snickered. "First rule of the Gallagher Grill-Out, don't take anyone too seriously." His mom gave Derek a small squeeze. "We're very happy to have you." Then she kept squeezing down Derek's arms. "Oh my, you're a sturdy-looking fella." A little of the Irish lilt emerged.

"If you could stop feeling up my . . . friend, that'd be swell, Ma."

"Lord, isn't *swell* just the right word for these muscles." Her eyes twinkled at Derek's biceps and his corded forearms.

"I think you're thinking *swole*. Chrissakes, mom." Dylan palmed his face.

"Nice to meet you, Mrs. Gallagher." Derek appeared delighted at this mortifying attention.

"Katie's fine, Derek. *Tommy*," she shouted out to Dylan's dad. "We've got two more strapping men to help with table duty."

Derek smiled. "Happy to help. Just point Dylan and me to what we can do."

Dylan's dad came around the side of the tent with a big crate. "Oh, c'mon, Katie, you know Dylan does better helping in here with you."

Derek's flicker of confusion made Dylan stiffen.

His dad put down the crate of flowers and kissed Dylan's mom. "The three big boys'll be in in a minute. They always do the tables." He clapped Dylan on the shoulder and then shook Derek's hand. "Heard a lot about you, Mr. Chang. Glad my boys asked you to come. You're right, Katie, this fella's almost as tall as Brooks. You're Sean's neighbor, right? Friend of that poor young goalie who passed away?"

A muscle ticked in Derek's jaw. "Yes, I am. Will Sean be here today? Haven't seen him for a while."

A shadow passed over Dylan's dad's face. "He's upstairs. Not sure if he'll be down. Have to see how he's feeling with all the people."

Something in Dylan's dad's reaction discouraged more questions. A noise in the corner caught Dylan's attention. Two more redheads sat on one of the big old rugs they always used to line the tent floor. Felicity held her niece in her lap, reading her a book called *A Young Girl's Guide to Fighting the Patriarchy*.

Derek elbowed Dylan in the ribs. "See."

As if to further illustrate the point, when his niece jumped down out of her lap, it revealed that Felicity's T-shirt was a cartoon-style uterus holding up a middle finger. Her shirt was knotted at her waist over an aggressively feminine, floral-patterned pink skirt.

"Nice shirt, Lissy."

"Mom's *pissed*," Felicity said in a carrying whisper.

Dylan's mom called back. "I think my daughter should be able to express herself through her clothing, but if all the kids start making that gesture, I'm going to burn that fecking shirt."

Dylan's oldest niece strutted up to Derek. "I'm Felicity."

"That can't be right because she's Felicity." Derek pointed at Dylan's sister.

Mini-Felicity lived up to her namesake with the look of pure contempt she offered Derek. "Multiple people are allowed to have the same name. I call her Aunt Lissy. Just in case you're *still* confused."

"Ahh . . . I had no idea. Thanks for explaining. I'm Derek."

Mini-Felicity gave a little approving nod and ran off, pulling off her T-shirt over the top of her bathing suit.

"Cal's daughter," Dylan said, and smirked. "Next year, you should bring your nephews and we can see what she makes of Lucas. They're the same age." The words "next year" gave Dylan a few seconds of anxiety, but Derek didn't react with anything other than amusement.

"Not sure the world is ready for those two to be friends."

Dylan's mother pushed a color-coded list into Dylan's hands. He and Derek dove into tasks. Derek was arranging centerpieces while Dylan was up on a ladder in the corner, patching a rip with duct tape.

When he climbed down, wiry arms grabbed Dylan from behind. He twisted to find himself wrapped in a hug from his favorite relative, Aunt Jeannie.

"Guess you couldn't come up with an excuse this year. Glad I made the trip out. Didn't know I'd get a glimpse of you. Missed your face." Her bright, blue-gray eyes twinkled. Eyes that were much more lined than the last time he'd seen her. She was thinner too. Felicity lived with her all through her undergrad out in Kansas. She rarely traveled away from her store in the last few years, so he was surprised she came.

"Shoulda known," Dylan said with a nod at the shirt Aunt Jeannie was wearing, twin to Felicity's.

"Aunt Jeannie buys me the best gifts." Felicity giggled and then started organizing the desserts.

A commotion built as Dylan's three brothers tromped in and stole Derek away from the flowers, yelling back words like "table duty" and "touch football" and "Gallagher initiation."

Dylan watched his . . . *friend* run off with his brothers with a twinge. It wasn't exactly jealousy. On some level he was happy that Derek fit into his family so well. Not that he had been thinking about it like *that*. Because that would be super weird since they hadn't even technically put a label on their relationship yet.

He stood at the tent entrance while all four tall men ran

through a field each carrying a large folding table from the garage as if it was one of those intense brute strength, Scottish Highland sports. Noticing Dylan, Derek stopped and grinned until Anderson yelled back at him asking if he needed a "wittle" break because the table was too heavy. Derek responded by lifting the table with one hand.

Macho bastard.

Derek winked at Dylan.

Felicity appeared and leaned on his shoulder. "I think that guy likes you."

"I dunno. Maybe." Dylan bit his lip to avoid beaming.

Just as he thought he'd been wrong to be worried, he saw Brooks carrying in a small sculpture that make Dylan's stomach sink into the ground.

"Oh *fuck*," said Felicity.

Chapter 36

Dylan licked the last bits of s'more off his fingertips after feeding Derek his third marshmallow. The sun had gone down an hour ago, and about thirty Gallaghers and Byrnes were milling around a large bonfire at the back part of the property. Kids stabbed marshmallows with the usual violence and lit them on fire as they had for the last twenty-five years.

Derek was seated next to him on one of the many mismatched quilts and picnic blankets laid out over the dry grass field. Fireflies blinked in the forest branches just beyond.

The day hadn't been bad. Well, it hadn't been all bad. There had been the usual awkward moments between him and his brothers, but the worst hadn't happened. It had just been the typical not-quite-teasing assumptions that Dylan was responsible for every minor mishap.

Thankfully, he didn't think Derek had heard whenever his brothers or cousins had *"done a Dilly."* It was annoying that even when he could *still* outrun his brothers, he had to endure digs about his athletic ability. Not that he gave a shit about that kind of teasing. The only reason he'd cared about his dad implying he couldn't carry tables was because he didn't want Derek to think he had ever complained about carrying tables. He hadn't.

Half the kids were running around with sparklers, much to Felicity's chagrin. She kept yelling at them to be careful or else they'd lose an eye or light themselves on fire. Her seven-year-old doppelgänger followed her around, refusing a sparkler in solidarity with her cautious aunt.

Derek slipped an arm over Dylan's shoulders and took a

sip of his Angry Orchard. The strictest Gallagher Grill-Out rules dictated limited alcohol consumption because of the high contingency of alcoholics in the family. Brooks, Anderson, and Dylan's dad had all been sober for years. For guests who did imbibe, only one alcoholic beverage was permitted each. Dylan's mom grew up with family gatherings devolving into drunken brawls, ending in the occasional overnight jail stay or broken skull, so she kept a strict tally on the coolers. Dylan drank his beer at lunchtime, but Derek had waited until all that was left were the ciders.

Gentleman that he was, he offered Dylan the occasional sip. The oddest thing about today had been the PDA. Derek was a much more casually affectionate person than Dylan would have thought. It was mainly strange because it felt very not-strange. Dylan had never brought a . . . friend over to meet his family. Ever. But no one said a word about it. A nice surprise.

He'd spent years watching his brothers and sisters and cousins bring significant others and later spouses to this event. He hadn't realized how much he wanted that. Watching Derek smoke his brothers in bocce was probably the most fun Dylan had ever had at a Grill-Out.

Derek finished his cider. As Dylan reached to take the bottle from him, Derek dragged his cold fingers over the back of Dylan's arm in a way that made Dylan anxious to get home. He tossed the bottle into the large recycling bin next to the supply tables where it landed with a *clunk* with the others.

Felicity stood beside the bigger table. "I hate amateur fireworks."

"We all know that. But no one's blown off their hands in the last twenty-five years, Lissy."

"Yet," she said ominously. She handed a lighter to Dylan. "Hide this."

"They'll just go get another one inside. Mom's got a million."

"I'll kill her if she's smoking again."

Derek slipped a hand in Dylan's back pocket, giving his ass a tiny squeeze no one else could see. Their backs were to the woods as they stood behind the towers of paper products and stacks of fireworks boxes. In the darkness, no one would notice Derek's hand. The covert contact sent a very specific type of thrill right down to Dylan's dick. He flicked the lighter on and off absentmindedly.

"Who's smoking again?" Derek asked.

"My mom. I think." Dylan shrugged. "Having Uncle Sean around the house has been a lot."

Derek's head twitched in a subtle, questioning movement.

"They think it's Alzheimer's," Dylan said quietly, watching the lighter flame. "Early stages, but it's not great."

"Damn. That sucks."

"Toss this in the recycling for me, Big D." Calvin lobbed his beer bottle toward Derek, but since Derek's hand was in Dylan's pocket, he couldn't get it out quickly enough. As he spun, he knocked into Dylan who was, unfortunately, still holding the lit lighter aloft. Avoiding knocking the fire into his sister, Dylan fell forward into the table, directly onto the pile of highly flammable paper napkins.

The engulfed napkins singed his skin. He dropped the lighter and pulled his sister away from the flames zipping down the fabric tablecloth. As if the disaster was happening in slow motion, Dylan reacted quickly, mind working quickly. His niece popped up from beneath the table like she'd been looking for something on the ground.

No.

There were a shit ton of sparklers and fireworks packages at the other end, right near her. Dylan grabbed the edge of the tablecloth and suffocated the fire completely just as Derek dumped the cooler of lemonade over the entire area. Dylan yanked the fireworks off the table and threw them into the cool grass as far as possible from any stray sparks, shielding little Felicity from the ashes. When he was satisfied all the danger was gone, he backed away from the table, breathing hard.

As if the volume of the world turned back up, the roars of laughter grew, overtaking the ringing in his ears. Brooks and Anderson were doubled over with laughter.

"Who gave Dilly a lighter?" His dad called out.

Brooks yelled back. "Felicity, come on. You know the rules about Dilly and fire."

Felicity's face was beyond outrage. "If Calvin wasn't such a lazy asshole and could walk the ten steps to the recycling bin, I wouldn't have almost got lit on fire."

"Language, Felicity," Anderson shouted back. "My kids are here."

Felicity's voice dropped to a venomous mutter. "Pretty sure they're gonna be very aware of the word *asshole* with a douchewad as their dad."

Derek grabbed Dylan. "You okay?"

Dylan caught his breath, speechless with what *could* have happened. Little Felicity had been three steps away from the side of the table with all those fireworks right there with her hair out and wild from a day of pool and sun. It could have easily gotten hit with a spark. Cal had grabbed his daughter once he realized what was happening, but he could have been too late if the fire had spread too quickly.

Dylan ran a hand over his hair. "*Shit.*"

"I'm so sorry." Derek shook his head and held onto Dylan's upper arms. "My hand was stuck and then my foot caught on the bottom of the table." His hands slid down to Dylan's wrists, checking him for burns, running his thumb over the pink scar on Dylan's palm from falling through the ceiling. "You didn't get burned?"

Dylan shook his head.

Felicity did her own evaluation of Dylan, checking his arms

and palms "You could have burned your damn hands off. Next time just wait—"

Dylan pointed to the sparklers and fireworks in the grass.

"Oh shit, little Felicity was right there." Derek whistled low, realizing what had happened and why Dylan hadn't waited for the fire extinguisher. "That could've been bad."

Felicity rushed off to make sure her tiny namesake was okay.

"Yeah." Dylan pointed to where the kid had been standing at the corner of the table. "I shouldn't have been holding the lighter like that, but *shit*."

Derek pulled him into a hug. "You cannot think that that was all your fault. God, Dylan. You could have really gotten hurt too. It was all a freak accident. More my fault than anyone's."

Brooks and Anderson pounced on Derek and Dylan. *"Is it time?"* they drawled in tandem.

"Oh, I think it's time," Calvin said.

"Time for?" Dylan's dad asked, but then grinned. "Oh . . ."

"Guys, please . . ." Dylan pulled away from his brother's grip. "No."

"Time for what?" Derek asked.

"Y'all are such assholes." Felicity said in a carrying whisper to Calvin. "Don't pull this shit this year."

"We need to give Derek the full Gallagher Grill-Out experience," Brooks said.

"It's just fun, Lady Lissy," Dylan's dad said, giving his daughter a little gesture that clearly said *What's the harm?* He grabbed Dylan around the neck and mussed his hair. "The boys really missed having Dilly here."

Dylan hadn't had a panic attack since he started his new medications, but he could feel the beginnings forming in his chest. Pressure rattling right beneath his sternum, breaths too rapid.

He counted in his head and backed away a few steps.

Chapter 37

Derek felt Dylan's absence beside him and turned around. "What's wrong?"

"It's s-stupid. It's all just a joke." Even in the firelight Derek could see that Dylan's ears had turned red.

"What's a joke?"

Brooks brandished a bizarre-looking sculpture thing like a Sizzler waiter with a dessert tray. "The Pickle Award," he said, in an affected voice that was obviously trying to imitate a radio announcer.

Abrupt, excited shouts erupted from all around them, making Derek jump. Everyone saying the same two words: *"Pickle Award."*

"What the hell is that thing?" Derek asked Dylan, but Dylan was biting the inside of his cheek and only shrugged. He kept adjusting his glasses on his nose.

Dylan shook out his head and then forced a smile that was so unlike Dylan's actual smile that it looked like some failed Madame Tussaud's version of his face. It was all wrong. He was breathing too fast. Derek had seen Olive have a panic attack, and hers were much more obvious, but if that's what this was, it was like Dylan was sucking the panic inside himself where no one could see it.

But Derek could.

"The year was 1998," said Brooks. "The first year of the Gallagher Grill-Out. And our sweet, young, eleven-year-old Dilly had been asked by our father to do a very specific job."

His tone was halfway between smarmy preacher and stand-up comedian. Derek did not like where this was going, but when Derek opened his mouth to say something, Dylan shook his head. He didn't want to be rude and cut into some kind of Gallagher family ritual, so Derek moved a little closer to Dylan. The weird phallic sculpture in Brooks's hands was supposed to resemble a giant pickle?

Anderson took the sculpture from Brooks. "It was a windy day, and young Dylan, we must admit, was great at tying knots."

"An expert at knotting, one would say," Brooks added in a reverent tone.

"Definitely the best knotter in the family." Dylan's dad nodded.

Felicity choked on her cider. She had clearly waited for this moment to imbibe in her single alcoholic beverage of the day. She leaned over to Dylan and spoke under her breath. "If any of them ever read books, I would think they were doing this on purpose, but—"

"You don't think your dad is well-versed in Omegaverse werewolf sex tropes?" Derek said dryly. At Felicity and Dylan's shocked expressions, Derek winked at Dylan. "I once took a little journey around the basics of smutty fanfic. As one does."

Derek *almost* had coaxed a smile out of Dylan. At least until the asshats started speaking again. Derek's patience with Dylan's two oldest brothers was waning. Rapidly.

"A-hhhem," said Brooks, clearly annoyed Derek wasn't hanging on his every word. The rest of the assembled guests were rapt as if watching a well-choreographed stage show. "Diligent little Dilly boy went out to the table with his small thing of twine. He managed to tie one corner. Two corners. Three corners."

"It's a little like David Foster Wallace wrote this, isn't it?" Felicity sighed.

Derek hid a smile behind his fist. "It never really occurred to me until this moment that the title *Infinite Jest* could be a pun on a melodramatic, long-winded, unfunny joke that never ends." Derek matched Felicity's volume. "Can't imagine why."

That earned a laugh from Dylan.

"It wasn't until that fourth corner that things went so very, very wrong. He'd used his wrist to hold down the tablecloth, and the twine got twisted in little Dilly's watch. And when Mom called him into the house, he ran off, right away."

"Always was a fast little sucker," Dylan's dad said.

"Not realizing that the knot in his watch was stronger than the one tying the string to the table."

"Oh shit." Derek grimaced at Dylan.

"He pulled every single thing off the table."

"And the only thing that survived was—"

A chorus of extended family voices joined in. "A jar of pickles."

"And so, our little brother Dilly inspired the Pickle Award." He held it up. "It's gotten a little discolored over the years, but it was green when we first made it."

Felicity held her cider bottle upside down to make sure she had sucked every last drop.

"Every year it goes to the person who did the most clumsy or absentminded thing of the day." Anderson grinned and gripped Dylan in a side-armed embrace turned headlock. "Dylan all over it, amirite?"

Brooks grabbed the small statute back from Anderson and handed it to Dylan. "We would've been disappointed if you didn't win your first year back."

Derek's hands clenched into fists. He'd always thought of rage as a hot thing. Like fire or lava or that time Olive dropped her straightener on his arm in the bathroom.

But no, Derek had already dealt with fire tonight. What was building inside him was a polar vortex. An explosion of sub-zero, icy fury.

As the party started to break up, the Gallagher kids and

their father gathered around the table cleaning up the ashes of the fire. Then the stories started.

While Dylan wasn't the only person who had "won" the award over the years, it all devolved into stories about Dylan. Sometimes they were just straight mocking Dylan's ADHD, and it wasn't even subtle. Every time Derek opened his mouth, Dylan shook his head. That stupid nonsmile was still plastered to his face, pretending he was in on the joke, trying to treat it all like this wasn't some decades-long humiliation ritual for a family's whipping boy. Did he endure this every year? Dylan was still holding that stupid goddamn quasi-phallic discolored pickle in his hands. His knuckles were white. His ears were bright pink.

"I found it." Brooks pushed his phone in Derek's face.

Dylan mumbled a pleading curse. "Guys, *please . . .*"

"Here's the photo of the first ever Pickle Award Ceremony." Brooks gestured to his phone. On it was a picture of Dylan as a small-for-his-age kid, crying and holding a large jar of pickles.

Anderson popped up at Derek's other shoulder. "Hysterical, right? So funny that that the pickles were literally the only thing that survived. Dylan. Dilly. Pickles. Dill Pickles."

Derek's nostrils flared. "Yeah, I get it, dude."

"I won last year, but the competition was less fierce since Dilly was sick."

As he looked up from the photo, Derek caught Dylan's eye. The little boy in the photo looked so broken while the man who meant so much to Derek was forcing himself to make that stupid face that was like the *Black Mirror* version of his perfect smile.

Something splintered inside Derek. He snatched the stupid thing from Dylan's hand and shook it out in front of Anderson. "This. Is. Not. Funny. None of this is funny, you giant jackass."

Felicity's voice broke the silence first. "Finally." She chucked her cider bottle into the trash. "Here we go."

Chapter 38

Dylan pressed his hand to Derek's back. Shit, the last hour had been miserable for him, but he hadn't wanted *this* to happen. An actual confrontation between Derek and his brothers? Not good. Derek twisted out of reach.

"Oh, come on." Anderson said. "He gets it's all a joke. Don't you, Dilly?"

"Uh . . ." Dylan said.

Derek flung out his hand toward Dylan, seemingly having forgotten in his fury he was still holding the "award." Held in Derek's fist like that, it looked even more like a misshapen, puke-colored dildo than usual.

"Just look at your brother. You think that's what he looks like when he thinks something is funny? Look at his face."

"What's wrong with my face?" Dylan asked, slightly offended.

"For starters, your ears are all pink, which means you're uncomfortable."

"My ears?" Did his ears actually turn red when he was embarrassed?

"And when he laughs for real his stupid dimples underneath his mouth come out, but now he just looks like he's in pain. Are you jerks even paying attention to the fact that it bothers him?" Derek growled.

Something about the way Derek said "dimples" helped Dylan shake the weight of mortification of the last hour. Derek noticed his dimples?

"It's a joke," Calvin said. While more measured than the

other two, he'd stood by and watched it happen, year after year. The relentless teasing. All of it.

It was Felicity's turn to do what Dylan had expressly asked her not to do . . . again. "That's the thing though." Her face was scarlet, as she marched all four feet and eleven and a half inches of herself to somehow tower over their three brothers. "It's not *a* joke. You're making *him* the joke. Like everything he went through before he got diagnosed should be some joke to shame him about—all the shit he had to put up with for most of his life. Oh ADHD, ha-ha, like oh look, there goes a squirrel! But do you know how hard it was for him? All the way until he was grown up. Do you know how hard it is for a man to ask for help because he's just not coping? Because I'm sure that shit's braver than anything you two jerks have ever done."

"It's braver than anything I've done recently too," Derek added in a controlled voice that hid most of his anger.

Dylan placed a hand between Derek's shoulders. "*Babe.*"

Derek's voice was a shattered whisper when he faced Dylan. "It was *hard* for you."

Felicity's anger was less lidded than Derek's. "It's not some stupid personality thing that makes him the quirky comic relief of our family. You dicks made his life harder. I've watched it my entire life."

Derek stood next to Felicity. "And tonight, he put out that fire and almost hurt himself to keep a little girl safe because he cares that much about you all. Only to end up a joke *again*."

"Dude, Dylan . . . I didn't . . ." Calvin seemed shaken.

Derek pushed in between them. "Don't *dude, Dylan* him. Felicity's probably told all you this crap before."

"I warned all of you when he was moving back that you fuckwads better not make his life harder again. It's probably just because you couldn't stand that he was smarter than you assholes." Felicity glared.

Derek again brandished the trophy at Dylan's older brothers. "This garbage stops now."

"It's okay. Really." Dylan pulled Derek's arm, honestly worried Derek was going to try to beat the shit out of the three enormous hockey players with a twenty-four-year-old plaster-of-paris pickle.

"Stop saying it's okay. It's not okay, Dylan." Derek held the pickle trophy between his hands almost like Dylan's mother held her rosary and addressed the brothers. "This 'award?' This making your brilliant brother relive an experience that is clearly painful for him every single year in front of your entire family like some ritualistic flagellation? This shit is *over*." Derek wound up like a major league pitcher and launched it into the woods.

Derek was shaking—actually shaking—as Dylan wrenched him into the dense woods where he had just hurled the Pickle Award.

They walked down the path far enough away that Dylan couldn't easily make out the voices from the field anymore. Dylan's feelings were so jumbled he didn't know where to start.

"Christ, Derek. I didn't need you to do that. And I've told Felicity before not to . . . *Ugh*, I didn't ask for your help—"

Derek's voice echoed off the surrounding trees. "Because you've been around this crap for so long, you're just accepting their bullshit even though it's everything you *told* me you hated last night. It's everything that makes you feel worthless. That's not okay." Derek pulled Dylan to face him. "You are not fucking worthless."

Dylan shifted and leaned against the trunk of a large tree facing away from the field. "It's a joke. I'm not the only one that's gotten it."

"That trophy is complete nonsense. And given the shape of it I'm not convinced that it's not *also* somehow obliquely and generically homophobic. Though I've never seen a penis that looked like that . . . But you know what, I hate those dickwads, and I'm just going to assume that's what their genitalia looks like."

Dylan's face wrinkled with disgust. "Please, could you not assume anything about my older brothers' genitalia? Like ever ever."

"Why didn't you tell me what you dealt with? We wouldn't have come."

"It's not always . . . Tonight, I was just shaken up about the fire. That's why I couldn't handle . . ." Dylan pressed his hand against the tree bark, the sharp texture distracting him from the weird stinging in his eyes. "It's not that big a deal. You didn't have to go off on them."

Derek grabbed hold of Dylan by his collar in a strangely gentle, intimate grip. "I . . . am . . . not . . ." His voice became something low and almost dangerous. He enunciated every word like he was struggling against the impulse to crash back through that forest and pummel someone. "I am *not* going to apologize for standing up for you. Ever. Those guys pull that shit again in front of me, and I will end them." The threat was a rumbling growl, some throaty feral sound. Suddenly, those fantasy romance books Felicity forced Dylan to read seemed a lot less ridiculous. Because as the last vestiges of bonfire light bled through the trees and lit Derek's face, it looked like there were actual sparks crackling behind his beautiful dark eyes.

"*Derek.*"

"Do *not* ever let someone make you feel that small again. Because you, Dylan Gallagher, are not fucking small."

Derek pressed his lips on Dylan's in a shattering kiss.

The kiss was everywhere. It was lightning, streaking down the muscles of Dylan's arms, his chest, his legs. Every shock of Derek's lips against his became a surge of pure kinetic energy. Derek's arms were braced on either side of him, pressing Dylan's back into the tree trunk. Every part of his body hummed with electricity. Flashes of real heat lightning and the tongues of firelight cast magical shadows over the planes of Derek's face, neck, and chest.

As Dylan slid his hands hungrily beneath Derek's shirt, the sound of unwanted raised voices knocked against Dylan's shellshocked consciousness. He was barely a quarter mile from his entire extended family including aunts, uncles, and about thirty-one cousins.

Dylan swallowed, breathless against the relentless pace of Derek's kisses. "You need to take me home right now."

Derek pulled away, his own breath hitching his chest. "I damn well am going to take you home right now. Your brothers and their immature bullshit can suck it."

"*No*, I really need you to take me home because if you don't, I'm going to ask you to fuck me right here against this tree. And I'm deathly afraid of tree snakes."

"Well, shit, now I am too." Derek yanked Dylan off from the tree where he had just been dragging rough teeth along Dylan's neck. "Say the other part again, Dylan."

Dylan grabbed Derek's face, which was still flushed with the irresistible effects of righteous rage. "I *hate* snakes."

"*Dylan.*" His hands circled Dylan's waist, so careful with him despite the near-snapping tension pulling his neck and arm muscles. "Please, say it again."

Dylan unbuttoned the top button of Derek's shirt. He played with the hair at the top of Derek's chiseled chest. "I want you to take me home, and carry me into my bedroom." Dylan slid his hand downward, slipping it inside Derek's pants, feeling the hardness grow against his palm. "And fuck me until I can barely sit down tomorrow."

Derek's eyes shut. His forehead dropped to Dylan's. He gripped the hem of Dylan's T-shirt as if he wanted to tear it off. Sweat beaded on Dylan's forehead from the heat of Derek's body pushing against his.

Dylan trembled. "Also, I need you to drive because I'm so turned on right now that I'm not sure I can keep it together behind the wheel." Dylan's hand shifted inside Derek's shorts, dropping further to cup and then squeeze.

Derek groaned his name.

"What do you think, babe?"

"You're going to kill me with this shit, Dylan Gallagher. Actually kill me."

***

The time alone when they got back to the apartment reminded Derek he wasn't done being angry. He was still seething about the last part of the evening until Dylan came into the bedroom, his eyes showing exactly how ready and hungry he was.

Derek's mouth found Dylan's again. "I'm still pissed you didn't stand up for yourself." Derek yanked off his shirt and tossed it on the ground at Dylan's feet. He cradled Dylan's head as they crashed into the wall, punishing Dylan with his lips and tongue. Ignoring whatever had fallen off the dresser. Ignoring the way the pictures on the wall rattled with the impact of their bodies.

"Good." Dylan's eyes glazed. He unbuttoned Derek's twill pants.

Derek lifted Dylan's shirt off and brushed the mussed hair from Dylan's sweat-slick forehead.

How could Dylan let them do that to him every year? Derek had every damn right to be angry.

Derek lifted Dylan and carried him without a trace of gentleness. As Derek threw him on the bed, nothing about Dylan's wild blue eyes suggested he wanted this to be careful anymore. But Derek would make this good for him. He'd go slow when it counted.

Dylan kicked off his pants and then splayed himself out on the bed. His hand moved toward the very full something as it bobbed against his abs, but Derek stopped him with a look.

Derek's mouth was watering. They'd discussed this on the way back. How to make sure that Dylan was okay. Dylan would tell him if he wanted to stop, but he didn't want Derek to hold back or act like any part of him was fragile.

Dylan trusted him.

Knowing that made Derek even hornier.

He licked the glistening tip of Dylan with a smooth, long swipe. Time became a haze of skin and pressure and heat. Derek's awareness narrowed to the twisting sheets and throaty noises that told him Dylan was ready for more.

"Condoms and stuff are in the bottom drawer."

Derek kissed the spot he'd just tasted and grabbed a condom. He ripped it open with his teeth. He rolled it onto his shaft and then coated it with lube. Dylan had rolled over onto his stomach with a pillow beneath his hips.

God, he was so beautifully eager as he looked back at Derek over his tattooed shoulder. Was it possible for Derek's cock to get even harder?

Derek climbed onto the bed. His hand sketched a long stroke down Dylan's back following the black lines across it and then the ridges of his spine before dipping further and spreading and exploring. He circled Dylan's rim, eliciting deep groans.

"Please . . ."

Derek didn't have the self-control to torture Dylan like he wanted to. That twenty-five-minute car ride and the sound of Dylan's voice begging robbed him of all of his patience.

He offered a single finger first.

"More." Dylan's hands fisted in the sheets.

A second finger joined the first. Derek's other hand traced the slope of Dylan's spine and then slid beneath his stomach to touch the pulsing presence there. Tender but not tentative, he let Dylan's panting responses guide him.

"Derek . . . *now.*" Dylan lifted himself higher. Opening. *Offering.* "I need you. I nee—"

And Derek filled him. Shaking, Dylan pushed himself, letting Derek deepen that pressure. The urge to move was almost too much for Derek. He used his hands to make sure every burn of pain was laced with pleasure.

"Do *not* be gentle with me, babe. Fuck me."

Oh, he would.

"Please?" The quiver on that last word made Dylan's demand a plea. A desperate invitation.

Derek let go like he never had with anyone else. He trusted Dylan to tell him if he needed to stop. He just trusted Dylan completely.

Was this *connection*? Not just the kind making Derek tremble as his hips flexed and bowed around Dylan's perfect ass.

These weeks of waiting for Dylan to be ready meant that in this perfect moment, he could give Dylan absolutely everything, because Derek felt *everything*. For all Dylan's claims on the drive home of wanting this to be angry and rough, it felt intense more than wild. The tempo was both more and less than something furious.

Dylan's praising whispers came on deep exhales against the mattress. Derek's hand covered Dylan's splayed fingers while Dylan arched and braced against the bedframe. Their fingers laced together.

But Derek needed to be closer. He pulled Dylan's torso flush with his, changing the angle and coaxing a stammered oath from the man beneath him. Derek's lips dragged over Dylan's shoulder, those lean back muscles bunching beneath his mouth. Sweat blended with sweat in a new rhythm. Even the slaps of skin against skin brought more of Dylan's almost worshipful words.

Everything slowed.

Thoughts blurred. Speech impossible.

All that remained was that intoxicating friction. The humming vibration of this beautiful man's sweet, whimpered noises. And that perfect slide of Derek's slick, eager hand.

Chapter 39

When they were both freshly showered and back beneath the sheets, Dylan lounged between Derek's ridiculous thighs reading a book while Derek dozed. Dylan hadn't stopped smiling for at least an hour. It was as if they'd done this for years.

Dylan's book sagged in his hand as he yawned. He checked the clock. He'd been reading longer than he realized. As he sat up, Derek reached for him as if he couldn't stand the loss of either Dylan's body heat or just his closeness. He hadn't been kidding about being a cuddler.

Impishly grinning, Dylan settled back between Derek's legs. Derek tightened himself around Dylan like a very sexy and sleepy sloth clinging to a tree branch.

"I kind of liked you all ragey and hypothetically violent to protect my honor." Dylan pulled the blanket over them both.

"I could tell." Derek's voice was hoarse. Probably from all the yelling he'd done at Dylan's brothers and then from all the yelling he had done in the last few hours . . .

"I'm worried it means I have too much internalized toxic masculinity." He sighed. "Or that I'm not a feminist."

"If it makes you feel better, I've never actually hit anyone in my life, and I've only ever used my sarcasm to shoot down someone's assholery. Never these guns." Derek flexed his arms.

Dylan laughed.

"Stop that." Derek covered a yawn. "Trying to sleep, and you're waking part of me back up."

"Sorry."

"Oh, somehow when we got out of the shower, I got distracted . . . so I forgot to ask you something . . ." Derek's drowsy voice trailed off.

"Ask me what?" Dylan braced but he wasn't quite sure why.

"On a scale of one to ten, how done are you with family drama right now?"

"Sixty-four."

"Cute."

"Why?" Dylan asked weakly.

"Because my mom texted. She and my new stepfather are hosting a dinner party next Friday, and she wants me to bring my new friend Dylan to dinner."

"And you . . ." Dylan winced. "This is a big night for you . . . Are you sure you want me to—"

"Yes." He kissed Dylan's forehead. His nimble fingers worked tangles from Dylan's damp hair until the hand lowered. He lifted Dylan's hand and swept a clumsy kiss across his knuckles. Derek nestled his head into the pillow without shifting from his sloth-on-a-tree-branch–style snuggle. "I really do."

Something about that unhesitant yes made Dylan feel bolder. "Speaking of things we keep forgetting to mention . . ."

"Hmm?"

"I just . . . I keep forgetting to tell you. My tenants are moving out in a few weeks, after I get back from the meetings. Could I . . . Would you want to see my house sometime?"

He'd phrased the question in an intentionally low-stakes way.

Like it was just a friendly tour and had nothing else riding on it.

"*Yes.*" Derek twisted to face Dylan, opening his eyes for the first time in an hour. "Yes. Absolutely."

Dylan tilted his mouth to let Derek kiss him. "Sounds good."

Dylan thought Derek had fallen back asleep until he shifted beneath him.

"My dad used to sketch plans for houses." The words were slightly louder than a whisper.

"Was he an architect?"

"No." Derek traced lines up and down the back of Dylan's arm. "He wanted to go back to school for it, but he and my mom had me so young—she was eighteen and he was twenty-two—he stuck with the engineering thing so he could help her pay for her school. But I remember this one plan for a house."

"What was it like?"

"Stone front, but sort of like a sprawling cottage. Five bedrooms, so my grandparents could come stay someday. A little library with a fireplace because he said the way American houses have unused living rooms was stupid. Open kitchen. Big dining room. A detached garage where he could tinker."

"He sounds like a dreamer."

"Yeah." Derek's hand rested on Dylan's diaphragm, lifting with each of Dylan's slow breaths. "Every time Olive made me take one of those wacky *Cosmo* quizzes, I'd always pick the one that ended up showing that my ideal date was sex at home in front of a fire on a bearskin rug." A sleepy laugh.

"Bearskin rug doesn't sound very ethical."

"The nineties were dark times. Remember?"

Chuckling, Dylan coaxed Derek's mouth into another one of those slow, deep kisses. "Sounds like you would've made a great hobbit."

Derek's laughter quaked beneath Dylan. "I thought you liked hobbits." He traced the Elvish across Dylan's ribs, even though he couldn't see it from his position. It was like he'd already memorized where it was.

Dylan's skin pebbled in response. "I do."

Derek's mouth pursed together and then parted. "That's convenient then."

Could Dylan really sleep like this?

Wrapped up in a goddamn delicious-smelling man who'd

just fucked him and then sucked him until he saw stars? A man who had invited him to a family event and would be coming to see Dylan's house in a few weeks?

Turned out, yeah, he could.

Chapter 40

They had been sitting in Derek's mom's driveway for at least five minutes, and Dylan was beginning to be genuinely concerned by both Derek's mental state and the structural integrity of the ancient-looking steering column on Derek's vintage car. Derek's knuckles blanched around the wheel.

Dylan undid his seatbelt. "So . . . are you excited to meet Bruce?"

Something softened in Derek's forehead, but his grip didn't relax. "For the last time, this is not a bit. We're not going to do this every time my mom's husband comes up."

"But . . . think he'll let me drive his car?" Dylan glanced around as if he were searching for the Batmobile.

"Well, on his website there's a photo of a bright-yellow commercial van with pictures of furry wild animals on the side—so still probably not."

"Are you saying I'm a bad driver? That's *mean*."

"You're the one who's mean. For the last time, his name is not Bruce Wayne. It's Ken Goh, and that fucker asked my mother to marry him after two dates."

"Right . . . so since they're married, does that mean we can ask him about the whole cave thing or just skip right over that to see if he has a cockney-accented butler?"

"I really hate you, Dylan Gallagher." Derek squeezed his hands over the leather of the steering wheel again. Would his hands just fuse there at some point? The key was still in the ignition. A garbled sound of frustration came out of his mouth which sounded a little like "Arrrrggjbbbflllr."

Dylan brought a hand up to cup Derek's cheek. "Babe, I was just trying to make you laugh because I'm legitimately worried you might break your car with your Hulk-like grip strength. This car is really old, you know." He pushed up from his seat and kissed Derek's offended face.

"This car is a classic." Derek's hands uncurled from the steering wheel and threaded through Dylan's hair as he deepened the kiss.

Thankfully the trees and bushes kept their parking spot beside the basement garage relatively private. Derek's mouth moved against his in that perfect way it always did. Kissing Derek seemed to make everything else fade. He hoped he could do the same for Derek right now.

They were both breathless when Derek pulled away. There was just enough space between them that they could look at each other. Derek's cheeks were flushed but his eyes had this odd look of confusion behind them that seemed in contrast with the perfection of the impromptu car make-out session.

"What's wrong?" Dylan asked.

"I . . . It's . . . *gahhh*." He grabbed the steering wheel again like he was a man overboard and it was a life preserver. "Do you feel okay about this? Being here?"

Genuinely perplexed about Derek's question, he shrugged. "I've always wanted to meet Batman."

Derek grunted, but again, his hands relaxed. "Have you heard the expression beating a dead horse?" Derek shoved Dylan's shoulder.

"Sure. Always sounded like something PETA wouldn't approve of." Dylan shook his head, not missing that tiny twitch at the corner of Derek's mouth that showed the laughter hiding there. "If I promise not to call him Bruce tonight, will you get me tacos?"

"You know there will be food there, right?"

Dylan jabbed a finger at Derek's chest. "*You* told me she

can't cook and I should eat before we went, but then Felicity called about picking the finishes for the bathroom and I forgot to grab a protein bar."

"Fine, we can get tacos." Derek touched the key still in the ignition but didn't twist it to remove it. Instead, he turned back to Dylan and draped himself over him, holding on with a ferocity he hadn't before. Dylan rubbed Derek's back with his fingertips, the tightness of Derek's grip giving Dylan that lovely mushy feeling inside. When Derek let go, he straightened Dylan's glasses.

"In case it wasn't clear, I really appreciate you being here." Tiny crinkles appeared along Derek's brow ridge.

"I-I'm glad to be here." Dylan smoothed a finger over Derek's forehead. "Tonight's going to be great. Really . . ."

"We'll see." Derek twisted the key, the old engine's growl ending with a splutter. Derek clutched the steering wheel again.

Dylan peeled each of Derek's hands away from the sun-damaged leather. "I think that steering wheel has been through enough without you squeezing the life out of it every five seconds."

"My mom's new goddamn husband has more balls than I do."

"Okay, I'm like super lost. Not sure how we got from steering wheel strangulation to the subject of your mom's new husband's balls, and I feel like bringing them up now is just going to make it really awkward when we meet them in five minutes. 'Them' being your mom and her husband, not 'them' meaning your mom's husband's balls."

"Dylan." Derek grabbed his hands and shook them once, eyes dead serious.

"Derek."

"The last person I like-liked . . . I told him, and he was just so conflicted about it. I thought we'd started something, but now looking back I realize it wasn't ever going to happen. But I was so *gone* on the guy that I built everything up in my head that if

I just tried hard enough I would fix everything, and shit would be good." Derek seemed *flustered.* Actually, legitimately Dylan-type flustered.

"Please tell me that this is not a long conversation about how you're still into someone else—"

"Will you be my boyfriend?" After Derek blurted out the question, he didn't give Dylan a gap to respond. "Or like *are* you my boyfriend already? So, if someone other than me asked you what I was to you, would you say, or maybe not even *say*, would you just think 'uh, yeah, Derek's my boyfriend' or would you be like nah—"

"Christ, you talk so much when you're weirdly nervous. Of course I think of you as my boyfriend. Just didn't really know when to bring up the whole label thing. Last time we tried to have that conversation we end up being attacked by your nephews and finding out your mom married Batman."

Derek groaned. "Not Batman. The bat man."

"Sorry. This won't ever *not* be funny."

"I changed my mind. You're not my boyfriend."

"Really?"

"No, dummy. Do you think I spoon everyone for an hour in the morning just so I can watch them sleep? Just you."

Dylan's breath caught in his chest for a millisecond. "Who is this *them* that you're spooning in the mornings? You're doing it not to watch them sleep but for some other reason?" Dylan grinned. "I'm hurt."

"I'm not sure who I hate more. You or the English language and its ambiguity with misplaced modifiers."

"Definitely me. So, when you introduce me tonight, you're going to say, 'Hello, please meet my brilliant and successful boyfriend, Dylan?'"

"That I hate."

"Obviously. Does the boyfriend label mean I can get extra tacos?"

"You're so needy."

"And a Diet Mountain Dew."

"Your eating habits make me want to die. Scratch that—your eating habits are going to make you *actually die.*"

"I just ate an apple."

"*Yesterday.* Goddamn it, Dylan."

"So, what you're saying is the point of this entire conversation about hating me, is that you—uh, like me?"

"Obviously." Derek kissed him. "Kay?"

"Kay."

A few minutes later, Derek stood facing the door of his childhood home, but he didn't reach for the doorknob.

"Do you usually just go in or knock?"

"Normally, I just go in, but now there's a man in there, and I'm not sure if I should still be treating this like my house too, or like her house with this new guy."

After enduring several moments of Derek's renewed indecision, Dylan pushed the doorbell.

"*Dylan.*"

"*Derek.* Babe, it took ten minutes to get you out of the car when we got here. While at least five of those minutes were extremely enjoyable, now I'm hungry."

Derek laughed in spite of himself. "How do you always make everything easier?"

Dylan blushed as the door swung open.

Chapter 41

Derek's mom hugged and kissed him before focusing all her attention on Dylan.

"This is Dylan—"

"Angela." His mom pulled Dylan into a welcoming squeeze as well.

"Dylan's my boyfriend." The last word came out hoarse, not because he had trouble saying it but because he was temporarily distracted by what was on his mother's hand. Specifically, the diamond the size of a marble sparkling on it. Given that this particular rock could probably be seen from the International Space Station, both Dylan and Derek were justified in staring as it caught the porchlight.

"Yes, Derek, I figured that was who this was." The corner of her mouth twitched.

Derek cleared his throat. "That ring. Whoa—"

"Isn't it beautiful? Finally got it back from the jeweler today. Had to get it resized." She held it up.

"Gorgeous." Dylan leaned forward to admire it.

"Come in. Come in." They took off their shoes and made their way into the house.

"It's so wonderful to meet you. Amy's boys haven't stopped talking about you."

"They're a wild bunch. Fun kids."

"Wild indeed." Derek's mom took Dylan's arm and led him through the entryway. Standing behind the beautifully set table were his oldest sister and Seo-Joon. The former was opening a wine bottle while the latter waved to them.

After pouring herself a large glass of wine and taking a large sip, Amy came over to greet them. Under the pretense of kissing her brother on the cheek, she whispered. "It's catered."

"Oh, thank god," Derek said.

"Are two of the boys coming?" Dylan asked, gesturing to the two extra set places at the table. "Or . . . ?"

"The Velcro baby's upstairs asleep and the others are with Joanna." Amy's smile seemed more forced than usual as she grabbed the extra places off the table. "I probably just went to autopilot. You know, sleep-deprived mom brain."

Derek didn't buy that for a second. Maybe Ken's college-age kids were supposed to come and she didn't want to make a big deal about it. They all had to know Michelle wouldn't . . .

"Hopefully no more gas station sushi for Joanna," Dylan said.

"She did mention she has new appreciation for her microbiology class. I was glad to hear it." Amy's voice dripped sarcasm as she filled glasses for Derek and Dylan.

His mom returned to the dining room. "Ken said we should go ahead and start." The bizarre thing was that his mom didn't seem upset, even though the inconsiderate guy was just blowing them off. And maybe his kids were too.

They all loaded their plates, and dinner continued the way most family dinners did these days, which meant it became a back and forth "conversation" (argument) about tax law between Amy and his mom. Seo-Joon was a patent attorney, but his main interest outside of that was Star Wars miniature figure painting. Derek figured this would be right up Dylan's alley, so he prodded the conversation in that direction, but it wasn't until Dylan interrupted Amy's and his mom's conversation that there was a subtle shift in the energy in the room.

"Whoa, whoa, whoa." Dylan said, whipping around from discussing the best paints to use for shading Wookiee fur to turn to the two bickering CPAs. "If you were doing that, are you saying there would be a tax advantage to *not* categorizing a business like that? Can you explain why? I'm a small business owner, but I never understood that. Just relocated everything to Maryland a couple years ago. Money stuff's pretty much my Achilles' heel. I haven't really been satisfied with the accountants I've been using." He shrugged modestly.

Pounced. Yes, *pounced.* That was the only word for what Amy and his mother did. They spent the rest of dinner mapping out sometimes-conflicting tax strategies for Dylan's business to the point where the guy asked for an actual piece of paper so he could take notes. If Derek hadn't been dating him and Amy's husband hadn't been sitting right there, his sister might have swooned when he asked some highly incomprehensible question about tax code that nevertheless made her light up.

Derek hadn't seen his mother this happy in a long time. Getting to monologue about the intricacies of the recent changes in IRS tax regulations with both a weirdly captivated audience (Dylan, despite what he said before about being bored by money stuff) and a bemused captive audience (Derek and Seo-Joon).

Derek had *thought* his mom was happy during that conversation with Dylan. Until a tall man in a yellow jumpsuit walked in through the door. His mother leaped up from the table and actually almost skipped over to the man with an expression of beatific delight on her face. The man who was . . . was . . . *whoa.*

He couldn't blame his mom for thinking he was attractive. Derek was honest enough to admit that this man with his shiny black hair and high, chiseled cheekbones and, honestly, rather impressive build was objectively attractive. The only problem was that Derek had *not* expected him to look ten years younger than his mom was. At a *minimum.*

Which meant—*oh god.*

Derek shot up to standing, making the dinnerware rattle. "I'm sorry, but how *old* are you?"

Every face in the room turned to Derek. Dylan was literally biting his lips together, probably to keep from laughing. Amy was pouring herself another glass of wine, and Seo-Joon had steepled his hands together like a bookie watching a horse race.

His mom, never the shrinking violet, walked over and smacked him on the back of his head. Hard. "*Derek*. Manners."

The new arrival took off his work boots and then stopped at the tiny powder room next to the front door, presumably to wash his hands after all of his various creature-related activities that had made him late to dinner. He had a wide, warm smile. At least, Derek would have thought it was warm if he didn't suspect this man was looking for some kind of sugar mama. God, please let him never think those last two words again about his mother. He needed to detox his brain. Or bleach it. A mental autoclaving.

The situation got worse when Ken came back in, and his mother said a thoroughly nonverbal and thoroughly horrifying hello to her new husband.

Derek plopped back into his seat and concentrated all his attention on eating.

"You okay, babe?" Dylan said under his breath.

"Totally fine. Why?"

"Because I think the steak's already dead, so you don't have to disembowel it."

Amy actually snorted. "I think *I* should keep Dylan," she said in an offhand drawl as if she was an Italian mob boss considering murdering all the members of a feuding family in order to steal a single talented lieutenant. She turned to Dylan and patted his hand, keeping her face deadpan. "I'll do *all* your taxes. Don't worry. I take care of my own. You'll be in very safe financial hands."

Seo-Joon gave his wife a highly affronted look. "Ames, stop trying to be a crime boss."

"Drat," she said. "Foiled *again*."

Seo-Joon lifted his palms in a possibly facetious show of shock. "Again—?"

Derek left the table to stand in front of Ken Goh, who looked like the kind of man who you'd seen as the hunky middled-age spy hero in a Hollywood action film.

Ken grinned. Like a goddamn hyena's that grin was. His teeth were too white and too straight for him to seem trustworthy. "Derek, it's so nice to meet you after we talked on the phone. Can't tell you how surprised I was when I came over here that first day."

His mom glared with her hands on her hips. "You told Ken I was an elderly widow living alone."

Derek's mouth fell open. "I did *not* say elderly. I might have said widow. I think I said grandmother. Which, you *are*. There was a potentially rabid family of flying rodents in your attic, Mom. I did what I had to do."

"Angie taught me a lot about expectations that night."

Oh god no.

Was Derek having a stroke? This had to be what having a stroke felt like.

Derek wished he'd accepted that second glass of wine when his sister said he might need it. He should have downed the whole bottle.

"And to answer your question, Derek, I'm forty-three."

Yes, this was absolutely a stroke. Derek turned back to the table, reading in Dylan's face that he had done the math too. His mother's new husband was closer in age to Derek than to her. To borrow one of Dylan's most recent favorite swears, *Jesus Christ on a popsicle stick.*

Derek tugged his collar. "Yeah, so that's my—er—boyfriend,

Dylan." He searched Ken's face for any sign of judgment, but there was none.

Dylan rose from the table and warmly greeted Ken. Stupid gentlemanly man that Dylan was. "It's so nice to finally meet—"

"Yeah, so Ken . . ." An irrepressible growling noise rattled Derek's throat. "What held you up tonight? You go on a lot of jobs on short notice? Just miss important family dinners a lot?"

Ken's smile stayed put. "I wouldn't normally have gone on a job tonight, but it was special circumstances. Angie told me I should go when she heard the situation. I still do calls when I'm short-staffed or when they're important." He gripped Derek's mother's hand, twisting his fingers around that iceberg he'd put there. "And, boy, am I glad I do."

How hard would it be to clean vomit off of his mother's immaculate white carpet?

"That makes sense." Dylan gave Derek's arm a prod toward the table. "So, we should probably finish eating, right, Derek?"

"What were the special circumstances of this 'really important' job tonight? Not judging. Just curious," asked Derek.

"Oh, yes that is quite a story, let me tell you." Ken Goh had one of those television laughs. Too rich and too cool to be real. The kind actors used on *Jimmy Fallon* when they were retelling some rehearsed story about themselves and trying to make it seem off-the-cuff.

Derek didn't buy it. He crossed his arms.

Ken exhaled melodramatically. "Raccoon got loose in a nursing home. Terrified the residents half to death. Turned out it made a nest in one of the dryers that hadn't been used in a while and had a bunch of babies who were crawling in through a broken vent. Then when someone opened it . . ." Ken playfully sprang at Derek, lifting his hands like claws and making a sound that honestly did sound a lot like a raccoon.

Jolted off-balance by the jump scare, Derek's feet tangled underneath him as he lurched back, clutching his chest. Dylan caught him before he crashed into Derek's mother's beloved Meyer lemon tree.

After Derek was upright and steady, Dylan lost it. And it had always been hard for Derek *not* to laugh when Dylan laughed, because it was one of the most wonderful sounds in the whole damn world. Everyone else seemed to agree, because within seconds everyone in the room was laughing too.

At the end of the dinner, his mother stood up. "We have another thing we wanted to tell you." For a moment her eyes flickered to the two empty chairs at the end of the table, but then she refocused and the sparkle returned to her eyes. "Since meeting Ken, I've been able to find a side of myself I didn't know I was ignoring for years."

"Please don't go into detail," Derek said before he could stop himself.

Dylan elbowed him.

"Derek Chang." His mother's glare was sharp enough even to cut through the rock-hard lemon cake they were all trying to chew as politely as possible. Unfortunately, the dessert had not been catered. "I'm still furious at you for making Ken think I was a day away from the old folks' home."

"I never said—" Derek gave up on the concrete citrus cake. His fork clinked down on his plate.

She *tsked* at him and took her husband's hand.

Derek's mom lifted her hands into waggling jazz fingers in exactly the same way Amy had. "Ken and I bought that Airbnb we were staying at near Disney World."

Ken's face gaped in a goofy grin. He took one of Derek's mom's hands and kissed it. "Angie and I are going to be snowbirds."

Derek decided to emulate Amy's current coping strategy and gulped the rest of his wine.

Chapter 42

When Derek got back to Dylan's apartment that night, it took a very, very thorough blow job and thirty minutes of being the little spoon to calm him down enough to close his eyes. But he still wasn't ready to sleep. "You still awake?"

"Yep." Dylan's mouth was pressed against Derek's back. He was clearly at least 85 percent asleep.

"What does your perfect life look like?"

"Are you thinking about this because your mom's about to be living her best life with her new super-hot husband or—"

"Can you *not* call him super hot?"

"Are we the kind of boyfriends who lie to each other?"

"No." Derek gritted his teeth. "But maybe just go back to calling him Batman instead."

"Maybe."

"Hmm . . ." Dylan tugged on Derek's shoulder, asking Derek to turn and face him. "What does the perfect life look like for *you*?"

Turning onto his back, he rested a hand behind his head and pulled Dylan on top of him. He loved Dylan's warm weight pressing on his chest, grounding him into the mattress. Derek considered. He'd never been asked it before.

"I guess . . . quiet. I don't like a lot of drama. Tonight's events notwithstanding. If I really think about it, I just want some space to breathe . . . like land maybe? A nice porch. Someplace cozy with just a shit ton of space for my books and my DVDs so they won't have to live in bins under my bed. Space for Gus to run around when I have him while Olive travels. If I could,

I'd sell my apartment and try to save up to get someplace with *space*. I like being a nurse because it's twelve hours and then done, but I feel like I want to do more with my days off. Maybe try to find a new hobby. Something stupid like gardening. Or maybe goat yoga."

Dylan's laughter vibrated against Derek's chest. "I've always wanted to know what happens if they poop on you."

"Scratch the goat yoga idea. I do want to read more. I don't know. I feel like the last few years have been one crisis after another."

"Olive's brother . . . and before that, and I guess *still* stuff with your sister . . . Did you know Michelle wouldn't be there tonight?" Dylan turned and rested his chin on Derek's chest.

"I figured. Not sure if she still speaks to my mom. But yeah, lots of crises."

"I guess even before that your dad too. You took so much on your shoulders." He caressed Derek's neck and over his shoulder blades. "You deserve a place where you could have peace. Drink your gross smoothies out on the porch and watch the sunrise."

"All of that." Derek took a deep inhale and then pressed a kissed to Dylan's forehead. "I know it's simple and nothing grand or exciting."

"Babe, all of my hobbies happen in my house or within a five-mile radius. Last year, I read an entire six-thousand-page book series in a week during that ice storm, and it was one of the happiest weeks of my life up until that point. Because I could just be in front of my fireplace. I felt peaceful."

"Yeah . . . I guess, I feel like that was really all my dad wanted. God, I hate he didn't get to have it as long as he deserved."

Dylan kissed Derek's jaw.

"He used to say some people loved to travel. Some people loved adventure. But that he loved *quiet*. I never thought that made him boring. I thought that sounded nice. Speaking of which, do you still have to fly out Thursday?"

Dylan sighed. "Yes."

"Still want to take me to see your house when you get back?"

Dylan's face brightened even in the dimness of the room. "Yes."

He'd mentioned the house more often since Derek found out why he'd rented it out. Dylan seemed to genuinely love the place and miss it. After all, the guy had spent two years fixing it up. It seemed like Dylan put so many dreams into that house. And now he wanted to take Derek to see it . . .

A lingering worry pinched inside him, distracting him from the anticipation of seeing Dylan's house. He *needed* to tell Dylan about what happened with Jake. He'd almost done it earlier, but he'd chickened out. He didn't want the moment asking Dylan to be his boyfriend to be ruined with explaining it. Since the Grill-Out they'd been too busy—both the good, sexy, exploring kind of busy and work and apartment reno busy—to think about Jake at all until tonight when he was about to have that conversation. The more things progressed with Dylan, the more what happened with Jake barely registered.

Bringing it up when Dylan was half-asleep was also probably not the best time. How could he even tell him at this point and make it clear that it felt like it wasn't even a big deal, when it was obviously a big enough deal before that Derek had intentionally avoided telling him the truth?

Dylan stirred, his eyes opening a sliver. "Did you remember to get the key back from Carol so Felicity could borrow one?"

Derek sighed. "I just got another copy made instead. She said to just leave it here in Sean's place when I went back downstairs in the morning." Yep, another way he was complete chicken shit.

"You know, I like you enough I'd go and march in there and take it from Carol, but . . ."

"But?"

Dylan pressed himself into Derek. "She's got birds." A yawn

muffled his next words. "You know what? Maybe we should get Daddy Batman to do it."

✳✳✳

Two hours later a call on Dylan's work phone woke him.

Dylan rolled off of Derek and grabbed his phone, pulling on clothes. Derek groaned but then snored and turned over. He snagged a T-shirt as he eased the bedroom door closed.

"What?" Dylan said into the phone. "I swear to god if this is about an error in that demo—"

"It's not." Chase said. "You missed the Pager Duty alert. There's a system outage. All hands on deck with the engineering team."

"*Shit.*" Dylan rubbed his head, dragging his hand across the areas on the side that were so much shorter now. "Call—"

"Already done."

"And you've sent me the—"

"In your inbox." Chase chuckled. "It's really a shame you quit *my* job. You were good at it."

"Just keep your phone on. I'll update you when I can."

"Well, I was planning on—"

"Yeah, not in a joke mood."

"Who got your panties in a twist this afternoon?"

"It's one o'clock in the goddamn morning here." Dylan turned on his computer, and while it was booting he grabbed his medication bottle and a drink. While gulping down the cold caffeine, he made a snack.

"Unlike you to actually know what time it is. Do you have a new lucky man in your life? Is that why you're a bit touchy about being dragged out of bed? You used to live for *this* action . . ." Chase's kind of assholery was so ubiquitous in tech, and he hated it. "I was kind of hoping we'd reconnect during your trip out. I rearranged my schedule so I could be back in the country for it."

"*No.*"

The gross, immature euphemisms and incubator frat boy wannabes with their hoodies and their casual misogynistic, homophobic bullshit. Dylan didn't miss it. And he hadn't been lying that Derek had absolutely nothing to worry about there. This minutes-long conversation with Chase made Dylan only more aware of how anyone else he'd ever been with couldn't measure up to Derek.

"Oh." Chase's voice stiffened. Clearly not what he'd been expecting. "I was just joking anywa—"

"Hanging up now. I'll be online in a minute." He took the snack and drink to his desk.

"The team's having a tag-up in thirty minutes."

"Wouldn't miss it."

The next time Dylan checked his watch for non-work-related issues, it was nine o'clock in the morning. He'd forgotten to set any of his usual alarms, but if he didn't pee and stretch his legs soon, he'd regret it.

Soon, but he couldn't stop now. He had two more things to do.

"Dylan?" a hand touched his shoulder. Derek was awake.

"So sorry. Hold on a sec."

He was so close to being done with this. He had so many things on his mind right now, stacking in his brain like a house of cards. He'd been on this program for five years, and this was one of the biggest disasters they had ever had. If it got a reputation for extended outages like this, especially right before that big client demo, the company would be lambasted in the news this week.

"Dylan?" The sound of his name was muffled, but some part of his mind processed it.

He held up a finger and then clicked and typed and moved between his monitors. Checking his email for updates from the team out west. Deleting stupid texts from Chase and trying not to panic when he was copied on emails with angry executives who were panicking about this impacting the big client demos next week.

Christ, they were doing the best they could.

His fingers sped over the keyboard. Lines of code scrolled on one side of his screen. He reran the new changes to see if it fixed the errors.

Crap. Crap. *Crap.*

Something was still not quite right. He pulled off his headphones and rubbed his temples.

"*Dylan*? What is going on with you?"

Dylan jolted, slamming his knee on the bottom of his desk.

"Jesus fucking Christ, Derek," He whipped around, blinking furiously to fix the dryness in his eyes. "I said one sec."

Derek was completely dressed. His mouth was hanging open with a mix of emotions on his face that Dylan was too tired to decipher.

"Dude, I was just checking on you." He shifted Gus's leash from one hand to the other. "For the record, you said *one sec* an hour ago." His face studied Dylan. "What's your Adderall dosage? If you're not careful, and if it's too high—"

"Okay . . . so I need you to not do the thing that people always do, which is to assume that I haven't *painstakingly* tried to figure out what works for me." He palmed his face, seeing that the medication bottle was still on the kitchen counter. He'd never taken it. No wonder he'd forgotten to set his alarms. He probably hadn't really moved in hours. He'd be paying for this tomorrow.

Derek shook his head. "I had a friend in nursing school who—"

"*Please* don't." Dylan was too damn exhausted to have this conversation. "So, for starters, for someone who gave my brothers shit a week ago about mocking my ADHD, trying to be a back seat psychiatrist is—"

"Oh—I wasn't trying to—"

"This always happens. People assume that there's a better option or that I'm not doing and didn't do everything I possibly could to figure out what worked for me. God, people never do this stuff about blood pressure medicine, why do people get so judgmental about—"

"I wasn't trying to be judgmental . . ."

"For the record . . ." Dylan sighed and rubbed his temples. "I *forgot* to take my Adderall when I got up to start working. Forgot it because I was distracted tonight. Which meant I forgot to do all the things that make me *healthier* while I was working. I'm not a tweaking college student taking Adderall to stay up thirty hours straight to cram for exams. I have an actual chemical imbalance in my brain. So, no, I don't think I have a 'dangerous addiction' to a controlled substance." Dylan barked out a self-hating laugh. "Ironically, my brain would remember to take my goddamn pills if I were addicted."

"I didn't say anything about a dangerous addiction."

"It's what other people say anytime they find out I'm on it."

"I was just saying this was just like last week when you went on some work bender and were barely sleeping. I didn't say anything then, but I'm just worried all of this is not healthy." His knuckles whitened as his hand gripped the leash.

"I need to get back to work." Dylan pulled the headphones on and swiveled around in his chair to his monitor. His head was still spinning. He just needed to finish this so he could sleep. Just a little sleep.

Dylan turned on music, and his fingers returned to his keyboard.

When he finished the next call with the team and got the *all clear* from management, he threw off his headphones. After taking a piss in the bathroom like that one drunk Tom Hanks took in *A League of Their Own*, he tossed his glasses on the side table and fell fully clothed onto his bed.

When he woke up, panic propelled him out of bed. *Shit shit shit.*

Everything he had said to Derek was true, but he shouldn't have said it like *that*. *Shit*, he'd gone from having one of the sweetest, tenderest moments with a man he . . . really liked . . . to petulantly yelling and messing everything up with him.

He flung open the door and something hit him smack in the face.

Chapter 43

Derek was honestly surprised Dylan caught the pillow, but the guy *had* supposedly grown up playing hockey. "That was for being a dick to me." He handed Dylan a Taco Bell bag. Somehow in the couple weeks they'd been together he'd noticed what Dylan ate when he was stressed or working. "This is because I was also an insensitive ass about your medication."

Dylan pushed the food onto the table and pulled Derek against him. "I'm *so* sorry. I just get in this hyperfocus zone sometimes. Interruptions . . . are hard. It's not an excuse. It's something I'm working on, and you didn't deserve that."

"I know."

Dylan looked Derek in the eye. "Do you forgive me for yelling?"

Half of Derek's mouth quirked upward. "That wasn't even yelling, but yes."

"It felt like yelling." Dylan's head bowed to rest on Derek's chest. "I lost it on you. I'm sorry."

"Trust me, no one who's ever worked in the ED would think you were yelling." Derek's hand wrapped around the back of Dylan's neck, rubbing it in that way that always made his face relax. He eased Dylan forward so that his forehead rested on Derek's chest.

"We need to talk about something else—"

A knock came from the door.

Derek's face made it clear that this interruption was expected though the timing might not have been. "You should get that, I think."

"I should?"

"Yes, but while you talk to him, can you eat your damn food so you don't keel over? I even got you a stupid large Diet Mountain Dew." He pulled away from Dylan and grabbed it from the fridge. "Even though that shit's disgusting."

Beaming, Dylan grabbed the bag again and then took a long slurp from the cup. "Talk to who?"

Another knock on the door.

"Ugh."

Dylan opened the door and inhaled an ounce of the Mountain Dew down his windpipe in surprise. "Dad?"

"I came by earlier too, but he said you were asleep because you had to work last night. Your friend let me take a look at what's going on downstairs, but I heard footsteps and thought you might be awake."

"Uh, okay." Dylan scratched at the back of his head, feeling how his hair was sticking out at every angle.

"Think we could talk for a minute?"

"Do you mind if I eat while we talk?"

"No, course not."

"There are a couple more tacos on the coffee table if you want them. Figured you'd be back." Derek's tone wasn't exactly welcoming. "I need to go downstairs anyway to check on my dog."

Dylan sat down on the couch behind the coffee table, and his dad sat beside him. He pushed the bag toward his dad even though his mom would be pissed about the cholesterol content. Tacos were a good choice for this. He could look down at his hands under the auspices of gathering stray cheese and lettuce. Being side-by-side meant more avoided eye contact.

Christ, this was awkward. Had he ever eaten alone with his dad?

Focusing on his body's immediate physical needs, Dylan bit

into the Crunchwrap and took a few sips of Mountain Dew. This stuff tasted like the actual nectar of the gods after a crisis all-nighter. He fiddled with the wrapper on a taco, ever aware of his dad's chewing and tense posture.

"Been wrestling with something all week. Your mom said I needed to quit my brooding and do something." His dad crumpled an empty taco wrapper and put it in the bag. It struck Dylan how different his parents sometimes were in almost every literal way. Right now, it was the way they spoke. His mom's almost musical voice was the opposite of his dad's gruff, slightly southern-sounding version of a Maryland accent. "Your mom says if it's keeping me up at night, I should talk to you about it."

"About what?"

"Was what Derek said true? At the party. Is that how you feel? I know your sister's been saying things like that for years . . ."

"Oh . . ." It had taken Dylan several seconds to catch up. The Grill-Out was just a week ago, but it didn't feel like that after the dinner with Derek's family and the emergency last night and the grueling week of repair work. "I—uh—I guess. Some of it. I didn't tell him to say that though."

"Never thought you had. The man just seems like he knows you pretty well."

Instead of answering, Dylan took a mutilating bite of his taco.

"You were always sensitive, kid. I didn't know quite what to do with you sometimes to be honest. Always thought it was because I let your mother name you after that poet instead of an Oriole like the others. You know, it wasn't the sensitive part so much as the fact that when you were seven years old you were already smarter than your old man. Your straight-talking little sister was sure right about that."

"Dad . . ."

"Just lemme get this out, and then if you want to kick my ass out of here, you can do it. Or you can let that nice fella downstairs do the job for you. Sure he'd like to. Can't say I blame him, to be honest."

"Alright."

"On that day when you were eleven, I sent you out there to tie those knots because I was half off my ass drunk. Couldn't see straight, and I was trying to hide it. It was the last time I fell off the wagon. I couldn't have tied those knots to save my life. Your mama asked me to go do it, and there was no way I could, so I sent you. *You.* Not your brothers. They couldn't tie a knot for shit.

"When it all went wrong you wouldn't stop crying. Saying it was all your fault. Saying you ruined everything, but all three of your brothers—they were just as boneheaded as me, even back then—they always wanted to protect you. They got the idea of telling you that you didn't ruin everything. All you did was save the pickles."

Dylan choked on a watery laugh. "That's why they used to tell me their favorite food was pickles all the time. Honestly . . . I just thought they were just shitting on me."

"I reckon I can't lie to you, there was a lot of that too. We shouldn't have let this go on so far."

"It's okay—"

"It's not though. Some of the stuff I've said and they've said. We've made it worse for you, haven't we?"

"Sometimes."

"Don't bullshit a bullshitter, son. It took that ball-busting sister of yours coming out and calling us on it for it to get even a little better on that subject too. We know that." He patted Dylan's shoulder and stood. "I won't keep you anymore. Just also wanted to tell you how much we like your man. Even though he yelled at us. Fighting for the people we love is the Gallagher family way, after all."

"Oh—he doesn't. I mean, he hasn't said . . . so, I don't know that he . . ." Dylan crumbled his napkin into a ball. "I think it's too soon to say that, Dad."

"Now see that there." His dad snapped him to attention the way he did when he'd been a kid.

"What?" Dylan looked around, not knowing what his dad was talking about.

"You saying that. Now *that's* you just being stupid. All the rest of the stuff was just us being stupid."

Dylan huffed in amusement. "Okay. Uh, thanks? I guess."

His dad did a quick scan of the room. "Bring me the keys to this place when you go on your trip out to California. I'm going to get a little more work done on it while you're gone, okay? Everything you've done so far looks great. And . . . ask that man if he'll let me take another look at what's going on in his place too."

"I really can get it all done."

"I have no doubts that you could, but Sean's *my* brother. I love him." He reached forward, and instead of patting Dylan's shoulder again, he rapped his scarred knuckle on the table a few inches from Dylan's hand. "Don't forget to ask him if he's okay with me and my guys doing some work down there myself while you're out of town."

"Sure, I'll ask him."

The front door opened and closed.

Dylan stared forward for a long while afterward.

When Derek came back, he brought Gus with him and sat down next to Dylan on the couch. "You okay?"

"I think so." Dylan put the remains of his second Crunchwrap down and wiped his mouth.

Derek spoke before Dylan could. "You were right about the Adderall. I've basically gone down an internet rabbit hole about ADHD today. Figured I should know more . . ."

Dylan pulled Derek into a kiss. It wasn't a casual kiss, but it wasn't a long one either. He tried to put a lot of real, honest things into the kiss, but it didn't seem adequate. What his dad said about Derek loving him was still echoing in his head.

"What was—"

"I-I never thought I'd be with someone who would react to me being such a jerk by d-doing something sweet like researching ADHD and my meds instead of . . ." His voice broke on the last word. "Thank you."

"It's not a big deal."

Dylan wouldn't let Derek minimize this. "It's an enormous deal to me." He took Derek's hands in his. "Do you forgive me for what I said this morning? I really understand if you're still mad. It was an overreaction. Being sensitive about feeling like a broken mess isn't an excuse for exploding at someone who's trying to help me. I know you like helping people. Fixing things. It's something I really . . . admire about you."

Derek frowned down at their hands.

"You okay?"

"What you said about me fixing things—" Gus cut in, licking and sniffing the spot where Dylan's dad had been sitting, looking for crumbs. Derek nudged Gus away.

"I didn't mean it in a bad way. I just meant . . . I never want to feel like you need to sugarcoat it with me. I'm not fragile, and I didn't realize until talking to my dad about stuff . . . So much of *everything* I went through with them could've been avoided if they'd just been honest with me, and if I told them how I felt too. And that's not to excuse what they did, but I'm just saying . . ."

Derek squeezed his hands. "Honesty's really hard if you're trying not to make something a big deal. But I'm glad you were honest with your dad . . ."

"I liked that when I pulled some shit like this morning you were honest with me about it. And threw a pillow at my face."

"It was between the face and crotch, but since you weren't

wearing your glasses . . . and also, I have a vested interest in your crotch area."

Dylan nestled his head into the angle of Derek's neck. "You don't know how glad I am to hear you still have a vested interest in my crotch area."

Derek cringed. "I'm really regretting ever putting it that way."

"I'm really regretting repeating it."

Dylan's phone dinged.

> CHASE
> The CEO bought you a plane ticket for tonight. They want you onsite NOW leading into the demos because they've decided that no one else is competent, and I guess even though you don't actually work here, you "were impressive" during last night's shitstorm.

> CHASE
> Double your typical fees.

Groaning, he held up the text messages to show Derek.

"You want to go, don't you?" Derek measured him.

"I *want* to make sure I can help them get everything right so I don't have nights like last night."

"You should go then."

"Okay." Dylan smiled and then typed out a text. "You know . . . one of the things about being okay with myself as I am is the ability to acknowledge my weaknesses and ask for help when I do need it."

"What are you saying?"

"You strike me as the type of hyperorganized person who's really good at packing for last-minute cross-country trips. Help me?"

"Oh, Dylan Gallagher." Derek affected a romance movie-esque voice. "I thought you'd *never* proposition me in such a way."

Dylan smacked him on the shoulder and then tackled his boyfriend horizontal.

Packing could wait a little while.

Chapter 44

Derek scanned the board at the charge nurse desk. His phone buzzed in his pocket, breaking his concentration. His body had been literally aching for Dylan. He'd been gone for over two weeks, since he'd left early. His flight got in this morning, and the hospital was too short-staffed for Derek to call out. They had talked for hours on the phone most nights and had perfected the unsubtle art of FaceTime sex, but Derek needed him back in his arms. He also needed to stop being a coward and have a conversation he'd been avoiding for weeks. It had been easy to make excuses when Dylan was dealing with stuff with his family or when he was on the other coast, but the excuses stopped tonight.

> DYLAN
> Making sous vide steak tonight because my brother brought by some meat. How do you like yours again?

> DEREK
> Practically mooing.

Derek was starving, and Dylan was a great cook when he took time for it. Derek had finally gotten back into the routine of going to the gym before work, so his body would appreciate every extra ounce of protein. That conversation with Dylan from the night before he left had stuck with him. So many of his choices had been about his family and being there for them. Olive was happy. His mom, well, as much as he hated to admit it, she seemed happier than she had in years.

Dylan had no end of interests and hobbies. He was always mentioning some past obsession and what he had learned from it. He kept talking about how excited he was to be moving back into his house.

He also kept saying he couldn't wait to show Derek the house when the tenants moved out. And every time he mentioned it, Derek's stomach backflipped.

What the hell did that *mean*?

What the hell did Derek want it to mean?

> DYLAN
>
> I'll tell him next time to just leave the cow alive. Honestly, Gus would probably get along with a cow.

> DEREK
>
> If it were a small enough cow, they might look like family.

> DYLAN
>
> Also, my brothers want you to come with me to their last game of the summer season.

Derek glowered at the phone.

> DYLAN
>
> Stop scowling at the phone.

> DEREK
>
> How did you know?

> DYLAN
>
> You scowl every time I mention them.

He flexed his arms, enjoying that soreness from his workout yesterday. But even the catharsis of a grueling lifting session couldn't make him forgive Dylan's brothers. Dylan wasn't as good as Derek at holding grudges. While he hadn't fully forgiven them, he seemed strangely pleased at the idea of them wanting him around *without* the threat of them ragging on him or awarding him a plaster wiener.

> DEREK
> Your brothers are assholes.

> DYLAN
> True, but they haven't stopped apologizing since the barbeque.

> DEREK
> Fuck their apologies.

> DYLAN
> Ngl, it's kind of hot that you're this pissed on my behalf, but things have been better.

Derek's smile faltered. Memories of the barbeque still made his hands curl into fists.

> DEREK
> If I ever hear the words Pickle Award again, I'm really gonna deck someone.

> DYLAN
> Can you keep that energy for when you come home tonight? Seems like we could figure out some ways to channel it.

Derek shifted his weight in his swivel stool.

DEREK
Stop giving me boners while I'm working.

DYLAN
Whoops. Guess you'll have to stay behind that desk
for a while. Off to marinate. Tootles.

DEREK
Tootles is a stupid word.

DYLAN
Kay.

A call came in on the staticky EMS dispatch radio. "Twenty-six-year-old pregnant female with a possible right patellar dislocation. Arriving in ten minutes."

As Derek entered the pre-arrival into the computer system, he thought about all the least-arousing things he could imagine. Once he could stand without embarrassing himself, he went to warn Joni. It wasn't that ERs didn't like pregnant people. It was just that sometimes it turned into a clusterfuck tug-of-war with labor and delivery if a very pregnant person came in with something that seemed possibly *not* pregnancy-related, which the ED doc then decided *was* pregnancy-related, leading to many unpleasant phone calls before the on-call OB would accept the patient. It sucked.

A dislocated kneecap should be straightforward though. But *shit*, to have that kind of injury any time was awful, and during a pregnancy would be brutal.

The stretcher rolled in with a tiny young woman on top of it with two curtains of black hair hanging down as she braced herself over her an enormous belly. Her leg was splinted.

Derek blinked. "Michelle?"

His youngest sister forced a tentative grin at him before she held up her hands and wiggled her fingers over her belly. Just like Amy had. Just like his mom had. *"Surprise."*

"You're . . ."

"Pregnant? I think so. At least, all the signs point that way." As the stretcher bounced on the threshold, her grin shifted into a grimace. She took the kinds of deep breaths she'd used while trying to master a difficult ballet move.

"Michelle . . ."

She spoke through a clenched jaw. "I'm fine. It's not that bad. The bouncing is . . . not ideal."

Derek tried to minimize the jostling of the stretcher. "Your kneecap is literally in the wrong place."

"Could be worse."

"It could be worse like it's still attached to your leg?" Derek guided the ambulance stretcher back to the private room he'd assigned.

"Well, yeah. I think that would be a lot worse." Tense tendons flexed in his sister's neck.

"You okay to move to the bed, ma'am?" the medic asked.

Michelle's eyes darted from the medic to Derek, forehead wrinkling and lips tight as she nodded. "I think so?"

Derek twitched his head at the medic. "You stabilize the knee. I can move her myself. If that's okay with you . . . ?"

Michelle nodded gratefully.

Even though she was pregnant, Derek had no trouble lifting her. OSHA wouldn't have approved of the technique, but it was his Michelle. After a quick exchange with the medics, Derek and Michelle were alone. She folded her hands in her lap and stared at them. God, she was *very* pregnant. He'd guess close to term, but on her slender frame it was hard to tell.

"H-how long have you been back in town?"

She looked up and scanned his face as if she were reading something there.

"What?" Derek tilted his head in confusion.

"She *really* didn't tell you."

"Who?"

Her head bowed again. "Mom." She picked at a hangnail on her thumb. "I didn't want you to know until I had stuff figured out, and then—"

"Do you have a good ob-gyn here?" Derek's mind revved into overdrive. He had so many questions. So many new things to be worried about.

"Actually, I—"

"If you don't, I can get you a recommendation from friends." His mind scrolled through the list of things she'd need. "Do you have a crib yet? I have another friend who's getting rid of one. And if you need a car seat, I bet—"

Michelle growled.

The sound was so startlingly reminiscent of the little girl who used to pounce on his back as if she were an attacking cat that he whipped around. "Is the pain getting worse? My friend's the doc today, and she should be in in a couple minutes, but I can see if—"

"I knew I should've made Zach drive me to the other hospital. But he *insisted* on calling 9–1–1."

"Wait, Zach? Your ex Zach's the father? Hacky-sack Zach? The dude that couldn't go to high school graduation because he got caught hotboxing in the principal's Porsche Boxster? *That* Zach?"

Michelle scowled. "He was making a *political* statement." She shook her head and pointed at his face. "All of *this* is exactly why I told Mom not to tell you. You can't help yourself. You didn't even wait for my answers before you launched into your"—she imitated Derek, making his voice a grating and robotic tone—"must-save-Michelle-from-her-inevitable-screwups mode. You couldn't just be normal and say 'Omygod, congratulations, well done on growing a human.' I don't know. Anything else except going into Mr. Fix-It mode about something I'm excited about."

"That's not what I was trying to do . . ."

"I know I didn't do it like Amy did with her and her perfect husband spawning their four *academically gifted* children." She put her hands on her hips. "And also, Zach hasn't done hacky sack since twelfth grade. He has a medicinal card now *and* drives a Tesla."

"How did hacky-sack Zach get Tesla money? Did he buy stock in puka shells?"

Michelle contracted her face. "I don't need these hints about *my* choices. I want you to let me try to fix things myself. You've always been like this. Of course Zach's not good enough. No one is. No one can live up to your expectations. And when we don't, you have to take charge and fix us."

"I'm sorry. I was just surprised. I'm sure Zach's a stand-up guy right now. Congratulations. I *am* excited for you. I *am* happy for you if you're happy. I don't want to fix you. You're perfect the way you are. I *never* wanted you to be like Amy."

"Yeah, well, saying I'm perfect doesn't quite fit with you trying to control everything in my life. Like before, I was *handling* it. And you wouldn't *butt out.*"

"You were handling . . . what?"

"I spent weeks meeting with a financial counselor. I had a plan mapped out to consolidate the debt and pay it off on my own. And all that time was a waste because you violated my privacy and opened my mail. And after you kept calling me and texting me like you were wanting me to treat you like a *hero* for trying to save my credit scor—*fuck.*" The word became a groan and she leaned over her hands, digging her knuckles into her forehead.

"*Please* let me get you something for the pain."

"No." She took several more breaths. A tear rolled down her nose, and he didn't even have the courage to offer her a tissue to wipe it away. "You can't fix this, Derek. Ever since my injury . . . I'm in *pain*. All the fucking time. But I'm angry because *this* is what really hurts and you couldn't see it." Instead of gesturing to her wrapped and splinted knee, she rubbed her sternum over her heart. "Every time it gets messed up, it reminds me that I lost everything because of this goddamn knee. The thing I loved more than anything. My career. My future. Every fucking dream I had." Michelle wiped more tears from underneath her eyes in smooth strokes that preserved her makeup. "I don't even think the credit cards were the real problem. You . . . you couldn't let me just be sad. You needed to control it. Just like after Dad with all of us. You had to try to fix it too."

"What . . . what are you talking about? What's *Dad* got to do with this?" Acid rose in Derek's throat. "You said you were going to lose your home. You said you could be okay if it wasn't for your mortgage. I didn't want to *control* you—"

"You did. You always did. All our lives, you couldn't just be my brother when I was sad or crying or feeling things. You assumed this *guy-in-charge* mode. When I could dance, I couldn't even miss a day of rehearsal ever without feeling like I was disappointing *you*." She shot him a glare. "Why couldn't you ever just be a human? Be a normal brother? I didn't need a . . . replacement."

"That's not fair. I was just trying to do what Dad asked me to."

Her jaw hardened. "You know what's not fair? My dad died. I don't even remember him, Derek. He is never going to meet my *daughter*."

"Daughter?" Derek blinked away tears.

"You wanted to fix everything so much that I didn't even want to ask about him because you said talking about him made Mom sad. I was a first grader. I didn't know how messed up things were. I threw my entire heart into ballet because you made me believe it would actually mean something if I kept pushing myself. My career with the company . . . it was all I had." She sniffled.

He couldn't even argue that. He still hadn't grieved his dad. But had his intense desire to do what his dad had asked him backfired and meant his sisters hadn't either?

The idea made him want to throw up.

"Ballet's gone for me." She snapped her fingers once and then her shoulder slumped. "I had *nothing*. And I was so pathetic you didn't trust me to be an adult and make my own choices about the messes *I* made."

"Just tell me what I can do. I'm sorry." Something was shredding in Derek's chest. "I'm sorry. I didn't know what I was doing. I was a stupid teenager who'd made a promise. And I screwed it up back then. And I screwed it up when I paid off the cards."

"I don't need you to *do* anything. If I did, I would've asked. I just needed you to be my brother. I *needed* to be broken for a while. I needed you to be okay with me being broken. I just didn't want you to look at me and only see something broken. But I just don't know . . ."

"What don't you know?"

"You don't even understand what this is like." She gestured to her knee again. "You've never loved anything like I loved being onstage."

"What does that have to do—"

"I don't even think you *can* love something like that. It would mean you'd have to actually take a risk." She shook her head almost pityingly, twisting her slim fingers in her lap. "You've always had the same friends. Same life. You're always drawn to the easiest thing."

"Hey—"

"I *knew* you'd judge me being with Zach again like it was some kind of backslide. It's why you never really found something like I found ballet. Never *loved* something like that."

He blinked.

She dug her hand though her hair and clutched her scalp. "You haven't even ever had a long-term boyfriend, and I didn't want this pregnancy to be one more thing like that when I—I . . . can I just get some tissues?"

He yanked open the drawer beside her and handed her a box. She blew her nose.

"I love you, Michelle. And I'm sorr—"

Her head shake cut his apology short. "I want to love her like . . ." She ran a hand over her belly. "Like I loved ballet. I loved the blisters and sweat and blood because it also brought me the stage and the lights and the applause." She smiled up at the overhead lamp as if even the memory of those performances made her feel something so intense, she couldn't hold it all in.

Something like . . .

Stupid, lovesick, radiant joy.

That's what glowed on her face. Even in the pain and grief when all she had left was a memory of it. That passionate love still glowed inside her.

"Michelle—"

"I don't think you know how to love broken things." She met his gaze for the first time since the tears began. "That boyfriend you left me that voicemail about—think he'll live up to your standards?" A flash of regret passed over her face as she said it, but she didn't take it back.

Derek couldn't have felt more torn apart right now if he were the one on the stretcher. It was like she reached inside him and pulled out his true self and then made him see just how pathetic and small he was.

After a quick knock, Joni pulled back the curtain. "I'm so sorry for the delay, Ms. Chang. I'm Dr. Sutton. Are you okay with me talking in front of your bro—"

"Derek, can you stay?" Her anger seemed to have retreated beneath a breathless surge of fear that dislodged Derek's heart.

"Yeah. Of course."

"I consulted your new high-risk OB to discuss the best plan for your knee and pain management for now. I've put in some orders for medications approved in pregnancy." Joni's eyes flitted to his with enough sympathy that he was sure half the unit overheard the conversation. "We're going to get some X-rays and an ultrasound taken before—"

"But last time they just put it back in? Can't we just do that? I tried to do it myself at home like usual, but—"

An irrepressible strangled sound escaped Derek, but Joni's understanding and silencing look kept him from saying anything else.

"This has happened before?" Joni surveyed the joint beneath the splinting.

"Before I was pregnant, once, and then since then . . . a few times," Michelle said.

Derek had to clamp down on his lips with his teeth to stop himself from asking anything.

"Hmmm . . ." Joni nodded. "Unfortunately, because of the way this injury looks with the generalized swelling beneath it, and especially with the last stage of pregnancy too, I really need to make sure there's not any other injuries or blood clots before I manipulate the joint and the leg. Pregnancy hormones can—"

"Okay." Michelle hugged her arms to her chest and turned toward the bare wall as if suddenly self-conscious "Is the radiation from the X-ray . . ."

"The small amount of radiation from the X-rays won't harm the baby at all. In this situation, the benefits outweigh the risks." Joni's firm, calm voice seemed to ease Derek's fears as well. "Can I get you some Tylenol now while we wait?"

"I don't need it. It's not too bad as long as I don't move. Ice would be good though."

"Let me know if you change your mind. I'm going to do a quick physical exam now."

"I'm good now, Derek." Michelle had retreated back into the stoically in-control persona she used to pull on her pointe shoes. "You can go. I . . . I think it might be best if someone else was my nurse." She didn't look at him or say anything else.

"Okay."

After asking another nurse to grab the ice, Derek headed back to the charge desk. He tried to read the patient board four times before he knew he couldn't do this right now. He needed a minute. He asked someone to watch the desk and headed outside the large double doors at the far end of the unit.

A wall of sweltering humidity hit him as he walked out into the ambulance bay and sat on the alcove ground. The ambulance that had brought Michelle was gone, so the long concrete loading dock was empty. Distant cars drove past. Summer birds chirped. A breeze rustled the branches in the small cluster of trees shading the parking lot. The air smelled like diesel and freshly cut grass. The world was exactly the same as it had been half an hour ago.

He tried to do one of his meditation exercises. Anything to stave off this growing ache.

Ever since his dad died, Derek thought he needed to be *everything* for his sisters and his mom. He liked being the one who helped, not being the one who needed help, because he'd promised his dad he would handle it. Handle everything. He'd tried to fill that role with Olive, too, after Jake's accident and death. Though in Olive's case he'd been better. He'd encouraged her to find space to grieve.

But Michelle had been right. He hadn't ever opened up himself to anyone new.

Was she right about why?

Was he so overbearing and arrogant that people didn't feel like they could screw up around him?

Even Dylan had mentioned his fixing-it *thing*. Derek drew his knees to his chest. He pushed his weight onto the brick wall behind him.

"They said you came out here." Joni sat next to him.

"Everyone heard everything, right?"

She winced. "Those doors are not very soundproof."

"Shit."

"She said . . . her fiancé's outside, and that she'd prefer if you stayed away from her room. I think your sister's really sad and angry about a lot of things right now."

"Yeah, a lot of things and *me*. I don't blame her."

Joni put a hand on his knee. "You know a lot of that was misdirected anger, right? Probably some guilt and depression too. And excruciating physical pain. You *did* help her. You *did* try to make her life better. What she said about your dad—"

Derek stood. "I should go check on the other patients."

"I think she was saying a lot of those things at you, but she was really saying them to herself."

"I really wish that were true."

As Derek finished his shift, he tried to ignore the nagging uncertainty plaguing him. Joni tried to make him feel better, but nothing she said could make this better. He'd failed Michelle before. Today had been a test, and he'd failed.

DYLAN
Can't wait for dinner. See you soon.

Derek weighed the phone in his hand. Just as he started to text back, he caught sight of his sister being wheeled out of the lobby in a wheelchair by a grown-up version of their neighborhood's high school pot dealer toward an illegally and poorly parked Tesla.

Admittedly, Zach did look more like a banker than a stoner these days.

Maybe Michelle was right.

Maybe she was right about a lot of things.

He took a step forward toward the parking lot while Zach brought the chair back into the vestibule area in front of the waiting room.

"Dude, my baby's tired and doesn't want to talk to you right now." Zach still had that affected surfer inflection.

Yeah, he hated this mofo.

"I'm just walking home." Derek lifted his hands and side-stepped the guy, stifling the frustration and hurt in his voice. And failing. "But I *love my sister*. If she needs me, I'm there. I might have made big mistakes . . . b-but . . ." His voice broke. "I was missing him too. I was a kid too."

He didn't know what he wanted.

He didn't know what he expected.

But he got exactly nothing.

The Tesla sped off, leaving Derek alone outside the hospital. He couldn't fix this with her. He started to doubt whether he'd ever fixed anything. Or could ever fix anything. She never told him she'd been working with a debt consolidator. Just like she'd never told him about the credit card bills in the first place. She hadn't wanted his judgment. And today, just like she predicted, Derek became the toxic overbearing brother who did what he thought was best without considering her feelings.

Instead of turning down the sidewalk leading to his apartment, he headed onto the winding path to Baker Park.

Chapter 45

Derek was lucky in so many ways. He didn't experience dark depressive days like Olive. Or have panic attacks, except for that possible one when he thought Gus was lost. But he was prone to pushing his feelings down. It's how he started working out. He lifted weights until the normal weight on his shoulders felt lighter. He pushed himself to do as much as possible even when all he had to do was ask for help and things might be a little easier.

Now it felt like everything was crumbling on top of him just like his ceiling had, making him rethink how he had been feeling even before seeing Michelle. Had he really been that happy? Was he destined to screw up his relationship because he expected people to be perfect or tried to fix them?

At sixteen, Derek learned to hold tight to the people he loved. Olive. His mom and sisters. And Jake. Now Jake was gone too. What was it about a new loss that made the old kind feel just as present? Michelle's face when she talked about dance had been the strangest mix of grief and the memory of happiness. She'd said she'd thrown herself into dance because she wasn't allowed to grieve for Dad.

Derek had fallen for Dylan.

Fallen *hard*.

He'd never felt this way before.

Was all of this just his own version of dance? Was it something that would give him broken toes and a busted knee and years of pain for the price of short-lived happiness?

Dad was taken.

Jake was gone.

Michelle hated him.

Maybe that was all that stupid, lovesick, radiant joy was.

Just another thing that could be taken away from him.

The idea of losing something else right now seemed like too big a risk.

When he reached the top of the stairs down to his apartment, his front door flew open. Dylan rushed out wearing those paint-splattered work jeans that rode low on his hips with an equally paint-splattered shirt. The way he adjusted his glasses made Derek's heart hiccup in a way that was definitely not medically possible.

Something ached in Derek's chest.

Something that changed everything . . .

"Where have you been?" Dylan gripped him by the shoulders, eyes scanning him.

Derek flinched. "I . . ."

Confusion glimmered on Dylan's face. "Bad shift? Where'd you go? It's nine forty-five. I thought . . . I thought you were coming up for dinner."

"Shit, nine forty-five?" Derek was taken aback. He'd walked for two hours? He'd been lost in memories. It had sped through his mind like the B-roll of the dead wife in one of his favorite movies.

"I even called the hospital. They said you clocked out at seven thirty, and I don't have anyone else's number that I could think to call. I was worried."

"Dylan . . ."

"What?"

Derek had never been as strong and capable as he wanted to be. He'd been a dumb emo kid who'd tried and failed to "fix" a heartbroken family. A family that didn't need to be fixed.

They needed to *heal*.

Derek needed to heal. He still needed to heal.

Dylan's jaw tightened. His glasses sparkled in the street-lights. He was almost shaking with what appeared to be anxiety. And something else.

There was a time a few months ago when Michelle's words would have rooted so firmly in his head, they'd have sent him running back to the life he had been trapped in for so many years. But he was different now. Joni was right. There might have been truth, but like Joni said, she was angry and sad and hurting.

Old Derek might have forced himself into his most confident swagger. He would have said some bullshit like *"This was fun, dude, but given that we're neighbors right now, the hooking up thing's probably not the best idea. You know what they say. Don't shit where you eat. Or whatever."*

Old Derek would have believed a trapped life was safer, just like pining for Jake kept him from getting hurt.

Dylan's hands dropped from his shoulders. "You're scaring me, babe. What happened tonight?"

Derek dropped his backpack on the ground and pulled Dylan in a potentially bone-crushing hug. Dylan rested his head on Derek's chest. One of his favorite things about Dylan was that so far he never ended a hug. It was like when he was hyperfocused on his work at that intense workstation. Every part of his consciousness stilled in a hug. Derek pulled way too soon this time because he couldn't hold back the words anymore. None of this was fair to Dylan. Life was precious. He didn't want Dylan to spend another second without knowing what Derek had figured out.

"Dylan, I . . ."

"What's wrong?" Dylan's frantic gaze flitted back and forth between Derek's eyes as if he were trying to read the thoughts behind them.

"I have to tell you something."

"I want to tell you something too. But first can we—"

Derek's partially latched door pushed open. Gus galloped up the stairs and onto the sidewalk. He jumped on Derek just as the small form of a woman popped out from behind the azaleas like a pastel jack-in-the-box from hell.

"I knew it, Mr. Chang."

Chapter 46

Dylan was a mess. He couldn't pay attention to anything that angry woman was yelling. Was Derek going to break up with him? He hadn't even been angry Derek was late. He'd been panicked. Last time that happened, Derek had been assaulted. Dylan had even taken Gus for a walk up and down Derek's normal route home and hadn't seen him.

He'd been about to beg Derek to tell him what the heck was going on when that goddamn Carol Taylor literally jumped-scared them out of the bushes.

Carol's tone anticipated righteous comeuppance. "I've caught you red-handed this time."

Derek sighed.

Another woman strolled up. At first glance, the two women could not seem more different. The stranger was several inches taller than Carol, and while Carol normally wore the kind of thing you'd buy in a Florida hotel lobby after your kid threw up on you in the airport shuttle, the other woman wore a crisp, tailored suit and held a briefcase. But their facial features were nearly identical.

"Janice, this is the one harboring a banned breed."

Janice, who must be her sister, leveled Carol with a look of irritable pity. "I told you to stop micromanaging the other residents. I didn't buy this building and let you head the HOA so you could bully the other residents into leaving bad reviews on the property management group."

"I'm enforcing *your* rules."

"Well then, just fine them both. I don't understand why

336 * Andie Burke

everything has to be so dramatic with you. Can't you even handle the simplest of things here yourself? I don't know why you make me attend these silly HOA meetings." Janice's finger swiped over her phone screen.

"I was waiting until I caught him with the monstrosity. I haven't seen the dog's legal owner in weeks."

"Just *fine* him then," Janice spoke the words slowly and more loudly than necessary, as if she doubted Carol understood them. "And kick out the monstrosity. If you can't handle little things like this, I'm just going to have to fire you again. Doing our parents a favor isn't worth these headaches."

"The monstrosity's name is Gus." Dylan squared his shoulders to Carol. "And technically he's not illegal."

Janice narrowed her eyes at Dylan and then evaluated the dog. "He's here, and he's clearly a Great Dane mix, and the HOA rules clearly spell out—"

"That a banned breed cannot stay in a single unit for longer than twenty-four hours."

Carol cut in before Janice could say more. "Exactly, and that dog—"

"Will be switching off between my uncle's unit and Derek's. Of course, no more than twenty-four hours at either. As long as he needs to." Dylan reached a hand behind him. "To the letter of the rules."

Warm fingers interlaced his. Dylan couldn't help the broad smile on his mouth at the look of utter horror on Carol's face.

Janice seemed to be rethinking her initial assessment of Dylan as an opponent. After a bored shrug at her sister, she nodded. "Fine. Whatever. Just let them keep the animal here."

Janice's heels clacked on the sidewalk as she walked away with Carol arguing with her every step of the way.

"Hard to believe Carol could have a worse sister." Dylan led Derek down the stairs to the door to his unit with Gus following behind.

When they got to the bottom, Derek stopped and shook his head. "I should've told her I wanted my key back."

Dylan smirked. "To be honest, I think you'd be better off changing your locks. Karen probably made a copy of that shit so she can sneak in at night and pretend to haunt you or something. Or sic her parakeets on you. Or smother you with one of her Mary Kay makeup bags."

"Death by MLM Karen," Derek said in a dark, ominous voice. "Not the way I want to go." A noise like something being knocked over came from inside the apartment. "What was that?" The apartment was super dark.

"Oh . . ." Dylan grimaced. "Yeah, so. . . ."

"What's going . . ."

"*Surprise!*"

Chapter 47

Back pats and shoulder squeezes came from all sides as Derek's eyes adjusted to the brightness.

Felicity ushered him in with a hug. "What do you think?"

He'd been holding off on hiring someone for the final finishing work until after he paid off his next credit card bill. But it was all done. It looked better than it had before the incident. So many of the tiny imperfections all over the apartment were fixed. When Felicity called him a few days ago and said that they needed to turn off the water again and asked if he wouldn't mind staying in Dylan's apartment for a few nights . . . he just accepted it.

Dylan trailed them as Felicity showed him where she'd fixed the tilework in his bathroom and everything that the others had done.

Derek looked at Dylan "How did you—"

"I didn't know anything about it until I got back." Dylan smiled. "They finished Uncle Sean's unit too. Everything's done." He ruffled his hair nervously. "My dad brought some of his guys over yesterday. He was up there when I got back from the airport." Emotion swelled behind his eyes. "Said he couldn't have done the rest of the job better than I'd already done it, but that he wanted it to be done so you and I could focus on other things."

Felicity ran a finger over the grouting as if checking for an invisible imperfection. "Dylan said you were thinking about selling at some point, so we figured you'd need to get the other stuff fixed. Surprised?"

Derek bent to squeeze the tiny ginger into a warm embrace.

"Thank you. Seriously, this doesn't seem possible." As he took it all in, he felt taller. Like a fraction of gravity had disappeared. He felt dizzy. Almost giddy.

A large grocery store sheet cake was out on the kitchen table. Pink and purple flowers decorated the edge and yellow elegant cursive reading *Glad we could fix your shit*. A blocky print parenthetical below said NO MORE PICKLES.

"I picked out the cake," Brooks and Anderson said at the same time. "No, you didn't, asshole." Again, they said in tandem.

Felicity pushed a piece of cake into Derek's hands. "It was probably Calvin."

"I—I don't know how to thank you all for this." Derek rubbed his eyes as warm pressure arrived on his arm.

"Seriously, guys. Thank you." Dylan stole some of the frosting off Derek's piece before Derek could yank it away.

"Get your own, jackass."

With a smirk, Dylan hustled over to the cake while two of the large Gallagher brothers converged on Derek, pulling him over to the small table in the living room.

"We need to talk to you for a second," Anderson said in a low, discreet voice.

"Hard to believe this is the way things are turning out." Brooks nodded.

"Uh—I guess?" Derek said, nonplussed. A sugary frosting flower melted on his tongue.

"We were so glad you brought Jake to try out that day," Anderson said.

"You remember that?" Derek asked.

"'Course. We just wanted to tell you, we're really sorry about what happened to Jake. And with what happened between you . . ." Brooks tapped the plastic fork tines against the plate and then dragged them through it like he was raking sand in a Zen garden. "We didn't want you to think . . . We know these last few years have been really hard. Life's shit sometimes, man."

"But sometimes people find a way to be okay. He was such a good guy. Thought the world of you, Derek. That's why we knew so much about you. We had thought it was a little brother thing at first, but . . . we finally figured it out." Anderson huffed a sad laugh. "Felicity would just call that heteronormative thinking. Until we asked what he was planning, and he said second-chance romance, and then told us to shut the fuck up."

"And he'd be so happy Derek's happy. Right?" Brooks elbowed his brother, still speaking in that whisper. "Wouldn't Murphy be so happy Derek's happy?"

"Hundred percent. That last time we saw him, he told us he'd gotten sober and asked for help planning a date with some guy he thought was too good for him. We didn't know who he was talking about, but he went on and on about it." Anderson lowered his voice and moved to shield the conversation further. "We were going to give this to you at the Grill-Out, but then . . ."

"You kicked our asses real good," Brooks finished.

"Give me what?" Derek set down his cake.

"The team's coach found this in Jake's hockey bag. His sister brought the gear back to the rink to donate a few months ago. Coach found it in the inside pocket. He figured it might be important to someone. Finally got a chance to go run up and get it from him the day before the Grill-Out. Even with what's happening with you and Dilly, figured you might want it." Anderson handed him a folded-up photo.

It was the last one taken on that damned disposable camera. Derek's stomach sank. It was a really flattering photo of a shirtless Jake, who'd just taken off part of his Halloween costume, smiling at the camera in that broad way that made him look a little like a giant, blond, classic Hollywood movie star, his arms on display as he held the camera out. He'd pulled Derek close, and Derek's hand had dropped to rest on Jake's thigh. He was smiling, kind of, but mostly he was looking at

Jake. Even though Derek still had a shirt on, nothing about the photo was subtle. He felt nothing beyond discomfort seeing himself back then, now knowing what he'd been feeling was just an unhealthy combination of gratitude, hero worship, and a defense mechanism against grief. He'd always miss Jake, but all the other feelings were gone. They wouldn't have been right for each other in the end.

A hand clapped down on his shoulder. "You can let it out if you need to," Brooks said, obviously misreading the expression on Derek's face.

Derek shook his head. "No, I'm not upset abo—"

"We also wanted to tell you if you ever need to talk, we're your bros now. We deserved that verbal ass-whipping. You're everything Jake said you were."

"We were rooting for you two. Just like we're rooting for you with Dylan. Whatever you need, man." Brooks's voice tightened with genuine emotion.

Derek refolded the photo and slipped it into his pocket.

"What'd they give you?" Dylan's strained voice broke through the conversation, making the two Gallagher brothers and Derek all jump.

"Nothing," said Brooks at the time Anderson shrugged.

If an expression could shoot shards of glass, Dylan's brothers would have been a bloody mess. "I swear to god if that's a baby photo or something else embarrassing I'm going to kill you both. I thought we were past this bullshit."

Derek was torn between being thrilled Dylan was standing up to his brothers and utterly disgusted with himself for being the reason Dylan needed to. Procrastinating was about to bite him in the ass. He knew it. God, Derek was such a coward.

"You said tonight wasn't going to be a thing like before." Dylan looked between his two brothers. "Was I stupid to believe you?"

"It's not what you think." Derek winced.

"Okay . . ."

"It's really not," said Brooks and Anderson together as if they had both caught a lifeline in tandem.

"Then what the hell did you just give my boyfriend?" Dylan still wasn't shouting. His arms were crossed in front of his chest. He stood his ground, squaring his shoulders to the two taller Gallaghers who seemed to shrink. Derek knew Dylan well enough to understand. Dylan Gallagher *had* to take a stand with this because he was proving to himself that he wasn't still that little boy left holding a pickle jar. He didn't need Derek or Felicity to defend him tonight.

Derek sighed. "It's just a photo they found of me and Jake. They found it in his hockey bag and were giving it back to me."

"Jake Murphy? It's just a photo of you and Jake? Then why . . . *oh*." Devastated understanding clouded Dylan's face.

While the two brothers were complete boneheads, whatever they saw in their youngest brother's expression shut them up.

"What about Jake Murphy?" Felicity asked as she entered the room. She said the name with a kind of fire Derek recognized. She must know the full story, or enough of it.

"Um—"

"Did y'all say Jake Murphy?" Cal said, coming in after getting off a phone call outside. "Such a great guy, right?"

"Uh . . ." Felicity's knuckles blanched around the fork in her hand as she tried to understand why Dylan looked shattered.

Calvin was too busy cutting himself cake to notice the transformation on Dylan's face. "Sure do miss that guy. Not just on the ice."

"Hey, Cal . . ." Brooks shifted his weight.

"Um . . ." Anderson said.

The grating sound of Calvin's hand digging through plastic cutlery muted their attempts at stopping the conversation. "Great guy. Life of the party. Would do anything for anyone. Thought

Derek hung the moon too. Of course we didn't realize what was really going on between you and Jake until right before . . . you know." His mouth was full of cake when he turned, offering Derek a misplaced sympathetic nod. "So sorry for your loss, man."

Derek had never watched a trainwreck in slow motion, but as Dylan's ears went to an as-yet-unseen shade of magenta, he knew just how bad this was.

"Jake Murphy is *Derek's* ex?" Felicity looked to Dylan for a confirmation he couldn't give.

Because Derek messed up.

"Seems like it," Dylan said in a cool, measured voice.

"Oh . . . uh . . ." Felicity said. "But I thought . . ."

"It's why we knew Derek was such a great guy. Shouldn't have brought it up tonight, but it's just . . ." Calvin grinned and gathered his brothers into a group hug, converging on Dylan, who was caught in the claustrophobic middle. "We know Dad came and talked to you, but we're all so sorry. Seeing you happy just makes us so happy." He pulled Derek to join. "It's all we've ever wanted for him."

Felicity stood beside the cake, holding the knife as if wishing she could carve Derek into pieces with it.

Anderson ruffled Dylan's hair, knocking his glasses askew and trying to break some of the tension. "Why do you think we asked Big D to come to the Grill-Out? We saw the way you guys looked at each other, but we've *learned*, you know? Not making the set-up mistake again."

Derek cringed.

"But that doesn't mean we can't just support you guys falling in big gay love," Brooks said.

Felicity scowled as she wrapped up the cake and took it to the kitchen. The fridge door slammed audibly. "It's late, guys. I hate to break up the party, but I need someone to drive me back to Mom and Dad's." She lowered her voice and spoke directly to Dylan, but unfortunately with the group of men still locked in a weird affection scrum, they all could hear her. "Or do you want me to stay so I can help you pack tomorrow?"

Dylan's head twitched in a negative.

"Come on, Lissy. Let the guys have their own celebration." Anderson tugged her ponytail.

She whacked him.

Calvin brandished his phone. "Sarah's been texting me that one of the kids is being a little shit, so I gotta go relieve her anyway. I'll drop you on my way, Lissy."

"Alright." She wrapped Dylan into a fierce hug all while pointedly glaring at Derek. "I'll be back in the morning."

Derek was roped into helping them carry one of their ladders to Calvin's truck. When he came back, Dylan sat on the floor next to Gus. Gus's large head took over his lap, and when Derek stepped forward, Gus looked at him without moving an inch from where he was. Derek was probably being paranoid, but it was like Gus knew Dylan needed his protection.

Dylan's face was all concentrated angles—an expression Derek had only seen when Dylan was at his workstation. There was no fidgeting. It was as if there was a problem in front of him, and he hadn't worked out the answer.

"I wish I could stop myself from asking if the photo was like . . ." His breaths sped up. "Was it a . . ."

"Oh my god, *no*. As much as I think your brothers are complete fuckheads, they wouldn't have brought a photo like that here." He gritted his teeth together until his jaw cracked, and he slid the photo from his pocket. No more lies. No more hiding anything. "It was just from the last time I saw him."

Dylan scanned the photo. His teeth sank into his bottom lip so hard Derek was worried he'd start bleeding. "The last time you were *with* him?"

The word *with* held so much. Derek didn't know what to say.

Dylan's hand swiped across his face. "I remember him being

really good-looking, but I guess I never really thought about it in the context of the type of guys I've seen you with . . . They *all* kind of looked like Jake, didn't they? Hudson . . . Hudson could've been his younger brother."

Derek blinked. "What?"

Dylan looked down at the photo again, his thumb right over Derek's face, over Derek's odd not-quite smile. "You could've just said you didn't want to talk about him yet." Dylan handed back the photo and rested his hand on Gus's belly. "I'm trying to work out why you said what you said. You know, I wondered because it seemed like you were avoiding the question, but I thought I was being paranoid. I didn't want that insecure part of my brain to screw this up."

"I fucked up, Dylan. I'm sorry."

"Are you still . . . I know he's gone. And I'm so sorry he's gone. My heart is breaking for both you and Olive after hearing what you lost tonight. I didn't know what he was like with other people. I didn't see the best side of him that night . . ."

"Jake was . . . Jake . . . Everything your brothers said was true. But he had his own shit."

"I think I pushed you into starting this with me, and you aren't ready. It's too soon after losing someone so important. Maybe that's why, but . . ."

"*No.*" He was just feeling far too much to think clearly, but Dylan needed to understand. "I put Jake on a pedestal. I know that, and I was wrong."

Dylan's head dropped. "I can't compete with some perfect guy. I'm sure that's selfish of me to say given everything you've been through. But I just started to think that I *don't* deserve the shit my family has put me through, and I can't . . . I'm so fucking messed up, Derek. I am not *that* guy. The perfect, confident, cocky, life-of-the-party . . ." His gaze flicked to the folded-up photo in Derek's hand. "And I get it that if he was what you wanted and you ended up with me—"

"Can you stop for a second?"

"It's not about you having dated him. It's about . . . *shit.*" Dylan's voice shook. He wiped his nose on his shoulder.

"Can I explain?"

Dylan's sadness shifted into something else. "I asked you. I *fucking* asked you. We sat in that restaurant, and you looked me in the eye. Christ, it wouldn't even have been a big deal no matter what your answer was as long as you told me the truth or even said you weren't ready to talk about it yet. But you didn't do either of those things. And then later . . . you were talking about *him*, and you intentionally didn't say . . . *He* was the guy you were 'so gone on' and then he was conflicted about it. You could have told me then too."

"I know. And I tried to tell you, but I kept overthinking it. I didn't want to bring it up while you were gone because I thought it would've made it seem like a bigger deal than it even was. I didn't want to be with him even then, not *really.*"

"And you think me finding out this way was better?" Dylan's focus fell to the folded photo. "Losing him must have been unbelievably heartbreaking, and knowing you were hurting that badly kills me. I wish I didn't even have to make any of this stupid conversation about me. But . . . it just felt like a lie."

"I know it did." Derek wanted to leap at Dylan and tell him everything else he figured out tonight. He wanted to *fix it*. Of course he did. "Olive doesn't even know about what happened between us. In retrospect, it was kind of this weird thing, and honestly, Jake was completely right, and it never would have worked because whenever I woke up next to him, I didn't want to watch him sleep."

"So, you slept with him. More than once. I know that probably should've been obvious . . . Okay."

"Fuck . . ." Derek flinched. He was messing this up worse. "That's part of what I was coming back to tell you. I was walking tonight, and I had this moment where everything made sense. I needed to tell *you* about it. Before anyone—even Olive. You were the only one I wanted to tell."

Dylan's forearms rested on Gus as he put his fingers in his hair. "I don't think now's the right . . . I'm just trying to wrap my head around this."

Derek bent to meet his gaze. "Dylan, please. I was wrong. It was years of thinking I was completely in love with someone, but—"

"You thought you were completely in love with him for *years*?" Dylan's blue eyes were wet. Every contour of Dylan's beautiful face showed a devastation he'd only seen there one other time in a very different context. When he'd seen that photo on Anderson's phone of Dylan as an eleven-year-old kid holding the proof of everything he thought was broken inside him.

"It wasn't real. I know now it wasn't real."

"Real enough you didn't want to tell me." His soft sadness hardened into a waxwork mask. The mask that came back whenever he had shut down. "And you *knew* I wouldn't push the issue."

"I'm sorry."

Dylan shook his head. "Please stop apologizing. I'm not mad. Not really. You're grieving and hurting, and I get why you didn't explain. You were so worried about my fragile feelings that you couldn't be honest about your own. That's not fair to you." Dylan pushed up from the ground. "I-I need a sec." He braced an arm against the couch and took a few deep breaths before moving toward the door.

Derek stopped him in the entryway. "Please . . ." The depth of Dylan's emotion hit him like a brick wall. "None of that is true. Can you please let me—"

"No, I won't." Dylan twisted around. "Derek Chang, I've watched you take care of *everyone* else around you at the expense of your own happiness. Over and over and over again."

He gestured to the apartment. "You did all this just to give your sister a break."

"I shouldn't have though."

Dylan locked eyes with Derek. "I've worked too hard on *not* hating myself to be with someone who thinks they need to protect me or rescue me or manage me from knowing the truth. I'm *not* a broken thing you need to fix. And if you think I am, this isn't going to work."

There was nothing but silence.

The words mirrored what Michelle said. Derek couldn't reply. He'd screwed up enough people already, hadn't he?

Dylan opened the door, and Derek let him walk upstairs alone.

Chapter 48

Dylan sat on the floor of Uncle Sean's apartment as more banging came from the front door. One of the last things he had done was re-key the lock since he had no idea how many people Sean had given keys to. He'd given the extra keys to his dad for the Realtor.

Felicity seemed pissed her key wouldn't work. She banged on the door again. "Just let me in."

Why couldn't everyone just leave him alone?

He'd be out of here in less than twelve hours. He'd spent the day moving the bigger stuff. He'd loaded as much as he could into his Jeep yesterday, making several trips when he knew Derek was working. Derek never took back permissions for Dylan to view his Google calendar. It was a little like reverse stalking. Today, Derek was not at work, so Dylan would be doing the brave thing. Hiding the entire day in this locked apartment.

It was like the Parakeet Karen calendar.

Dylan needed to be back home. He knew this was ADHD burnout. He'd been through it before. The weeks in California out of his comfort zone had already nearly wrecked him, and then . . .

"Open this damn door, Dylan Gallagher, or I will propel my height-deficient self through it, and if I break my shoulder, it's on you."

More banging.

"If that Karen calls the cops again, they're definitely going to arrest me this time, so open the goddamn door."

"Everything okay?" said a different voice outside. It took

Dylan a second to place that voice. He'd only seen Joni, Derek's doctor friend, a couple times since that first day after *the incident* when she'd bandaged his hand and checked out his ribs like some ethereal medical sprite. "Sorry to intrude, but I heard you yelling and just wanted to make sure everything's okay. Are you Dylan's sister? I'm Derek's friend."

"This jackass won't answer his phone. And I think he changed the locks because Uncle Sean's selling the apartment, but I'm freaking out."

"You think something's wrong?" Joni said.

"I don't know. He's gone radio silent before, but not usually from me." She kicked the door this time. "Can you just open up?"

"If you're really worried, we could call someone," Joni said, a note of growing concern in her voice. "When did you last hear from him?"

"A week ago."

"We could call the non-emergency line, and—"

Dylan wrenched open the door. "Jesus Christ, Felicity, I'm fine. I just want to be alone."

Both redhead's mouths fell open.

"What the hell happened to you?" Felicity asked, probably taking in his unshowered, disheveled appearance. She pushed inside. "You should come in too. We need to find out what the hell is going on between these two."

Joni frowned at Dylan. He gestured to the couch, resigned to his fate and unable to suppress his need to know how Derek was. Joni sat next to Felicity, and Dylan shut the door behind them and locked it.

Felicity pulled out everything edible in the fridge and put it on a plate and then pushed it in front of Dylan. "You look like garbage. If you don't eat, I'm taking you to the hospital."

"*Are* you okay?" Joni asked tentatively.

Dylan placated his sister with a bite of cheese. I'm fine. Couple work projects have kept me busy. That's all." The last word came out like a tremor. He tried to eat one of the baby carrots, but it was slimy so he spat it out.

Felicity faced him. "What happened?"

Dylan slid the plate onto the coffee table. "How's he doing, Joni?"

Joni shifted in her seat. "He called out of work three days in a row. Said he was sick. He . . . uh . . . had a hard day at work the last time I saw him, so I was kind of hoping *you* could tell me actually. You haven't heard from him?"

"No."

His sister leaned her head on his. "Come on, Dylan. You've got two emotional support gingers at your disposal."

"There's nothing to say." He dug the boniest part of his knuckle into the spot between his eyes, remembering how Derek's eyebrows used to furrow together during those sweet, earnest moments.

"So you broke up with him?" Felicity asked.

"I-I didn't want to be one more thing that he gave up parts of himself to try to help, Lissy. You saw what he did for his sister. What he did for Olive and her dog. That's the kind of person he was."

"Why's that a problem if he wants to be with you?"

"Because he's obviously still in love with Jake Murphy. You saw how protective he is. He wasn't willing to be honest with me about it. Probably because he didn't want to hurt me. I gave him a chance . . . and he just let me walk away."

"Derek had a tough time that day . . ." Joni said.

"He's been having a tough time for years. And I'm not going to be another obligation."

Joni patted Dylan's shoulder. "Why do you think you were?"

Because Derek wanted a Jake Murphy. Even Dylan Gallagher had too much self-respect to sign up to be a consolation prize.

He needed to escape this conversation. He'd seen how much

Derek had been put through because of him already. He'd had to deal with that horrible end to the Grill-Out night. He'd had to deal with Dylan yelling at him and being insecure and needy. He'd had to deal with him falling through his ceiling.

"I need to figure some shit out. I think he does too."

Dylan needed to be alone. He needed to lose himself in something else. He needed a new distraction. A project. A book series. A hobby. Anything to keep his mind off Derek Chang and how Dylan was not enough. He'd been too much of a coward to tell him what he felt. To ask him what he was so desperate to ask. He'd been too scared.

It was just one more sign this wasn't right. He pulled his crooked glasses off his face and tossed them onto the coffee table next to his plate.

Joni placed a hand on Dylan's right hand and Felicity placed one on his left. He pulled his hands away and leaned forward, body shaking. He pushed his fists against his eyes to try to stop what was happening. The two hands rested on each of his shoulders now, giving him a few slow pats and just letting him go.

When he found the ability to speak again, he managed to get one sentence out. "I just want to go home."

Chapter 49

Derek walked up the hill to the graveyard gate just before dawn. It was misty for summer, the damp coolness out of sync with the coming heat. Movement caught his attention from the corner of his eye. She was already there, leaning against a tree. They hadn't discussed it this year, but then again, he hadn't been answering his texts or phone calls lately.

He smiled through blurry eyes.

Olive held out her hand with an open palm, and he sank to the ground when he saw what she was holding. "I figured you'd bring them too, but I picked some up just in case." She reached down and folded Derek into her arms. "I made you a promise."

Derek was eighteen years old, standing in his parents' room. His mother had asked him to do it because she couldn't. *"It's been two years almost to the day, why now?"* he had asked her.

She'd cried more and said she couldn't keep looking at it every day. Not for another birthday. His dad had always made a big deal about their birthdays and his own. His father loved holidays. Derek didn't blame his mom for being struck hard by another birthday without him.

Derek could do this. He could fix this. He should have already done it.

He tackled the closet first, carefully folding each of his father's suits into a box to take to a charity that gave them to unemployed men for job interviews. He went through the dressers, bagging up everything else for Goodwill. The last thing in the room was the nightstand, and for some reason it seemed more personal than the clothes.

He filled the next box with books and papers. His hands hit something all the way in the back that must have gotten pushed there to make room for all the medication bottles. He pulled out his father's thick-rimmed black glasses.

He had sat down with the glasses in his hand, holding them and unable to move.

Olive showed up at his house unexpectedly like she often did back then. He didn't know how long he'd been on the floor holding the glasses.

She wrapped her arms around his shoulders. "I'm so sorry. God, Derek. You should have told me you were doing this. I would have helped you."

His voice shook. "I shouldn't need help. This was my responsibility."

He wasn't a child anymore. He should be able to handle everything.

Olive shook his shoulders violently to force him to look at her. "Just because you're *capable* of doing something by yourself doesn't mean you have to do it alone." Her next squeeze practically cut off his oxygen.

Jake showed up later. He packed the bags and boxes in his truck while Olive led Derek back to his room. He was still cradling the glasses, and his dad was still fucking dead and all he could think about was Anna Chlumsky screaming about Macaulay Culkin not being able to fucking see in his fucking coffin.

That afternoon was the only time he cried for his dad. That afternoon the day before his dad's birthday, he wept on Olive's shoulder for hours, never letting go of those busted, old, cheap plastic frames.

Olive slept over, never leaving his side. When he'd woken, it had been the middle of the night. Olive sat up and held his hand. It had been his idea in the end. He knew what he needed to do. He grabbed a spade from their shed. They went to the graveyard, dug up a small patch of ground next to the head-stone, and buried the glasses inside.

Every year afterward, Olive had met him at that tree at dawn for this small ritual that was all his own. Every year she brought a pair of glasses, and he left them on top of where he left the other ones, not knowing what happened to them. Every year he *wanted* to walk up to the grave by himself, but he just couldn't. She always asked the same question at the gate.

"Do you want me to come with you?"

Every year he said yes, because being alone with the grave would make it all more real. It was easier to clutch her hand and bring her with him because he couldn't think of anything worse than losing control and feeling the grief.

Now, Olive stood in front of him again, holding another pair of glasses, while the first blush of morning fanned out from the horizon.

"Do you want me to come with you?"

On that long walk after seeing Michelle, he realized he'd been trying so hard to push down his feelings that he never could heal. He tried to do so much alone that he'd messed shit up. But in other ways, he'd clung so tightly to what he knew, to what was safe, that he never opened himself up to new things. And that's what he'd been doing all these years when he wanted to sit and talk to his dad alone, but he'd been too terrified to take that step and open himself up to feeling all of it.

Because if he broke down, how could he still be the one who fixed things?

He needed Olive to be here at this tree because she loved him and believed in him even when he screwed things up. He needed her to hold him until he could breathe again so he could take these next few steps by himself.

"I think I'm going to go talk to him alone this year, but do you mind waiting for me?"

She nodded and kissed him on the cheek.

He walked to the grave and set the glasses in front of the headstone. He'd never been here completely alone before. He came with his sisters or Mom with flowers and incense in April. But now it was silent as he faced the gray granite engraved with his father's name.

He sat and began to talk.

✳✳✳

The sun was up when he walked back out to the gate.

Olive crushed him into another hug. "You okay?"

"No." His voice was hoarse. He must have spent at least an hour talking to his dad. He hadn't talked this much in days. He hadn't seen anyone in days.

"Good. Sometimes it's okay to *not* be okay, I think."

"I think I might need help with this. I think I should've gotten h-help a while ago . . ." He could barely get the words out. He broke down like he had when he was eighteen. There was something cleansing in letting your body give way to every bit of stifled grief. He'd read a theory about this once. Instead of trying to ignore the pain or distract yourself, you focus on the pain itself. And it allows your mind to pick it apart and experience it in a more functional way.

With every shudder and sob in the shadow of that big maple, Derek dove into the pain until he almost drowned in it. Every breath was jagged. Every muscle screamed. He felt that profound *lack*. That emptiness that came with death. All those moments that had been taken from him.

Because his dad was dead.

Exploring those vacant spots seemed to fill them slightly. As if the act of acknowledging them made them easier to bear.

God, this fucking sucked.

Grief wasn't just sadness. Anyone with a vague awareness of psychology knew about the stages of grieving. Kübler-Ross.

Denial, anger, bargaining, depression, and acceptance. Like it was really that simple. Fuck it, he wished it was really that simple. Grief was fear too. Fear of letting go of what you lost because letting go seemed to devalue it somehow. Guilt because being the happiest you've ever been reminds you of everything that person missed. Derek had watched his dad fade away into an existence of unbearable pain, so at the end there was also . . . relief. Which brought him right back to guilt.

"Fuck those stages."

"W-what?" Olive pulled away, looking around as if Derek had cursed something she would see. "Am I missing something?"

"Kübler-Ross." Derek flung his arms out as if the name explained everything before wiping his face on the back of his hand.

As always, Olive was right there with him. "Yeah, I hate that bitch too." She hiccupped, a strange, strangled sound somewhere between a laugh and a wail. "Why didn't I bring tissues? My purse is in the car."

Derek dug into his slacks and found two things crumbled at the bottom of his pocket. A receipt from Sumittra that made him want to cry some more and a small silver key chain he'd carried with him since he found it.

"I'm ready to go." Derek sighed.

Olive linked her arms with his and pulled him to her car. She grabbed her purse and tissues first, then she handed him a small cup and poured cold brew coffee from a thermos into it. It was already swelteringly hot, so they climbed into her car and blasted the air-conditioning.

"You glad you went alone?" Her voice was still a little unsteady.

"I think I needed to."

"I'm proud of you."

He made a dismissive noise in his throat. "Don't be. I've screwed up everything."

He told her what had happened with Michelle. With Dylan. All of it. Even what happened with Jake. He was sick of lying. He was sick of keeping secrets. He was sick of pretending he knew what to do about any of it.

"What's that?" She pointed to the silver key chain he was still clutching.

It was engraved.

PEACE

The neatly wrapped box had been in his apartment on the table beside his bed. He hadn't found it until Dylan had left. There was a card scrawled with a few lines of Dylan's handwriting. He pulled it out of the center console of his car and handed it to her.

> I should've watched more of your movies, and then maybe I could do this better. I know I'm not Heath Ledger, and this isn't a Fender Strat, but maybe a key with an open invitation for <u>always</u> could be almost as good? I really hate the idea of missing you. —D

Olive shifted in her seat and then smacked him on the back of the head.

"What was that for?"

"For starters, you need to go get your goddamn man."

"What?"

"Secondly, how oblivious do you think I am? Of course I knew you had a crush on my brother. Didn't know you slept together." She wrinkled her nose and made a gagging motion. "To be honest, I'm gonna try to forget I know about it now. I think you already know this, but you and Jake would've never worked. Yeah, for a while, I felt the way every girl with a perfect gay best friend and a perfect gay brother feels, like wouldn't it be nice if they would just both stop being lonely and get together. But *no*. You guys. Not a chance."

"Jesus, Olive, don't hold back."

"When have I ever? Jake was obsessed with traveling. And his job. And he wanted to move around someday. You are the biggest homebody ever. You hate hotels, for Chrissakes. And just for the record, you never *once* looked at my brother the way I saw you look at Dylan the one single night I saw you with him."

"And I hated him back then."

"Bullshit. Y'all had that *I want to kill you and fuck you* chemistry dripping out of your eyeballs at each other. You looked at him like you wanted to gobble his ass up."

"That is the grossest mixed metaphor for attraction I have ever heard."

"Admittedly, it wasn't my best, but my point stands. Look at you, you're a mess. But the good kind of mess. Something about your time living with Dylan got you to this point."

"To be a mess?"

"*Letting* yourself be a mess. A point when you're ready to feel things. Really feel them deep down in the sucked-up marrow of your soul. You took such a big step today."

"You go up to New England for a month and come back quoting Thoreau?"

"Christ, no. *Dead Poets Society* was on TBS last night, and I stayed up and watched it with Stella's dad."

"I hate that fucking movie. That ending? What the actual—"

"*Gaaaaaahhhh.*" Her annoyance must have grown beyond words, devolving into half growl, half shriek. She smacked him again. "*Derek Chang*. Stop changing the subject. What do you *feel* when you look at Dylan?"

The entire world slowed.

He leaned forward and gripped the dashboard. The unfurling

feeling in his stomach was halfway between nausea and that lifting sensation when you drive over a hill too fast and it feels like flying, but it also feels . . . it also feels like *falling*.

What did he feel when he looked at Dylan Gallagher?

Chapter 50

Dylan was alone, but he was home. In his house, at least. Felicity had started her semester, so she wasn't coming by anymore with absurd excuses or camping out in his guest room. Before, she would just come and sit while he read or come help him fix something that his renter's kids had broken. They'd watched the three DVDs he'd accidentally stolen from Derek countless times without Felicity complaining.

Last night there had been another system outage, and it felt amazing to lose himself in the predictable complexities of a work crisis. He'd taken his medication. He'd taken his breaks and eaten. He'd done all the right things. He'd been setting firmer boundaries lately.

The sound of a car in his driveway dragged him upright from where he'd been dozing in an Adirondack chair on the porch. He fixed his glasses and walked around the house. He stopped dead at the sight of Derek's ancient Dodge Dart, and Derek himself leaning against it with his hands in his pockets, wearing a gray striped Henley and black twill pants. His hair was longer than usual, and his chin was stubbly rather than perfectly clean shaven.

"You said there was an open invitation," Derek said, looking up through lowered lashes. He held up the key. "For always . . ."

Dylan stared, feeling miles away from the self he was when he had scribbled those words on the card. He'd been right to hate the idea of missing Derek. For the last few weeks, missing Derek felt like being ripped in half. His brain was still struggling to know how to say any of the things he wanted to say or ask any of the questions he needed to ask.

He opened his mouth, and something unexpected came out. "Can I give you a tour?"

Derek smiled. "I'd love that."

Derek followed him inside. Dylan pointed out the old stained glass he'd refurbished. The cozy front room with the fireplace. The small but well-apportioned kitchen with its vintage-styled appliances and large island. He led him out on the back porch and down to the elevated, partially covered cobblestone patio that looked out onto a garden and the large field with a duck pond and small dock in front of the woods. He showed Derek the barn he was still in the process of restoring.

When Dylan's voice was gravelly from speaking too long, he returned to the cobblestone patio at the back of the house and sat on the narrow cast-iron bench that looked out onto his small work-in-progress garden.

Derek sat beside him. "I'm not going to lie, I feel a little like Elizabeth Bennet visiting Pemberley and then conveniently figuring out she's in love with the man right after she finds out how nice his estate is."

Dylan whipped around. "What did you say?"

"Why are you acting so shocked I know about *Pride and Prejudice*? My best friend is an Anglophile bisexual. *Pride and Prejudice* is like OG bi panic fiction. Don't even get her started on the 2005 version. In Olive's words—do I want to *be* Keira Knightley's Elizabeth Bennet or do I want to—"

"That wasn't the part I meant." Dylan grabbed Derek's shoulders. His glasses were drifting down his nose, but he didn't bother to fix them. "Say the last part of that sentence again, please."

Derek gently pushed Dylan's frames back up. "It doesn't really apply though because I knew I loved you long before I came here to your fucking amazing house. How many blow jobs would you need before you agreed to dive into your pond in a billowing white shirt and then just walk out of it slowly?" Derek touched Dylan's hair. "You have the right hair."

"Jesus Christ, can you just be serious for a second?"

"Yes. I can be serious." Humor shifted into intensity.

"W-what did you say?" Dylan's chin trembled. The sound that came out of him was definitely not a sob. Nope. It was just a very sob-like manly emotion sound.

Derek's eyes were glittering, reflecting that misty morning sunlight as if each dark iris was flecked with stars. "Today, when we were in the car at the graveyard, Olive asked me how I feel when I look at you."

"You were at the graveyard? Christ, is everything okay—"

"Now you *focus*." Derek pointed from his penetrating eyes to Dylan's. "Dylan."

"Yeah?"

"She asked me how I felt when I looked at you, and it was weird because normally that question might freak me out or make me implode, especially since I know I majorly screwed things up. But still, the answer was so easy, I just blurted it right at her." He took several slow breaths.

Dylan's body practically vibrated. "Are you going to fucking tell me?"

"What do you think I'm trying to do, jackass? I thought about finding a marching band for this moment just because it would probably make you shut up and listen to me, but—"

"You don't think I'm worth a grand movie gesture?" Dylan stood to face Derek.

Derek grabbed hold of his shoulders. "I think you deserve *everything*, Dylan."

Dylan's breaths quaked in his chest.

"I'll start with raw honesty." Derek cradled Dylan's wet face in his hands, his thumbs brushing away tears. "First of all, I love your perfect house because it's *you*. Everything in it is you and your hard work and your amazing skill and patience. I love that you can lose yourself in things because you have these talents you feel so strong and passionate about. I love that we keep each other on our toes, and we have different strengths and interests but there has never been one single moment with you when I've been bored. You make me laugh. I've never—not for a second—thought you were broken or needed to be fixed. Even when I thought I hated you, somehow we just fit. We've always fit."

Dylan could only nod.

"There was never anyone else who made me feel this way, and there *could not* be anyone else. I'm so sorry if I made you feel otherwise by making that really bad choice about keeping my history from you, but what you said about competing—t-there's . . ." Derek's voice cracked.

"There's . . . ?"

Derek took in a deep breath. "Dylan Gallagher, every single time I look at you all I feel is stupid, lovesick, radiant joy."

Several moments passed. Nothing existed except the little space left between them and the very tangible something filling both pairs of eyes.

"K-kay," Dylan said in a splutter.

"*Kay?*" Derek released Dylan's face. "I bust out *stupid, lovesick, radiant joy*. And you give me *kay*? A single letter."

"Or three, depending on how you look at it." Dylan's face crumpled. He sat down on the cobblestone and looked out on the garden below in absolute stillness. No fidgeting. No shifting his weight except to lean against the bench behind him. Derek rested a fist on a patio pillar.

"I have to know what you're thinking, Dylan."

"I'm sorry for the *kay*. It's just that I'm—I'm—I'm . . . *Christ*, Derek, you come here with th-this beautiful declaration, this poetry, and I love you so much that honestly when you first showed up I was terrified I was just hallucinating you because

I've missed you so much over the last few weeks it feels like an actual organ is missing from my body. Is this what it's supposed to feel like? Because it's fucking awful." He patted the place on his chest where most of the hurt collected when he tried to sleep in a bed that felt too big. "I hate it."

"You hate it?"

"Goddamn right I hate it." He stormed down the couple steps to the garden and paced in front of one of the newly cleared-out beds.

"Alright."

Dylan scraped his fingers into his scalp. "It feels like everything is completely out of control. I thought if I could get home, I'd feel better, but *no*. Derek goddamn Chang is in my brain forever, and I didn't know how to get him out." He braced his forehead on his open palms.

"So what do you want, Dylan?"

"Want? I want you here. I want you and all your shit. Your DVD collection and the romance novels you're embarrassed about—they aren't fucking Olive's, Derek." He gave Derek a pointed look at then continued to pace. "When you were describing your perfect life in your perfect house, can't you see that it's here with me?" He had to take a couple more breaths before he could finish. "Don't you see that this place is perfect for us? It's perfect for you because *I'm* perfect for you. We're so perfect together, and it doesn't make any sense. Nothing makes any sense. Isn't it just way too soon to be thinking about this? I'm scaring you off, aren't I?"

Derek stopped Dylan's pacing by pulling him close. He let the pressure slow Dylan's anxious shaking before he slanted his perfect mouth over Dylan's trembling one. When they parted, Derek took a step away but didn't let go. For the first time during this conversation, a ghost of that obnoxiously cocky smile Dylan fell in love with was back on that obnoxiously hot face.

"Let's try this again. One more time." Derek nodded as if he were helping Dylan cram for a pop quiz. "Dylan Gallagher, what do you feel when you look at me?"

"Stupid, lovesick, radiant joy."

The cockiness vanished. Derek's eyebrows scrunched together, and then he covered his face. His shoulders shook, but he managed to get out one stuttered syllable. *"Kay."*

Epilogue

Derek handed his best friend another set of tissues. In her defense, her dress didn't have pockets, and his jacket did.

She whispered into his ear. "Do you remember when we were fourteen and watched *My Best Friend's Wedding,* and we swore that when we were twenty-eight if we weren't married, we'd marry each other?"

He tried to keep his face in a suitable pleasant and respectful expression as he whispered back. "Twenty-eight was really the age they were in that movie? Now I just feel old. Why'd you bring that up?"

She blew her nose and dabbed her eyes. "I'm just really glad we didn't decide to do that. Oh *shit.*" She stuffed the tissue wad down the bust of her dress and then hurried forward.

His best friend always kept it classy.

A warm touch on his back made Derek turn. He pressed a hand to his heart as he took in the sight of Dylan dressed in a three-piece gray suit. He hadn't ever seen Dylan in that suit until today, and *fuck, yes.* That one had been the right choice. God, he was relieved they did the first look thing, or else Derek would have needed to pull out his tissue packet again, and he was down to his last two.

Dylan's eyes were red as he blinked, sniffing once. The glassiness brought out the blue. It was really two different shades of sapphire and ocean marbled together. After kissing his forehead, Derek held him closer as he watched the processional advance ahead of them.

"Need a tissue?"

"Nope." Dylan's Adam's apple bobbed, and he tugged at his collar.

"Stop that." Derek reached over to straighten his pocket square. "And good, because between Olive and that sister of yours, I'm nearly out."

Dylan laughed at that, which seemed to help him manage those brimming emotions. Derek was, of course, fine with his fiancé crying, but . . . their photographer was expensive, and Dylan said his only goal of the day was not to blubber on camera.

A small ruckus at the front drew their attention away from each other. A feat in and of itself. From what Derek could see, Lucas had smacked his younger brother for taking the ring pillow. While Dylan's niece, the firecracker named after her aunt Felicity, had yelled something that might have been *Death to the patriarchy*" before throwing her basket of flowers and snatching the silk pillow from the tussling boys. Michelle's laughter at the commotion woke the baby strapped to her chest, her daughter's screams drowning out the piano.

"You didn't actually give them the rings, right?" Their small family wedding was quickly looking more like the Kidz Bop mosh pit despite the best efforts of most of the wedding attendants, several aunts and uncles of Dylan's, and one very frazzled justice of the peace who thought he'd be officiating a wedding, not refereeing a riot.

"Give our rings to that group of feral monsters?" Derek narrowed his eyes in offended disbelief. "Heck no." He tapped his pocket and then pulled out the small box.

"Have you looked at them yet?"

"Just when we tried them on at the store, why?"

Dylan smirked. "Just look at them."

"Look at the WWE match happening over a stupid pillow?"

"No, jackass. The rings."

With a small intrigued exhale through his nose, Derek drew the blue velvet box out of his pocket. He pulled out Dylan's ring first, holding it up in the light after seeing that it was inscribed. Derek's face spread wide as he read the etched words on the inside of the band: STUPID, LOVESICK, RADIANT JOY.

"I was lucky that was under thirty characters."

Derek pocketed that ring and took out the one Dylan would be putting on his finger. At first he thought there wasn't an inscription at all, but he turned it. He had to swallow back tears again because it was perfect.

"You like it?"

He didn't answer, but he did reach into his pocket for the last two tissues, because in small, thin letters it just said KAY.

Acknowledgments

Thank you to my editor, Lisa Bonvissuto, for loving Derek and knowing he needed a happy ending of his own. Thank you for being kind. Thank you for your brilliance and your patience.

Thank you to my agents, Mariah Nichols and Bob Diforio, for giving me this shot at making my precious dreams come true.

Thank you to Kerri Resnick and Guy Shield for creating this stunning cover and infusing it with all that perfect enemies-to-lovers angst. Thank you to editor Christina Lopez. I'm so excited to work with you more in the future! Thank you Nicole Hall (your comments made me laugh) and Ginny Perrin (sorry I'm still not good at capitalization and hyphens). I am so grateful to Crystal Shelley of Red Pen Rabbit for your keen insights on Derek's heritage. Thank you to Kejana Ayala, Alyssa Gammello, Austin Adams, and everyone at SMPG who helped this story get found by readers.

To my author friends—thank you for answering my questions, helping me talk through things when the imposter syndrome vibes were strong, and supporting my books: Ruby Barrett, Tim Janovsky, Susie Dumond, Sarah Adler, Mazey Eddings, Chip Pons, Erin Connor, Chloe Angyal, Gretchen Schreiber, Lana Ferguson, Mae Marvel, Rachel Runya Katz, and others. Also thank you for writing fantastic books. I'm especially thankful for Courtney Kae and Falon Ballard for their incredible *Happy to Meet Cute!* podcast. (Seriously, go listen right now.) And, of course, thank you to bookseller extraordinaire Mike Lasagna for hyping my book on that podcast at a very crucial moment.

I am also *so thankful* for my local bookstores and booksellers. Y'all make author dreams happen. Thank you for always making me feel so welcome when I visit, hosting events, organizing book clubs, asking me to sign stock, and overall supporting me as a clueless debut author during the release of *Fly with Me*. Curious Iguana (Bonnie, Emelia, Elna, Lauren, Shelby, and others), East City Bookshop (Laynie-Rose, Amy, Maggie, Destinee, and so many others), People's Book (Mylo, Megan, Matt, and others), and Scrawl Books (Leah, for moderating my first-ever authory event). Also thank you to the team at Barnes & Noble Gaithersburg, Maryland, especially Taylor and Sarah. Love getting to stop by on my lunch breaks and see your smiles.

Thank you to *every* reader who picked up *Fall for Him* or *Fly with Me*. It feels utterly magical to know that people across the world have spent hours with my characters. It's hard to wrap my head around it. Thank you for your DMs and your posts and reviews. I love hearing from you. 🖤 Thank you to the nurses and all the health-care workers who have read and reached out to me about these books. So much of my inspiration comes from what you do and what you face every day.

Thank you to the people who often don't get enough shoutouts but who patched me up this year, both physically and mentally—my therapist, psych NP, dermatologist, neurology PA/NPs, local EMTs, ER nurses, and a very kind ER doc who asked me what tropes my book had (and his supercool reader wife who had appropriately educated him on the topic beforehand). ***My fellow chronically ill neurodivergent besties will understand how important these folks are.

To my dearest most kindred-est spirits. I would not have survived this last couple of years without you: Erin Dixon, Mary Pollard, Natalie Priani, Cassie Sanders, Chelsey Saatkamp, and Ciara Trexler.

Thank you to my radiology besties—Becca Gabby, Kathleen, Marla, Chaya, and Viktoriya. You're all awesome.

Haley, Lauren, Liz, David, and Kimberly—thank you for being in my corner.

To Taylor Swift for somehow always dropping new albums around my traumatic life events, and to Boygenius, Noah Kahan, and Lizzy McAlpine, none of whom will ever see this, but somehow can see inside my soul.

To Kayla (sorry about the snake encounter) and Ellen. Thank you for being on my team always.

Karen Jonas, I'm not sure how to express how much you mean to me as a person and a creative. It's been <number redacted> years . . . and *jfc* I couldn't do life without you.

And finally, to Amelia and Emerson—you kiddos are the most precious core of my heart. Being your mom is the best thing I'll ever be. Thank you for your hugs and snuggles. The biggest honor of my life is getting to watch you grow. I love you.

About the Author

Andie Burke writes romantic comedies in between her pediatric RN shifts. She lives in Maryland with an alarming number of books, ultrafine-point pens, dehydrated houseplants, and two small humans. As you read this, she's probably listening to Taylor Swift or finding a new hyperfixation for her ADHD brain.